flag on the date

M L Chambers

flag on the date

Book 4
Mountaineer Footballers

M L Chambers

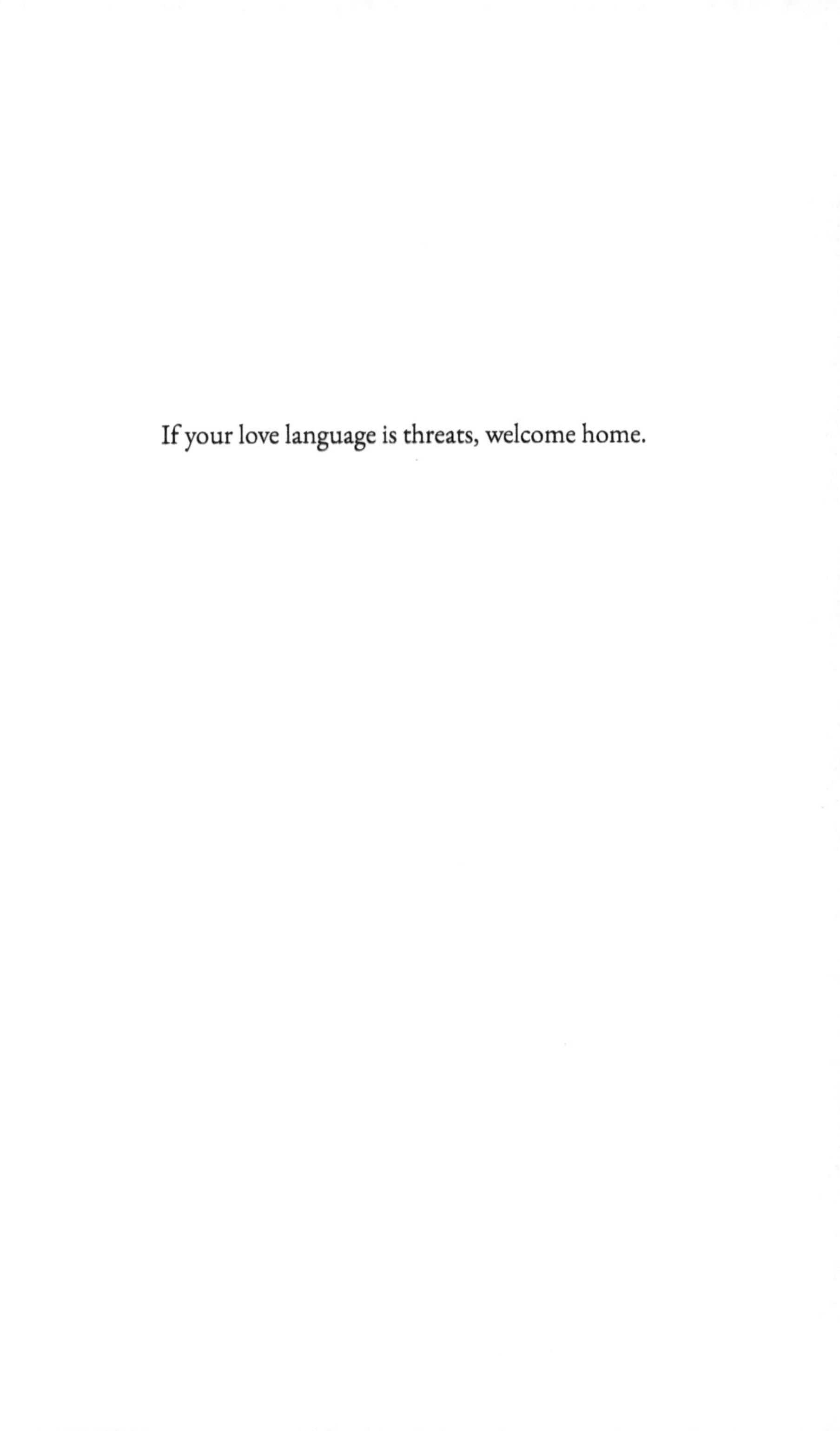

If your love language is threats, welcome home.

CHAPTER ONE

ASHER

S TANDING WAS AN ELUSIVE, ever out of reach desire. A sober man's game. There was no feeling in Asher Laughlin's legs. They'd started numb, but the static fizzled between the cheap apple brandy and candy corn Jell-O shot. Now, feet hooked on the bottom rung of his stool, ass hanging off the rounded wood top, he only vaguely registered the notched metal footpads stinging his shins, like iron chains binding him to a ship's mast. And he was capsizing.

Under the peg legs of his chair, the sticky bar floor pitched and rocked. Sea spray in the form of cran-vodkas and vegas bombs dusted the back of his neck. Foam splatter from overfilled pints turned the butcher block bar into a sordid slip 'n slide, streaking the dye of his rising stack of cardboard coasters.

One on top of the other: Green Empire Brewery, Burlington Beer Company, Four Quarters Brewing, The Alchemist. He'd taken a tour of Vermont's greatest breweries without venturing five miles from the airport.

You won't learn what you like until you try something different. Go far, try new things, put yourself out there.

Marianne Schulman's final speech had been an ad-lib of a dingy poster tacked behind her folding table desk. Asher had considered the orange songbird studded sunrise behind the words and set his teeth. *Go far* set his legs bouncing. *Try new things* made his stomach churn, and the pièce de résistance shrink-wrapped his skin onto his bones until blood ceased to flow. Until he was dizzy and sweating. Wrenching on the gaping neck of his Goodwill-buy-the-pound t-shirt as if it was coiling around his esophagus like a ruthless cobra.

Why couldn't she have quoted the infographic on the rampant spread of mono?

The day after the infamous Last Words, Asher committed to play football in Indianapolis. Sixteen minutes from the hospital where he'd first met Marianne Schulman.

Three years later, no more informed about infectious mouth diseases, he was drafted by the Bengals. An hour and forty-eight minutes away. And in orange and black, Asher went everywhere. Private jets shuffled him around like he was stars expanding the universe.

"Another?"

"Sorry?" Vertigo struck as he swung his chin to the barkeep. She wore a silky yellow mini dress and an axe stuck out of her tight blonde curls. Thin red syrup trickled down her temple, cut across her cheek, and pooled in the subtle valley above her lip.

When she overturned his empty pint in the dishwasher, he spotted black lace underwear and shut his eyes. The tip jar was vacuum packed with cash. Men in costumes fighting to shove in wads of ones wrapped in a single twenty. But only if she was looking. No good deed without proof.

"Another Heady Topper?" she asked Asher, ignoring the flailing hands and swishing tails on either side of him.

"No." He'd gone far. Now he had to try new things. "What's left?"

"Let's see." She swiped through his coaster rolodex, bending across the bar, the white end of a sucker sticking from between her lips. "The only draught you haven't tried is the Oktoberfest, but I can make you something better than that."

Asher shifted, plucking the velvet knot at his neck. "Just the Oktoberfest."

Caribbean blue eyes clocked him. "It's bad."

"I don't care." *Just leave. Now.*

Before he punched double Charlie horses into his dead thighs and had to do it himself.

"Oh, you will," the barkeep insisted, leaning close enough for him to identify the sucker as Blow Pop and the flavor as grape. Revolting. "My boss dumped a lethal quantity of red dye 40 into the keg. It clumps and clogs the lines, leaves huge heads and—"

"The Oktoberfest." Blowing out a series of quick breaths to gain control, Asher flattened a twenty on the counter.

Irritation blazing, the axe-head snatched the proffering and abandoned him.

Finally.

The Google reviews for The Hand were a mixed bag of *lost my ID there, never found it, cheap, strong drinks*, and *the staff are apathetic asswipes*. Needless to say, he'd been immediately intrigued.

He could put himself out there so long as it included being incomprehensibly blitzed while manning a lone barstool and avoiding eye contact with a blasé bartender.

The costume helped too. Immensely.

Glass shattered from the depths of the dancefloor, a mere slap of grating sound in the cacophony of music and mingling. Didn't stop him from flinching, from forcing the pads of his fingers into the hard bone of his knee. He heard it like the sole reverb of a police siren in the school parking lot. Fear carving into his spine and scooping out melon balls. Irrational, insane fear that two gun-toting uniforms would kick open the Crown Vic doors and apprehend the resident reject.

His eyes darted to the entrance, choked with a shifting line of eager partiers, bottlenecking at the bouncer's inspection. They weren't looking at him, didn't care. Hadn't heard.

A muddy, dark red pint slammed onto a wet, black cocktail napkin. Bubbles no bigger than a pin's head fizzed along the glass walls like barnacles on the Red Sea.

"No refunds," the barkeep said as she slid him his change with stained red fingertips. "Beer was seven. Eight—"

"Keep it," Asher returned, peeling his hand back from hers. "Just—" *Stop looking at me. Stop talking to me. Stop.*

His hands tingled as he pried the napkin free and mopped up the mess. "Thank you," he muttered to the heinous pink foam, at once deliriously thirsty and terrified to drink.

What are you still doing here? Leave.

Leave.

But he wouldn't, would he? Not after coming so far. Asher never did things halfway.

The bar stool on his right—and left for that matter—had remained empty since he sat down. Owed to the wide angle of his elbows and spread knees, and the you-better-be-fucking-kidding glare he'd been serving since he lost sensation in his ankles.

But examining the lousy crimson vortices in his beer distracted him. And before he could plug his nose and chug hazy carbonated blood, the stool next to him swiveled, a lone knee slid into the center.

"Quite bold, aren't you?"

He would've ignored her if it hadn't been for the accent. Lilting and charming and so politely British, his mind waffled between strictly sweet nannies and over-educated globetrotting princesses.

Not the world's greatest detective.

Creamy, flawless skin, long dark hair pinned to stay in harshly executed curls. The latter notwithstanding, Asher immediately knew who she was. Tweed three piece suit, curved black tobacco pipe, and calf-length brown frock coat.

Under the bartender's attention, she pointed to the plastic blue Pepsi Cola cup clutched in her brown leather glove like the two had met pre-party to discuss refill signals.

"Really, it's admirable," came that prim and proper accent. "A fuchsia pint. Does it taste like hibiscus?" Her cup was swapped with a twin, ice dancing around a narrow black straw. "I'd guess not. Beer's too bitter. But still captivating to look at. More men should drink pink, don't you agree?" She turned to rest an elbow on the bar and looked straight at him.

Smiled.

The spinning lights reflected off round wafer thin glasses.

Asher waited for the sweat, for the heart palpitations, for a thousand bad scenarios about how talking to Sherlock Holmes would end. His head in a freezer. Her head in a freezer. Extraneous body parts getting traded on the black market.

Waited. Felt himself nod.

Again. Nodding, a multitude of agreeing, conversing nods instead of wrestling back deformed prophecies.

His mouth was dry, but his hands were steady, calm. His heart hadn't shot to haphazard. With a single curve of her lips, she'd evicted the tension from his body.

Trapped him.

Without locks, or chains, or the temptation of a hard, yellow cheese. Asher was rigged in place as well as if she'd stunned him with a kiss. He didn't dare escape. Inexpressible gratitude bubbled at the sudden lightness in his chest. The people she'd stripped from his focus. Narrowed his life down to her and him.

Her lips pressed tight. "Or maybe you chose pink to discourage conversation?"

He was staring at her mouth. Nodding. Unspeaking. Suffering the worst mental lapse of his life.

She opened her mouth. Closed it. Lifted her cup. "Happy Hollow's Eve."

The sight of her, elegant and witty and friendly, wending into the crowd leaving him, threatened to put him to his knees.

Chapter Two

Carrie

RESOUNDING TRIUMPH. MASSIVELY SUCCESSFUL. Doubters be gone for Carrie Huston and her tireless flirting efforts—back by popular vote—had won again.

Even in her head, it didn't sound convincing.

Diana wouldn't believe a word of it. She'd spin Carrie around and send her careening back into the fray for more man-hunting. "Rebound or revenge," Diana had said, surveying the cloaked denizens. "Doesn't matter. Pick one and commit."

For some long-lost reason—three tequila shots in thirty minutes—Carrie had agreed. She'd straightened her spine, licked her baby hairs down and committed.

But the singular, silent rejection from lonely boy Romeo was ten too many after Rhett and his blithering, *I thought I texted you,* as he scrambled for his skid marked whitey tighties. As if a text would excuse him for banging his—completely platonic, she's not even pretty—fellow sandwich artist against the plexiglass spit shield.

There'd been shredded baby spinach and sliced turkey everywhere.

Now if she even smelled Subway, she got a manic, convicted-murderer-willing-to-strike-again face. Not the cold-blooded, wrong-place-wrong-time, sorry-I-chopped-you-into-bits-and-chucked-you-in-the-river. She went full blown obsessed. We're talking cuts-letters-out-of-Highlights-magazine-to-taunt-her-victim-before-she-slits-their-throat-and-stuffs-them. Googly eyes included.

None of which she'd ever say aloud.

Shoulders hunched, Carrie scuttled further into the pulsing crowd, adjusting her hat to mask her right side—phantom style. At five-ten, with hair down to her butt, gawking was commonplace, but at a clear six feet and change in her heeled penny loafers, she felt like an escaped circus freak.

Diana said Carrie looked like a witch-hunter, had wanted to zip tie Katana blades to her tweed blazer.

Declan—Diana's tall, thin shadow of a brother—had argued for a fully functional rifle clipped to a leather harness.

The Lovatt siblings did not understand the artistry involved in costuming, and how quickly anachronism destroyed months of meticulous prep-work. They just liked artillery.

Struck with a surge of affection, her attention skated to the entrance, where the Lovatts stood sentinel. Out of their typical devouring black, they resembled zombies in blaze orange STAFF tees. Pale skin, dark hair, purple swollen bags under their eyes. They gripped slender blue flashlights like they were nightsticks, and watched every incomer like a pig with an apple in its mouth and they were starving.

Carrie snorted into her ice water. They liked artillery and money. And violence. Though, the last was only astutely inferred.

But hell, they knew how to party.

The Hand was like she'd never seen it. Overhead, temporary lights strobed tangerine and fuchsia and magenta. Music with a hip bouncing bass leached from humongous rental speakers. White streamers—toilet paper—drooped off wide wood beams like listless ghosts and the trio of skylights were frosted to mimic graves.

However, the biggest change was the patrons. Fitted flannels and ripped jeans had transformed into tutus and trench coats. Eyes shone from behind masks, or not at all, hidden under a persona. Witches, zombies, Captain America, a flying pig, that pervy guy from Grease.

Their first Halloween rave and The Hand reached fire capacity two hours ago. A line of werewolves, mummies, and overpaid baseball players shivered outside, suffering a bleary autumn drizzle for a chance to dance under single ply decor.

Happily and not above patting herself on the shoulder, Carrie was the only Sherlock in sight. Her hand stitched overcoat and hat were hotter than boiling sap, but she was one hundred percent authentic English detective.

Her best look to date. But the gender bent Sherlock meant she'd donned leather heeled boots, which, while authentic to the era, were absolutely atrocious to walk in. She'd rather do the worm on sun-drenched asphalt than stuff her feet into air tight leather again.

How did Diana do it?

Cut vents? Suffer trench foot?

Stifling the urge to pant, Carrie checked her timepiece and wet her lips. Was this historically accurate? Was Sherlock perpetually dehydrated? Was that why he was so finicky?

While Ariana Grande Thank-You-Next'd her heart out, Carrie finished her lap and found she'd executed a perfect circle. *Dammit.*

Keeping her hat artfully tipped over her glasses and her back to the Failed Flirtation, she leaned against the sticky bar and flagged Megan—masquerading as the first girl to die in any horror movie—to order the ultimate thirst quencher.

From behind her, a gravelly voice asked, "Where's Watson?"

Fucking a tuna scooper.

Slowly, Carrie angled to eye the object of her botched seduction. Perched on the edge of his seat, cloaked in black, his thick forefinger traced the BBCO logo of his bloody beer.

Now he wanted to talk? Where was he fifteen minutes ago when she'd hacked pathetically at the ice wall surrounding him?

"Could be late." This time his voice was low, and even, and invading. Each word fitting noise canceling muffs over her ears until the music, the chatter, and constant rush of the sink became fuzzy, and all she heard was him. "You keep checking your watch."

"How should that concern a ..." She tipped her head at him, searching for clues through the strobing lights. "Vampire?" She faltered over the word, having never heard it in a British accent.

Because her knowledge of the Queen's English centered fiercely on historical BBC dramas and *Pride and Prejudice (2005)*.

In her defense, Sherlock understood and acknowledged the confines of reality. Thus, the mangling of an occult word was canon.

If there was a costume contest, she'd so win. Decimate. Thank the judges' panel with the word indubitably.

A short, low laugh clipped her ear, stroked along her spine like warm rain on the beach. He pointed at his top hat and plopped a bubbled plastic knife next to his beer. "Jack the Ripper."

Black velour cape. Play knife. Boxy hat. Shaggy black sideburns.

She let out an incredulous laugh. "How perfect that we met, then. Now I won't have to track you down to find justice." She collapsed onto the stool next to him, turned.

Froze as their gazes locked. Her earmuffs engaged. She forgot the revelers swarming the bar, the dangerous volume of Diana's Makin' Money playlist. It was just them, poised inches apart in a decadent burgundy glow that made everything seem rehearsed.

His gaze drawn to her mouth, the swipe of his tongue over a deadly white canine. The flex of his hand over his thigh. As if fighting the desire to touch her.

Carrie craved to capture him. The shadow of his hat over impossibly dark eyes, the jagged length of his jaw, the swallow stuck in his throat. In a sea of half-assed Powerpuff girls and gold chained Jokers, he was every bit the dangerous killer. All deadly temptation.

He shared a slight grin. "Dear Holmes, surely you know it wasn't anyone but I who lured you here."

"As if the greatest detective in her time would knowingly walk into a trap."

"Perhaps she would in order to face the deadliest man of his time." His huge hand closed around the rubbed silver chain dangling from her jacket pocket. "Perhaps, even knowing it was a trap, she couldn't miss the opportunity to meet her match."

He tugged the overused timepiece free and deftly unlatched it. "Only ten," he observed, thumb stroking the fogged antique glass. "Hardly late enough to add to the body count."

He held her hostage with the gentle stroke of his thumb and his low murmur. His willingness to join her game.

Somehow, miraculously, Carrie avoided an honest to goodness fit of vapors, swoon-off-the-back-of-her-stool as the scent of him struck. Ice topped mountains, harsh peaks and jagged white stone cliffs. Fresh and treacherous.

"Too far?" he asked at her silence, quickly returning her watch and taking a long swig of his beer. His mouth came back stained a grisly red.

If he were Jack the Ripper, his Most Wanted poster would earn him a Times Square Billboard partnership with Alani Nu. Kosmic Killer. Bloodberry. Cranberry Crush.

Wide shoulders. Hard, square chin buried in fake, black scruff. He didn't sit. Too banal and pedestrian for the likes of him. He waited, stone still, like a claw hooked gargoyle at the edge of a skyscraper, surveying, stripping the passing world of its glamours.

"The contrary," she said, commandeering the elegance of a Mayfair Lady to squash the butterflies in her stomach. "For the world's foremost killer, I expected less critical thinking, and a far more insidious blade."

His smile gleamed. "For just one night, I want to be something other than a homicidal deviant. I want people to look past the murder and see me. A man. With feelings other than bloodlust and carnage."

She gave him an openly speculative glance. "That's what all gentlemen say before they string a lady up."

"Not tonight, not with you. Tonight, I'm just Jack."

How could one man possess such charm? Carrie smiled as she snatched her drink and held it up. The heavy glass was cold soaked, alerting Carrie to the whole body flush Just Jack gave her.

He met her glass with his, pausing short of a clink.

"To uncommon friends," she cheered.

A curl of his lips, a pierce of white teeth. "To ending our friendship."

They clinked and drank, and his dark, heady gaze soaked into her skin, revived dead cells and made new, circuitous connections between the taste of gin and the tight feeling in her stomach.

Drinking more than a sip, more than a glug, she returned her glass to the bar, but before she let go, Jack's fingers curled around hers, sliding it from her hold.

"Holmes." He drummed his knuckles against the counter, turning her drink under the light. "Movies or books?"

Carrie grinned, cracking the triple layer of her Ultra White Creamy foundation. Sherlock didn't have freckles, and in the time of his life, it would've been most uncouth to be anything but pale faced. "The TV show. Benedict Cumberbatch."

"Wow, and I thought Downey Jr was the kingpin. I've been bamboozled." Jack stopped his inspection of her drink and flashed long, insinuating lashes at her. "It's purple."

"Yes."

"It looks radioactive."

Swiveling on the bar stool, she hooked her toes around the metal rung. Not exactly ladylike, but kicking her feet like a giddy teen was a dead giveaway to her growing attachment. "And your lips are red."

"Keep drawing attention to it and I'll color match yours, dear Holmes."

Call it. Time of death on Carrie's dry spell. Three blushes past ten.

Executioner: Just Jack.

"Gin, maraschino, lemon, and creme de Violette." She ticked her fingers, remembering the day she'd discovered the mesmerizing shiny purple liquor in Diana's skunked cabinet and gone bug eyed as she begged for a pretty drink. "It's prolific."

"Gin. That's what you're drinking? Gin and cherries and flowers?" He exhaled loudly, mimicking a disappointed parent. "Holmes." He groaned, covering his face in his palms.

She was laughing, spinning in her seat. "What?"

"Holmes," he repeated, hand sliding over the thick blend of her trousers. Five fingers dug into her skin, guided her to him. "Look at me." She couldn't breathe. "Who is forcing you to drink this? It's inconceivable. If you like the color, I'll melt some blue raspberry ranchers in my beer. Do not subject yourself to milked pine needles."

Her cheeks ached from smiling, and her thigh was an inferno under his touch. "It's good."

"Yeah, if you're an alcoholic stranded in the arctic with a lone tree to keep you company. There's not a soul in here choosing gin." He was shaking his head, an exasperated grin on his face. "Holmes," he said again, and it made Carrie want to race to the DMV to officially change her name.

"It's good," she defended as she jabbed her pointer at his pint. "And you're essentially drinking paint."

"I'm being festive," he countered, dragging knuckles down the side of his glass. No tattoo on the back of his hand. Which meant he'd been in The Hand before Diana doled out stamps. A long time. Alone the entire time. "I'm in the spirit. I brought a knife to a goddamn dance fight."

"No to dancing?"

"Honestly Holmes, if it weren't for you, I'd have loosed a bag of marbles on the floor already."

"I'm sorry if my presence is ruining your delinquent behavior."

"It is," he insisted with a smirk. "Dammit, my foot's tapping because of you. You can hardly look at me, too busy smiling at the dancers."

Her eyes widened, and her feet unhooked as her knees turned to jelly. She wiggled in her seat, accidentally brushed his knee with hers. Felt it like an electric shock. Dove for her drink.

He was partially right. Yes, she enjoyed dancing, but she kept turning to keep from blinding him with her idiot I'm-planning-our-next-three-anniversaries grin.

Her smile dimmed as she stirred with her cherry stem. "I don't get it."

"Me either. Gin is essentially poison. It's snake juice."

"Stop," she teased, struggling to maintain her accent. "How are you single?"

His brow arched. "Ah. The elephant in the room." Although his smirk was present, his words were hollow, as if he'd known and dreaded her asking. "The question that's been circling." His jaw flexed. "You know why I'm single."

"Your work hours are killer." She waited for the rumble, the chuckle she'd balance a red ball on her nose for.

He made a fist, sucked his teeth. Didn't look at her. "You were here. Before. You swept in like you were ready to petition parliament, and when you started talking—" He shook his head.

Endlessly dark eyes sought hers. Searched. "Holmes, I thought it was likelier you were undercover FBI talking to three dudes in a dog washing truck than talking to me."

His hands were shaking as if nervous, but he appeared savage, capable of every gruesome deed of a homicidal deviant. The playful mask corroded.

Their gazes tangled, and Carrie felt her muscles tighten like she was at the top of a roller coaster, staring down a triple loop upside down drop and her seatbelt was loose.

"I nearly fell off my chair when you smiled at me. Me, out of everyone here, and the second, Holmes— The very second you turned, I knew I'd lost."

"Lost?" She tried keeping her voice light as she grappled with his confession. Swallowed the lump in her throat, poked her cherry to dive under the ice. "Is there a game afoot?"

"One involving a great deal of casualties." He bent forward, staring as though entranced, licked his canine. "My sanity, my pride, my plans for the future."

Suddenly, Carrie wanted that tongue inside her mouth, his teeth sinking into her lip, biting, sucking away the pain. His intensity made her quake, so she teased, "You're too charming to be tied down, is that it?"

"This is the first non-mandatory party I've been to since I was eight. Good beer, a fun crowd, the music's been on fire, and I'm desperate to leave." Jack's gaze was riveted on her, his eyes so dark they reflected the pink strobe. "Or I was."

She understood at once. He was an introvert.

Halloween in a packed bar as an introvert.

She slid her gloved hand along the grain of the bar top until her pinky brushed his. "Why'd you stay?"

"Because a very important woman asked me to put myself out there. She told me to try new things and see the world, and when I put lilies at her grave, I don't want to feel like I disappointed her."

"Did you?"

He tipped his head back, hat slipping up on his forehead. "Asking a lot of questions, Holmes."

"Detective, remember?"

His eyes shut, the exposed line of his throat revealed a bracing flex. "I think she'd be proud of what I've done, what I made for myself, but the rest— I don't know. I should've done more, tried harder. I should've followed her advice sooner. I should've told her what she meant to me every day for the past twenty years. I should've thanked her."

Twenty-years, Carrie's heart wrenched. His mother, he spoke of his mother. She searched for the appropriate response. The apology, the soft murmur of support. But those never made Carrie feel better.

A faint smile touched her lips. "You still have time." She nudged her drink over. "Here. Try it."

A dangerous flick of his gaze to her. Refusal, she braced for it.

Then he shook his shoulders. Picked up her swirling purple cocktail, shut his eyes, and drank.

His hand slowly slid away. His eyes flickered open, slashed to her, dipped to her mouth. A smirk. "That's terrible, Holmes."

But he was grinning.

And it was dazzling.

Time slipped after that. Beyond reason and logic and everything Sherlock was grounded in. This immovable thing, this concept known and fixed, it compressed and shrank, disappeared under her feet. She didn't move, didn't talk to anyone but Jack. Laughing and smiling. They spoke of nothing and everything. The songs he liked in middle school. How Carrie spent six years growing out her bangs.

When a slash of cold air replaced the near constant heat of jumping bodies, Carrie glanced over her shoulder.

It was late. Late enough for more people to be leaving than coming.

She crushed a cherry between her teeth and broke the spell. "They're going to kick us out soon." Her accent had gone cockney over the fourth dose of gin. Wrangling it back to polished seemed impossible.

"I don't want to go," Jack said, staring at his beer. The Oktoberfest turned an odd, old blood brown when it went flat, but he was insistent it was the most palatable thing on the limited menu. As if he'd tried the rest already.

His eyes never met hers, restless hands on the hardwood. "I don't want to leave you and I can't ask you to come with me because I'm drunk and there's nowhere to even take you."

Carrie felt her insides warp, harden and snap. "That's alright."

Had that been an Irish accent?

"It's not." He exhaled sharply. "I've lost my fucking mind. Did I conjure you up? I'm waiting for the walls to bleed or the ceiling to crumble, anything to tell me I'm in an alley with vomit on my lap, and you're a construct of my lonely fucking mind. A torture device."

His fingers scratched at the tie of his cape, stopped and reached up like he wanted to pull on his hair. Stopped again.

Carrie thought he might be blonde. Pictured the lovely golden curls of a surfer, colors that shone under the midday sun.

"I'm terrified of what comes next." He spoke quietly, like the truth required subservience. "I can't leave, not when all I want to hear is your laugh. I can't make myself move if you're not coming with me. I want to steal you away and never let you shine for anyone else." He blew out a breath, and wet his lips, tongue nicking his tooth. "It's pathetic, but—"

She closed her eyes tightly, desperate for him to finish his sentence.

He didn't.

"The worst." He scrubbed a hand down his face. Laughed darkly. "The worst of it is that I don't care. I want every thought. I want to keep them, horde them for myself. It's wrong. I know it. I see right and wrong, but I can't do right in this. Holmes," he sighed on her name. "If you were a butterfly, I'd already have you pinned, needles in your wings so I could look at you whenever I wanted to feel."

Carrie swallowed, her fingers trembled.

He emitted a callous laugh. "I've ruined it."

"You didn't." Her voice was less than a whisper, a rasp.

"You're shaking."

"Ignore it."

"Ignoring you would be like ignoring the oxygen in the air. Impossible to survive." He tightened his jaw, downed dark, filthy burgundy, still not looking at her, hand firm on his glass. "So what now? You splash water on me, and I wake up?"

"No," Carrie murmured, fighting her instinct to grab him, to kiss him, to give him every word. "We live here. In this moment."

Where perfection existed.

Chapter Three

Carrie

"You're into bestiality?"

Water squirted from Carrie's mouth and doused the lap of her purple sweatpants as she sent wide, what-the-fuck eyes to her best friend.

"No animals." Diana Lovatt's husky voice hit the smudged corners of the inch thick plexiglass observer's window and scattered across the cement room. Gray walls dappled in black and one very disturbing spot of brown.

Diana was as unbothered by the stains as she was by the heavy fog of foot sweat and BO.

"Animals are either adorable—" She paused to make a crude gagging sound and bounced the edge of her racquet against the thick rubber edge of her Vans. "—or a nasty comparison. Do you want people likening you to a cow? An ostrich?"

Carrie scrunched her nose. She firmly believed any and all comparisons to giraffes, elephants, and yeti should be left in year ten.

"What about a sexy cat?" she countered, picturing long red nails wrapped around a furry orange tail. Delicate black whiskers painted across her cheeks, a sexy lace choker with a silver bell. "That's a classic for a reason."

"Until you cough, and some sod accuses you of a hairball." With force, Diana slammed the burgundy ball onto the pocked wood floor and whacked it.

Here we go again, Carrie thought.

Begrudgingly, she watched the rubber ball of death soar, flinching as it smacked violently against the wall. Only at the last possible second did she react, generating maximum effort to give chase. Her lungs burned and her thighs quivered like she was breaking through the ribbon at the end of the Boston Marathon.

Racquetball.

Whatever happened to chasing butterflies? Naming clouds? Picking dandelions?

Sure that her ears were bleeding from the pounding thwack of the ball, Carrie lunged toward the ricocheting rubber Death Star. Her arms were imitating overcooked noodles, and the back of her tongue was coated in iron.

They were not coming back.

Not ever.

Not if Diana first learned how to, and then proceeded to beg Carrie for a rematch.

It wasn't just that Carrie possessed the athletic prowess of a long rotted pumpkin; it was the infuriating inability to think while a fist-sized bullet played pinball with her very precious, highly vulnerable bones.

With a swing and a capital M: Miss, Carrie ducked as the ball struck the window behind her. A wave of brown hair blocked her view when it came shooting back and slapped her calf.

"Stop hiding," Diana instructed steadily.

Carrie blew hair out of her mouth.

A bob. Ideal in theory: adorable, fun, easygoing. A complete transformation from her pedestrian brown sheet of hair into Avant-Garde. Or as Avant-Garde as hairstyles got in little Burlington, Vermont.

Eight months after the Great Chop, Carrie understood why Debbie at Hair Force had double checked the style. "A bob?" she'd asked as she'd tied off Carrie's ends. "You're sure?"

Of course, Carrie was sure. A new style plus fifteen inches for Locks of Love? No brainer. Snip, snip. Make with the transformation.

The questioning tone was—in retrospect—warranted. Turned out bobs were impossible to put up or pin back. And when stuffed under a hat—

Well. Diana made enough phallic jokes to demolish Carrie's knitted beanie collection.

The layers were a hassle. Bobby pins and claw clips treated her scalp like a scratching post. The ends stuck to her lip gloss, and if she missed a tweeze, she twinned with Lord Farquaad.

This was all to say, never get a haircut because your boyfriend convinces you it'll distract from the winter weight you packed on.

A bob was not a thinning hairstyle.

"What was wrong with the park?" Carrie separated a wayward strand from her eyelashes. "I saw a hawk."

And there wasn't rubber shrapnel.

Used to hauling kegs, corralling drunks, and spending ten-hour shifts on her feet, Diana hadn't shed a speck of sweat. Might not have the glands for it.

Carrie had once tried describing her best friend—while under the influence of an addictively tart sangria—and she'd proudly settled on Cadbury Egg Beautiful.

In retaliation, Diana referred to Carrie as a pink starburst about yay high.

Carrie may have been drunk on sun, peach stained wine, and Diana's throaty laugh when she said it, but it held strong. Fit perfectly.

Diana's skin was creamy and supple, porcelain, free from scars and scabbing, untouched by wrinkles and pollution. Her thick, wild mane of hair was the same shade as a powerful brew of English Breakfast, and she had eyes like dusk in the early fall. A decadent bronze that warmed and cooled with the moon.

Delicate features. A slight frame.

In short, Diana was undeniably universally beautiful.

And an utter disaster to photograph. Light fractured over her like wet paint down a windowpane, slipping and sliding, fighting to stick. Failing.

In the frightfully early hours, usually when Diana flipped the lights on for last call at her bar, Carrie would rest her chin in her hands and admire. Fantasize about capturing Diana's inhuman symmetry.

That symmetry—the understated lines and subtle palette—was the creamy, heavenly sweet, homogenous center.

Which Diana coated in a hard chocolate shell of ripped Blink-182 concert tees, oversized leather jackets, and jeans with more holes than seams. Her resilience to her own demure nature only cranked up the allure. A hard shell cast around such fragile beauty.

And deep—center of the earth deep—in that ooey gooey center laid a ghost pepper waiting to singe and permanently alter your taste buds.

No, a better metaphor didn't exist.

Cadbury Egg Beautiful. Special prize inside.

By the by, how the two women became friends, much less stayed friends, was one of Carrie's favorite mysteries. Oatmeal cookies and chain mail. Teacups and Metallica.

"It was too bloody cold." Diana's black nails sank into the maroon ball. "And my paints dried out and that hawk shite on my All Saints jacket."

"You don't actually know that it was him." Though the beady eyed turd had looked quite smug hovering overhead.

"When I said you should be more discerning, I didn't mean with me. Taking the pro-side of an argument is making me queasy."

As if anything could scare Diana. "Please vomit," Carrie intoned with a half-smile. "At least then, they'll ban us for life."

"What's so bad about racquetball? It's good for you. Gets your blood pumping. You've even got a bit of a sweat going."

Carrie peeled her *Sabrina Jeffries Men or Bust* shirt from her chest and lifted an eyebrow. She was drowning in her 'bit of sweat'.

Diana ignored her. "Most importantly, it's free."

Oh, how the words both wrangled and delighted Carrie. Losing her job at Sam's French Fry's had been a lifetime low. A day marked in grease soaked history. She missed the under the table, taxes-who cash like a missing limb. Like a missing ventricle. But she didn't regret it. Losing her entire support system had made her biggest dream come true.

Professional photographer.

No more crammed photo sessions after a double fryer shift or canceled shoots caused by ice cream machine malfunctions. All photography all the time. The business card switch was thrilling, but full-time photographer didn't include overtime and a free hot dog every six-hour shift.

When Carrie suggested she and Diana replace their standing happy hour drink with a walk by the lake, she'd been a mess of frayed nerves. Mostly because Diana had thrown her boots off her desk and immediately checked Carrie's skull for a missing chunk.

There was a moment—not a proud one—wherein Carrie had considered feigning a heinous brain contusion, complete with crossed eyes and a goopy string of drool. But her wallet of air and overstuffed SD cards didn't even cover after work frosé, so she forged ahead. In between listing how many fingers wiggled an inch from her nose, Carrie admitted everything. She was stretched so thin, you could see right through her.

After the big, forever humbling reveal, Carrie denied Diana's two loan offers and a flat out cash gift.

Then, not eight minutes later, the goth queen was stomping size five Doc Martins down the boardwalk.

"It's very loud and aggressive," Carrie pointed out, might have shouted it. She feared she'd never hear the tick of a clock again.

Before Diana could dole out another whack, Carrie scrabbled for the ball and asked, "How long do we have the court reserved?"

With a peek at her chunky men's watch, Diana shrugged. "About another five minutes, but it's not as if there's a line. The kid at the front desk was clearly watching porn."

"He was reading, and you were being unnecessarily nosey."

Diana looked at her like she'd not just missed an exit, but like she'd driven them straight off a bridge. "He launched over the counter to hide his phone and then gaped at us with saucer eyes. It was porn. You're too trusting."

Carrie's mouth opened, but nothing came out.

"Wash your hands before we leave," Diana added with a curled upper lip. "I knew the YMCA would be filled with perverts. Tell me you didn't sign us up for that step class."

"I was too late. It's already full."

"Small miracles." Tossing her racquet on the floor, Diana sat in the middle of the square court and leaned back on her palms, feet outstretched before her.

The soles of her shoes read *Look* and *Away*.

Pleased that combat hour was finito, Carrie collapsed too. Legs splayed wide, chest heaving. As her fingers danced along the tight plastic weave, she figured there was some accuracy in Diana's statement.

Not the porn. The kid was barely sixteen, and he was working. He wouldn't.

But Carrie had only recently admitted to herself—in the darkest moments of the night—that she might benefit from a raised level of wariness.

"What about a cop or a ninja?" Diana used the corner of her thumbnail to scrape at a stubby streak of black beside her hip.

Carrie's stomach turned. "I want to be …"

"Sexy, I know. And I'm pitching sensual gold. Nurse? Milkmaid?" She snapped her fingers. "Cut straight to the chase and be a stripper. Or pole dancer. Bloody hell, be a lady of the night. It's Halloween. There are sexy nuns."

A cross and garters? "Absolutely not."

"What? You're suddenly religious? Saw Jesus on your toast this morning?"

A wry smile reached Carrie's lips. "No." Though her pink pop tart icing had been the spitting image of Westminster Abbey. "I just don't want to be obvious or common, and I don't want to look like a completely different person. I want him to see me and remember. I want …"

Ignoring the pinch of the cold, hard floor on her tailbone, Carrie closed her eyes to envision what would be the most romantic moment of her life. Dust particles freezing midair, sound ceasing, her lips tingling as she sat in the same stool for the fourth and final time.

She'd turn. He'd smile. His pinky finger would brush the outside of her thigh. Fire would light her blood, she'd lean forward, his hand would slide up over her tense muscle, inward.

"What?"

Carrie jolted at Diana's question, flushing at the lurid derailment of her fantasy. "Huh?"

"You want what?"

Staring at the gnarly red paint strokes on Diana's soles, Carrie said, "I want to watch his eyes widen until his entire perception of me changes and he suddenly realizes that one night isn't enough. That I complete him in the same way oxygen gives life. Then he'll caress my cheek and tell me we're perfect together." Her breath was coming out hard as she finished, her eyes glistened.

"Hyper realistic expectations," came Diana's flat response.

Rather than argue, Carrie shrugged. Diana didn't get it. Didn't believe in soul mates or love at first sight.

"How about next week," Diana went on dryly, "we'll go to the botanical garden where you can play *does he love me, or does he love me not* with a mum and I can find a sturdy vine to hang myself?"

"No guess as to what you'll be for Halloween. Crabby old witch."

Diana kicked her foot out to smack Carrie. Stopped two inches short.

All bark, no bite. Good for Carrie's wellbeing.

And the city at large.

"You don't even know his name," her friend reminded as she stood. Five minutes up. "You know nothing about him. You've spent three days together and since the leaves turned, he's been all you've talked about." Diana pulled Carrie to her feet, tone changing from practical detachment to gentle concern. "Your eyes are two floating hearts, and they terrify me. I want to shut down the bar just to avoid the fallout."

Carrie's heart nosedived. "You wouldn't."

"I can't afford to, but I should. It's just ..." Diana toyed with the skull on her necklace, stroking the mandible like one would a kitten. "It's not like you to seduce someone."

"It's the best idea I've ever had," Carrie insisted, taking Diana's hand as a tight feeling squeezed her chest. "He's the most reliable man I've ever known. Every Halloween. Ten o'clock. He's there. Waiting for me." Broad shoulders level and straight. Two drinks in front of him. A pint of the seasonal and an aviator, extra garnish. "For three years, I've been too chicken to ask for more. It's time. I'm not getting any younger. The adventure starts in T-Minus thirty days."

Carrie had done the math.

Three dates over three years. She was twenty-nine now, and if they kept their current pace, she'd be the oldest *Say Yes to the Dress* participant in the history of ... history.

It didn't matter how much lace or how many pearls she added if it was her casket getting wheeled down the aisle.

"What if he doesn't live here?" Diana asked, relentlessly pragmatic. "Are you going to move? He could have a family in Philadelphia. Tiny little pirates and axe-murderers."

Carrie flinched, unable to fight it.

"I shouldn't have said that," Diana blurted, softening, regret pulling her gaze down.

"You're right. He could be another Justin." Who's kids' names were Heidi and Tim, grades four and six. Information that would've been nice to know before she drove her rust-mobile to

Franconia, New Hampshire, only to be caught breaking into her boyfriend's kitchen by his wife.

Carrie knocked now. Forcefully, with knuckles. Searched high and low for doorbells.

Clutching Diana's hand, Carrie struggled for the right words to explain that in her soul, she knew Jack. Knew he was different, and that she was destined to be with him. He was the end to her string of bad dates.

Settled on, "But he's not."

Diana dragged her in for a hug, smelling cool and woodsy. Like she'd rolled in fresh wood shavings and eucalyptus. Meanwhile, Carrie's sweat cast mismatched crescent moons under her boobs.

Was her left boob really that much bigger?

"I should be a bloody witch for Halloween," Diana muttered, heaving a sigh, two ring studded fingers massaging her temple. "I'm worried you're going to get hurt. When was the last time you even had sex?"

There were no secrets between best friends. But Carrie could under no circumstances admit it'd been less than six months since Travis talked his way back into her bed. He'd been so apologetic and dimly tender, lugging daffodils stolen from the park with the roots still attached. Carrie folded.

Shonda Rhimes was to blame. Never watch *Bridgerton* alone.

Now, her precious baby Camry was scattered across the junk-yards of Georgia.

Carrie dabbed at her sweat stains. "Does it matter?"

"Maybe you should give it a go. It might knock those goofy cartoon hearts out of your eyes."

Diana viewed sex like a vitamin. Low on D? Grab some at the Kinney's and pick me up a travel-size aloe while you're at it.

Snagging her bulky camera bag off the aluminum viewer's bench and hauling it over her shoulder, fierce resolve poured over Carrie. There would be no men, no temptation, no distractions for the next month.

Because she chose terrible men. Men who called her the wrong name, men who had secret families, men who stole her car.

But Jack—

He was different.

Attractive, smart, funny, with enough money in the bank to order a drink without checking the price or counting out dimes. A Vermont twelve out of ten. A New York eight, according to Diana's conversion chart. He was the last of the gentlemen. Honest and kind and mannered. He listened to her. Remembered her. Respected her.

Carrie Jenkins; photographer, knitter, crap racquet baller.

There would be no other men. No other mistakes. Jack was it. Her forever.

Diana didn't understand. Couldn't. She used men like Kleenex. Didn't matter if they were bad or good, she never found out before she dunked them in the trash.

Jack wasn't even his name. It was a moniker. A label. An idea.

Without knowing his name, his hair color, where he lived or what he did, Carrie knew more about him than Diana bothered to glean from all of her conquests combined.

Two racquets and one terrorizing ball abandoned at center court, the friends hurried their way past the front desk, skirting around a pair of toe-tapping old men, each bedecked in goggles, sweatbands, and knee pads.

"Court's for playing," the bald one sneered, face souring when Diana showed him straight, white teeth in response. Not a smile.

Latching onto her friend's wrist, Carrie shoved her bulldog through the exit, and whispered into her ear, "He's you in like two decades."

"That makes you the flabby chinned knee-high socks one."

Warm calves? Yes, please.

Carrie laughed and raised a hand to block the sun as the brisk air nipped wet skin.

Overhead, flocks of geese intent on escaping for the winter weaved between dreamy wisps of clouds.. Fall had come as it always did in New England: heartrendingly potent.

"Oh!" She spun on the sidewalk, dry auburn leaves crunching underfoot. "What about a serial killer? But not what you're thinking. I'm a box of Trix with—"

"Puns are not sexy." Cold air scooped Diana's dark curls and spun them tighter. "Killing on the other hand—"

A phone cut her off on the first ring. Ever the workaholic, Diana answered without preamble, barking out concise orders as she checked her watch. Shifting the receiver out of range, she lifted her chin and smiled. "Declan confirmed, he's found him."

Finally.

Chapter Four

Asher

H AD ASHER BEEN A nanosecond slower, the bird's egg blue box would've hit him square in the chin.

And had he not already wrecked his body for the day, he'd have caught it.

But since practice had indeed beat the ever loving shit out of him, Asher only tightened his jaw as the finest of Tiffany and Co's wrap jobs collided with his front door like a slop of mashed potatoes in a cafeteria food fight.

Better not leave a mark.

He stifled the warning in his throat with a tooth cracking clench.

Maintaining a businesslike calm, Asher loosened the cuffs of his Armani and hung his jacket, carefully straitening the folds in the tapered sleeves. Some of the tension left him.

Fuck, it was hard to step back into it. He'd either forgotten or been out of practice too long.

For close to twenty years, Asher had people pleased. A maladjusted introvert who'd starve before taking the last serving of baked beans at the table.

He might as well be eight again, skinny knees knocking together under his desk as he assured Mr. Garber the family tree unit didn't make him feel excluded.

He wasn't born into foster care. He'd been almost three when CPS found him on the interstate with blackened feet, scabbed knees, and a full diaper.

Asher had bought in to the stories. The rumors of what it took to be adopted. How to get your photo on the famed family wall. A bedroom. Hugs and pets, and someone to pick you up from school when you were sick. Packed lunches complete with little hand-written notes.

If you met the criteria.

Every day, Asher had tried. He perfected his manners. Didn't yell *mine* when someone took the working train. He never hit. He didn't eat more than he needed, he washed all the dishes in the sink even if he only used a spoon. Dressed respectably, never made a mess. But every day, Asher got older.

And he'd believed those stories, too. Old kids never get picked. So he doubled down. Worked harder. Trained himself out of a lisp, became the fastest counter in his class. He lived with his head down, lived to conform to the child someone sought.

He'd moved in with Dave and Lisa Batting on his eleventh birthday. They were full time foster parents, who cared mostly for infants. Lisa was a neonatal nurse, and Dave liked football. Neither wanted a preteen. But they had a spare room in the basement and Marianne convinced them Asher wouldn't cause problems.

There were rumors about foster parents, too. Nasty gut churning rumors. Violence, and drugs, and hate. Step out of line, get the belt. Do it again, get out.

He hadn't known Marianne trusted the Battings. Just the stories. He'd figured if he never left his peeling tennis shoes in a pile, never left a cup in the sink, or forgot to trash the diaper pail, the Battings would forget he was there, alone in Dave's Colts memorabilia room, staring at a signed Peyton Manning ball, trying not to breathe too loudly.

The Battings were not like the stories. They didn't pack his lunch, but they didn't backhand him either.

And Asher started to think they'd adopt him if he was even better. So he'd spent every night in the nursery, listening to the baby's coos, counting down the hours until he had to warm the first bottle. He had a knack for predicting needs, for determining what each baby needed. White noise, a night light, a diaper change at two in the morning. If he kept the babies happy, the Battings would be happy. They'd want to keep him.

When Asher turned thirteen, Marianne informed him that his biological parents had abandoned him on the highway. No one knew how far he'd wandered. A dad in a gold minivan had called the police, thinking he was a body, not a boy.

The next year Asher went out for football. And when stern Dave patted his back, Asher's hope had flared, hot and penetrating.

The Battings moved a second crib into his room.

At sixteen, Marianne told him there'd be no point in adoption. Confessed she hadn't realized he was still trying.

Because he'd never asked for it. Because it'd be rude and selfish to ask.

He had become so desperate to please others that he never revealed his greatest desire.

"You seemed so happy with the Battings," she'd said, pushing her chrome cat eye glasses to rest on long white hair.

"They aren't parents," he'd whispered, burying his white-knuckled fists under his thighs. "I wanted parents."

"Lisa and Dave like you."

He'd pushed harder into the thin cushion of his chair, pressed the soles of borrowed sketchers into the depressing brown government carpet. "Yes," he'd whispered when he'd wanted to overturn her desk, when he'd wanted to shred the motivational posters from her walls, when he'd wanted to scream that Lisa and Dave also liked cloudy fucking mornings and discovering their coffee hadn't gone cold, but no one ever wanted to hug that.

The next time he'd met with Marianne was the last, and she'd stung him one last time. *Get out there. Try something.*

Another box flew at him. Black with a genuine silver inlay. Excellent quality, and judging from the way its corner punched a hole in the drywall, the luxury market had discovered rebar.

"These are women's," came Burton Kilbride's growl as he tore through the meticulously organized offerings.

Huh, Asher mused, examining his teammate's bloodshot green eyes and scruffy overgrown beard. It was impossible to differentiate a furious Burton and the everyday model. The deep crow's feet and protruding neck veins were becoming permanent.

"It's all shit. I don't want any of it," the tight end snapped, swiping another box from atop Asher's solid black walnut desk. Pawing about, searching wildly, Burton emulated like a self-righteous grizzly hunting for beef sticks at the bottom of a cheap Igloo freezer.

Designer orange rocketed through the office's French doors and across the vaulted foyer, razor sharp corners aiming to puncture.

Exhausted, Asher stayed nimble, dodging flying Hermes with a side step along the checkerboard marble tile.

Burton made eight million dollars last season, but if he loitered too long on the street corner, well-meaning loose change would wreck his coffee before the first sip. Mesh shorts and an overstretched *Where's Champy?* t-shirt paired with stained socks and too narrow sandals and the man demanded to be paid in gold.

Like a fucking Bond villain.

And not just any gold. Rare pieces. Priceless. Special collection, be-on-a-list-to-get-a-name-to-meet-someone-who-may-have-a-connection gold.

Asher sawed his jaw to stop from exploding.

For now, he needed the Boar's help.

He'd panhandle the entire Yukon to find her. Then he would lay into Burton for being a self-serving egomaniac and general misery to be around. The entire Mountaineers' team walked on eggshells around the big bastard since his divorce. Four. Years. Ago. Meanwhile, Asher got regularly flayed for having a poor attitude because he didn't want to sing Kumbaya with the Scooby Gang.

The rub of his molars muddled his rising irritation with a soothing white noise. But even that sliver of peace was interrupted by Dr. Delane's nasally warning, *Stop grinding, or you'll be the first twenty-five-year-old with dentures.*

An impossible task.

Yanking his collar up to get some breathing room, Asher gritted, "Gold is gold. There's no women's or men's."

A velvet lined necklace box struck the vulnerable skin behind his knee.

"Watch it." Asher felt the words rumble in his chest.

Burton dangled a thin woven chain from pinched fingers like it was the gruesome entrails of a roadkill opossum.

"Oh, there's a fucking difference," he growled, Vanna White bending the 24 carat gold to his wrist, taking the clasp and snapping it. Clean in two.

"You absolute fuck—" Asher snarled, snatching the broken ends from the black tile. "That was Harry Winston, you oversized troglodyte—"

"You undersized gremlin—"

They spoke at the same time, sporting matching scowls, tight chins and pinched, hate-filled eyes.

Fuck. What the hell was he doing? Twisting his palm, Asher locked his jaw and fixed a stern gaze upon the woven chain.

He was losing it.

Three years and he was splintering. Unhinged. Desperate to find her. To have her. To feel her voice wash over his skin.

He'd brokered a deal with the devil for her. Sacrificed his good judgement, compromised his morals, his beliefs and the worst of it, he couldn't—not in the deepest valleys of his soul—make himself regret it.

"You asked for flash," Asher said tightly. "You didn't specify anything else."

Burton's nostrils flared. "I don't fucking like you."

It bounced right off. Who did the thirty-four year old like? He was dropping friends faster than two burst engines on the team jet. Bitter, temperamental asshole. The day his stats dropped would be the day Burton lost everyone.

Asher fisted the chain. "The top drawer of my desk—" he said, aware he was grinding his teeth to keep his tone amenable. *Play along. Play his game.*

A sudden tightness gnawed at Asher's nerve endings as Burton made himself at home.

He hated having someone in his place. Hated dealing with this asshole. Hated Miles for pairing them up like two rotten apples thrown out from the bushel.

Wood rattled. "It's locked."

Teeth throbbing, Asher emptied his pockets onto the credenza and lined up his phone, keys, and look—dentures would fit beside his wallet. Just there. A top and bottom. He could set out bowls of Listerine for soaking while he gummed down a chicken Caesar.

"Where's the key?" No hiding the aggravation in Burton's voice.

Asher relaxed his jaw and shoved a straining fist behind his back. "Tell me what you found first."

The groan of leather drew Asher's attention. If Burton was fucking up his chair—

But the Boar was sitting, fingers poking at the ornate lock inlaid in the dark wood.

A slice of tension released from Asher's soul. Having Burton in his space felt like throwing open the shutters during a tornado watch.

Their common manager, Victoria, liked to tirade about the state in which the Boar had left his PNW house before he joined the Mountaineers' ranks. Used warm and fuzzy words like *Chernobyl* and *Hiroshima* as she made frenzied, obscene gestures.

But where else could they meet? Clandestine updates on the turf were impossible with fifty-one other Mountaineers sniffing around. So the Peak was out. And he refused to let Burton Kilbride sully the only other place in Burlington he liked.

This, Asher decided, was the true cost of being a homebody.

Remaining steady at the door, Asher inhaled through his nose and unbuttoned the top two—fuck it, three—buttons of his oxford, rolling up the sleeves as he mapped a path through lethal Cartier boxes.

He had cash.

A teetering Scrooge type stack in his closet banded in bank certified blue rubber. He wanted to charge into the walk-in, yank the Armani, the Gucci, the McCartney off the racks and pile his arms full of greenbacks until Burton was satisfied, until he had answers.

"Cash I got," he'd said when Asher first asked for help, grinning like a wolf happening upon a freshly snared rabbit. "You'll give me something better."

Ridiculous, crotchety, difficult fucker—

He shut his eyes, unclamped his jaw. This was the only way. The last rock unturned. Get the information and—

Wood cracked.

Echoed in the vast space of his office, a violent shear bouncing off clean, hard surfaces. Asher's eyes ripped open. The hand turned legs of his desk shuddered. A drawer ground along its rails, not sliding, dragging. Grinding.

Burton made a throaty noise. "Bulgari." He withdrew the platinum plated serpent broach. "Vintage."

"You broke my—"

"She's dead."

Terror slashed into Asher. Overpowering, malicious.

His stomach plummeted, shot down so fast, he braced for the floor to crumble, to freefall ten floors and flatten against the cement of the building's parking garage. He staggered. His back smacked the wall, and he sagged against it, pressure building painfully in his chest. Light-headed, dizzy, sick, his mouth fell open, sweat coated his spine.

He was numb, but his heart suffered. He grappled with his shirt, with buttons, needing air. He was shaking his head, looking at his hands, the floor, his keys. "No. She can't. No. I—"

"Or in witness protection," Burton kept on, attaching the pin to his chest. "She's a ghost. No sign of her. Anywhere."

No sign wasn't dead. No sign was—

Bastard.

His heart kept contracting, trying to beat and wondering *why? Without her, it's—*

"You said dead, you—" Asher sounded like a man possessed, growling and snarling.

"Ah, ah, ah." Burton wagged his finger, a smirk making his ugly mug more terrifying. "This is only a down payment. Piss me off and I'll leave. Take the information with me."

Asher's mouth snapped shut, and he stiffened. Slowly, he crossed the vestibule, fighting the return of the dizziness.

Burton smiled.

"She's not a ghost," he reiterated sharply, rubbing the butt of his palm against his chest, performing mild CPR. "She's real and she's—"

"Duncan's combed from Virginia Beach all the way up. Everything on this side of the Mississippi. Raided costume shops, stolen security tapes, asked after your girl in every corner. No British bits running about with porcelain skin and hair down to their ass. Call off the search."

"You said Duncan was the best. That he could find people. That's what I paid for."

"He *is* the best. The fucking Kilbride of private investigators. He gets dirt every time, no matter how clean someone appears to be. Ex-military. Professional hacker. A shadow in the midday sun. He's never failed. He could find you a fucking personality. It's not his fault. It's you. Your shitty memory. Brown hair. White hair. Black hair. No height. No weight. No goddamned name."

Asher glared at the ceiling, cracked his neck, left, right, then settled his glare on Burton. *Don't grind your teeth. Don't.* "I wasn't taking goddamn measurements when we were together."

"Mistake one."

Asher rolled his tongue on the inside of his cheek as his eyes narrowed. No other option, he reminded himself. He'd played every card, stalked every lead.

Stomaching Burton's tyrannical accusations, loosing the Boar free in his house. It was nothing.

He'd crawl naked over shattered glass to find her, live with the shards embedded into his skin for the rest of his life. She was his only peace.

Scrubbing a hand down his face, he strode through the parted doors into his office. "Next time, Kilbride," he said, steps harsh on the refurbished maple floor. "I'll strip her down and take photos."

Burton's coarse laugh echoed.

People pleasing wasn't all ass kissing and manners. It was building a connection. And Asher would construct one of skeletons and ash if it got him what he wanted.

His teeth were dust when he made it to his corner of refuge. His bar cart. An extravagance he never imagined having. The tangle of silver trimmed hardware, nested crystal decanters, three levels of arabesque etched glass. A lower level wine rack designed to fit only pre-1900s reds.

Lavish edging toward gauche. It'd been spoiled in mold, the glass shattered, and missing a handle when he found it. Restoring it cost him more than his rent, but he hadn't blinked.

1854 was carved into the bottom panel.

Careful not to smudge the antique, mirrored surface, Asher scooped pelleted ice into a lowball glass and doused it in gin.

One glass could propel him through this meeting. And when it was over, when he could stop pretending to find Burton's crassness charming, hopefully he'd be blitzed enough to forget he knew Burton at all. Drunk enough to soak in the silence, turn off the lights, his phone, and his mind until he was there. With her again.

"Gin?" Asher offered, not a hint of humanity left in his voice.

"Clear liquors don't work on me, boy." Burton crouched beside Asher, peering at the finest alcohols money could buy, and frowned. With meat hooks for hands, he knocked the bottles about like they were expired strawberry mint wine coolers. Sniffed a decanter of Johnny Walker Blue. Snorted.

Making space, Asher perched on the arm of his camel desk chair, watched his ice float and spin. "You better not have come here to tell me you found nothing."

Burton turned with an amber filled lowball. Whiskey or brandy. Though he wouldn't put it past the Boar to guzzle rum straight.

"Duncan hasn't quit," Burton informed. "But he needs more information. How do you know it's her? Year after year? Could be you're drunk enough to—"

"It's her. Every year." Asher's eyes refused to focus on the trees shaking outside his window, seeing instead the foggy outline of Holmes. "Right on time." He'd set his heartbeat to her presence.

He knew her in his bones and blood. In his dreams and dark, delinquent nightmares. Holmes was the candlelight he prayed under. She pulled the sun into his day and never let the moon wane too thin for him to miss its cover.

But if he crashed into her on the street, would he recognize her?

Without the elaborate hats, the cherry stem dancing in her fingers, without her quirky accent, and spun sugar scent?

Guilt reared.

He might've been drunk and nervous and depressed, but the moment he heard her voice, watched long gloved fingers tug at the tip of her old, checkered hat, he'd understood exactly how fucked he was, meeting his soul mate when he couldn't pace a straight line.

She alone was the reason he'd taken the offer to play for the Vermont Mountaineers. Sure that fate would draw them together.

"It's her," he said again, rougher, a throb in his jaw. "Even when she looks different, sounds different. Even if I couldn't recognize her. I know." He tried to call her image in his mind, but she blurred, the curves of her face molten like shimmering mercury.

His patience wore thin waiting for her to fill the empty spaces. He was done. The emptiness was spreading, carving into his body, consuming his thoughts.

"I need to find her. I've spent so long waiting for her, for fate or destiny and I can't anymore. Won't. I need—" He felt Burton's piercing stare suddenly, and remembered himself, switched the words. "I'll pay."

Burton rubbed his jaw, glaring suspiciously at Asher. "You remember nothing? No scars? Marks? Moles? One tit bigger than the other?"

Dread hitched onto Asher's heart and yanked, dragged down and down until the muscle ripped and shredded. His ribs poked wide holes into his lungs, and he thought he might be sick.

"No. She wears makeup and—" And it was dark, always dark, and loud and they were drinking.

Asher closed his eyes for the first sip. The hair on his arms lifted at the unmistakable juniper essence. His lips felt the warmth of a true smile.

Cut short by a loud knock on his door.

Burton's bushy brows knitted in offense. "Who's that? You don't have friends, Laughlin."

He threw a glare across the room. "It's your mother."

"Should've said ex-wife, I'd have believed you."

Asher scoffed. Not even he was that cruel.

"We're not as different as you think, son."

That's what Asher was afraid of.

Sucking air through his teeth, he drank again, relishing the burn of fire racing down his throat, spreading over his chest, and pooling in his gut. He exhaled. Not enough, but it calmed the edge. In ten steps, he opened the door.

Looked down.

Clenched his jaw. "No."

Chapter Five

Carrie

T HE ANGRY, LOW RASP of Asher Laughlin's voice made Carrie's heart thump too hard, and she felt the sudden urge to hide behind the door. As if she were a cotton-tailed bunny and he was awake from hibernation three months too soon.

She tamped down all notions of fleeing once she looked up.

He stood head and shoulders above her, but the smug way he looked down at her was born of cruelty, not necessity. As if he well knew she'd sacrificed half her day for this exact moment.

And he didn't care.

"No?" she repeated, hoping she'd heard wrong, cursing herself for the plaintive plea tied to the word.

To stand this close to him felt surreal. Forced Carrie to recall her first encounter with the elusive Asher Laughlin. She'd been sprawled in the opposing team's end zone, elbows rubbed raw from the dry Bermuda grass. He'd charged into frame while she'd been adjusting her ISO. Number thirty-one draped in Mountaineer Green.

She'd never glimpsed such harsh cheekbones before, or such astonishingly beautiful features. The structure of his face would have made Michelangelo's mouth water, could've stopped the dark ages with a single look.

Finding her muse had been like discovering a well of ancient, dangerous magic in the marrow of her bones. Magic she'd dipped a toe into and gotten consumed limb by limb. Terrible magic that made her forget to blink and breathe. Possessed her. Glued her lens to his form. Bound her inspiration to a field, a game. A sport.

His hair was onyx and messy, his hazel eyes were bloodshot, and lines bracketed his mouth as if he had no choice but to frown. His white button down was half tucked into slacks, rolled up his forearms. It gaped at the neck, and the collar jutted up awkwardly as if he'd been fighting it. Though she couldn't say if he'd won or lost.

He had angled inky brows, tanned skin, and a perpetually red nape, as if he spent all his time looking down on people.

He looked smug and rich and miserable.

Which meant he photographed like a long-lost Hadid sibling.

"No," came Asher's growl, complete with bared teeth.

No? After marching up 116 steps with a thirty by twenty print of his face balanced on her head? After 116 steps of self-imposed noogie? Her pinky finger had enough static to score its own nuclear code.

She'd sweet-talked Artie—full time building security, part time small batch granola influencer (@GranolArt)—for two hours to get a fob swipe into the Hub's exclusive windowless, whitewashed stairwell. Because apparently, a follow and flood of likes didn't make the cut for elevator status.

She should've ordered the seasonal batch. Petit Pumpkin Spice.

"Not no," Carrie returned, sticking her foot across the threshold before he could slam the door in her face.

His eyes gleamed with feral intensity. "*No.*"

Don't meet your heroes, folks.

Viscous oily rage blistered through her, fueled by stale pocket pretzel rods and weak lobby coffee, and 116 steps. Carrie slapped her palm against the sleek oak paneling of his door. "*No.*"

He folded his arms. "No."

Final answer.

Her breath hitched, her clothes shrunk, and her lungs forgot the warm comfort of oxygen. Violence was becoming an option. "Do you say anything other than 'no'?"

The edge of his mouth quirked. "No."

"For feck's sake," a gravelly voice interrupted. "You sound like whiny, spoiled children."

In the narrow gap between Asher and the doorjamb, Carrie spotted a thick, gnarly beard and wild hair. Burton Kilbride. Number thirteen, the tight end for the Mountaineers. Relentless on the field, brutal and domineering.

Off the field too, it seemed.

Asher didn't acknowledge the Boar lurking in his hallway. His glare was steadfast, disgusted by the flotsam jamming up his doorway.

"He's talking to you," Carrie pointed out helpfully, foot slipping over his Old English vibes black and white tile. Slick. Had he waxed it?

No, he probably had people for that. People like Carrie who responded to Craigslist ISO ads every time her piggy bank's ribs protruded. Looking for a professional floor waxer? Carrie had a half burned Leaves candle and a can do attitude.

"Me?" Asher asked, affronted.

"Ha!" She had two feet past the threshold. "Got you to say something else."

Moving closer, looming, he offered a quick, disgusted snort. "Leave before security drags you out."

She went stiff. "Artie would never."

Hazel eyes trailed from Carrie's converse to her mauve Align dupes before losing interest at her yellow *I'm about to Snap* crewneck. A clip art camera holding up the text. "Who the fuck is Artie?"

"You don't know your own—"

"I don't have time for this," Burton interjected, his slight Irish accent muffled by the metal screw cap between his teeth. A boxy bottle with a big matte black label hung lazily from two fingers, chinking against the intense brace enclosing his knee.

Four o'clock seemed early to be carting personal liters.

The knot in Asher's throat bobbed as he twisted to his teammate, jaw tight. "You'll wait," he hissed.

Carrie's lips slashed upward in a victorious grin. *Yes. Ha!*

She only needed a few minutes to ask and then another couple for him to sign. Working quickly, she spun for her print, excited to explain, and—

A hand pressed into her spine and pushed. Between the tile and her reach, the shove sent her crashing sideways. Carrie squeezed her eyes shut and braced for impact on the nasty patterned-to-hide-upchuck hall carpet.

But before she could even throw out her arm to minimize smackdown, Asher was hauling her against his chest. His forearm banded around her, warm and hard, just under her boobs, and yanked them together.

The act of their bodies pressing together reminded Carrie of the deeply satisfying snap of a fully charged battery pack into her camera.

This close, he smelled like gin and ice.

She shivered as pleasure scorched down her spine and relaxed into her heroic duke. Then, like a true lady, she spat out the split ends attached to her tongue.

"Shit," Asher growled, still clutching her tightly. "Do you have hollow bones? I barely touched you."

Right. Not a heroic duke. A ruddy rogue. "You pushed me! When I had my back turned."

"You were gonna flash me."

What. In. The. Name. Of. Queen. Victoria.

She rotated in his hold and discovered a small nick along the smooth ridge of his jaw. A temporary slash from a hasty shave. She felt the magic swirl, call her to wade in to the steaming black lagoon.

Heat tingled and spread up her arms, the starting creep of hyper fixation. Her questions flipped like pages in the wind. *What other marks did he have? Where? How many had she missed because of his uniform, the chin strap, his lime green mouth guard?*

A phantom draft slammed the door shut behind the, and a quick scan revealed Carrie's most desperate desire and her greatest fear had come true: they were alone. In a hall of sealed doors and in case of emergency exit instructions.

Counting in for five and out for six, Carrie breathed away her tunnel vision to say, "I wasn't going to flash you."

Immediately, Asher released her.

They locked eyes. She had him right here, at her mercy, a captive audience. She opened her mouth to ask him for her favor, to beg for it, ready to answer any question, assuage any worry. "Would it really be so terrible to see my boobs?"

No.

The blood drained from her face and pooled in her throat in a hot, suffocating flush.

Congrats, you blew it. Big time. What a humiliating disaster.

Eyes wide with abject horror, Asher scrubbed knuckles over his scar, as if it still smarted. "Do you want to see my dick without warning?"

Don't answer, it's a trap. "Does that even happen?"

He scratched the back of his neck, swaths of black hair falling over his forehead, heat was subtly rising in his cheeks. "I'm led to believe it's an epidemic. For example, if you have AirDrop on in a subway, or—"

"Not dick pics," Carrie said, irritation searing her from the inside out. "Flashers. That happens? Women crawl up to your Rapunzel tower just to expose a sweaty nip?"

He peered at her. Clenched his jaw.

She was right. Carrie smiled with a sick kind of glee. "That's what I—"

"Yes."

"What?"

"I said *yes*, brat." He towered over her from a foot away, like he was afraid to touch her again. "In the last year alone, four have crawled. Why do you think there's security in the first place?"

"F-four—"

Behind him, the door cracked and opened. Asher was fast as lightning. He snatched the handle and yanked it shut, his fist covering the entire bronze knob. "What do you want?" he snapped to her. "Sixty seconds."

His forearm flexed against a pull from the other side, blue veins appearing as he held strong.

Carrie could make an entire exhibit dedicated to that arm. The corded muscle bulging under expensive shirtsleeves. Warm bronze skin, dusting of black hair, impossibly long, capable fingers. Even his nails were clean. Like he'd scrubbed the beds with a bristle brush and stored a file in his wallet. Buffed and neat. But what Carrie liked most was the simple watch banding his wrist. Brown leather no wider than a ruler, a slight sheen as if it was conditioned regularly, but the spotless metal crowd suggested it'd never been set.

Stop.

Sixty seconds.

Lurching into action, she retrieved her print from the wall.

"I'm Carrie," she started, wishing she'd planned a speech. She hadn't predicted this to be so formal. She made an adorable little curtsy, smiled, and kept the print tucked toward her knees, bubbling with excitement. "I'm a professional photographer and I have an incredible opportunity for you to—"

"No."

She felt the corners of her mouth fall, her eyebrows scrunch. "We're past no, Asher. I—"

"No"—the door pushed open and he slammed it again—"You think you know me because you've seen me play, but you don't. Because if you did, you'd emphatically know I'm not interested in your little opportunity." Slam.

"Motherfucker!" Burton shouted, banging on the wood.

"You have to—"

Asher cut her off. "Times up."

"No." It couldn't be. She needed him.

"If you don't remove yourself, I'll call the police and Artie can kiss his job goodbye."

***

"YOU REEK OF BEEF, darling." The way Jill's body contorted to avoid the stench wall added weight to her claim.

"It's lamb." And Carrie had stopped smelling it entirely. Full assimilation in five blocks. She couldn't even smell the sweet overripe apples littered along the sidewalk.

The downtown bus stop was located directly under the Kebab House's black and green awning. As if navigating public transport with a mega poster of a smoking hot dude you crushed on wasn't humiliating enough, now do it with a thorough meat soak.

"It's wretched," Jill said. "COVID rules. Three meters."

Exhausted, frustrated, Carrie stopped in accordance with Jill's raised palm. "We share a wall. You know this is not enforceable."

In her prime, Jill had been a dancer on Broadway. The backbone of the stage, the unsung star of the show, the bringer of crowds. Pretty much the Broadway version of defense wins championships. Her prime had been about thirty years ago, not that she'd admit it.

Today she'd styled a thin rainbow striped scarf with a loose beige jumpsuit. No shirt. Just a narrow black bandeau underneath. Carrie avoided staring straight at her neighbor's nipples. So. High.

Diana referred to Jill's style as Sexual Harassment Prone Art Teacher.

Wrong.

Pot Brownie Childless Aunt energy. All day. With an expansion pack of stick-it-to-the-man.

Unperturbed by logic, Jill narrowed her gaze. "Paul will enforce it."

"Paul loves Kebab House. His picture's on the wall for eating an entire shank."

"Yes." A proud smile touched her lips. "He's a positively voracious eater."

The ensuing smirk led Carrie down a dark, lascivious path involving wrinkled bodies and steak sauce. Yuck. "How lucky for you."

"And what of your man?" Jill asked.

"Which one?" If Carrie repeated her macabre ex history one more time, she'd summon a jilted poltergeist. Gaslighter. Cheater. Orc porn guy. Cheater. And the latest mistake: a literal car thief.

"Him," Jill said, entering the zone of marjoram, coriander, and gristle to tip Carrie's print face up. Gray eyebrows dove into her hair as she blew a low, appreciative whistle. "He is ..."

Insufferable, egotistical, a destroyer of happiness, hater of Carries.

"Delicious." Jill sighed.

"Yes." Utterly delectable.

She could still feel the heat of his glare stroking her up and down. Likely charging her with a fashion crime. Straight to jail. Four to six months. No probation.

As she'd walked from Elmwood stop to her little cul-de-sac, Carrie had pondered intensely how he'd gotten so deep under her skin that she still felt him there. His gaze stripping her down. His palm sizzling on her spine. His fingers wrapped tightly around her ribs.

She'd met plenty of bad men. Indolent, conceited, delusional. Hell, she'd *dated* those men.

Asher though ...

Every second with Asher clawed into her, hooked into her muscle, and gnawed. Intent on destruction.

He'd smelled like gin.

Gin was reserved for her lips. A heady burn to suffuse the butterflies Jack gave her. Sweet, wonderful Jack who despised gin.

Carrie's eyes slid to the portrait. Darkness gathered behind his multihued eyes, protecting secrets and stories Carrie yearned to unearth. Stress thickened his jaw, snapped his eyebrows together. A crack split his lower lip, a wet red slice dividing the sunburned pink. No face should be that stunning. Pensive and passionate. Fascinating. Befuddling.

Capturing him was intimate and overwhelming.

A whisper of a breeze dusted the back of her neck. Carrie went from blazing hot to subarctic.

Jill cut her a look. "You have punched your way into his chest, seized his bloody heart, and squeezed for this photograph."

"He's symmetrical."

Holding wisps of her faded lilac hair off her cheeks—she'd recently taken to recreating purple shampoo dye trends—Jill shook her head. "He's beautiful, yes. But you've made him marvelous. Who is he?"

Carrie felt a blush. "Asher Laughlin. He plays football."

"Obviously." Her neighbor waved a hand at the helmet, forgetting the time she confused croquet and baseball. A cultured Lady's' lawn game and an excuse to get drunk on a Tuesday. "But why do you hate him?"

"I don't."

At Carrie's attempted shrug off, Jill snickered. "Please," she crooned. "You practically cursed his name when you spoke."

Because she loathed him. "I'm entering this piece in an auction to raise money for the Green Mountain Cancer Alliance, and I went to ask him to sign—"

"He refused!" Jill spat next to and on Carrie's shoe.

"Worse." She lifted her eyes to Jill's foggy gaze, which was intrigued and delighted in the way only a true gossip could be. "He didn't even let me ask. He told me to leave."

A theater worthy gasp. "He didn't."

"He literally pushed me out of his apartment. Like I was a moth wandering toward a light." A horny moth.

"The audacity!"

Quickly, Carrie gave Jill a complete rundown of the incident, from a decline in her follow ratio to the stupid gorgeous tile, through Asher's no chorus, and finally her fifteen second minute.

When she finished, Jill's jade ring was stroking the short sprigs of gray on her chin. "Don't go inside today," she said. "Spend the night with your mouthy friend, or better yet, find a man and slide between his sheets."

"Why? Is your carbon monoxide alarm going off again? I just replaced it." Now hers was out of batteries. And honestly, it didn't seem like a terrible way to go.

"The beeping has ceased," Jill said.

"Then what? Water heater on the fritz? Garbage disposal backed up? Another cave in?"

Townhouses in the Old North End were uncommon. Because of its primo location, the neighborhood was expensive. And old. 1800s rubble construction old. Homes sold as estates, and tiny, defunct corner stores survived off the big three: toilet paper, 1995 Bordeaux, and truffle oil.

After her mom lost the fight with ovarian cancer, Carrie had vowed she'd make a home out of 21 Nice Way. She adored the lemon yellow siding, the three mismatched stoops. Even the soggy, over-trodden yard was scrappy and enchanting, surviving in the shade of two brilliant orange maples. There were always flowers by the mailbox, and the flag stayed permanently raised for Jill's write-in campaigns.

Her home was dilapidated and delightful, and a massive F-you to the monstrosity framed across the street.

Sure, it had never been 'up to code' or 'mold free,' but Luisa, their old landlord, kept the water warm and the walls square. Ish.

But it'd been three months since Luisa sold the place.

An entire summer of burned out fridge bulbs, clogged drains, and daring, circus worthy Reginald break-ins.

A misty look crossed Jill's narrow face. "Paul pulled the headboard from the wall so I do think structural safety is no longer a concern." Her lips pinched in a futile effort to stop a secret. "There's a note."

"A note?"

"On your door."

"My door? What's it say?"

"Here." She dug a hand into the wide pocket of her chic and slouchy onesie. "Take two of my gummies. Wait thirty minutes and then read it."

Carrie ignored the pineapple shaped gummies, her stomach knotting around the single Kebab sample in her stomach. "They can't evict us, Jill. We have lease agreements. Stringent rules. I'll fight for the both of us." She was never giving up her home. It had been her mothers, and it was all Carrie had left of her.

"Is that why you're out here?" She touched the elderly woman's elbow, seeing her as frail and thin instead of chic and agile as horrible thoughts rioted in her head. "Did they threaten you?"

"No. It's—" Jill pointed at the labyrinth of framework going up across from their lot.

Relief—as well as agitation—washed away the fear.

Carrie tried to avoid looking at it. All summer, she'd listened to the obnoxious beeping of excavators carving out the basement. Then it was groaning cement mixers and creaky cranes. Now constant, off beat hammering.

"It's *them*," Jill hissed. "Gentrification should be illegal. I've had rats and mice and urine on my stoop on the Lower East Side, but never such filth as this!"

Carrie followed Jill's horrified leer to the sidewalk, which was coated in an ultrafine, tan sawdust.

"I need your camera to take pictures for the chief of police. Paul has a connection. He's getting a mighty citation for littering on our street. I'll fine him out of a roof."

A new attempt to end construction. Carrie slotted its potential efficacy between the two-day hunger strike and distracting the workers with her sexuality.

The guys had loved seeing Jill in shimmery hot pink spandex and knitted turquoise leg warmers. So had Carrie. It was like seeing a baby in a tuxedo. You couldn't tear your eyes away.

"I think you'll need the 10-18 mm lens for this," Carrie observed, looking over her shoulder to see her mopey, dragging footprints. "I'll set it up for you. All you'll have to do it point and click."

And then she'd warn Chuck, the head contractor, for wave three of his demise.

Picking up her print, Carrie bid Jill goodbye and started across the lawn.

Dinner waited in the form of rolled tortillas and a chip off the Tollhouse cookie dough log. She'd eat in front of her TV with her legs crossed while she edited the dog poop out of last week's engagement shoot.

Alone, with no signature, no car, no hotdogs, and a sun-blocking mega mansion ever widening across the street, Carrie felt like the wilted sunflowers next to her mailbox. Hopeless, defeated and dull. As if there'd once been life in the citrine petals, but it'd been squeezed out. Wrung free of the last golden drop. Her print submission was supposed to revive her, zap away the helpless feeling.

Donating it was something she could offer like a capable, in control adult with consistent water pressure and less than three comfort water bottles.

But she'd failed that, too.

Staggering up the front stoop of 21B Nice Way, avoiding the rickety railing—termites—she wiggled her key into the deadbolt and spotted the flash of white stapled to her purple door.

Jiggling with increased veracity, Carrie set the edge of the canvas on her shoe, hoping this was at long last a sign of life from their new landlord.

She skimmed as she added her elbow into the wiggle, lifting and twisting.

She froze.

Rent increase.

Blinking, Carrie widened her eyes. This note wasn't the jittery scrawl of Luisa's blue fountain ink. It was typed. Stapled. Collated in legal 8.5 by 14, addressed to Miss Carrie Huston.

Key surrendered to the lock, Carrie tore the page free, and jumped past the first terrifying line. Rent hike. Starting in November to counter increasing taxes and compete with rising neighborhood values. There were notices and charts. And near the bottom: the amount.

Double.

Rent was doubling.

Carrie couldn't breathe. She kept blinking, faster and faster, hoping the words would change. She staggered back to find air, shook her head. Swayed.

"Excuse me Ma'am!"

Ma'am on top of this.

Feeling like she was underwater, Carrie half turned, cold expanding from her stomach, pinching her elbows, her wrists. *This can't be real. It can't.*

The little boy in knee high blue socks and a sash was a figment of her imagination. His hovering mother carting a Red Rider's worth of popcorn kernels was a mirage.

"Would you help me pay for a camping trip with all my friends?" the imaginary kid asked, kicking a yellow dandelion head off the sidewalk. "I need a bunch of gear. Sleeping bag. Tent. A hammock. Matches."

"No matches," his mother scolded.

Rent doubling.

Don't, Carrie.

Head shaking, she croaked, "How much for the smallest one?"

"Thirty-six dollars."

Because why wouldn't it be? "Might as well give me two."

Chapter Six

Asher

*D*EAD.

Asher couldn't escape it, but he kept peddling, absurdly trying to end the restlessness.

The whirl of his stationary bike fan drowned out the energized crowd.

She's dead.

It corroded his skin like goopy boiling hot tar.

She's dead.

He cracked his knuckles. Any second, he'd charge onto the field. Replace the Mountaineers' defense to rip back the lead, wreck their momentum with a single pluck of Wray's tight spiral.

Dead,

No emotion, no details. He pictured two policemen huddled in the entry, black shoes on his tile. *D-dead*, they'd stutter, hats scrunched in their hands, exchanging uncomfortable side glances.

Asher gnawed on the moldable plastic of his mouth guard like a feral wolf. Fury wove through him like poison seeking to annihilate.

Dead.

Except if she—

He couldn't even fucking think it.

If she wasn't ... here. Wasn't with him anymore. How would he even know?

How many hours would he sit there, demanding for her drink to be remade so the flavor stayed fresh, the ice crisp. How many excuses could his fucked up mind generate? Lost, sick, tired, busy, forgot, doesn't love you. Never loved you.

If she's dead, I'm dead.

The thought brought an acid taste to Asher's tongue and a firestorm of outrage choked off his sorrow.

He refused to look at Burton, splayed on the bench, cocky, reviewing plays on an iPad with an arc of coaches around him.

If she was dead, he was dead.

Good, a venomous voice quipped in his head. Hers. Her voice. Carrie.

The image of her, her doe green eyes, soft chin, and mussed brown hair lingered in his thoughts.

Tasting metal on the back of his teeth, Asher dug his elbows into the handlebars, ribs pushing in, biting and snapping at his lungs.

Dead. It had slunk through his mind like magma spreading into crevices and hardening, cracking to brittle shards when he'd opened his door and found the opposite of his Holmes. Black freckles, renegade glare, that little jab of her finger.

It'd felt like a sign he was chasing after a mirage. His perfect woman no more.

She couldn't be dead.

Be gone, be away, be busy and lost, but do not be dead.

"Have faith!" Coach had shouted in the locker room. He'd written it in white ink across the polished mahogany lockers. "Without faith, we can't build trust and without trust, we all fail. We lose."

He'd been referring to Lincoln Wray, their new quarterback, signed last minute, flown into the mountains halfway through preseason. The offense had bucked against the choice. He wasn't special. Not like Rose, their previous QB. Wray was mellow and confident and accomplished. He was three yards a play wins games. Controlled.

The opposite of Rose's frantic throws and flashy setups.

But Asher heard Coach's growl and ran with it. *Faith.*

Holmes had to be alive.

"Can you answer my mom?" Riley Moore's head popped in front of the twenty yard line, trademark grin upside down, hands on his narrow hips.

Despite the fall chill, the wide receiver was caked in sweat. Wandering trails trekked from his cropped black hair down dark skin to the rich evergreen of his custom cleats.

"My cousins are in town," Riley continued, used to bearing the weight of conversation. "And I got everyone jerseys. It's the gift that keeps on giving. But then Mom says she feels bad because there's so many 44s in the stands." He tapped the number on his chest with a smirk. "I told her to get used to it since I'm the clear fan favorite. But you'll never guess whose jersey she wants."

Asher straightened his shoulders without losing his pace. "Let me guess. I'm giving it to her myself? Game used never washed. And don't worry, I'll pay the fines for another lost jersey."

"Don't be a dick, okay? Smile and wave and when she sports"—Riley gagged—"thirty-one, pretend it doesn't bring shame and dishonor to my family." He pointed past the crammed Mountaineers' bench to the families and friends section. The only section in the Peak without dabs of traitorous blue. Just pure mountain green.

"I'm never dick to your mom."

"You gave her a handshake at Christmas. I spent three days cleaning up that meltdown." He shook his head. "You were allergic to her perfume if she asks. Which is super convenient for me, because I never have to buy *Sexy Ruby by Michael Kors* for her ever again."

Shame ran through Asher, alongside guilt. "We'd just met."

"The Moore's are huggers."

An understatement.

Twisting in the saddle, Asher smeared on a fake, blasting smile and waved blindly. Odds were the entire section was stacked with Moores.

Alarmingly close knit people.

Not text-chain and linked calendars close.

No, they were twelve in a bed, Charlie and the Chocolate Factory close. Hand crafted Arbor Day cards and watching home videos on Wednesdays over barbeque close. Matching tie-dye family vacation to Barbados shirts close.

At first, Asher had been jealous. Soul achingly jealous. Then he was petrified. Because the moment Riley introduced Asher as a friend, the Moore clan opened up like the jaws of a great white and devoured him. Standing invitations to dinner. Updates on the extended family. Probing questions about his life. Mrs. Moore sent a celebratory fruit basket whenever he had a hundred yard game, and a consolation chocolate basket when he didn't.

Never in his life had Asher been more uncomfortable than when Mrs. Moore told him how proud he'd made her.

Now in his closet, Asher had two Moore family Christmas sweaters. Screaming Green and Radical Red. They itched and couldn't be dry cleaned. The sequins were double sided and created little piles of glitter if bumped. Encased in protective film, he'd tucked them between his favorite black Valentino and the pinstripe Brioni.

Supportive, ostentatiously kind, and overly trusting, the Moore's overabundance of love was why Riley didn't have a single worry line. Why he only ever had excitement in his eyes, two endless pools of hope and positivity.

Befriending the six-six Alabama graduate had gone against Asher's instincts. People made him anxious, and combative, left him exposed. And Riley was his direct competition. A wide receiver, a damn good one. It was idiotic, self-destructive, downright twisted to entertain talking, much less bonding with the guy.

But shit, two years ago, Riley didn't leave Asher a choice. Kept smiling, joking, sharing until Asher was watching a VHS of nine-year-old Riley eating a churro on a tilt a whirl.

Mounting the warm-up bike next to Asher's, Riley bent to grip the handles and slowly pedaled. "Thanks for the extra tickets, by the way," he said, watching the Patriot's line set. "Mom wants us all to get dinner tonight. Fancy Italian. No menu prices kind of place. She deserves it. But after that, you want to go out? Miles is AWOL, so I need a wingman. Preferably one who won't tell my mom I'm a no-good womanizing miscreant."

"I told you. I'm too busy."

Riley's eyebrows shot to his forehead. "Yeah, but I thought you were kidding. Like when you told me I wasn't the next of kin in your will."

He was, so Asher said, "It's October fifth already. The house is studs, Burton's fucking with me. I can't help you, find someone else to blow smoke up your ass."

Asher's comment left Riley doubled over with laughter. "Is that what you think you're doing? Helping me?" He wiped at the corner of his eye. "You scare every woman that approaches."

"I'm not scary."

"Not scary like Dracula, no. You're scary like what's this guy's deal? Which actress will portray me on *Dateline*?"

Asher stuck his finger in his best friend's face. "Fuck off. I don't touch anyone. I don't even flirt."

"I'd rip out my liver to see you flirt."

"You're that desperate for lessons?"

Riley was laughing too hard to hear him. "Flirting would be infinitely better than flat out ignoring them or drilling them your creepy specific questions." He sighed and placed his hands on his hips again. "You can't ask beautiful, single women if they like to 'dress up'. They think you're a furry."

Asher blinked. "A furry?"

"Search it with incognito on." A pause. "I'm just saying, you're not the Casanova in this duo. You're not even Woodhouse to my Snoopy. You're the antithesis of smooth."

Asher was well aware. "I have questions."

"Then ask straightaway, where were you last Halloween?"

If only it were that easy. "Even if she says the right place, it doesn't prove it's her. I need better answers. Does she know 1800s history? Who's the Whitechapel killer? Does she like him?"

Riley slid him a look. "Might not be a bad idea to weed out anyone pro-serial killer."

"Holmes is," Asher said. "I don't care about the rest."

"Good. Because they are not lining up to be yours."

Not news. "Why invite me, then?"

"I use your intense energy to scare them into my open arms." Riley grinned a perfect dimpled smile. "It's easy. See that poorly adjusted sad sack who's pining over an imaginary woman? It's me or him. And my house has four walls."

Sarcastic ass. Asher felt a ghost of a smile on his mouth. "Fuck you. You can't do anything without me."

Riley punched him in the shoulder. "You're a polite tag-a-long."

Liars, the both of them.

Riley Moore could charm the panties off a nun with a head cold and a broken dick. And Asher would denounce all human interaction if he could maintain his sanity.

"Whoa," Riley choked back a laugh, slouching back to rest hands on his lower back. "October Asher ..." he trailed off. Shook his head. "I'm excited to witness it." A mischievous smile. "Do you keep a little calendar in your locker to check the days off until Halloween?"

"Oh, yeah." Asher squirted Gatorade into his mouth. "Candy hearts behind each door."

"Be mine." Riley chortled. "Fuck, you are so whipped. Soon I'm going to be the last single guy on the team. I'll have to mingle for eleven."

Asher had to laugh. "Doing God's work."

"Someone has to. I give a wicked best man speech. Ya'll need me. Except Burton. He'll be alone forever."

Sweat swept down Asher's spine. *Alone.* He picked up the pace.

He wasn't alone. He had Holmes.

"Is she pretty?" Riley asked.

On cue, flowers and houndstooth and stripes flooded his brain. "More than anyone else in the world." And he didn't even know her eye color.

Riley had learned about Holmes through sheer dumb luck.

Last November, he'd stumbled in on Asher during a sloppy drunk spell. Riley had cleaned the explosion of red bull vodka vomit from Asher's bathroom, hid the bar cart, ordered wings, and forced Asher to watch Fast and Furious movies until Asher's conscience had a shoddy Italian accent.

The truth spilled out.

Not spilled. Splattered.

Burst out in a rush, the story spouting from a broken faucet. "There's this girl. She's ... my soulmate. I don't know her name. Only that she's perfect. She's it. Everything I've ever dreamed of. When she's with me, I feel whole. I love her. I love her. I love her."

If she was dead, he was dead.

"I think I'll come," Riley announced, suddenly serious.

Asher rolled his eyes. "Better do it on the white lines or you'll be breaking news."

"Hey. No. Cut that shit out." Riley dragged his pointer across his neck. "My mom is like twenty yards away. She doesn't know I lost my virginity yet, and we don't talk about what she found in my special time drawer."

Asher belted out a laugh.

But Riley was still serious, fingers tapping his chin, lips tight in concentration. "I'll come to The Hand. Meet her."

Asher's heart pounded. "No."

Do you say anything other than 'no'?

"What if she's a freak, or a killer? What if she tries to steal your identity?"

Steal it? He'd give it. "How can she? She doesn't know who I am."

"What if she's married?"

"She's not." He sure as shit hoped she wasn't. He could never bring himself to ask if she was unattached. She had to be. She wouldn't see him if she wasn't. She wasn't like that.

"You're building her a house." Riley tilted his head. "You need to at least—*Fuck*."

Asher jerked his head up. His gut clenched as the ball soared end over end through the uprights. Two sets of black and white arms raised. Whistles blew. It was good.

Time to work.

***

POWER WOUND THROUGH ASHER. Trampling his veins faster than his blood could pump.

On the field, under his helmet, was the only place Asher felt free.

Anticipation gathered in his sinew and swelled, exploded as he cut left with a sharp pivot. His calves bulged as he sprinted, legs corded and roped in tension. Ten yards passed. Twenty.

He went blindly, trusted his quarterback, trusted the line, trusted that his route would pay off.

The ball wasn't meant for him.

He was the feint, racing for a Hail Mary, dragging apart the zone defense. A ploy. A distraction. He groaned as his thighs clenched and forced himself to take longer strides.

Faster, get to the end zone, confuse the safety.

He had to sell it, convince every player on the field, every beer guzzling fan in the stands, and every analyzer up in the booth that he was expecting the ball to kiss his gloves any second.

A rush of awareness battered him as a blue and white defense-man matched his stride. Panting, Asher pushed on, arms flexing, teeth clenching. He reached his arm out and grabbed at the flapping jersey.

Pulled.

Pushed.

He broke right, glanced back, and there it was. The ball. The ball that didn't belong to him but found him, anyway. He coiled, dispelling his remaining strength to unleash himself into the air.

Leather touched his gloves, and he struck, attacked it with his fingers, clenched and yanked it into him. Precious, precious cargo. He smiled as he fell, too far lateral to recover. He pointed his toes to drag the tips of his cleats inbound. Every muscle trained to be rigid and resolute. To fight nature. Battle the urge to collapse, to protect himself, to brace as he landed on the cold, hard ground.

He closed his eyes.

Darkness. His heart beat. Gasping breaths.

He opened them.

The stadium erupted.

Adrenaline flooded his system, washed the pain from his bones. He didn't consider the rapidly forming bruises as he spiked the ball in the end zone. As he pumped a fist in the air. Hands smacked his back, his helmet.

Nirvana.

He swiveled to watch the score change. To behold the heady, delicious fucking proof of what he'd done, what he'd made. A good thing. He did good things. Elation coursed through his blood.

He stepped back.

His cleat rocked sideways, forced him to twist. He jerked to recover, but his ankle was caught. Tangled.

He went down. Hard. And a lone cry of pain broke him from euphoria.

Not his pain.

Hers.

CHAPTER SEVEN

ASHER

F UCK, HIS JAW HURT. And his beard itched. Had itched for the last hour, and Asher struggled to keep from clawing at it like a rabid, self-mutilating squirrel.

This year, he'd gone grisly and rugged, all masculine power stacked in a glued Jenga stack. Cardboard axe, red buffalo check flannel, thick suspenders, and a fur lined hat. He'd fucking committed. Glasses, full beard, socks that said: wool, not machine washable.

He'd worked on it for weeks. Lumber-Jack.

Victoria had said he looked ultra fuckable.

What she meant was hot. As in sweltering, sweat dripping down his back, pooling in the crack of his ass hot.

The Hand had transformed. Darkened, evolved. Light came as burgundy and plum, staining walls shrouded in black cobwebs. His pint had a skull and crossbones drawn in the foam, and the disposable sleeve to catch spillover bore a skeletal hand giving the finger. Even the music differed. No more pop, no more hits, the sedan sized speakers vaulted out sinister, grinding rock.

Halloween.

On steroids.

Grimy and gross and delinquent.

Sweaty.

Beside Asher sat a flower. Hair too white to be silver, shimmering and brilliant, brighter than the most magnificent star. Eyes electric thousand-volt laser blue, and pink, pink—fuck, he loved pink—lips. She'd weaved a flower crown of the brightest colors into thin interlocked braids, and a cream dress puffed out at her middle. Long mint green lace gloves ran up her arms like vines climbing a trellis.

She looked part fairy, part twinkling supernova, and utterly breathtaking.

"*Midsommar*," she'd explained when she saw him, curtsied—*a British greeting?*—and asked if the smoking glass was hers.

An aviator. Different too. Served with dry ice that puffed fog into her mouth before every sip. She'd purred when she tasted it, spilling the pretty purple over her gloves when she brushed aside his axe to sit.

She thought he'd stared at her because he'd been trying to place the costume. *No.*

He'd stared because how the fuck was he so lucky? He'd been a monk in a past life. The kind that lived off dead grass and never swatted a fly.

She'd come back.

He'd put the odds of her returning at a million to one. As the days neared, shortened, as dark and cold swept in, he got more paranoid. What if she met someone? Put on a white dress with a big veil. Grew a round belly and glowing skin. What if she'd left civilization? Traded cell phones and Roman calendars to live in the Andes? What if—

What if she just forgot?

What if meeting him had been another Friday night? He'd been another Ripper. What was a typical day for her? A kaleidoscope?

He hadn't changed. Not in a fucking year. Not really.

Yes, he had a new team, new contract, new apartment, new state. But Asher was the same.

Alone.

His memories didn't do her justice. The tender fold of her ankles as she sat was more gentle and deliberate than he recalled and her accent an entire cadence lower, but it was her. His Holmes. Out of loafers and tweed and in butterfly heels and a linen skirt down to her calves.

They didn't catch up.

Didn't ask about their time apart.

There was no time apart when they were together. It was sequential. One after the other. They slipped back into it with the ease of putting on a favorite pair of mittens before shoveling snow, knowing they'd get wet and eventually freeze in the mold of their fingers, but it was okay. There'd be hot chocolate and cookies when they pried them off.

Asher had always craved that.

Braced for it as he snuck into the dark house, knocking ice from his hair.

He'd ordered a beer when he arrived two hours ago. Opened his throat and tossed it in like Shamu taking a fish after a flip spectacular.

Another. Another.

A fourth and fifth because he needed to occupy his hands. Kept wanting to put something against his mouth. It couldn't be her mouth.

He couldn't tell if it was the air, the atmosphere that The Hand conjured that made him so thirsty, so twitchy, and desperate in his seat. He was a slave to the tap of glittery green nails on the bar, to the oscillating twist of her stool.

He'd rather find out Santa was a chain-smoking pervert than learn Holmes wasn't real. This woman who understood his jokes, delivered her own like it was a second language she sank into with him, as easy as breathing. The sharp shooter, gin drinker, sugar scented star who laughed and teased and smiled and stopped to gaze at him. Said the most serious things in the sweetest tones.

She'd come back.

He repeated it when he felt himself about to edit his words, strip down the truth, lighten the edges. *Stop.*

She's here.

Because of him. Because of the stuff no one else ever gave a shit about. Not his money, not out of pity, not because she recognized his name.

She promised to get the next round each drink, only to be beaten to it, and stubbornly leaving her tip on top of his.

Then, new this Halloween, his own delicious, addictive, king-sized Kit Kat treat, she'd offer the first taste to him. And because he was a masochistic bastard, he'd take it.

She was right. The gin burned. Brutal and potent, but he kept taking longer sips, thinking this was what she tasted like and finding it less and less atrocious. Fresh and citrusy and just a little bit sweet. His mouth watered when she nudged it to him.

She was perfect. Period. Full stop.

"My mom sewed," she said dreamily, smiling, plucking a fat yellow petal from her crown and setting it to sail in his beer. "She'd ask me what I wanted to be for Halloween on the first day of school. An astronaut. A lobster. A cheerleader. Two years in a row." She smiled ruefully. "And she'd make it. Functional stargazing helmet, sharp piercing claws, hand tufted pom-poms. And I'd get so embarrassed because everyone else had the same cat woman costume or ninja and I was dripping in custom ribbons like I was something special."

He watched his flower swirl on the red, bobbing against the bubbles. "You are special."

"I don't know about that." A pause. "But no teenage girl wants to be special. We wished we were zebras in the middle of the herd." Her brilliant eyes shone in the dark, and her pretty smile could have belonged to an angel.

"No one here hasn't looked at you and stared, Holmes. You could never fit in."

"I don't want to anymore. Now I want someone to like me, even with a wreath on my head." She ditched her cherry stem on his napkin. "Did you dress up when you were little?"

"No." He was staring again. At the blush on her pale cheeks. "I would've if it meant meeting you earlier."

"Why didn't you?"

Because Halloween was trouble. Because he couldn't risk it. Because Asher never found the courage to ask for a costume. So superfluous and stupid. Not want a good kid did.

He spun his pint and watched the flower suck down into a vortex, get crushed.

"Too shy."

She gazed intently, tipped her head. Her eyelashes sparkled like shooting stars. "I like shy."

Of course she fucking did. He clenched his teeth hard enough to crack a crown.

"But you don't have to be shy with me," she said. He glanced at her, cursing his glasses for the disjointed view. "Tell me what you're thinking."

Marry me.

"I like being alone, but lately I only want to be alone with you."

She leaned closer, chair spinning. "And what would we do, alone together?"

Asher noticed the blood rushing toward his dick at the same time she set two gloved fingers on his wrist. Could she feel his pulse exploding beneath his skin?

He caught her fingers.

She gasped, intertwined their hands.

A muscle in his neck throbbed. "I'd peel these gloves from your fingers with my mouth, pry those silky sleeves down the perfect curve of your shoulders. I'd leave the flowers in your hair, make love to you until the bed and the floors were drowning in petals, until my hands were stained pink and purple and red with pollen."

She was so close that he smelled every note in her perfume, the demure vanilla and thick, heavenly cream. Her lips were just a hair's breadth away. He wanted to taste her tongue, lick down her throat, inhale her scent, everything. "I'd have you until we didn't feel alone."

Her lips parted, blue eyes wide. "We aren't," she murmured. "This moment, this spot, will always be with us."

She moved before he could ask for more. Suddenly standing, a daffodil petal drooping into her lashes. Her eyes were hazy and slightly bloodshot. Her skirt had a new crease in it.

She didn't consider a hug, a handshake, a wave as she faded to the words of a soft goodbye.

If she was right, if he wasn't alone, why did he feel raw and desolate?

He ripped open his phone and shook his head at the glowing white numbers. Two a.m.

Chapter Eight

Carrie

CARRIE STARED AT THE blinking red and green and blue lights on the dashboard in front of her, and while she usually equated pretty glowing dots with garlands and crackling fires, the only word slinking through her mind was mainframe.

It was possible Christian was mistaken and she indeed did have a concussion.

Although why *server* and *data* and *integrated circuit* were circling wasn't because something got knocked loose.

It was as if she'd thrown the opposite switch.

Her ardent love for the past, for leather ledgers and abaci, for solicitors poring over line of successions had been swapped for hardware and networks and escape keys.

She was short in this upside down world. Her feet didn't touch the ground, just hovered above the black corrugated floor, leaving her to swing and kick and bounce with each turn and every pothole, seatbelt sawing at her neck with the same ease as slicing steak with the dull side of a plastic knife.

Carrie leaned closer to the gleaming colors, squinting to find them attached to the long ends of switches and the underside of knobs. Unlimited possibilities. Push the bright blue dot or smack the unbroken row of glowing yellow lines. The glaring red light looked like an eject button.

A fire truck was the perfect place to have a complete mental breakdown, she thought for no particular reason.

"Not that one." Trent's hand shot out to block her reaching pointer.

She bent it back, eyes darting between him, the road, and the steering wheel, stomach prepping for the ten ton truck to flip and roll.

But they kept neat in the lanes of Elmwood, rolling through a yield sign.

He arched a blonde eyebrow at her, and Carrie realized he could maintain control of the rig with his pinky and blindfold in an electrical storm.

Embarrassed, she tucked her fingers into a ball.

Trent grinned. "Because that's my favorite to push." And push he did.

The first siren whoop earned a discordant mess of howls and claps and shouts from the backseat.

A boot collided with the back of Trent's headrest and with a final wink to Carrie, he turned the siren off and slapped an arm behind him. "I'm driving you—"

"I'm trying to sleep!" Kenny groused.

Laurie's hand snapped up like a teacher's pet, "Yeah Sarg, and I was gonna cut off Kenny's mullet once he passed out."

Carrie opened her mouth, on the verge of spilling that she'd led Trent down the mischievous road of illegal siren use in residential areas—she'd read the posted signage—but sealed it shut again. If she heard her voice, scratchy and weak and shameful, she'd lose it.

And then the crew would really regret gracing her with shotgun.

"You love my mullet," Kenny muttered. "You're all still jealous 'cause I got Christina Aguilera's autograph."

"This again!" Trent grumbled. "As if I'm not a clear Dion guy,"

All three in the back erupted in unison, "So this is Christmas!"

Carrie smiled at a joke she didn't get as she brainstormed a non-sexual way to invite four firefighters to stay with her for the night.

So like, I have this great loveseat. Sleeps three. Easy. And Laurie, you can sleep on the floor next to my bed with your phone light on, so I don't wake up screaming.

"Is this right?" Tent called over the mewling, wide biceps flexing as he steered down Nice Way.

Rather than shout over the self-awarded encore, Carrie threw him a big thumbs up plus exaggerated head nod.

I'll call each of your families for you, she added to her proposition. *No one can say no to a crying spinster fresh off hospital drip.*

"Whoa!" Christian called from his spot behind the driver's seat. The bill of his backward Mountaineers hat jabbed Trent ear as they turned. Christian wasn't wearing his five-point harness and his white BFD shirt wasn't near tight enough, but he'd sang Lavender Haze to Carrie while they rode in the ambulance, so naturally he had a thick black band on his ring finger. He grabbed onto Trent's headrest. "Remember the Class A we had here?"

As Trent guided the rig into a controlled, squeaking stop, he narrowed his eyes at Carrie's decrepit yellow townhouse. "Yeah. Two years ago, right?"

Last year. But she was living a mute lifestyle. Which meant she couldn't explain that Hubert in 21C had been moon soaking his crystals when his arrowroot and eucalyptus soy candles decided to eat his highly flammable drapes.

She'd give her left boob to have malachite in her pocket right now. And Axinite.

They jerked to a stop. The seatbelt yanked on her shoulder.

Fuck the crystals.

She wanted codeine and fentanyl. And ice cream.

The hulking engine cut off in time for the truck of literal heroes to hear her high-pitched whine.

I rescind my sleepover invitation.

The ensuing silence echoed.

"You okay, champ?" Christian asked, unclipping his seatbelt to kneel next to her, lowering his voice to that soft, do-you-know-who-you-are EMT tone he'd employed on the field. Such pointed gentleness set her off.

Complete with cottonmouth, her elegant assurance of sanity came out as: "ohmeI'mfinegreatinfact."

She could hardly hear herself around the throbbing pulse in her ears.

Tears slid down her face. New tears, mixing with the old, dried salt trails of hours past.

Funny, the first cry of her day had been the result of a breath-taking sight. Tears conjured from keeping her eyes anime wide as she peered down her lens. She'd ignored the bite of whistling fall wind in the name of football. For untold grace and violence.

Those tears had been biology's revolt. Her eyes wanting her to blink, to warm, to stop gawking and banish her trance, clear the glob of drool from her chin.

Eye strain was a familiar enemy. One Carrie didn't bow to.

Not when Asher Laughlin was competing.

She'd meant to ignore him, never take his photograph again, crop him out of team shots for eternity. *Number thirty-one? Must be part vampire. He's not showing up.*

It'd explain his ornery attitude.

A single glance demolished her vow of animosity. Rude and impetuous and obnoxious, the camera didn't discriminate. It fawned and coddled, led Carrie's hands around like a plastic pony on a kid's carousal. She'd never get off the ride.

He was vicious and suave. Two hundred pounds of brute strength, a man who made his living breaking out of holds while cradling a ball. He was contradictory and magnificent, and she had an entire game of thirty-one.

She could like him, she'd defended as her camera chased him to the sidelines, watched his helmet come off, dark hair wet and shiny like polished obsidian, if only a little, if only his face, and hands and the straining bulge in his biceps.

"We can stay as long as you like," Christian's voice yanked Carrie back. Holding her gaze, he took her good wrist and turned it over in his palm to test her pulse. "We're in no rush tonight."

Three nods of agreement.

Why didn't she become a firefighter?

"I'm sorry," she mumbled, a sad, broken record. Prone in the end zone, strapped in the ambulance, screaming to get out of St. Agatha's. *I'm sorry. Sorry. Sorry.* She couldn't do it. Any of it.

She'd felt like she was in a flooding submarine, a depressurized plane, on the Nile with a hole in the hull. She couldn't survive it.

The stench of over-bleached sheets and latex gloves. The sound of gurney wheels clicking across the tile, the intercom paging doctors.

It crushed her with memories.

Waiting at her mother's bedside. Listening to strained groans as she struggled through sleep. Laugh tracks dinging faintly on the television. Carrie's shaking fingers pinning her mother's palm to the bed, so she didn't rip out her IV. Her dad permanently altering his hairline as he argued with the insurance company.

Forcing the past deep, deep down, Carried focused on today. This horrible day. How she'd pathetically failed to ignore the raven haired wide receiver and ended up trailing him with trembling fingers hovering over the shutter.

It had paid off.

The smile. The euphoric, private grin he'd shared as he'd crashed into the end zone was worth it. A reward for hard work. For spending hours hunched on the sidelines, shivering and starving, crying. Her muse had provided.

She'd stretched to get the shot, joy bursting through her when a cleat caught her thigh, snagged in the loop of her camera. Twisted.

Flattened her.

Carrie's world had gone fuzzy. And it was unclear which round of tears came next.

There'd been many.

Some sobbing, some sniveling, all regretful.

Her cheeks had run with tears from the lancing, horrendous pain. From shock, from embarrassment, then from the reserved pampering of the medical teams rushing to help. Laten gloved hands buckling her onto the stretcher, lifting her into an ambulance. Voices telling her to be calm, asking where the pain was concentrated.

Such insistent fussing had been new to Carrie. That, plus the beautiful drip of painkillers into her system, had thrown her into round fourteen of wallowing hysterics.

At some point, she'd figured, her eyes had to stop. The tear ducts would tire, and her body would shrink into a desiccated Hollywood version of herself.

Not yet. Carrie wiped her nose with the extra fabric of her hospital gown bunched at her hips. "Does anyone have an extra tee?" Trent asked the back row. A flash of white, a shirtless Kenny—nipple rings—and then Christian was drying her cheeks.

There was a rock in Carrie's throat. She tucked the fraying ends of the thin cotton gown into her jeans. "I'm fine," she lied.

Trent, Carrie quickly deduced, had no discernible red flags. His socks, though black was not a direct match to his blue slacks, were a bona fide pair. No obvious holes or frays. He was clean shaven, short hair tamed by a dollop of gel, and when he checked the time on his phone, his background was a big-pawed Pitbull. Which

Carrie staunchly preferred to a secret second family or a sonogram of a third love child.

He reminded her of a Count or a Lord.

An Earl.

And Christian, with his double dimpled smile, channeled Victorian era industry tycoon. Not as formal in the clothing, but no less mannered or kind.

"Where are your discharge papers?" Christian asked, spotting them before he finished his sentence and taking the stack from her lap, tossing them to Trent, who started flipping.

She'd been stupid. Laughably stupid.

Crying because she was a terrible adult. Because her shoulder hurt.

This morning, eating CrunchBerries with no milk, she'd been struggling.

But now—

Medical bills. Humungous, grotesque, uninsured medical bills. And work—

The Mountaineer's PR would grab and smash her field access badge. Make banned-for-life posters with Carrie's face. She'd never photograph a game again. Never smell the shredded grass and dirty sweat. Never sunburn the back of her thumbs.

Never photograph Asher.

Christian beheld her unharmed left arm. "Can you hold your camera in one hand?" A fresh swell of tears escaped. "Carrie?"

"No." Ears burning, she hastily dried her cheeks. "No, it's too heavy. I need both hands to shoot."

Calmly, perhaps repulsed, Christian wiggled Kenny's shirt from her iron grip. It'd grown so dense with water, she thought he might wring it out, but he discarded the soggy cotton on the plastic center console.

"What even happened?" Laurie asked. Christian had been the only one on the game day EMT team.

Mind in turmoil, fingers fidgeting in her lap, Carrie shared her best recollection. She told her story like a fireside horror story. How she'd arrived to the stadium early to get the front spot in the designated photographer's area. Excited, bright eyed, and bushy-haired. Extra batteries, layers, gel insoles. Then she described in excruciating detail how Asher's foot caught on her lanyard.

The fall.

However, she carefully left out the moments after, though she refused to consider why.

She'd been delirious, she supposed. She'd remembered it wrong. *Right?*

His solid, muscular body sprawled on top of her like a cozy weighted blanket. Strong, gloved hands wending over her arms, cupping her cheeks, brushing the hair from her face. Gently wiping away her tears.

His voice had been gruff, near desperate. "Where does it hurt?" he'd asked, hovering atop her, braced on an elbow and knee, smelling like sweat and grass and cold air. "You have to tell me, where's the pain? C'mon brat." The desperation in his words had echoed through her.

Then there was the moment of realization. The horror and guilt when he'd discovered her arm, limp and non-responsive. He'd wrenched his glove off with his teeth before coasting unsteady fingers into the scoop of her neckline. Scorching calluses slid over her bra strap, down, pushed.

She'd gasped, arched, expecting pain, squeezed her eyes shut.

Gone. In his hold, the agony faded, tamed under his touch. His thumb traced the lines of her face, the sweep of her cheekbones, the soft curve of her jaw. Her lower lip.

"Shh..." he'd whispered, hot breath tickling the line of her throat. "Breathe now. Yes. Good. Like that. Just breathe through it. Tough. You're so tough."

He'd told her she wasn't alone, he wouldn't leave her. He was proud of her. She was doing great. The combination of his low praise and the slow sweep of his thumb over her parted lips caused her to lose her breath again. Worry she might suffocate with a pounding heart and blazing skin.

She'd opened her eyes and gasped at the radiant green encircling his irises, at the flick of his tongue over his lip. He was so close. Impossibly large—the kind of large that made Carrie feel small—and devilishly handsome. Deviously so. Even grass covered, even wrecked. A card shark with aces up his sleeve, a distraction around every bend. Rich eyes, regal nose, the precise scar on his chin.

"I have you," he'd said, sliding his hand into her hair.

She'd believed him. Let the fear drip away. *Asher had her.*

He'd tipped his head up to yell for help, voice angled with a brusque, dangerous edge. Carrie had felt people surround them, poke her legs, talk around her.

Asher's hold remained. His ragged voice lived in her ear. "I have you. I'm here, I'm staying." A vow.

She'd peered up at him, weathered by exhaustion and grime, and she'd seen something.

A softness.

Concern. Something hesitant and cherished. He'd refused to release her gaze. They'd froze together, their breaths coming hard and fast, somehow synchronized.

When the tip of his nose scored hers, the intimacy of the motion awoke something deep and raw within her. An emotion sharper than hope, stronger than want. It'd tugged at her from her center and by some miracle, she'd forgotten she was hurt. She'd inhaled, closed her eyes.

Smelled sweat and grass, icy-hot, and plastic. Blood. Asher.

Awareness had flooded her. A shocking zap she distantly identified as trust. She'd soaked up his every promise. Felt protected. Safe.

Her breaths evened and time slowed. She'd almost—

Well, she'd almost smiled.

Until two of his teammates yanked him off her, shoved him back. A wicked curse had sounded from his throat, nearly feral.

She'd reached out and shouted but her arm refused her brain. Laid limp. Useless. She'd been forced to watch, helpless, in complete anguish as the ref snagged Asher's chest pads.

He was yelling. They both were. Pointing at the ground, pushing. More players got involved. A yellow flag appeared. Another. Whistles.

Asher was removed forcibly from the field.

She'd twisted to watch, to follow, saw him throw his helmet, watched it bounce when a flashlight blinded her.

Alone, the elements unleashed on her. Blaring sirens, flashing lights, blistering wind. A small army of medics asking questions, prodding her body, twisting her shoulder. Christian's calm smile.

Trust. As easily broken as it was forged.

"That's shit," Trent muttered, removing Carrie from the memory.

She swallowed, ignoring the goosebumps on her arms. "After he fell, I don't remember much other than Christian offering me a ride home"

Only the embarrassment of trusting Asher. The feeling of security and warmth and then being immediately shown how misplaced that trust was.

Carrie pulled on the thick white strap of her sling, trying to straighten it to lie flat across her chest.

"Well, hey," Christian said to her. "I put my number—"

Three radios blasted at once. "Available units. We have a reported passenger vehicle fire on Route 17.

CHAPTER NINE

ASHER

T ENSION TALONED UP ASHER'S spine and dug into the nape of his neck as he entered the bedroom. No peace came. No restfulness or warm, homey rush.

He desperately wanted to blame the missing walls, but he knew better.

Sawhorses, coils of electric wire, and pallets loaded with flooring dotted the room. A thick, creased sheet of plastic covered a blue table saw. The cement subfloor wore a heavy layer of sawdust and wrinkled leaves, interspersed with nails and flattened cardboard boxes. Overhead, the night sky was a turbulent navy, clouds of dark gray and black drifting by, the moon a distant glowing white.

He turned and faced Charlie—call me Chuck—Kelton. The head contractor had rusted keys in one hairy hand and an empty Dasani bottle in the other, having obviously just gotten to the site.

Chuck's shoulders and neck were hunched, as if he'd carried one too many support beams, and his buzz cut revealed scratches and cuts tearing up the skin outside the protection of safety glasses.

Wood creaked from deep within the house. Dirt and dust tickled Asher's nose. "I expected more."

"We had delays with the materials."

"Deadline hasn't changed."

Chuck Kelton didn't appear nearly as terrified as he ought to. Not when there were a dozen other contractors who'd leap out of a warm bed to take a call from Asher and his multi-million dollar project. "Every tiler, dry waller, and electrician would need to work overtime to finish."

"Approved."

Chuck stepped back, inching towards the exit. *Huh*, Asher must still be projecting pissed-the-fuck-off despite showering the game off and donning his Burberry two piece. What gave it away? The muted tone? The industrial clamp in his jaw? How he'd shouted for Chuck to get his ass up and working at one a.m. on a Sunday?

Asher had no desire to be here, but he sure as hell couldn't be in his apartment. Not without having to buy the entire building to cover damages.

The stadium was off-limits thanks to his abrupt ejection from the game.

They ejected him. For wanting to stay with her, for refusing to leave. Fury and disbelief continued to roar through him. And something else. Something like regret and guilt.

He'd given her his vow. And they'd shredded it from him. Cole Seeder hauling him sideways. Miles Santos ramming the butt of his hands into Asher's chest.

Riley's frantic, "Coach is freaking" in his ringing ear.

Who cared about Coach? Asher was fucking livid. Mostly at himself.

Chuck swayed forward and planted a palm on a two-by, keys flapping in the night like a wind chime. "That kind of overtime will increase the budget three fold."

"Approved. There's no price too high. I need it done. It's a gift."

"Some gift." Chuck crooned. "But even with the overtime, the weather—"

"Is only getting colder. Hire another crew if you must. And get the damn roof up." He cast an objectively threatening look at the man building his future. Cargo pants, a sherpa lined flannel, wad of mint chew packed behind his cracked bottom lip. "Or I may forget to recommend your services to my teammates."

"Right, you see, a month isn't enough. We're working non-stop." Was his voice wavering?

Asher straightened, checked his watch, and leaned in closer. "I've been up since four, Chuck, and when I stopped by, the lot was empty, then I worked all day but when I stopped by again, it was still empty. Which part of that is nonstop?"

"We can't work this late. Neighbors complain."

"Let them." He'd lost too much time to building permits and inspections. Nasty words from a neighbor in their bath robe wouldn't deter him. "And it's twenty-five days. Not a month."

Asher drew his fingers over a wide window gap. "Skip the finishes, we'll leave that to the Mrs."

Chuck's probing gaze shot over Asher's bare fingers in question. In judgement.

Asher snapped his hand back and buried it deep into his pocket. Think him insane. He didn't care. She'd be his. If he couldn't convince her with words, he'd do it with the house. With his gesture. He was putting himself out there, just as Marianne advised.

Sweet and soft, and starry-eyed Holmes deserved the world. Asher aimed to start here and expand until she had it.

He paced a circle in the wide space. Walk-in closets so disgustingly big they were cavernous, a shameless en-suite that could fit a bath for five. *Should the bed face the door or the windows?*

Windows.

She could rise with the sun, stretch under hazy, golden light.

"And get a quote from a landscaper. She likes flowers."

"The shingles are on back order, since the pandemic, it's—"

Asher's jaw sawed. "Give it a steel roof."

"Economically—"

"This isn't a conversation. We're not discussing options. It's decided. I'll cover whatever cost. Afford any fees you deem necessary."

His molars ached. How could every lead be cold? Three years. Searching for three. Years. He *was* insane. Skin crawling, stomach clenching insane. Desperate and pining. Frantic.

"What about the extension permits?" he asked as he surveyed the eyesore across the foggy street. The stain on his vision. A dank, dilapidated yellow leviathan. He'd shred it. Replace the view from the kitchen sink with trees and flowers.

Chuck spat brown into his bottle. "Coming along. Need approval from the city."

"Get it."

A judgmental grunt came from the contractor's throat. "They're nice, you know. Good people."

"You've met them?" Asher asked, making a final inspection of the room.

"Only two."

Would this conversation never end? "Two."

"An older bird and a young thing," Chuck continued needlessly, following Asher to the front of the house. "Carrie's real friendly, gives the boys ample encouragement. Keeps 'em sharp."

What were the odds of Carolyn Huston taking a nickname?

Asher didn't have time to mine the thought before Chuck carried on, "She used to bring by blueberry peach cobbler after day shift, but she lost that job. Now it's donuts. They're pretty good. Dense, but not heavy. I like—"

Asher quit listening. He stopped in his tracks in the front entrance, cool wispy mist snaking between his ankles. Across the street, a tall, curved figure balanced on the narrow handrail of the center stoop. A woman. Pressing spread fingers into the garish siding, reaching.

His gaze clung to her, to the exposed arch of her spine, the panels of her shirt fluttering open in the breeze.

He knew only one woman reckless enough to balance on that flimsy wood rail eight feet off the ground. It wouldn't be a fatal drop. Not for him, tucked shoulders, loose lats. For her, it was certain death.

The strain of her fingers upward indicated she wanted to go in through the window, flagrantly ignoring the purple door beside her knee.

As Asher's gaze raked over her, he saw the painted rail slant left, saved from crumbling by two shaky pin supports. Those tenuous holds spurred him into action.

Sheared sections of pallets clattered underfoot and then the hard pack of asphalt stung his shins as he sprinted. One long leg lifted to the wall, as if siding equated a sturdy foot hold.

"Yes!" He heard her gasp when her fingertips stroked the sill. Then he heard the rusted screws and rotted wood team up to belch a horrendous croak.

She didn't see him until she was falling.

Asher seized her from the air, sweeping her securely into his arms, and twisting to escape the railing as it shuddered to the ground. She gave a high screech of shock at the rattle of wood, drawing her legs and feet into his chest.

Asher fought the urge to steady himself as the entire world tilted. For a horrible minute, he wondered if the earth was about to open in the middle of the misty crabgrass and devour him.

It *was* her.

Carrie.

And he was furious. "What were you thinking?"

"Asher?" Her voice was barely there. A whisper.

A surge of wind picked up the blunt ends of her hair and tossed them. Rich brown shining under the shimmering moonlight. Her arm wound around his neck, tickling his nape. She tipped her head back. Oil slick lashes scraped his jaw.

And a completely natural, totally expected male response hummed into his blood.

Fuck.

He lifted her higher, ceased noticing her freckles, the light graze of her fingertips, the soft curves draped across him. She was liquid, like a cat in a vase, finding any air between them and filling it with warmth.

Her eyes shut as a shiver broke through her.

"Carrie?"

She went rigid, retracted her arm and jabbed his throat. "Let go of me!"

Asher choked, and Carrie released a pained groan as she spun free of his arms. There and gone as she pushed him away, staggered backward. Lost her footing on the dewy grass.

"Shit," he coughed, lurching back as she crashed forward. She met the damp earth with cheek and elbow, groaning, and rolling to her side, cradling her arm.

She had a sling.

Apologies floated to his tongue. Useless words to smooth over the pain. To solve nothing. Vows rushing in their wake. "Fuck. Let me help."

"*No,*" she snarled, recoiling, blowing thick hanks of hair from her face. "Don't touch me. I don't need help. Leave"

He should. Victoria had ordered him to stay away.

No, ordered wasn't right. She'd jabbed her freshly painted fingernail at him, wild outrage blazing in her glare. "Do *not* talk to her," she'd warned in the locker room, her red latex dress squeaking loudly as she paced the lush carpeting. "Protect yourself. Go home. Stay home. Do not be dumb. Do not make this worse."

She hadn't wasted another second on him before marching back to the field, complaining about ballistic man children.

Since Asher had seen the black-haired manager yank Burton Kilbride—the biggest, nastiest footballer in the league—around by his earlobe like a toddler on timeout, he listened.

Sort of.

Usually, he didn't require instructions to not intervene. He stayed away, maintained a well-trimmed, razor wire barricade. Impenetrable. Him against the world.

Except he'd made a promise.

"*You*." Her voice was a growl of disgust, and she wore an expression like he'd stuffed Santa down the chimney and lit a fire under his ass. Curls of smoky night air rendered it impossible for Asher to track her hands as she pushed to sit, her right arm limp in a polyblend crayon blue sling.

Wrapped around her shoulders was a thin hospital gown, knotted messily to accommodate the sling. Flappy, cloudy blue sleeves swallowed her elbows, and the neck gaped wildly, revealing a line of black freckles across her collarbone.

She'd ventured outside in that? In scraps?

She looked so small. Fragile. Cowering in the mist.

The same feeling he'd gotten when the officials had separated them awoke. Intense possession, fierce protectiveness. Smothering a snarl, Asher sank to a knee, took off his jacket and slid it over her shoulders.

"You," he returned, sounding like he ate nails for breakfast. "What happened?" Dumb question.

Her almond eyes were narrowed as she gazed at him. She stared.

"Carrie?" he tried, wishing to jab her with a stick, the same way he'd check a washed up body for life.

Her name in his rumble seemed to jolt something. She bent forward and placed a shaking hand on the cold, wet grass. Before she need push up, he was hauling her into him, setting her feet carefully on the ground, balancing her by her hips.

"How can I help you?" he asked. "What do you need?"

The moonlight was liquid silver over her skin, dripping between her freckles, spinning them into onyx stars.

Army green pants gripped her waist and hung loose at the knees. The pink laces on her sneakers were untidy, wayward aglets mounting escape, like she'd been in such a rush, she'd forgotten how to tie them. And tears, one by one, cascaded down her cheeks.

"What do I need?" She pushed him and stumbled back a step when he didn't move. "Is that a real fucking question? How about a restraining order?"

"From me?"

"Who else is casing my place? Is there a sick little team of you camped in the shadows, plotting to ruin my day?"

He crossed his arms to refrain from angrily fixing the loose thread in her neckline. "You broke into my building—"

"Artie and I follow three common accounts."

"—broke into my building," he went on, skin feeling too tight. "Wedged your way into my fucking apartment to pitch multilevel marketing bullshit and the next time I see you—and I don't want to see you—you're scaling the wall like you have untapped Spidey powers with one fucking arm."

Her beautiful eyes, lit by the moonlight, met his. "Spidey powers?"

"And excuse me for rescuing your bird bones from dusting out on the ground." His hands slipped on their own accord, curved against the paper thin gown at her waist, clenched. Low and lush, and furious, he whispered, "But yeah, fuck me for ruining your day."

"Rescuing?"

He inclined his head at the question. Let her correct him. She was standing, breathing,

Her glare did not waver. "Get off my property."

He met her glare with one of his own. "Surprised you didn't try that one at my place."

"This is *my* house."

He cast a glare at the canary tear down. "If that's true, then why the break in act?" he asked, tense and defensive. Territorial. "Why not walk through the front door?"

"Because while I was laying flat on the field in untold pain—"

"Untold pain," he scoffed, angrily cuffing the sleeves of his jacket into the pockets so they stopped flopping around. "It's a dislocated shoulder, not a stab wound."

"Untold pain! Writhing in agony, I didn't reference a laminated checklist as the medics rushed me to the hospital. Not the first thing on my mind after I was steamrolled by a jackass."

"I—" The air compressed from his lungs. He'd tried. He'd tried so damn hard. He'd been dragged like a screaming child torn from its mother. He'd fought.

"*You*. Everything is about *you*," she snapped, and Asher almost burst out in laughter. "There couldn't possibly be a world out there that doesn't involve you, people who don't know your name or see your face when they close their eyes. Get off my lawn."

So she could kill herself? The words escaped him without thought. "Make me, brat. See how far you get."

She puffed a quick, disgusted snort. "You are so patronizing. You think you can give me orders because of you've got a little prick?" An eye-roll big enough to gain its own gravity. "How'd you like it if I called you brat, huh? Not so much?"

"It would be an improvement from jackass, but I'd prefer you come up with something original instead of copying from me." He sliced her a smirk, adding viciously, "Brat."

The brutal way she looked up at him told him he'd won. Until her mouth curled at the edge and a determined glint erased his confidence. "Yes," she said. "Leagues from now, I'll be the villain in this story."

They seethed at each other. Breathes fogging in the night.

Carrie's hospital gown whipped against her neck and dread sunk into his chest as her fingers clumsily caught the end.

"*Fuck*," he choked out before he could stop it.

A sling. A concussion. What else? Bruises? Internal bleeding? Did he get the ribs? He clenched his thigh to keep from spreading his hand over her torso and drawing his finger along each bone.

He'd done that. Given her searing pain with each inhale. Every flinch a red hot iron poker in her shoulder. News coverage of the game said a dislocation was one of the worst pains a body could endure without blacking out.

Unbidden, he saw her, hair splayed out in a crown around her, tears sliding down her cheeks to her ears, shuddering, staring at him, clutching him.

He'd left her.

Fuck.

He assessed the decrepit tacky yellow townhouse, it's narrow sidewalk and rail-less steps.

You've done it now, Laughlin. You got involved, and now there's a crying half-dressed photographer yelling at you.

Call Victoria, logic said. Dump the girl on his manager. She'd fix his mess.

Call, he told himself as the icy breeze nipped his skin, raised the hair on his neck. *Dial her number. Hit call. Wait for the rings.* He crossed the leaf cluttered lawn, strode up the walk and *fuck—*

Call.

Now. Dial and call. Talk.

Fuck. He couldn't abandon her.

It didn't have to do with the fact that she was beautiful or crying or that in his place, Holmes would've offered her own bed, cash, and an hour long hug. Not at all.

Might as well commit. Flicking the quietly crying photographer a final glance, he stripped out of his shirt and swallowed a groan against the cold.

"What are you doing?" She was whispering now, glancing nervously at the street, backing away from him. A swallow stuck in the line of her throat. Her cheeks were red.

"Go ahead. Run." He had a two minute split.

She was striding for him before he could finish setting the bait. "Stop it," she hissed, chasing him to her stoop.

Angry and tired, and fucking cornered, he wrapped his shirt around his knuckles and closed the gathered buttons in his palm. "Stop what?"

A pause. Her eyes traversed the spread of his torso, heating, searing, until she abruptly jerked her gaze to the street, just to be contrary. "Stop *this*," came her breathless whisper.

"You don't even know what I'm doing, and you're telling me to stop. Ever considered this might be for you? You might like it? Even thank me?"

"I'm not so hung up for men that I'd want you."

He twisted, feeling his abs contract and her gaze was there again, burning through the skin. For a moment, he couldn't draw a breath. He made a fist. "Yeah, you find me disgusting, don't you?"

She locked eyes with him. "Repulsive."

"Horrific."

"Abhorrent."

Was he smiling? "Attractive."

She snorted. Scoffed. Wedged her free hand into the wrapping of her sling. "No."

He *was* smiling. "Liar. Thought you didn't like that word, brat. Or is it just when someone says it to you? Not used to being denied? Always getting special treatment because you have a pretty smile and tight jeans."

"I am not a brat."

Right. "How many other people got personally escorted home by a fire squad?" He'd seen the truck while waiting for Chuck's arrival.

"They—"

Asher punched clear through the lower left glass pane of her front door.

Carrie yelped. "Reprehensible!" She raced up the steps, but Asher spread his feet to protect her as he knocked the jagged remains from the frame, reached inside and undid the bolt.

"There," he said, shoving the door in and shaking the shards from his shirt. "You're welcome."

He expected her to slam it in his face, call him contemptible or depraved while her heated gaze scalded him. Maybe she'd hit him, grasp a nasty shard, and threaten him with it.

Instead, she was quiet. Her lower lip disappeared into her mouth, her eyes exploded to moon wide.

A surge of regret charred Asher's pride. His stomach flopped onto the concrete. He thought about giving her his wallet, his phone. Threatening *himself* with the glass.

"No," he said, hands raising, shaking his head. "No. No no no."

She burst into tears.

Chapter Ten

Carrie

CARRIE COVERED HER FACE with both hands. She knew he'd seen her crying, but there was something to be said about not dousing a flame in gasoline.

"No," she hissed past a strangled sob. "Not now."

Five minutes quicker. Three if she left the window unlatched. Three minutes and she'd have missed Asher entirely, never gone gooey in his arms only to be mansplained his heroics.

Three minutes faster and she'd be inside. Collapsed against the wall, knees curled into her chest, sobbing until she was lightheaded and exhausted. Until her eyeballs hurt more than her shoulder.

Except nothing seemed to go her way.

Beside her, Asher wore an expression of horror. Through the gaps in her fingers, she saw him actually step backward on the stoop, as if toppling over the ledge was more tempting than suffering her tears.

"Just leave," she sputtered, sniffling and trying to wipe away the mess with her flimsy, awful sleeve. If she got snot on his jacket, he'd probably charge her for it.

"You're good at that. At least this time you didn't promise to stay." Her filter wasn't functioning. The tightly woven mesh sheet between her brain and her mouth popped a hole. "God, why did I even fall for it? Every loser that smiles at me or makes me feel special. Then they cheat and lie and steal, and I'm shocked. Why? It's a sickness. I'm sick."

"Loser?" came his reply, voice ripe with offense.

Naturally, he skirted past Carrie's horrible revelation to the part about himself.

Narcissistic, impossible, six-pack having jackass.

"Leave," she ground, shaking her head, clearing her cheek with the other sleeve. "You broke my door. You win this round. Skip the victory lap, and let me wallow alone."

"No."

The single word sent an unholy flush through her. "No?" The fog sunk into the grass. The moon flung into the ocean, and every owl, raccoon, and night crawler stuck up their legs to play dead at the pure disdain in Carrie's voice.

The bastard smirked. "*No.*"

Through damp, tangled lashes, she peered over his bare chest and the cords of his neck to the stern line of his jaw and finally his eyes, twinkling.

She was going to punch him. Right in the mouth, until his smirk was smeared in dripping crimson. She felt it building in her, adrenaline and anticipation and bloodlust, like a snowball rolling down a hill, packing on hard layers. Her first slugger.

Before she could bunch her fingers, he was gone. Stalking into her home, glass crunching beneath his boots, turning to diamonds on the original hardwoods.

"Jesus." Asher grimaced at the state of her cluttered hallway. "How do you live like this?"

Suddenly, Carrie had more pressing problems than whether to aim for his mouth or his eye.

"Don't look!" she screeched, rushing inside, shoving him into her book tower so she could slam her coat closet shut before he witnessed the crazy.

Outside, they were on even footing. Known exclusively for their actions, but here ...

Most people didn't keep wedding level ballgowns on a dress form in the hall. Once the latch clicked, she used the sides of her converse to kick sewing needles and ribbons scraps into the abyss.

Heaving a sigh of relief, she turned, and he was in her kitchen.

"Don't look at anything," she repeated harshly, rolling up a placard of runaway gold lace and shoving it in a random cabinet. The door creaked. Something—a thousand things—budged it open. She slapped her hand on it, and kicked the where-else-would-it-go drawer shut, spinning around to find Asher, see where he'd snuck next.

But he was staring at her, surrounded by pistachio green cabinets and a bleeding heart chandelier, looking like a USDA certified snack. Unnaturally handsome. Midnight brows slashed upward, eyes feasting on her discomfort.

Heat poured into Carrie's face.

Nothing was dirty. Leave a crumb out and Reginald would find it and squawk a victory cry. But no volume of vacuuming would make her place less than a mess.

Asher Laughlin was not messy.

Based on a fleeting glance of his apartment and the amount of starch pressed into his jacket, she knew how he functioned. A place for everything and nothing out of place. Order and organization. He slammed the door on little cookie entrepreneurs, denied wrapping paper sales, and destroyed candle purchase forms with an industrial shredder.

"Ever heard of a landfill?" he asked, poking loose acorns around in her cherub spoon rest.

She snatched it from him, stroking the white porcelain. "That's an antique." Declan had gotten it for her at a flea market.

But Asher wasn't listening. He was making big gasping sounds in her living room.

Carrie ditched her buttons on the stove and hurried through the rose archway. *Shit.*

Her nest.

"What in the—"

"I knit." As if that explained the sheer quantity of blankets and pillows and yarn balls clustered around, draped over, and stuffed under her cream love seat. "I have restless hands," she clarified, tiptoeing over the thick carpet, as if she were approaching a feral wolf and not a home intruder. "I made six hats watching *Bridgerton* season two. I gave them to the animal shelter."

"You knitted dog hats?"

"The homeless shelter only wanted gloves." She'd overstocked them with hats because she'd been too terrified to actually watch during *Pride and Prejudice and Zombies*.

Asher's mouth formed a flat line as he lifted her dish towel, turned scarf, turned blanket, turned king sized blanket, turned ship sail. A riot of heathered pastels and sparkly silver. His gaze slid to her.

Ignoring him, Carrie carefully aligned the hand painted cement coasters on her tufted blue ottoman.

"Of course you knit," he said.

And something in his tone, the accusing, unsurprised, entitled tone, made Carrie instantly furious. "Of course?" She scarcely opened her mouth to hiss it.

Asher shrugged as he moved past the lilac section of her mega blanket onto periwinkle. "Look at you."

She was across the room before her next breath, yanking her ineffective ship sail from his hands. "What is that supposed to mean?"

"It means you look like you knit, brat. And you do. No need to get offended." His brow arched wickedly, and his tongue flicked at his teeth to shred a smile. Smother a laugh. He was laughing at her. "You're have a trigger temper. So touchy."

Nobody in her life had ever accused her of a short temper. Nobody used *Carrie* and *temper* in the same sentence.

Gullible. Disorganized. Frivolous.

Never temperamental.

She scowled up at him, reeling more blanket into her arm. "You didn't say it like that."

He cocked his head toward her, pushing wide fingers between robin's blue loops. "Enlighten me then, brat. How did I say it?"

"Like I'm knitting myself to death, alone and sad and pathetic. Wasting my life away in yarn and BBC dramas and forgetting dinner, but never losing weight." Carrie's chest rose and fell and only when her voice came back to her did she realize she'd started to shout.

Asher was unfazed as he stepped into her, gathering the heavy mega blanket between into his arms until they were no more than stitches apart. His untidy black hair reflected the warm tones of her lamps, and his hazel eyes reminded Carrie of a delicious caramel apple, bright granny smith green and golden brown. Towering above her, he emulated an infuriating, stunning archangel.

"Or perhaps," he said. "I meant that your house is a cash register away from being a Jo Ann Fabrics. There's knitting needles next to your spatula, and—"

"*No.*" She gave a piercing look, dug her heels into the carpet and wrenched on the blanket. "You said *me*. Look at *me*. Not my house. What'd you mean?"

"You wanna do this?" he asked calmly, as if she were a child asking to arm wrestle.

No.

But it'd been *no* all week and now it was two in the morning. She was an arm down, there was a hole in her front door, and she was sharing a blanket with—and actively hating—her greatest muse.

"Yes." Her gut twisted. "I really do."

"Alright." He wet his lips. "Look at you. Look at your freckles. Look at your hair. Your mouth. Look at how people treat you. Opening doors. Handing out free rides, saving you from breaking your damn leg, even though it might teach you a lesson. You're alone and sad and whatever else you want to call yourself because you want to be."

Her fingernails sank into her palms. "I'm not."

Asher wasn't done. "You tell yourself you're knitting because you're alone, but you know if you had stopped when this was a blanket and charged outside, you'd be facing a nightmare. Because you don't want to be with anyone. That's why you're alone. It's your choice. You're not a victim, you're not pathetic, and life isn't swindling you."

He smelled like nature, like dew and apples, and wet leaves. She could feel the heat coming off his skin, droves crashing against her. He curled over her further. Not looming. Not with the tilt of his head, the low dip of his chin. He was matching her, meeting her. If she rocked forward, pulled a loop closer, their foreheads would collide.

She forced her tongue to move. "Then what am I?" she breathed, watching his pupils dilate, watching darkness spread until he had no color, until he was black hair and midnight eyes, so much like a killer, Carrie leaned even closer.

Her hair scraped his cheek, the blanket pulled taut. Her pulse raced, thundered inside her chest, but she was still as stone. Straining. "Tell me."

He couldn't be done. He couldn't finish there. Negative. He was so negative. Telling her no, explaining what's she wasn't.

He breathed out slowly. The gin was gone. Replaced by something sweet, like buttercream icing.

In that second, she'd realized she was starving, craving. The tip of her nose brushed against his.

The warmth of his silent gasp seeped into her skin.

"*Please.*"

"Me." His voice lost the purr, the rhythm he'd had. It was harsh and angry, jagged and raw. "You're just like me."

Chapter Eleven

Carrie

"Y ou open it."

Carrie blanched at Diana's suggestion. "Me? You found it."

"It was on your porch."

Diana reached over Carrie's plate to grab another pancake, rolled it up and chomped the end.

"Does it smell?" Carrie asked, breaking apart her hashbrown and stuffing it in the middle of her egg McMuffin. They were in her kitchen, flamingo-ing next to the fridge so Jill couldn't see, smell, or hear the crinkle of the McDonald's brown bag. One more rant about the dangers of sodium and it might stick.

Mickey D's was a home cooked meal in Diana's book. Medium fries and chocolate shake no lid were as healing as Great Grandma Lydia's potato leek soup. Guaranteed to cure scoliosis.

To cook would require Diana a kitchen, which Carrie wasn't convinced Diana possessed. They'd been best friends for ten years and Carrie suspected Diana rented a room in a haunted mansion.

Coffin bed, personal poltergeist, radioactive goo leaching from the walls. Where the weekly sage burning escalated to a full-blown exorcism. Every time.

If Diana had a place at all.

Carrie would also believe it if Diana's People magazine—an accidental subscription she now enjoyed—went straight to the Hand's mailbox.

If Diana wasn't at the bar, she was with Carrie, fighting with Declan, or getting her dose of vitamin D.

Meanwhile, Carrie tried to step foot outside as little as possible. It wasn't because she detested nature or humanity like Diana, it was simply she felt closest to those she loved tucked away in her slice of Nice Way.

Initially, it was because she got to use the same rooms her mother once occupied, and stepping inside on a bitter December night felt as comforting as a warm hug. Then, at some unidentifiable point in the last six years, her home started doing that for others. Declan, when work took him to dark, dreadful places. Jill, when throbbing arthritis robbed her of a perfect Chassé. Diana, whenever heartless bruiser persona chafed.

Nice Way was an escape.

Last night, Asher turned it into a dungeon.

You're just like me.

He couldn't possibly be more wrong. He was a rich bastard who wished everyone was as miserable as him. Judging her home, mocking her hobbies.

Carrie knit because she already had love. Every year waiting for her. Excuse her for not searching it out in the meantime.

What was his excuse?

Gun to her head: despicable absence of charm, courtesy, and introspection.

Sleep eluded her for hours, kept shaking her from bed to gather all her loose ruby corset buttons into a dish, fold her blankets, rearrange her matriarch themed teacups into order of beheading. Asher had rubbed on her nerves, blown into her space and treated it as if it were a crime scene.

It wasn't until Diana was pushing inside, brown bag pinned under her elbow, steel bat in her grip, that Carrie realized she'd let Asher do it. Flatten her.

For the second time in ten hours.

Diana had found The Bag. Waiting in the crisp morning air on her stoop next to Carrie's camel leather camera bag, and her cheapo baby blue crossbody. Everything there. Pink fuzzy keys, Barnes and Noble membership card, birthday cake ChapStick, and knockoff lip oil. Her phone, complete with satellite visible sparkly case.

An irritated Diana had gone through the stockpile, checking every piece of lint in.

After weeping in front of her mortal enemy, hours of frantic organizing, and one vivid, wholly violent dirty dream about a raven haired rake—getting her purse back was a good way to start the week.

And then there was The Bag. The little white parchment bag.

They'd used tongs to carry it into the kitchen for a full autopsy.

Carrie smooshed her Mc-hash-muffin and stared at the it sitting on her stove. "What if it's explosive?"

She should call Trent. Her gaze flickered to the hall, at the end of it, the hole in the bottom quarter panel of her door. It made Carrie think of a jack-o'-lantern with a missing tooth.

"Could be a finger." Diana poured brown sugar into her oatmeal. "Bloody and swollen. Purple and—"

"It's not a finger."

"Too small for a head," Diana argued. "Unless it's not human." She bent at the waist like she had x-ray vision. "Somebody could've snared a squirrel. Chopped it up with a chef's knife, tortured it and sent it to the tiny rodent guillotine."

There went breakfast. "Why do you have so many details? And why are you so chill?"

A shrug, lazy and unaffected. "Bags show up all the time at Casa Lovatt." Her tone implied a squirrel's head would be preferred to whatever she found.

"It's not any of that." Bodies didn't show up on Nice Way. Especially not fuzzy, cute headless bodies.

Diana kicked up an eyebrow. "Then open it."

Carrie fondled the plastic clip on her sling, chewed on her lip. She couldn't open it.

Because only one person would have folded the edges of the bags so crisply. Bent the corners at an exact ninety-degree angle. Only one person would ensure the bag remained immaculate, despite being the product of a ding-dong ditch.

She knew because she wanted to photograph it. It's resplendent clean lines before her shattered door. Like a gift from an angel.

A misnomer.

That's how far gone she was. She was no longer obsessed with the sharp angles of his face. Now it was his bold technique in everything, his refusal to be anything other than himself.

When she looked inside, she'd want to take a picture of that too.

"No." No. A word she wanted to scrub from his mouth. "Why would he do this? Who does he think he is?" Carrie pointed at the bag accusingly. As if this were an interrogation and the bag was seconds from blabbing under the pressure of bad cop and who-gives-a-fuck cop.

Diana rolled her eyes. "Let's trash it. If he asks—which he won't—we'll say Reggie snatched it."

"Reggie had egg rolls last night." A deep freezer offering.

"Asher doesn't know that." Diana reached for the bag. Stopped. "Did you give him the plum sauce too? It's a game changer."

"Yes," Carrie said, unsure how refined Reginald's palette could possibly be. He ate banana peels. "Stop!"

Diana snatched back her fingers. "We have to do something. What if it's a bomb on a timer? I think I hear clicking."

"That's Jill's metronome." Carrie grabbed the bag by the throat. If someone was going to touch it, it was her. "I'm doing it. Have a resuscitation kit at the ready."

"Whoa!" Diana lurched across the oven, diving for Carrie's open laptop and hitting pause on the upload. "Who's that?"

Carrie turned, armed with Asher's name and a vindicated smirk. Diana finally got it. The appeal, the agitation, the bone deep obsession, but her tongue stuck to the roof of her mouth. She frowned at the photo. "Lincoln Wray?"

"Lincoln," Diana murmured, near covetous, gazing at the man in the Mountaineers' jersey.

"He's the new quarterback. Lots of fans." She tilted her head, taking in the QB's long face, pointed nose, thick dark eyebrows. "He's my new target." Wasn't like she could ask Asher for his signature again.

At this point, it'd became a principle. He didn't deserve to participate in noble deeds. "I snapped a few of him. I'll have to search for a decent one."

"What's wrong with this one?"

Besides the amateur angle, lousy focus, and shoddy lighting? Carrie twisted to her friend. "You like him."

The vile goth barkeep shuttered back down over Cadbury features. "Sod off." Diana rolled her eyes. "He caught me off guard."

Carrie didn't believe it. "Because he's hot."

"Because he doesn't look like a football player. He looks like—" She clicked ahead to a shot of Lincoln stretching to unleash a spiral, body taut with focus. "I don't know." She narrowed her gaze, chasing the firm tendons in his forearm. "Smart, almost. Players are supposed to be meatheads with no necks. He looks—"

"Bored?"

"Tortured."

They looked at each other. Carrie grinned. "You want him," she accused haughtily. "He looks like your next serving of D."

"Bloody hells. I'd point out a cow on a sheep farm too. It's an oddity. Doesn't mean I'll shag it."

Carrie's cheek burned from grinning. "Yeah right." She snorted. "A football player. Jeez, Diana. What a cliché. Do you think you'll wear pigtails to his game? Put on a jersey and join his fan page?"

Her side hurt from laughing, picturing it.

Diana's lips flattened into a straight white line. "You deserve this." She ripped apart the staple on the bag.

They looked down.

Carrie's heart stopped. An orange bottle, and a box of ginger green tea. Her prescription of horse sized pills she wished came as strawberry gummies.

"Drugs and tea," Diana harrumphed, clearly disappointed no world ending destruction had befallen. "At least there's something for each of us." She snagged the bottle and Carrie let it fly even though she needed ibuprofen like adorable otters needed tiny round pebbles to cradle.

There was a note. Written on the back of the winding CVS receipt. Capital letters, blocky, neat, severe determined lines. No room for alterations, for regret.

Ice and repeat brat.

-it's not little

A threat or advice? And the sign off. She ignored the way her stomach flipped.

"That means it is," Diana muttered, holding out two pills for Carrie and a yellow coffee cup. "If it wasn't, he'd attach a photo or drop trou for you. Jotting it on a note is major small dick energy."

Carrie kept silent and stared at the words. He'd picked up her prescription. He'd brought her tea, got her camera.

I have you. You're so tough.

"Good taste in tea, though," Diana said, sniffing the package. "No Lipton BS."

Carrie blinked and found tears in her eyes.

"Oh no," Diana caught her hand. "It's okay, sweetie. What's wrong?"

"Why did he do this?"

"Regret? Remorse? A temporary embolism?"

"I've been waiting for good and this. *This.*" She crushed the paper bag. An urge to punch rising again. "This is what I get? A jackass who has a robin hood streak? The rent hike. The fundraiser. I spent three years photographing the middle school volleyball team and stuffy golf tournaments to get access to the Peak, to take actual pictures. Four games before I'm out with an itchy, hideous sling. I'm almost thirty. What am I doing? Where's my fucking karma?"

Silence fell in the wake of the question.

Diana cleared her throat. "It's right here." she reached into the pocket of her Beetlejuice hoodie for her money clip. Undoing the metal tab and peeling hundreds free like they were off-brand Kleenex. "How much to cover rent?"

"I'm not taking your money."

"Then how much for the Lincoln photo?" She slapped cash on the counter. "There's twenty-five hundred."

"Take it back or I'll soak it in plum sauce and stuff it Reggie's gullet."

"I consider it a steal for a Carrie Huston shot."

Carrie ripped open her fridge and grabbed the purple plastic bottle. "I'll do it. I'm not mooching off you. You need it."

"I'm swimming in cash," Diana countered lazily.

It was true. Diana had stuffed mattress level money. But she wasn't hoarding. She was saving. Had been for years. To open a second bar. And she finally had enough for a down payment. Carrie refused to postpone Diana's dream. Not anymore. No more surprise Diana paid a few bills to get Carrie back for drinks last week.

Like a bucket of coronas was equivalent to Carrie's Visa statement.

"I've got it covered. I'm just—" Carrie swallowed. "I want Jack. I want to stop struggling alone."

Diana set down the pills, yanked the strings of her sweatshirt tight, and forced deep concentration into the chipped metal on the toaster.

Hurt. Hiding it.

"Not alone," Carrie corrected quickly. "I'm not alone. I have you—"

"I get it," Diana returned rigidly. "But you can't honestly think you're mooching off me, right? I owe you."

"*Ha!*"

Folded arms. A pause. "You want to go upstairs and fake laugh?"

Point Diana. "I love you," Carrie said as she wrapped her mini Cadbury egg in a one-armed hug. "So much." She set her chin on top of Diana's head, breathing in her cedar perfume. "What would you do if you were me?"

"Use the upper cabinets in my office." Carrie pinched her. Diana growled, but finally cinched onto Carrie's waist. "If I were sweetheart pinchy Carrie Huston, I'd charm the shit out of your landlord, get a rent extension, and then I'd call the mountaineers and blame them for your shoulder."

"Is that all," Carrie said dryly.

"I'd also probably shag this Lincoln character because he is not small."

"That's a cup, not a bulge."

"It's a big cup."

Chapter Twelve

Carrie

THE **CONTRACTOR AB INITIO**— Carrie flipped the packet ahead a few pages. **xi: Force majeure.** Closed the damn thing and reached for her phone.

Scalding hot tea sprayed across the counter.

"Shit!" She hopped up from her stool, crossed legs untangling as tea seeped through the threads of her flannel. "Ouch," she hissed, scuttling over the peach tile, frantically undoing her buttons with one hand.

Heard a slow drip onto the floor. "Shit!" A green pool was spreading, flowing over the edge, and all of her kitchen towels were crocheted and adorable and priceless.

The contract. Her Mountaineers Field Access, sub-heading Private Photographer contract. She launched all twenty odd sheets into the stream.

Paging through it for loopholes, for disability, for workman's comp was pointless when she didn't speak four languages or have an advanced law degree.

She hadn't even read it before signing. She'd been so excited to try something new, to use the big lens. And then her muse.

Ten days ago, she would have tossed her firstborn in a basket to keep her field access. Now her badge dinged red at the Peak's south entrance.

Not like she could photograph anyway with her sling.

She heard steps on her stoop before a knock or a shout or a doorbell ring. Turned out, those six square inches of glass were a real muffler between her and the outdoors. "Coming!" Carrie called. What immaculate timing to meet her new landlord. When she was using a legally binding agreement as a mop. Carrie dumped the soppy pages in the trash and rushed to the door.

A good first impression was imperative. Once they met, once she saw Carrie's sling and big friendly smile, and sniffed the quarter cookie log baking in the oven, she'd fix the broken glass and ease the gas on rent. Girl to girl, they'd find a groove. Like her and Luisa had, planting daffodil bulbs while laughing about the times Carrie split her rent check into three late payments.

Smoothing the strap of her sling, Carrie rushed for the door, fingers scrambling with the latch.

"Morning."

Carrie's hand stilled. Her body stilled. Her heart too.

"*You,*" she growled, dropping her hand to slam the door.

Asher shoved his foot in the jamb, let the wood crush it. Grunted. "These are Italian. Handmade."

She pushed harder. "Leave."

"You're pinning me in place," he commented dryly, giving voice to the obvious. "How can I leave?"

Oh. Carrie opened the door.

Asher strode right inside, brushing past her and down the hall to her kitchen, appraising the watercolor rug runner like it was a bloody pelt.

"Wow," he said. "You cleaned."

She almost laughed at the idea she thought she'd be rid of him. "No, I didn't."

"Huh. It's better in the light then." He opened the door to her stairwell and glanced up. "Isn't this a two story? Can't you store yarn wads up there?"

"What are you doing here, Asher?"

Shutting the door, he slipped his hand into the pocket of his navy slacks. His button down was tidy, thin striped green, and his eyes were blazing. "You called me."

"Funny." She'd give a eulogy in the same tone.

"Is it?" he drawled, finding her cream teacup and trapping the teabag's flagged end between his fingers.

She snatched her cup from him before she realized she'd moved chest to chest with him.

"Think hard, brat." His voice was low and silkier than she'd remembered.

The air squeezed from her lungs as she felt the unmistakable pulse of heat between her legs. From him, his finger pad, smudged with black ink, running the rim of her ginger tea, from his strong firm thighs against her cozy lemon sweatpants.

"I didn't call you." Was that her voice? Breathy and quiet and strange? She curled her hand around the porcelain, the remaining tea searing her palm. Her nipples hardened against her bra. "I don't even have your number. And I wouldn't use it if I did."

His finger dipped into the tea and then he flicked it at her, spraying her parted lips. "Liar." He stepped back before she could shove, resting his hips against her sink, the picture of ease. "How's the shoulder?"

That punching feeling returned. She swept the tea off her lip with her tongue. "Still fucking dislocated. Thanks for that."

"The place looks better, but you are just as sour, huh?"

"I am not—" She moved to poke him, but her shoulder screamed in pain. Her teeth clenched.

Asher was there, taking her teacup as a wave of mortification washed over her. She didn't need help from him.

"Did you take your pills?"

"Are you here to shove them down my throat? Is this when I learn they're cyanide?" He'd clap as her skin turned blue and her mouth foamed.

A barely there smirk as his eyes dripped to her chest. Lingered over the unhooked buttons. "C'mon, brat. I'm a man. I have better things to shove down your throat."

"You—"

"Hi! This is Carrie Huston from unit 21B!" Carrie froze at the sound of her own voice, at the phone in Asher's palm. "We haven't met yet!" Pause for giggle before her high pitch fake cheery phone voice continued, "A few nights ago, the glass of my front door shattered. I think a stone or stick must've hit it during a storm. Anyway—"

"No. No no." She grabbed his hand, muted the voicemail. "No." He couldn't be.

He wasn't her landlord.

"Oh, yes." With a spin of his wrist, he was holding her hand, covering it in his fist, displaying split angry red knuckles. Proof of her lie.

"I can't believe you left a voicemail," he taunted. "Three minutes. I had to listen. And from my inspection of the damage, it looks like you broke it."

He released her.

She lurched backward, hip knocking into the cabinet. "Are you kidding me? You're literally red-handed."

"Yes, but being caught in a lie makes you seem very guilty." He searched the cabinet above her electric kettle for space that didn't exist. "If it were truly a natural disaster, I'd gladly replace the whole thing for you. That's the kind of landlord I am. Understanding. Accommodating."

Carrie was shaking with fury.

"But since it wasn't." He went one cabinet to the left, movie theater cups and plate bowls. "My hands are tied."

She gritted her teeth. "You cannot leave me with a hole in my house in the middle of October."

"I wouldn't have helped you at all if I didn't think you'd freeze to death." He scratched a fingernail at the tape keeping her microwave shut.

Punching seemed inevitable.

A thought occurred. "Why would you break it? You own it, you must have keys."

"I don't carry a janitor's ring of keys with me." He dropped to a crouch to search under her sink. "And you were desperate to get inside." He stood, scratched his jaw and then started on the drawers.

A tornado.

He was a tornado in her kitchen. Chucking debris and working wildly. Ink blot hair falling in his eyes as he dug through drawer after drawer, creating a constant ruffle of thick paper and sliding silverware.

She had nothing left to say to him but, "Stop."

"Why?" He pulled open another drawer and lifted a crocheted oven mitt. His lips curled at the corners. "Do these actually work?"

Obviously they didn't. She twisted her elbow to hide the burns. "There's no way you're my landlord," she muttered to herself. "Because there's a conflict of interest. We have history. You shouldn't be able to land lord me. I have rights."

"You do," Asher agreed, rifling through serving spoons. "As in you have the right to move if you're dissatisfied with management, and the right to not fucking call me and lie." He slammed the drawer shut, locked eyes with her and he raised one imperious eyebrow. "Three minutes of what was essentially rambling. I might have believed you if it'd been a text."

"People used to write hand written missives, spritz them with their favorite perfume, seal them with wax, and pay a shilling to send them by hackney. Door to door delivery. I'm not writing a text."

The storm ended.

The air sucked out of the room, the crackle of energy, of ricocheting electrons siphoned into Carrie's stomach, brewed there in equal parts fear and anticipation.

Asher laughed.

Laughed. A breath of air scented with snow and mountain rain and peppercorn wafted over her as he raked his hair back. Shot her a smug look. "Maybe the women did."

Carrie spun in indignation, violently steeping her abandoned tea. Screaming would only guarantee Asher's smugness, so she held back. "Men did too."

In a single stride, he was behind her. Right behind her. Wrenching the teacup from her, sliding it out of reach. "Men who owned their wives and had mistresses. What is the number of syphilis deaths involving a quill? Off the top of your head?" His warm breath found the delicate crevices of her ear. and Carrie's heart surged supernova. "Everything seemed great back then. Balls and royals and servants. But they were also fucking their cousins, oppressing the poor, and colonizing. So how about we stop idolizing the past."

He pushed off her, the storm returning as he worked double time searching her kitchen.

"It wasn't all bad," she challenged.

"You're right. Gambling and prostitution were legal. Truly a golden age."

Figured that's what he'd applaud. "Families spent time more time together. Friends held week long parties in the country. Couples courted publicly, with chaperoned dates and grand wedding announcements. There was no ghosting, sexting, or one-night stands.

Asher pinched his eyes shut and sighed at her ceiling. "Of course you're a romantic."

She ignored the comment. She refused to go down that road again. "Not to mention, the craftmanship far exceeded today's standards. If a dress tore, it was mended, wood was refinished, furniture fixed."

"Excellent point," he claimed, startling her. "I knew you'd see this my way."

Carrie fumbled with a response as he turned, a naughty gleam in his eyes. She tapped her nails against her sling, watching as he strode the length of her kitchen like Reginald on a—

"Wait. Don't open that!"

Chapter Thirteen

Asher

On his best day, Asher struggled to let his guard down around people. The struggle intensified in unfamiliar surroundings, with uncontrollable factors, no set schedule, or clear purpose in conversations.

Holmes was his exception. Her calm, sweet angelic features settled his anxiety better than a deprivation tank. She was a glorious haven. Utterly perfect for him.

He should have hives from just stepping foot in Carrie's house. A headache from spotlight bright white walls. Nausea from the sugary, melted butter scent percolating her kitchen. Vicious palpitations from the mismatched hardware on her cabinets, gold rods and silver pulls and leather tassels.

Everywhere he looked, it was too cluttered, overly sweet, and *hers*.

That was the crux of it. *Her*.

He wasn't comfortable around her, but he was far from anxious. Carrie Huston and her bright blue sling made Asher crackle. A thin layer of ice about to break, flames about to raze.

Made him want to consume and destroy. Ravage and devastate. Fuck and fight.

"Wait. Don't open that!"

A sheet of frost showered Asher's upper body, scattered down his slacks, and splattered at his feet. Cold and wet slunk through his clothes as he stared at the burned out light of her freezer.

Jaw locked, he brushed a bank of white flurries off his belt's edge. Turned to face his tenant.

She muffled her laughter with her palm, but twinkling eyes gave her away.

Freezer maintenance lectures flew from his mind. Dammit, it wasn't funny.

A smile tugged at the side of his mouth. "That's a lot of pizza rolls."

"They're nutritionally dense."

"I'm sure," he mocked, withdrawing a small bag of triple cheese. Then he pilfered the tape from her silverware drawer and skimmed the top of her mail heap for junk.

"Hey," she snapped as he upended her pile of old newspapers. "That's a federal offense."

"No," Asher replied. "The sheer quantity of flammable herbs hanging over your oven is. This is grabbing garbage and fixing your problems." He retrieved the marble rolling pin from its spot beside the bread ties—insane organizational system—and dropped it into her sling hand.

"Oh shi—" With a little squeak of surprise, she surged to hold it with two hands.

In the confusion, he stuffed the pizza bag under the strap of her sling atop her shoulder. He couldn't ignore it. She was in pain. Tiny winces when she moved too quickly. Barely there.

She hissed, trying to tilt away from him and the cold, but he held her firm, making sure the frozen bag would stay.

She shot an angry look up at him. "That's sensitive."

That explained the goosebumps and hard nipples.

"If you iced it, it wouldn't be," he informed, pulling hair free of the plastic. "Lift the pin ten times using only your wrist. Keep your elbow still, and your back"—he drove his knuckles into her spine—"straight. Like that." His instructions finished in a whisper as she arced against his hold, shoulders spread, neck elongated, gaze like smoke, completely unreadable.

He let go of her. Stalked over her ridiculous faded Milky Way rug and set up shop at the door, squaring his stack of junk mail and ripping it in half.

"You're a doctor now?" Carrie's dry accusation was punctuated by her butt hitting the wall.

"Not since I last checked." Another rip.

"Then why would I listen to you?"

Oh, for the love of— "I've dislocated my shoulder four times and recovered well enough to keep playing. So maybe I know what I'm talking about, and you should be grateful for the advice."

Her eyes went blackhole wide. "Grateful?"

Before eruption, he asked, "Do you want your door fixed or not?"

"Yes."

"Then start your reps."

She raised her rolling pin. Once.

Twice.

Asher returned to stacking, eyeballing the size of the empty pane.

"I'm not moving," Carrie told him confidently. "Raise the rent. Go through all of my drawers. My mom used to live here. I won't leave."

She wouldn't have a choice. "You sound sure."

"I can outlast a rich kid playing land lord."

Ink as black as night crumbled from his fingers onto the white block of papers as he wondered which part he should correct first. The only one that affected her. "I don't do anything halfway, brat. When I bet, I'm all in. Your lease stipulates that rent can't be more than double every three months. So give me a couple months and we'll see how long you last."

All summer he'd had lawyers dissecting the lease, searching for an eviction gap or right to terminate. They'd found only one answer. Gouge the tenants.

He'd happily do it to achieve his vision for Holmes.

Nothing halfway. He nearly winced at the truth of it. Finally, he was close enough to his goal to see more than one potential outcome.

If he lost, he'd lose everything.

"Why did Luisa sell to you?" Carrie asked, and he glanced back at her.

"Same reason she and her four sons and extended family are going on a ten-day cruise for Thanksgiving break. She understands what's best for her. And you will too." It was beyond his ability to sound remorseful.

"Back to threatening, but I'm not scared of you." She glared up at him with such ferocity it made him ache.

Forced him to wonder how'd they interact under different circumstances. If he'd get the full force of her smile. They'd discuss history. The Regency and Victorian eras. He'd tell her he'd studied it all, desperate to understand the appeal. Pored over compromising marriages, outlandish behaviors, and rudimentary medicine. Yet in a single breath, she'd highlighted what he'd overlooked, as if it were all see saw.

He dismissed the fantasy entirely. There was no outcome where they became friends. All in meant removing Carrie from the equation.

He dropped down to his knees, hunting for the end of the tape. "You have no reason to be. Eight more reps."

Her pretty mouth fell into a pout. She lifted the rolling pin. Let it drop.

"Seven. Whose shirt is that?" Not that he cared.

She glanced down at the flannel as if she'd forgotten herself. "Why can't it be mine?"

"It's too big, the buttons are on the men's side, and it smells like—" fresh air and snow and cold. "Stale. Besides," he paused, "it's not something you'd wear."

"How would you know?" She scowled harshly as if he had never noticed what she wore. Yellow sweatpants and purple leggings, and bright shirts with cutesy sayings. "Oh, the look at me. You think you know me so well, don't you? Judging my freezer."

He knew she'd never pick out a gray flannel. "Whose is it, brat?"

When he caught in her stare, she was no longer angry, but instead curious, calculating. Cautious. "Why does it matter to you?"

His whole body drew tight. *Why did it?*

He shook his head. She kept doing that. Leading him in the direction she wanted, tangling him up in words until he forgot where he started or what his point was. "I was engaging in casual conversation, but now you've dodged the question twice, so I'm guessing you're too embarrassed to say."

She narrowed her gaze. "I am not."

"You have a tell," he told her, using the edge of his nail on the tape roll. "When you lie. It's obvious."

"It is?"

His thoughts splintered, jumping between ripping the damn shirt off of her or making her do it in front of him. "Whose shirt?"

"My ex's, Travis. We broke up right after we reached the have-a-drawer-at-my-place stage. If you break my leg next time, I'll be in orange basketball shorts."

"Mutual split?" *Why do you care?*

She snatched the blue painter's tape roll from him, peeled the end free effortlessly, and thrust it back. "Actually. I ended it," she said softly. "After he stole my car."

"What?" Asher yanked out too much tape.

"Technically, he borrowed it to go to Pensacola to help his sick grandmother. But that was five months ago. I haven't heard from him." A flash of hurt crossed her face, narrowing her eyes and scoring lines around her mouth. "But I would've ended it before that."

"Why?" Why was he asking?

She looked at him as he ripped the tape with his teeth and pressed it along the panes' outside edge.

He guessed she'd skirt it again, avoid. But she tipped her head. "There was no intensity."

He should not have experienced pleasure from the answer. "Intensity."

"I never missed with my heart. I didn't lose track of time with him. I didn't reach for his side of the bed when I had a nightmare." She rubbed her lips together, as if searching for the words. "And I wouldn't have loved him if he didn't love me back."

For a single, wild moment, a vision flashed of the intensity they might have. Here, with the breeze whistling his tape, with her arm pinned. How she might gasp when he grabbed her, how her skin would warm if he lifted her up, pushed her against the glass of the door so he could taste that warmth on his tongue, find her scent beneath the snow. Would she call it intensity, when they're hands chased each other, when they couldn't breathe from kissing? Would she cry out and reach for him, hold on and pull?

He'd let her pull. Yank him in.

Asher froze, staring at the box of blue lines. Carrie Huston with her freckles and her curves was not the woman Asher wanted touching him.

"Give me seven more."

This time she stuck her bottom lip out, and the swirled white and gray stone pin sagged. "It hurts. I don't like it."

He resisted the urge to smile. "Okay, fine. What's his last name?" There was a smooth sound of tape being torn.

"Hanger."

"Seven more and I'll report Travis Hanger to the police for car theft."

She pushed off the wall. "You will not! His grandma—"

"Is dead. But alright. I'll pivot. Seven more to stop me from tattling."

For three full reps, she watched him carefully as if trying to see inside his mind. Her face was a lesson in composure, a slight bend of her neck. Her soft stare made him want to stick out his chest, change the subject.

He stuck his tongue to the roof of his mouth.

"Why do you care?" she asked quietly.

He ignored the question. "Why'd you share a drawer? If you didn't have intensity?"

She lifted her good shoulder in a shrug and approached him. "Because intensity is consuming and disruptive and when you're with them, it can be the best thing in the universe, but when you're apart ..." she trailed off.

He felt a light sweat break out on his face. Didn't dare speak.

"It festers," she finally decided.

A word to describe the raw gape in his soul, the spreading black. *Festering.* "Yes," he agreed hoarsely and clamped his mouth shut. Festers.

She came to him slowly, like she saw the sludge circulating his system and was afraid to contract it.

"It's like suddenly discovering you can breathe underwater," she continued, wrist rocking. "And now your world has tripled in size, and you're desperate to discover it, but you'd have to leave everything behind first."

He threw a cautious glance at her.

She didn't look away from him, both huddled next to the door as if he were off to war, as if they'd just settled who got the dog which days.

"Not always." He let his gaze travel over her. "It can be yelling. It can be muttering why the fuck am I doing this when you jump onto a balcony when you should just leave her?"

"Punching a window?" Her soft voice made his chest pound violently. Her toes touched his.

Desire flooded every part of his body.

"Slamming a foot in the door," he said.

It could be her. Intensity. This. The missing air he knew he'd find on her lips.

"You did it first."

Wrapping a hand around the back of her neck, Asher bent over her, finding her pulse with the tip of his thumb. "I'd do it again."

A ragged sound escaped her. Shock. Appall. Delight.

He wanted it for himself. "Brat."

Her eyes fluttered closed and he could see plain down her shirt to a lack of bra, just the swells of her chest, flecked with black spots.

"What's that smell?" she murmured, suddenly leaning against him, her hand on his stomach. Low. Low and he was hard as steel.

Asher's lips brushed hers, finding air there. Life. "Is something burning?"

"My cookies!" She shoved him back with a gasp, and the rolling pin crashed onto Asher's foot.

"Fuck," he growled, bending in half as Carrie escaped to the kitchen.

Metal slammed. A loud groan. Then a shout. "This is not indicative of my leasing lifestyle!"

Seducing men or setting fires? Because both seemed firmly in her wheelhouse. She was a car wreck he couldn't resist. Messy and cluttered with emotions as fleeting as snow in October.

A wrench in his plans. A complication he couldn't handle while he was festering.

He finished the door. "Text if you have other problems."

"I'll call!" she shouted back. He heard a violent sizzle of cold water on a hot pan.

"Do not call."

"Calling!"

Chapter Fourteen

Asher

TINTED WINDOWS. LIFTED BED. Chrome hubcaps. Ten to one, fucker spread oil onto the highway. Pumped regular in the premium only tank. All flash, no substance.

Asher knew every car in and out of Nice Way. The electrician's van, Chuck's bronco, 21A's red mini. But this— "Who the fuck is this guy?"

Chuck didn't turn to answer. "The boyfriend."

Travis.

Asher ducked under the rising trusses and rushed for the road. The second his feet scuffed the centerline, the truck swung around and the horn exploded. Aftermarket. Obnoxious.

But Asher tuned out tens of thousands of screaming fans every Sunday. He didn't flinch at a souped up horn.

This man had hurt Carrie. Stolen from her. Wedged himself into her life in clothes fit for a youth basketball coach and betrayed her. Asher itched to do damage. Inflict pain.

The blaring horn stopped. Before Asher opened his mouth, it was there again. And so were the brights. To what end? Taunting the golden sunshine? Idiot.

Uncrossing his arms, Asher offered two choice fingers to the driver.

From the corner of his eye, he spotted Chuck waving his tape measure, a yard of shiny yellow plastic wagging. Warning him, shouting.

Fifteen years of striving to be liked.

Now Asher was working the other way. Not giving a shit if people hated him, so long as he achieved his goal. Reclaim Carrie's car, and ransom it for her change of address.

"Clear the damn road!" the driver yelled, honking again.

"There's no through traffic here." Asher shrugged, seemingly helpless. As if traffic cams clocked the trucks three drive-by's of 21 Nice Way.

"Make room, boy! Or I'll stab the gas."

Asher buried his hands in his pockets, projecting ease while his legs tensed. "I've got a team of lawyers thanking you for giving them a premeditation defense."

"This is fucking America!"

"Exactly." Asher's smile was a feral thing. "And I'm about to defend my fucking property in a way that'd make the founding father's proud."

The promise was barely out of his mouth when the hideous purple door on the opposite side of the street burst open and out spilled Carrie Huston.

Naked.

Fucking *Christ*. The fight coursing in him switched teams.

"Hey!" she called, bare feet shuffling down her front steps. A joke of a towel in unicorn pink clung to her, ends sealed together by her hand at her chest.

Asher had never in his life wanted to approach another so much, but he remained in the street, unconvinced he hadn't been hit. This wasn't a dream.

Then he heard the whistle. The sudden absence of spitting nail guns and grinding table saws.

It was Hell.

She was sprinting across dried leaves in the lawn, wet hair like a mirror, dark strands sticking to her forehead and jaw. "Asher," she said, kicking an apple core off the curb and dashing over the hot asphalt. "I see you've met Paul."

Say goodbye Paul, Asher thought darkly. No witnesses.

Not for this. Carrie's olive skin shone. Silky and wet. Shoulders, cheeks, and nose scalded red from steam. He'd known she was beautiful, but he'd meant it in the same manner as a sunset. Bright colors, gentle curves.

Standing before him was a solar eclipse. Light ceased to exist expect the liquid shimmer of her skin, a corona of silver and gold, flecked with black. Magnificent, so stunning his eyes strained.

He couldn't look away. That was a problem. The problem.

The curl of her fluffy towel teased above her cleavage, fitted tightly around her thighs, left long lovely limbs for devouring and threw wicked, delectable ideas into Asher's mind.

How much pleasure he could wring from her without even touching the towel? How much more with the towel cushioning his knees?

Asher rushed to intercept her, catching her arm and using her momentum against her to spin her into his chest, her toes dancing onto his Nikes. Her skin steamed with heat. She smelled like snow and vanilla. He resisted the urge to grin, to growl.

"Have you lost your mind?" he snapped, heart pounding.

"You started it," she whispered darkly, expressive features twisted with anger.

He tightened his grip on her. "How did I possibly—"

She leaned past him, not listening, her water swollen fingers permanently marking his bare forearm. "Paul, I got you popcorn. And before you ask, it's wasn't for some out of touch foundation. It was for a scout project." She sounded entirely herself, as if nude on the street was normal.

Paul, from inside his truck, asked the question of the year: "Where are your clothes?"

Asher still wanted to put an end to him.

"I didn't want to miss you," Carrie explained loudly. "And it takes forever to get dressed with my shoulder."

"Ya know," Paul returned, shooting the shit. "Jill bought me a robe and I use it."

She nodded eagerly. Asher barely refrained from mentioning that a robe would be just as damn difficult. What she needed was a poncho. Down to her knees.

"A robe is an excellent idea," Carrie gushed. "I'll put the popcorn in the mailbox."

"Popcorn," Asher growled against her ear, teeth grinding a slow, even rhythm. "That's your rush?" His grip popped off her slick, soapy biceps. He reset it at her waist.

She pretended not to hear him, but her lips twitched. "It's cold, Paul. I have to get back inside for shampooing, and Asher's going to fix my oven light." Green flashed to him. "Aren't you?"

Asher had a brief vivid impression of slippery wet and warm and then the scrambling to usher her backward, away, into a deep cave with an enormous stone he could haul over it.

"He better," Paul grumbled.

"He's so handy!" Carrie mocked, and though he didn't dare look down, he could hear her smile.

He was deprived of the chance to see it. When she looked up at him, she was scowling, ripping free of him. "Stop pushing me."

Asher shoved forward, lifting her, moving close so there was no risk of tripping. "Stop making fucking conversation in a towel with a trespasser."

"I came out here to save your ass." Her tone added an unsaid, *you fucking idiot*. "Paul is a former marine. He served tours. Despite the bullet in his body, he has a full head of hair."

Like Asher didn't? "You couldn't wait for pants?" he asked with a calm he did not feel.

"And use the towel to mop up your blood?" She was trying to protect him, but he wished she'd stop. He wanted her to be cruel. To embrace the fire in their meetings, to burn and blaze.

"You brat—"

In a miraculous display of wiggling and shimmying, her smooth wrist slipped from his grasp. She fluttered away quickly but mindfully. Tiny, premeditated steps like a child struggling to respect pool rules. He wished he could throw her into the deep end.

"Get inside." A threat.

"I'm already out here," she returned sharply, tugging open her mailbox. "What if someone's written me?"

"American Express can fucking wait."

"Sure," she drawled, "but the charming duke can't. Or the rakish earl, or the most eligible Marquess on the island."

He almost laughed at that.

"See." She flashed a plastic placard at him. "Bed, Bath and Beyond coupon to current resident."

He did laugh at that, but immediately squashed it. Grabbed her arm. "A romance for the ages. Inside."

"Fine." She started off on the yard, casting him a salacious sideways glance. "You know I'm perfectly covered. I have dresses smaller than this, tighter too."

He'd like to compare to be sure.

"This hides everything." Her fingers walked a wobbly line up and down the pink. "It's thick and—"

"It's removable." He wound his hand around her elbow again and dragged. "You could hide in your blanket for twenty and if you told me, you were naked, I'd have the same sinful thought. With just one pull, one tug, you'd be on display. No zippers or buttons or fucking socks to pry off. Everything. And with a towel it's worse, because everything's wet."

"I see." She arched to peer in his eyes, damp hair teasing his chest before she turned to the house.

And he followed, his hands clenched into fists. The grass was soft under his shoes and cold water soaked into his toes as if it were the latest breakthrough in runners, soaks up twice the stagnant rain, but fuck if he cared.

He smelled vanilla.

Wrapping his fingers over her wrist, he gave her a gentle tug, and after a moment, she eased her weight into him. "Hurry up," he commanded.

"You don't trust yourself with me."

He locked his jaw at the lazy amusement in her words. The reminder was harsh and instant.

"You need zip ties and duct tape and rope to make sure nothing happens. Because you're attracted to me."

"Nonsense." He needed chains.

She stopped talking. Stopped walking.

"You hate it." She was grinning, teeth gleaming white.

Mint. She'd taste of it. Clean and fresh and crisp.

"*Yes*."

Her grin turned into a smirk, and the firm clasp of her hand eased. The towel sagged. "Hate how much or hate that it's me?"

Yes.

Perhaps it was the greatest irony that her smirking while outlining his hate set his entire person ablaze. Asher covered the hand holding her towel and squeezed. "I hate how much of my time you take up."

She smiled at that. "Think about me when you're alone, do you?"

"Whenever I undress and find the black bruise on my foot."

Her smile grew. "What a predicament for you. Karmic retribution."

Haughty. He switched his hold, to keep her blocked from the construction viewing party, first her right upper arm, then her left, a dance. "Door. House. Clothes."

"Me. Man. Mad."

"Don't say you didn't have the option." And then, in two swift moves, he had her folded over his shoulder.

Chapter Fifteen

Carrie

I T WAS CERTIFIED SACRILEGE to be sprawled over the broad shoulder of a grumpy Greek God and be stuck fretting about what percent of her cooch was out.

Yes. Her heart still pounded at his hissed admission. To stay steady, Carrie pressed her palm into his stomach and her mouth dropped open. Taut and warm and rippled with obliques. Her toes curled in the air, ankles crossing in pleasure.

Seeing was not believing.

She'd seen the hard lines of his torso, ridged with muscle, corded everywhere, rippling as he moved like waves washing ashore. Impressive and intriguing. But to feel it, have only the soft fabric of his shirt between her fingertips and his scorching heat. Carrie wanted to unwrap him like she used to on Christmas morning. Half feral, ripping and tearing, frantic and hungry.

Against her wishes, her fingers spread over him, lower. And suddenly Carrie felt the heat coming off him everywhere. His shoulder poured into the curve of her stomach, his banded hand burned the back of her thighs, his swallowing throat at the indent of her hip.

He started up her steps and Carrie slipped, hand shooting downward. He caught her before she slid beneath his belt. He exhaled sharply.

"New property rule," his voice was a winter storm, brittle and ruinous. "Clothes are required on the lawn."

She craned her head back and saw it. Her mother's aubergine door, with an eyepatch in the glass. Sad, yes. Made worse by the psychotic care Asher put into his patch. He'd used his own rent hike announcement to seal the exterior, and painstakingly folded it so anyone who dared to admire her entrance had to read:

Respectfully,

Asher Laughlin, Proprietor

She'd missed it the first time because she'd been too focused on the double rent whammy. Now, every time she gazed up at her beloved home, she read it. All thirty-three wretched letters.

The most exquisitely devious idea unfurled in Carrie's mind. He loathed her, yes, and she despised him silly, but he'd confessed attraction.

Sweet, toxic revenge hatched. Him leaning over her with a dark, tortured expression, mouth grazing hers. Carrie cackling.

"Please." Carrie sighed dramatically. "You can do better than that."

"Consider it carved in stone."

"How incredibly disappointing." She waited, but he wouldn't take the bait. Preoccupied with letting himself inside and shooting threatening looks behind them.

Honestly, she couldn't tell if his furious gaze was aimed at the crew across the street or the lump of her ass and curl of her legs dangling wildly.

She fidgeted atop him. "You're carrying me naked over a threshold and you're thinking of rules. I expected more."

A low rumble came at that, and her breath caught. Then, "More?"

Oh, yes. She was delighted with this plan. His steps slowed over her runner, a furrow formed in his brows. "I only mean, Paul got a lawyer threat. I don't even get a little spank?"

He set her down even faster than he'd picked her up. Left her damp body swaying on the edge of her living room carpet. She tightened the hold on her towel, a sudden chill breaking up her arms. "A warning would be nice. I get dizzy."

Asher didn't care. "Who's Paul and why are you buying him popcorn?"

"He's Jill's man friend."

"Jillian Hark?" he asked. "The woman who delivers a laundry bag of nickels and dimes to pay rent? Purple hair. Bifocals. She's dating lifted truck Paul?"

Ah yes, Jill's anti-bank lifestyle had spun into a cash boycott.

"There's not a thing wrong with Paul's truck." How Paul was the center of this discussion made Carrie want to scream. "And you shouldn't have antagonized him. He's been our neighborhood watch for the past four years. He makes me feel safe when I'm walking home."

Asher watched her for a long moment before he asked, "You don't feel safe here?"

She used to, in her car, in her quiet dead end. "How can I with the constant flux of strangers next door?"

"How does Paul help with that?"

If she didn't know better, she'd mistake his tone for genuine interest, as if he too wanted to play white knight.

Fuck, now she was picturing him on a horse. A stallion, his onyx locks ruffling in the wind, white oxford billowing, whipping against corded muscle.

You're seducing him! she reminded herself

"He follows me home from the bus stop with his low beams." Cold was sinking in fast, the ends of her hair were drying. "He's old world. Doesn't want to offend Jill's honor by driving me around. I think his security passes are some twisted form of fore-play."

He narrowed his gaze on her. "Foreplay."

The word, in that dark, disdainful tone, launched into Carrie's cozy home much like a wrecking ball. Obliterating all sense.

"I called you."

She could have just given him a whip. "I listened to all of your voicemails." A smirk. "A year of my life I'll never get back."

When did the punching plan go haywire?

"Well?" she drawled.

"Well, what?"

He was going to make her ask again when he'd come here pre-cisely to answer her request. For what purpose? To gloat? It only made her hate him more. "Aren't you here to fix my oven light? It broke."

Most things would when trapped in tight quarters with a flaming log of cookie dough.

His hand balled into a fist. "I'll buy you a flashlight."

"If I'm paying twice my rent, I expect better living conditions."

"Then I suggest a dumpster."

She wanted him to leave. *Now.* "Let me guess, you throw out every card you get, every gifted trinket because it serves you no purpose in your cold, hollow home."

He came closer, and they were toe to toe. "Why should I care about a sloppy signature under a cheesy Hallmark slogan?"

"Because they're thoughtful."

He watched her intently, as if she were the last ruby leaf on the maple, and he wanted to see her fall. "It's pointed thoughtfulness. Look at me, I thought of you. Give me credit."

She snorted. "Bet your locker was stuffed with roses on Valentine's Day."

There was a pause, as if he realized that admitting just that would be better announced with confetti and dancers. But then he said, "Yeah and I drove a Maserati and was class president, and Beyoncé asked me to prom. Tell me other shit about my life. Why don't you?"

If his voice was anything less than savage, she might have felt guilty. Instead, she hissed, "You're such a jackass."

"Yes," Asher agreed harshly. "I fucking am. And I honestly can't believe it's only now you've noticed it."

Going by the bitter tone, she knew better than to confirm. He hadn't said it for her sake, he'd said it for his.

"Too distracted I'd bet." His dark, simmering words taunted as he stepped closer, eyes slipping over the curves of her shoulders, lower, lingering.

Carrie clung to the corners of her towel, pressed her feet into the carpet, suddenly feeling less brave.

He reached for her and brushed a lock of hair behind her ear. "Amazing." His nail scraped her earlobe. "Isn't it? How much you let slide when you see something you like."

He wanted her to agree.

Admit her skin tightened in his presence.

No matter how badly it did, how forcefully her heart raced under the sear of his lingering touch, she wouldn't.

She didn't step back, didn't flinch or cower as he prowled closer, came to loom over her, hand smoothing over her damp hair. Asher did a lot of things she hated: fixated, argued, dressed like an upper class workaholic, but he'd never purposely hurt her. In fact, he'd repeatedly stopped her from going ass up.

"Is it hard?" Carrie breathed out quietly.

Asher's black brows shot up and Carrie would eat a dirty sock to keep the intrigued gleam in his eyes. The caught breath in his throat.

Ever so slightly, she leaned into his palm. "It seems hard," she whispered. "Constantly pretending to be miserable, acting like you didn't get the big three." She was silently fuming beneath her murmurs, always fuming around Asher. "Looks, brains, brawns," she listed. "The big three. How terrible. And more money than you know what to do with."

"Funny," he snarled, dropping his hand. "Haven't you looked me up? Read the headlines? I know you're interested."

Heat roared on her cheeks. "Without a doubt, you'd tell me if there was something even remotely flattering."

"It's not," he said.

A thousand imaginary Daily Mail articles sprung to mind. *Player Kills Coach. Beyonce Abandoned in Limo. Teen Hocks Maserati. Burns Love Letters.*

"As I guessed."

"You still don't want to know?" he asked. "Not a bit curious why there'll be no remorse when I scratch Carrie Huston off the lease?"

"I'm not at the edge of my seat waiting for you to take a spin with the sharing stick." Fury was in the rearview mirror. "I don't even remember who you are when you leave my sight."

"Yes, you do," he whispered darkly. "And you hate it."

Her own words chucked back in her face.

Asher's hissed yes.

Here it was. Her ace.

Carrie allowed a smile spread slowly across her cheeks, blinked slowly, let her pointer wander across the bare length of her collarbone before she met his gaze, and said, "No."

His lashes flickered, and immediately the lie stung her mouth. He looked hurt as he leaned away from her, as his attention glued to her blank TV. She hated herself for letting it fly, more than she hated him for needling.

Instead of saying so, however, she hitched the towel higher, "Fix the light or I'll report you to the state."

Before he cut in with how wrong she was about reporting landlords, she charged to her bedroom, where she snatched her Target sweats from The Chair and shucked her towel. She had one foot in when she found her sling and grabbed for it. Not wearing it pulled on the muscle and hurt.

She'd have to double her Asher exercises today.

Putting her elbow in the smelly blue prison, Carrie caught her reflection in the mirror tacked to her closet door. White streaks of soap stuck to the tips of her hair, errant bubbles waiting to pop. *Shit.*

Could've stayed in the shower. Deep conditioned while Paul pummeled Asher.

Had to intervene, had to stick her nose in it, had to—

Oh no.

Had she turned off the water? Was the instrumental version of What About Us on its eighteenth repeat? She stumbled to the door. Paused.

Was he still here? How long did it take to change a bulb?

"Asher?" she called, hopping wet legs into thick cotton. "Asher!"

The door swung open, hit her ultra plush duvet and got stuck.

Carrie yelped, pants fused to her calves, a sling covering four ribs.

She spun to the bed and covered herself with the closest pillow. Frilly pink, embroidered with *That ankle tho* ended up sideways in front of her boobs and crotch.

Asher's knuckles were bleached on her doorknob.

Blushing, horrified, bridled from a case of terminal cotton-mouth, she gaped right back at him.

She prepared to read him his rights for ogling, for barging in, for being here—any number of things—because she could be as unreasonable as she wanted when someone walked in on her completely naked when she realized he wasn't even looking at her.

Fancy white sneakers sinking into her carpet, his fingers hooked in the crack of the door, he stared at a point beyond her. Past the floor pile of crocheted strawberry pillows, over her sunrise cloud bed, behind her water glass nightstand collection all the way to the enormous print of him.

CHAPTER SIXTEEN

CARRIE

"DID HE SEEM FREAKED out?" Diana asked, planting her wide black boot on the MDF sheet, and reaching for her hammer. "Nail."

Sorting through the nest of tarnished metal in her palm, Carrie selected the straightest, shiniest one and passed it into Diana's waiting hand.

"Because I have a secret shrine to him over my bed?" Carrie clarified sarcastically as she flicked dust off her favorite jeans, the denim painted with vibrant bursting daisies. "Honestly, he took it pretty well."

Mentioning it brought it crashing into Carrie's mind. The subtle tilt of Asher's head. The dart of his gaze back to her. And then, the violent slam of her door.

On his way out of her house, he'd shouted, "Your bathroom's flooded." Which, since she'd still been hovering naked in a sling and shampoo, had felt like punching down.

That'd been five days ago.

"It's not a shrine," Diana argued. "It's one picture." Diana could convince Carrie a face tattoo of a clown was no big deal if it meant making Carrie feel better.

"It takes up half the wall. And it's on my nightstand." She stuck a couple of nails in her best friend's outstretched palm. "He probably thinks I'm kissing it goodnight."

"Sweet, naïve Carrie. He thinks you're rubbing one out to it twice a day. Why is it in your bedroom?"

"Obviously because I never wanted him to find it." And Asher entering her bedroom had been as unlikely as Carrie inviting him there.

"You could've turned it around. Nail."

Yeah. But then she couldn't see him. Despite detesting the man, she was proud of her work.

Diana snapped her fingers. "Nail."

"Jeez. Are you on a deadline?" Carrie dumped her a handful. "You're a workaholic. I'm scheduling you an intervention. Any snack requests?"

"Bugles." She wiggled the tips of her fingers. "So I don't get bored."

To celebrate the last seventy degree day of the year, Carrie had planned the perfect cheap, lazy, gossip heavy girl's day. She'd de-spider webbed mismatched folding lawn chairs—a temporary loan from Jill—and set them in the only shade free spot in the yard, which came with views of the maple's shedding leaves, hot construction dudes, and the drifting patchouli smoke of Jill's incense.

Rigorous scrubbing of her favorite tiny tea set and a Pinot Noir from the renowned Ohio Valley were on the menu. And she'd topped it off with lap blankets, sunglasses, and a full Asher debrief. No flying balls or menacing birds.

Diana lasted less than thirty seconds. Parking the front wheel of her twenty-year-old truck on Carrie's curb, her boots had hit the asphalt, and she'd pointed a black tipped finger at the mini crane next door. "Bloody great view," she'd said. "Know what they're doing?"

Lifting the trusses into place. Whatever the fuck trusses were. She'd heard the beeping and shouting and explaining all night. Hammering and mixing, the crunch of energy drink cans and curses. All. Night.

Abandoning her bed when the sun came up, Carrie had walked to Dunkin, ordered a dozen of the prettiest donuts and a carafe of blonde roast and beelined for Chuck.

"You're an angel, Carrie," he'd said, flipping the box lid up and claiming the double sprinkle Long John. "Boys are going to worship you if you keep spoiling 'em."

"I figured you had to be tired. Working all night."

"Yeah." His response had come muffled by pink icing and strawberry jelly. "But it's the job."

"Still." She'd tipped the donuts to a passing worker, beaming as he snagged a crueler. "Tiring. You need a break. You look exhausted." Laying it on thick, yes. But Carrie was past exhausted, she was delirious and angry, and could she not catch a single break? Rent, her shoulder, the work hiatus, Jill's voracious sex life.

Chuck had shrugged, unscrewing a metal tumbler and filling it with fresh coffee. "It pays."

She'd waited there, lingering on the subfloor for him to add something like *it'll be done soon. We're taking next week off to experience the Wizarding World of Harry Potter.*

But she got no such reassurances. The look on his face had said, 'Saddle up, darling, you're in hell with the lot of us'.

Day drinking had seemed like the logical next step.

Until Diana's restless leg syndrome and constant, "I could do it better" had them marching across the street, claiming yellow hard hats and taking over front porch construction.

It was five o'clock, the birds were chirping, the sun was shining, and Carrie should be drunk.

Instead Diana was hammering her third stair runner, and Carrie was looking over her shoulder to make sure none of her soaked peach bath sheets had toppled off her railing into the mud.

How can a tiny bathroom contain so much water?

Diana tipped her hard hat up and swiped the back of her wrist on her forehead. Another hour and she'd be crushing Red Bulls with the team, hocking loogies, and complaining about unions. She liked this work. Difficult, sweaty, grinding. Doing shit with her hands.

Carrie got blisters tie-dyeing her sweatpants. A wonder how they were friends.

She never forgot that while Diana now planned extravagant parties and wore enough jewelry to break a metal detector, she'd made her money with a back breaking grind. Taking odd jobs as a roofer, a stonemason, chopping down trees, hauling kegs. They'd met when she and Declan were doing a stint grave digging. The day of her mother's funeral.

She'd been desolate, broken, felt abandoned, waiting outside the graveyard for the world to stop moving. Beautiful tiny Diana with dirt on her fingers, rock hard calluses, and a flashing head-lamp had found her. Asked if she needed a ride, and when Carrie broke down in tears, Diana showed her how to eat ten Swedish Fish at once. Not an hour later, Declan was making them Kraft Mac on a hot plate. They never asked her to leave, never said goodbye, just plied her with food and went on with their days. She stayed in their cramped studio for a month.

"I like intervention," Diana said with a row of four nails clutched between her teeth. "Add it to the list. The Intervention."

Giving up all pretense of help, Carrie planted her ass on the bottom step and grabbed her phone. "Should it go above or below The Rainmaker?"

"Below The Doctor obviously. I'm worried about the legality of that one." She drove the nail in with two whacks. "Don't want to be caught in court."

With the tip of her sneaker, Carrie traced a heart in sawdust. "Does it have to start with 'the'?"

"I have a theme," Diana said, bent over, four steps up. "Themes are the blood life of bar success."

"But The Doctor? It's clinical. What about The Funhouse?"

"And instigate a statewide clown nightmares? No." Diana brushed thick curled locks off her neck. "Instead of saying I'm going to get blackout wasted, think about how bloody fantastic it would be to say I'm going to The Doctor."

"Is Sunday good for the intervention?" Carrie teased dryly. "I'll have to move some things around, alert the media, dial some friends, arrange train tickets."

"You're my only friend and you don't want me sober. Trust me." Diana fell to a crouch, sweat dripping down her forehead.

Carrie smiled, reviewing the list of potential bar names, when a maniacal growl came from Diana. She jolted up, expecting to find a nailed finger of hammered toe.

Neither. Only Diana's narrowed eyes. "Tell me you're not texting him." *Him* could be anyone, so a lie here— "Carrie!"

Shit, what was her tell? How did Asher figure it out so quickly?

"We aren't texting," she blurted.

They weren't.

He was texting her.

After she'd left Asher a voicemail about how the latch on her bedroom door stopped working—because some meathead couldn't handle seeing a woman in chaste pillow attire—she'd received a single text.

Doubt there's any threat of peopling wanting into your bedroom.

Which had not only incited a fury in her blood, but it'd also made her grin. So she'd called him again on Monday as she waited for her ramen water to boil. "The front burner on the stove won't turn on. Come and fix it immediately."

When she was bloated with a thousand milligrams of delicious sodium, parked on the couch, his response came. Made her laugh.

You shouldn't be within ten feet of a stove.

Eat a vegetable.

She'd read it five times, hearing the snark and shaking her head, fingers hovering over her keyboard.

She'd lasted sixteen hours. Then she'd called about a clogged garbage disposal.

You can't get me to stick my hand in a dark, serrated hole. Flagging your call as an act of terrorism.

During the second call on the same day, she realized halfway through her message she didn't have anything to announce. No leaky faucet. No creaky cabinet, not even a fruit fly. She'd hung up. He'd texted.

Minus one for excess rambling. Balances out with a non-complaint rant. Chaotic neutral.

Her mouth had fallen open. She'd screamed into a pillow.

When she called at four a.m. two days later to tell him the radiator was hissing, he'd replied instantly.

You sound like a chain-smoker on uppers. Go to bed.

Then,

Wrap your shoulder in ice. It'll help.

As if she could sleep with the evocative image of Asher Laughlin spread out in his bed, listening to her voicemail. Head resting on his hand, a smirk tearing at his cruel mouth. The slow saw of his strong jaw, tongue wetting his lips. Texting her back. Twice. And despite all the reasons she shouldn't dream of him, she had. Vividly.

His hands, his mouth, his smirk on her throat, the green split in his eyes getting darker and darker.

"What about Jack?"

Cold doused Carrie.

She tucked her phone away. "I don't have his number."

"I know. I just mean, I like Jack."

Diana didn't like Jack, the penultimate, the crème de la crème, Vermont's premium man. On several, quite public occasions, Diana claimed men in masks were creepy and insidious. *What do they have to hide? Arrest record? Pedophilia? Is there a sewn on face under that mask? Cyborg?*

"What happened to only perverts wear masks?" Carrie asked. "Or he probably killed his mom?"

She shrugged. "He's growing on me."

Carrie stared, utterly floored.

"What?" Diana avoided eye contact. "He's great. He loads you up with compliments, spends money at my bar and then properly sods off for 364 days. What's not to like?"

A year ago Carrie would've wept at Diana's support, but as the clock ticked down, as her seduction neared, the butterflies in her stomach grew razors on the wingtips.

"I know that's *your* ideal man," Carrie said, fingers hopping between the white petals on her pants. "But I want more. I want ..."

To be wanted. For a good man to see her and want. To ignore the dishes in her sink, the cowlick that never curled, the slap of hair in her shower. Did Jack want her like that?

Last night as Enola Holmes charged across the TV, Carrie had almost screamed at a missed stitch in her costume. Six months spent crafting the skirts, the bodice, and whimsical tear drop sleeves. Her best work for him. Jack. To impress and dazzle but—

What if he'd seen her there? Wearing her pink and purple tie-dye, sucking blood off her palm thanks to a misplaced needle. A chunk of cheddar cheese on a napkin for a snack. Hair drenched in coconut oil.

Would he still want her when he saw the real her? Carrie, not Holmes.

"Sex," Diana finished abruptly. "You want sex." She pounded the last nail through and backed away to admire her work.

"Looks crooked, " Carrie said, just to annoy her.

"At least no one drew a penis on my sling."

"What?" Carrie jerked at the fabric, pulling the blue. In a futile effort to bond, she'd had Chuck's crew sign it like a pseudo-cast. "Where?"

"On the end, it's veiny. On the verge of coming."

"Diana," Carrie hissed, plastering her hand over it. "Ohmygod! You let me walk around with it? Who did it?" Probably Tarik, the electrician. He didn't eat sugar. *Congrats, Tarik, you're better than the rest of us gremlins.*

Stealing the black sharpie from the clip on her sling strap, Diana uncapped it with her teeth. "I'm kidding." She slashed a smiley face with X's for eyes next to Carrie's wrist. "You're penis free."

"Not funny."

"I hired a new decorator for the party. Good references. Ann Taylor style. Bet she could do a haunted medical ward theme if you wanted."

"Sounds fucked up," Carrie said with a smile.

"Right." Diana clicked her tongue. "We're going for sexy. But how sexy? Boobs covered in blood? Pasties scattered around the bar? Overtly phallic candlesticks?"

Carrie gave her the finger.

She didn't quit. "What are you going to be? A vampire? A vampire hunter? Vampires are really hot right now."

Carrie had an idea and forty yards of lavender fabric, but there was no universe in which someone, not even her Jack, would call it sexy. "I'm still brainstorming. What about you?"

"Working," Diana replied, throwing her head back, a hand going to her forehead in mock mourning. "Thus is my strife. Someone needs to switch on the lights at three a.m. and turn the

Goslings into ducks." She looked at Carrie and grinned. "I could rip Jack's mask off at midnight before he turns into a pumpkin."

"That's not how it works. At all. And don't you dare try to intervene. I am handling it."

Diana re-folded her safety blanket filthy bar rag and slotted it through her black belt loop. "Look, if you're really planning on shagging this guy, I need to know his name, what he looks like, and his social security number."

Carrie would like the details too. But she knew how he made her feel. Worthy, beautiful, important. And for her, it was more than enough.

Glancing at the finished porch, she hooked her good arm in Diana's. "Can we get drunk now?"

"Did you buy a bottle opener?"

"It's a twist off."

The barkeep scrunched her nose. Snob. "I have a better idea. But the daisies are not gonna cut it."

Chapter Seventeen

Carrie

Carrie had started her prep in June. Gathering fabrics, curating Pinterest boards, studying old sea faring texts—wherein she learned everything about piracy, from tracking trade routes to swabbing decks to the horrid poop stick.

Each week, a new accessory joined her ensemble. Beaded anklet. Feather for her cap. A gnarly **P** temporary tattoo. On top of her outlandish garb, black wig and full face of makeup, she'd worried the eyepatch was overkill. What if it fussed with her depth perception and she tripped in her perfectly tattered swashbuckling skirt and smacked face first into the bar?

Then she saw the parrot on Jack's shoulder, and every ripped stitch, every blister, and thwarted pattern became worth it.

All of her worries washed away, like a ship disappearing beyond the horizon.

He'd come.

Halloween had fallen on a Wednesday and through some unspoken agreement, it hadn't mattered to Jack or Carrie.

Ten sharp, there he sat, in an authentically weathered pirate's hat, hair hidden under a red kerchief, wide shoulders clad in a billowy cream linen peasant top. To the nines. No peeling sideburns or cheap crushed velvet. The arms of a kraken crawled up his throat and disappeared in his ebony beard.

He stuck out like bleached crossbones on a flapping main sail. Too polished, too trimmed, shoulders painfully straight. His knee rocketed up and down, flashing the curved hilt of a silver revolver under the black lights.

Two days from now, The Hand would resemble a mosh pit at a T-swift concert. Diana had been teasing a superhero Halloween for months. She'd even taped a wide red line on The Hand's pristine wood floors. DC fans on one side, Marvel on the other.

She was calling it the *vote of the century*, and *Vermont's final stand*. One of her flyers compared it to arch rivals entering the knockout round.

When Carrie had asked which team Diana supported, she'd snorted. "I scheduled the bloody keg delivery during my wax. You think I have time to watch movies?"

A neutral host—so long as both sides bought overpriced themed drinks. Iron Man whiskey shots and Joker Juice.

As Carrie floated through the crowd, she counted two Captain America shields, and four bat toting Harley Quinns. The staff were dressed as Spider-Man. Every which one. Red and black body suits.

Web nets covered the light fixtures, darkened the green and yellow *Pow! Bam! Wham!* signs on the walls. This week, The

Hand was dazzling and over the top, spitting out upbeat pop music and sparking the debate *is Wasp or Bane the women's?*

Tacky and thrilling and loud. Comic strip drink menus, roving Bat Signals, and two pirates sitting on the white gang plank, ordering off menu.

A sparkling, frosted purple glass slid into her palm.

"A peace offering," Jack said in a growl.

"Do we need peace?"

"If you don't, I do. Been talking to a bird for three hours, convincing myself you'd come." He turned and Carrie grinned. Eyepatch, beard, tangled gold necklaces, and kohl lining his midnight eyes. "Captain Jack Sparrow," he introduced with a bow of his head.

He'd returned as her Jack.

Carrie launched head first into her best Elizabeth Swan, accent coming swift and harsh. "I shan't say I'm surprised to see you dressed as such, Jack. Once a villain, always a villain."

"And how does Holmes reason her own dress? Undercover pirate for the British armada?"

She loved a backstory. "An entrepreneur, the first female pirate. I'll prove women aren't bad luck on the high seas."

He grinned. "You'll rule them."

They laughed, and Carrie felt light, lighter than she had in months because of him. Because he'd come. To talk to her, to drink red beer on a Wednesday night with a stuffed parrot pinned to his shoulder. Her last boyfriend said it was too much work to carry-out instead of delivery.

Jack would allow neither. He'd take Carrie out, show her off in whatever restaurant she wanted.

The hours slipped by quickly and became pillars in Carrie's heart, like hot molasses dripping over dry ice. They talked eye-patches and stripes and canteens. They talked weather and philosophy, if highwaymen were as big of rapscallions as pirates.

With his eyepatch on the left and hers on the right, they made the joke they completed each other no less than three times.

"I don't know," Jack was saying. "I think Spider-Man was a bad choice."

"Yeah, how are they peeing with the full latex?" She twisted to look around. "Still better hero than you were in your plastic floss string mask."

"That was the first costume I ever put on," he told her. "Like a real one that I went and bought. In college, I cheated the system, threw on an old jersey and called myself a ballplayer. It was a copout."

She stuck her cherry stem in the thumb hole of her fingerless gloves. Fought a smile. "Oh, and the single cape of fake velvet wasn't?"

"It worked," he returned, thigh hot against hers. "I met you. You wouldn't have talked to me if I were a player. I'm glad I tried."

She'd been floating on a cloud of gin and lemons, inhaling Jack's mountain peak cologne, sucking in his warmth, but his confession yanked her down.

"Why?" she asked softly, straightening on her stool. They'd never discussed the past. "Why did you try that year?"

He faced the bar, fingertips tapping his pint. "I don't know," he said. "I just had a feeling. I didn't know anyone in town, but I knew I wanted to do something, be someone else. I had the Uber wait outside while I was at Halloween express."

She looked at him, hunched over the counter, folding the corners of his napkin. "Then you waltzed in, dressed completely to the nines and made me look terrible." Dark eyes slatted to her. "Miss Holmes."

"Not so formal," Carrie replied, wondering the extent to which she had said it, and how much was Holmes. Or the gin. Her cheeks flamed red, and she added, "I don't really do things halfway."

"So it was a standard year for you?"

"No," she blurted. "A typical year is handing out caramels to tiny Cinderella's and Buzz Lightyears. A party is usually out of the question, but I like The Hand. I couldn't pass it up." She felt wistful suddenly.

"Sometimes I want to mock fate and scream in its face." She spun her retractable telescope on the counter. "Why do bad things happen to good people but then"—she swallowed to look at him—"it proves me wrong."

It was the ephemeral strands of fate that brought them together. Two people unlikely to ever cross paths. A shy gentleman and a hopeless romantic photographer.

"One inkling, one decision changes everything." Her pinky brushed his on the butcher block. "Fate gives me you, and I forgive all the bad because it led me here, to you."

His finger hooked around hers. His nails were painted black. "You're giving fate too much credit."

Her eyes went wide, riveted to their hold. "Am I?"

"Fate didn't wake me up yesterday and whisper your name. Fate doesn't yank me out of bed and send me to the costume shop. It's not a feeling pushing me, it's want. It's desire and drive." His voice was lower than it had been, quieter. Darker. "I am petrified of the day I sit here, and you don't come. I've been in this seat since the doors opened, for fear of missing you, unable to drink or eat because of the gnawing in my chest that I've made you up. All year I'm fighting fate to make sure I'm here now, alone with you."

Her heart pounded against her ribcage. Her fingers were strangling his.

"I think of you all year," he continued, holding her just as fiercely. "I think of you when spring comes, of the flowers in your hair, and I want to pick them and bring them to you. I think of white and black and brown hair under every kind of sun, and not a winter passes without you're accent gliding through my mind."

"You don't think it's fate?" she asked, hip on his, knees together. "That the man I want most I met on a whim? That we meet without talking, without planning?"

"You could wear any costume, Holmes. Sit anywhere in this bar and I'd find you without fail."

They're shoulders touched. She was breathless. "I'd find you first."

This was love.

In its truest, purest form, two souls finding each other in the midst of chaos.

Fate or not.

Chapter Eighteen

Asher

"SHE'S HERE," RILEY HISSED into Asher's ear, breath reeking of coconut and Malibu. So at odds with the ectoplasm green color of his drink.

Asher stood at the center of the pumpkin patch because he'd found it to be the place least occupied at any social event. And it offered Riley an excellent vantage of the entrance.

Heady Halloween was a spooky night out for adults to mingle, unwind, and have a fright. Riley's mom was the organizer of the party and, judging from the amount of gasps and bubbling laughter, she'd outdone herself.

Overhead, storm-dark clouds clotted the sky. Ominous and foreboding. Held off by strung blood orange lanterns and glowing skeletons the size of Asher's thumb.

Party goers clustered around the sheet metal *Texas Chainsaw Massacre* bars, the gore-tastic buffet and a host of devilish lawn games. Outdoor heaters kept the bitter chill to bay with dancing orange flames and a whipping bonfire was growing next to the band stage.

"She's fucking here!"

Asher jerked sideways, slamming a hand over his ear. "We've talked about inside voices."

Riley ignored him. "I knew she would be here. What do I do?"

If he was asking Asher, he was fucked.

Asher rolled his shoulders back and shook his glass. Not even the sear of straight gin sliced through the thousand apple pumpkin candle perimeter, little flickering flames corralling guests to congregate, and leading them toward the hay maze.

"You said there were gonna be kids here," Asher complained. He liked kids. They were nice and honest. Their hope hadn't been drained by the world yet.

It was the only reason he'd agreed to come tonight.

Lie.

He'd needed a distraction. And the house wouldn't work. If he stopped by to yell at Chuck, he'd end up banging on Carrie's door too.

He couldn't shut his eyes without seeing her body. Every dotted curve. Full, grabbable hips, tits that belonged in the hall of fame.

She'd seen the way he wanted her.

Worse, he'd seen how she struggled with her desire in return.

"You're not listening. She's here." Riley tapped his nails against his teeth. "Shit, I'm buying Ma a house for this." He knocked an elbow into Asher's shoulder. "Look. Behind you. Wait. Don't look."

"Moore, I don't care if your mom's here. I'll lay you flat out if you don't lower your voice."

People were staring and Asher was losing layers of enamel. Head and shoulders above the crowd, Riley wore bright cherry red sweatpants and a Behr perfect color match sweatshirt, and he glowed under the attention. Soaking it in as if he was part of the attraction, spinning, waving, flashing a smile only genetics made.

"Okay," Riley breathed. "Now, slowly, discreetly, turn around."

Grinding his teeth, Asher pivoted a half circle and planted his feet. Searched the dense crowd encircling the nearest bar. "Who am I looking at?"

"*Her*." The wide receiver pointed too quickly for Asher to see. "Diana. The goddess in black."

The bartender. "She's the one who promised to castrate you, right?"

"What I heard," Riley clarified sharply, "was a genuine interest in my best feature."

"Well, it's definitely not your face."

Riley didn't hear. "You ready?" he asked, tugging the strings of his hoodie from his collar, and tying a bow. "How do I look?"

He didn't look. "Like your mom still dresses you."

"Fuck you. Ma hates Gucci. She's Prada." He exhaled, drank more green goo. "Alright. Let's go."

They moved across the party with the same care they charged down the field, anticipating, reacting, cutting wide to accommodate the clique of women,, skirting close to the apple bobbing buckets, and slowing incrementally as they reached the end of their route.

From the corner of his mouth, Riley said, "You distract the friend while I instigate a meet cute we'll be telling our grandchildren about."

"No problem," Asher agreed, sampling his gin. "I'll tell her how you thought the hand sanitizer was breath spray for a month."

Riley shot him a irritated glance. "It was watermelon flavored."

"It was ninety-nine percent alcohol," Asher pressed.

"I was trying to be polite."

"You were drunk in the gym." He was grinning now, cheeks hurting from the pull. "How minty fresh did you need to be?"

Riley chopped Asher's ear. "If you do this for me, I'll leave The Hand to you for Halloween. I'll even make sure no one else on the team goes."

Sweat broke out on Asher's palms. No more joking around. "And you'll ask a Burton for a favor."

Riley stiffened. "You can't? He's a fucking maniac."

"We already have debts. You need to ask." If Asher asked for more, he'd get a face mask from his own line. "Yes or no?"

They were within hearing distance of the target.

"Fine. Deal. *Fuck*," Riley muttered. "You better distract like you're live depends on it."

"Deal." Asher smiled, easing back to let Riley do what he was born to.

Riley's walk became a saunter in the last two steps, his smile going wolfish, his gaze twinkling. "If you're here, who's watching over heaven?"

A wild tangle of deep brown hair spun around, and liquid gold eyes narrowed.

Riley's goddess wore shredded black shorts, boots made to kill, and a Nirvana tee with white and red paint splattered across the chest. "I carry a gun."

"*Diana*," a voice chastised.

Asher's life flashed before his eyes.

He'd walked away, but that voice followed him everywhere. He'd close his eyes, and have her over his shoulder, hands sliding over wet legs. Turn over in bed and smell the faint scent of the mountains. And he might have ignored it all. Until he'd seen her bedroom.

"You." Carrie's usual greeting lacked it's burn.

She was smiling. Asher looked behind him.

"You can't ignore me," she said, cocking her hip. "We made eye contact."

He had no desire to look at her. Not in that. Not in ... his eyes darted back—autonomous traitors. Heart pounding, he drank her in. Disbelief and tension and no small amount of pleasure coursing through him.

He swallowed thickly at the stretch of tight leather skirt painted on her legs. The black corset buckled over a Rolling Stones album cover. Silver hoops, a dangling dagger necklace, black circling her eyes, sending sleek slashes toward her ears. Even her sling was darker, mottled with black lines.

Fuck.

He locked his jaw.

She smelled like pumpkin spice and sugar and looked like a throwing star. It might not have been the bright pink towel and dewy skin, but it rendered him steel hard as easily. As quickly.

Then she gave him a little smile.

Guilt shredded him. "Don't you think you're too old to play dress up?"

The moment her smile slipped, he wanted to punch himself in the mouth.

Fuck, can't do anything right when it comes to her.

Because you want her.

Because when she wore black and leather and chains, he wanted to wrap his hand around the buckle of her bustier and crush her against him. And he wouldn't. The distance between them was one he'd never break, never cross, never tamper. She was another obstacle to his happiness.

He bit hard enough to crack a crown.

A single sentence and he'd wilted her. He swallowed the apology on his tongue.

They were supposed to tease, supposed to fight. They hated each other. He didn't care if he made her feel bad.

She took a long drink of bubbling blue and growled, "Don't go there."

A boundary. The only one she'd ever drawn.

Why this? His throat tightened around an onslaught of questions, which he managed to stifle only because of the sharp look in her eye.

"Oh, great, you two know each other," Riley said, staring at Diana's mouth. "It's kismet. I see double dates in our future."

Diana, Riley's ultimate crush, pursed her lips. She was the miniature, hairier, spot-free version of Carrie. Black on black, more chains and studs. Boots to break necks. She could be telling the truth about the gun.

She tipped her head to the side, sending coils of hair down to her waist. "I see twenty CC's of O negative in your future."

"I'm A positive, beautiful. But I find your discretion extremely thoughtful. Can I buy you a drink?" Guy had balls.

Diana tapped her shitkicker boot on the dead grass, flicking an irritated look up and down the tower of red beaming at her. "It's an open bar."

Riley thought for a moment and grinned. "Then I'll pay you."

Carrie's lips parted in objection, but Diana shrugged, looped her skinny white arm in Riley's, and led him into the fray, discussing cost per finger of whiskey.

Good for Riley.

Fuck all for Asher.

"So," he said into the empty air between him and Carrie. He drank. Scratched his chin as a horror house scream accompanied the band. Drank again. "We're chill with prostitution?"

Carrie cast him a knowing look. "If he calls her cute or beautiful or sweet, he'll be paying for his own murder."

"He'd welcome it from her."

"Another poor soul drinks from the River Styx." She exhaled wistfully and shrugged. "At worst, her brother Declan will add another John Doe to the morgue. At best she'll chew him up and spit him out."

"That's precisely what he's hoping for." Asher stepped aside for a tray of flaming shots to pass by, following it's weave through the crowd to avoid looking at Carrie. "Riley needs a challenge to function. Refill?" He nodded to her empty cup.

"You're still"—he threw back the final two fingers and hissed—"full." She nodded once. "Refill it is." She swiveled around.

"Not that way." Asher caught her arm and pulled her in the opposite direction. "It takes time for people to warm up to Riley. He's not as vivacious as me."

They're gazes slid together. Carrie's lip twitched.

As they got in line for the witch's bubbling cauldron, she turned to him, challenge in her gaze. "It's garbage that women are only desirable if they don't wish to be desired."

It was the last thing he'd expected, no mention of nudity or texts or photographs.

If she could forget it, why couldn't he?

Because it was painted on the inside of his eyelids. Carrie lounging on her pink comforter, naughty fingers walking down her stomach as she stared at him, and murmured, "Can you fix this?"

"It's ingrained patriarchy idiocrasy," real Carrie added, peering at the chalk menu.

"I agree," he said. "But it's a fresh take from a historical romance reader."

She shot him a dark look.

He smirked. "Face your spines in if you don't want people looking." They ordered quickly from the green-faced witch, Asher stuffing a twenty in the tip cauldron as they whisked away for others to order.

"Beer?" He didn't hide his surprise.

She licked foam off the lip of her dark, swirling pint of Okto-berfest. "What? Because I like pastels, I should only drink sherry out of a tiny crystal glass?"

"That and you have an entire set of sherry glasses."

"I'm getting in the spirit." She clinked her glass against his gin rocks as they walked, attention roving over the candles. "What now? Maze? Caramel apple station? Pumpkin carving?" She perked up. "Oh, there's cider."

"Hot apple broth? I'll stick to gin."

Her expression mirrored that of a child who just learned about the origin of babies.

"What?" he taunted, stopping momentarily for a group of couples to flow from the ring toss to the bonfire. "Not a fan of delicacies? Too refined for the beer guzzler?"

Her mouth popped open and red sheeted her cheeks. "Nothing's fun because I'm a grown man," she mocked in a low voice, wind rippling her hair. "I don't play games or enjoy myself."

"Is that supposed to be me?"

"Yes. Stick in the mud in e flat."

He literally played a game for a living. "Those are children's activities. If there were kids here, as was promised, I'd be at the head of the face paint line, rest assured."

Her brows rose. "Really?"

"Butterfly or turtle," he shot back. "Painter's choice."

She drank and then asked, "You like kids? What do you know about kids?"

"Only that I raised seven from infancy to their first birthday." He felt her gaze and swallowed.

Shit. He hadn't meant to say. But now, there'd be too many wrong conclusions if he didn't specify.

He glared at his boots, crunching through yellow curled grass, and pushed it out in one breath. "The foster home I was in had my room and a nursery. There was a revolving door of newborns, and I took night shift. Lullabies, warm bottles, diaper changes." Steamy showers when colic hit. Rocking. Singing. Counting tiny fingers and tiny toes.

Her irises flittered in the candlelight. "The night shift. Waking up to screaming and you liked it?"

"They weren't crying without reason. They were lonely or hungry or scared and I—" he stumbled, feeling a pang he hadn't felt in years. Longing. "I understood, I could fix it. If only for a while. I'm good at figuring out what people need. Babies, just like kids, are honest and open and if you show compassion, they return it. Kids aren't greedy or malicious."

Asher understood kids. He never felt like they were ripping him apart or judging him. He could be plain and honest.

"I'm sorry," she said after a beat of silence.

Asher stiffened. He couldn't stop the thread of offense he took at her words. The generic response to foster home. The pity and—

She lifted her chin, and the paper lanterns washed her face in warm melted gold. "I can't imagine saying goodbye to so many people I cared for."

A heavy weight squeezed his chest. The music quieted, the lights dimmed. She'd apologized for them. He ran a finger along the edge of his shirt collar, and softly, nearly too soft to be heard, he told her, "Thank you."

She nodded, and gazed out at the crowd, unaware he was crumbling at a few kind words. She swayed gently to the music, the lights drawing an auburn sheen to her hair. She was magnificent, beautiful lips curling at the sound of partiers laughing.

Asher would never fit in here. Mingling and socializing. But she would. She'd shine. Even without her bright colors. In liquid black, she shined.

She shivered.

Asher took a step closer, imagining what would happen if he hauled her into his arms. Would she nuzzle into him, languid and willing?

And what would he do if she did?

"You want kids?" she asked.

A dozen messy hands tearing up his shit, spending his money, needing attention? "Yes."

They stopped in front of the caramel dipping table, sprinkles and chocolate chips and candies laid in jeweled bowls. "This was my childhood," she said, plucking a dark chocolate curl from the pile and setting it on her tongue. "Activities." Soft eyes ringed in black found him. "Every day, I'd sprint through the school doors for my mom, so excited to see what she prepared for us, what adventure we were taking. Tie-dye station. Crayon stained glass. Pine cone bird feeders."

Asher didn't recognize a single word. He thanked the low lights for hiding it.

"I want to be that mom," Carrie said, pride and nostalgia filling her voice.

"You will." He knew it like he knew the sun would rise in the east.

Glancing back at the crowd, she flashed him a grin and quickly dunked her finger in the stream of the chocolate fountain. Licked.

Asher tightened his jaw to stop from smiling. "That's highly unhygienic."

"Yes. And it's quite fun." She dipped again, hissed, and stuck her whole pointer in her mouth, eyes wide. "And hot. Fuck." She shifted between her toes.

Avoiding the look of her lips pursed, Asher grabbed her hand and pressed the burned finger to the iced wall of his glass. "You deserved that for being a public menace," he told her, putting pressure on her finger with his palm, squeezing her into the cold. "Flouting health code for a taste. Too good for a plate."

"As if you've never wanted to do that. It's everyone's fantasy to take a swipe." A little smirk as she asked, "You've never given into temptation?"

He released a breath at the question. Didn't tell her *she* was temptation. "If I did, I wouldn't dip my finger."

"Oh right," she drawled. "My Lord only uses his desert fork and a square of pound cake to sample the delicacy of chocolate."

His heart threatened to give out at her pet name, intended to be mocking, but it struck him like a drug. He pulled his glass to his chest and with it her until there were scant inches between them. "Wrong," he murmured, defiant and aching. "I'd thrust my head under, open my mouth and swallow, brat. Let the heat burn the back of my throat and still I'd devour."

Her eyes shuttered closed.

He released her finger from his clasp and bent to put his mouth beside her ear. "Now. You're going to enter the maze, and I'm going to finish my drink."

She recoiled at once, glaring, angry. "Wonderful bonding suggestion. We can—"

"If I catch you before you find the end," he warned softly. "There'll be consequences far greater than a red mark on your finger. And brat?" He brought the gin to his mouth, held it there, cold biting his lip. "I'm fast. So if I were you"—he smirked—"I'd run."

CHAPTER NINETEEN

CARRIE

H OLY SHIT, ASHER KNEW what he was doing.

He'd told her he didn't do anything halfway. Carrie never imagined it'd apply to fun.

The maze was more labyrinth than line, and the deeper Carrie got, evading short dead ends, the fewer people she saw and the darker it became. Tea lights decorated the center path like magical fireflies guiding the way, except they had a penchant for mischief, for hauling her around a tight corner, giggling when a wall blocked her next turn.

That's when she felt him near. When she retraced her steps, his dark form would swallow the light as he stalked forward.

He wore his uniform—coal black trousers, pure white button down and over it, a tapered black coat that always made Carrie to throw blue paint on him. Mess him up, wreck his structure. Sink fangs into the barrier and shred.

Except it was never a wall. Asher didn't hide. He wore a shield. Seven first birthdays. Seven goodbyes. A crack in his armor revealed the man beneath. Gone was the man she'd known—the one who'd been cruel and contemptible, who'd spoken in threats and taunts. The man she'd have run through the hay bales to escape, clawing and digging one handed, breathless and panicked.

Now as she fled, she hoped he'd catch her. Because in the crack, she's glimpsed spinning silver, luminous as a shooting star.

Carrie burst around a bend, streaking forward, glancing behind her, grinning as beer spilled down her wrist.

When did she last have this feeling? Out of breath, adrenaline pumping, exhausted and glowing. Laughing, she took another corner and lunged back in startled surprise as she stumbled on a couple in a lurid embrace. Fast as she could, she backed up, her pants breaking through the whispering quiet.

"Carrie?"

Her mind went blank, her stomach dropped. She froze to see Rhett's beady blue eyes rake up and down her body. He didn't let go of his date, roaming hands tucked under the hem of her sweater.

"Careful there," he said. "Or you'll break the other arm."

Blood rushed in her ears. This was her life, wasn't it? Her horrible, shitty history rearing the moment she was smiling. She stumbled a step back, sucking in a breath, wishing for the hay to topple on top of her.

She hadn't seen him since—

"What happened to you?" he asked, his thin oval face contorting into a snide smile. "You look—" Another sweep of his gaze over her, joined by the blonde clinging to his middle, red lipstick on both their mouths.

Since she'd caught them getting nasty on the deli meats, Rhett shrugging while Carrie's future splintered.

"There you are."

She nearly dropped her glass at the words, the movement sending beer into the hang of her sling, pooling at her elbow. She barely had time to hide her surprise before Asher's strong arm wound over her shoulders, the rapid fall and rise of his chest betraying the speed at which he'd chased after her.

His lips lowered to press against her crown, and his murmured taunt sent fireworks off in her stomach, "You can't outrun me."

Carrie breathed in sharply as his fingers slipped under the short sleeve of her shirt, and he looked down, hazel eyes missing their streaks of color in the shadows. "I win."

She'd give him whatever he wanted to leave. "Let's go."

His stare veered at her plea, slicing to focus on Rhett. He curled Carrie tighter into him, under him, a dark shadow of protection.

"Oh my god!" Rhett's succubus gasped, peeling her hands from Rhett's belt to point at Carrie. "I know you. You were on Channel Four. I thought you died."

Asher stilled beside her, and through the twinkling lights, she watched his jaw click.

"Alive," Carrie informed with a shaky smile. "Asher, this is Rhett and his ..." she trailed off. "Employee."

"Justine, and I was promoted actually."

Probably from hard work and perseverance.

Fingers tracing over her arm, Asher cocked his head to Rhett. "Laughlin," he corrected. "How do you know Carrie?" His attention flicked between the group, assessing the tension, the avoidant glances. "I see." His touch stilled and his focus returned to Carrie. "Which one is he? The cheater or the liar?"

Rhett's smile vanished. "That was a misunderstanding."

"The cheater then." Asher's eyes hadn't changed. They remained on Carrie, watching with avid interest.

"Carrie understands now—"

"Does she." Not a question. Fuck-around-and-find-out energy wafted off him. No more gentle *thank you*s. Her little confrontation bot had returned. And it was glorious.

Rhett read it like a gunshot, puffing his chest out. "I don't know how that's your business."

"Do you really not." Asher's voice was dry as sand. Detached, as though he was hooked up to a lie detector and brim full of juicy secrets.

"I'm not the piece of shit for having needs. Everyone does. I—"

"Having. Needs." Asher's restraint was breaking, but his touch, the lone hand at her shoulder had roamed up to rest at her neck, and the fingers re-tucking hair behind her ear, were tender. More than treating her with care, he handled her with reverence, cherishing her.

The first man to ever draw her into his arms with pride. To behold her horrific thousand pound ex baggage and flex.

Carrie drank. Drank it all until bitter hops numbed her lips.

"Maybe," Rhett defended. "If she'd dressed more like this, I'd …"

He stopped his slow perusal of Carrie's body when Asher stepped forward. And even in the candlelight, it was obvious there was no fight to be had between the men. Asher's bulk and height epitomized strength and stamina.

Rhett was—Diana used toothpick—but Carrie thought he was at least a maypole. And that'd been her type, mostly. Skinny. Baggy jeans, Ed Hardy t-shirts. Survived on Sweet Chili Doritos and gas station energy drinks.

There'd be no fight.

"Finish it," Asher goaded.

Rhett swallowed. "I'm just saying she looks good." He slashed his gaze to her. "You look good, Carrie. Even with the sling."

Asher's mouth kicked up in a little edge. "No. No, that's not what you were going to say. You were going to say that if she'd dressed in a way that completely betrayed who she was, you'd have fucked her more. Maybe you would've kept your dick in your pants at work instead of being a stupid, worthless boyfriend."

Carrie couldn't summon enough air to gasp.

It was Asher as she had never seen him before, no longer mocking and egotistical, but riding a harsh wave of rage. Eyes intense and narrowed, pinning a deadly red dot on Rhett's forehead.

"She doesn't like wearing black and she'd never dress to please you." Rhett's breath rattled nervously, and his body slunk backward. Asher wasn't finished. "Say goodbye to Carrie and fucking mean it, or you'll be begging me to tell you goodbye."

Seeming to realize Asher was happy to comply with his threat, Rhett muttered a flimsy goodbye and towed his sandwich artist back into the maze.

As soon as the dead end was theirs, Asher released her. They hovered feet apart in the quiet. Rhett. The last person she'd expected to see, and Asher the last person she'd thought would come to her rescue.

And he had. Rescued her. Her unlikely hero.

"At least they're still together."

He cut her a look, and she saw the full force of his anger. "What the *fuck*. Carrie."

"What?" She clenched her empty glass. "If he's going to cheat, I'd rather it be with someone he's spending his life with than a rando. I never had a chance if she was the one."

She'd meant to comfort him, to show him she was unaffected, but she only made him colder. His body went completely rigid in front of her, jaw stapled shut. "You cannot be serious—"

"Wouldn't you rather lose to a team that won the Superbowl than a team that doesn't even make playoffs? There's a consolation—"

"You are not a consolation!" He yanked on the end of his hair, eyes ablaze. "*Fuck me.* Stop devaluing yourself, letting people make you insecure. Don't let anyone question the power you have."

Her throat constricted and all the affection she'd built for him vanished, as quick as a streak of lightning in a building storm. "This from the man who tells me my door isn't worth fixing and I sound like an addict!"

"What am I supposed to say when you call and leave those meandering streams of consciousness for me to wander through?" he snarled. "Tell you a deadbolt on a bulletproof door couldn't stop me from getting to you, or that you should save your middle of the night voice for someone who actually fucking deserves it?"

His low growl sent a thrum through her, feeding her hate. "If you said any of it, wouldn't it all just be for attention? Because you want proof you can be nice? Isn't that the point of flattery, of writing down your thoughts?"

"And here I thought texts were the spitballs of modern communication."

"From you, I'd agree!"

He stood there for a long moment, silent in the middle of their spar. He was so close she could see the burst of green encasing his pupil, and find the fading scar on his chin, ready to disappear forever. She was heaving. From anger, from desire, from the beer and the chase.

"I shouldn't have looked," he muttered to the stars, raven locks tumbling back until his face was clear sharp lines kissed by hazy moonlight.

Carrie crunched her hand into a fist to stop from grabbing her phone and photographing him. Confusion swirled. "At the maze?"

"At *you*." He swallowed and tilted to peer at her, eyes a shade darker than ever before, hazel swirling with a life of its own. "*Fuck. I shouldn't have looked. I should've been a gentleman. I should've closed my eyes and turned away.*"

He meant it, was torn up about it, the lines surrounding his mouth, the tension between his brows. Guilt. "It's alright."

The wide expanse of his shoulders spread, straightened as he walked her into the wall of hay. As he wrenched the buttons at his neck free. And then he was staring, unwavering. "I don't regret it, though."

A flush of visceral heat rushed over her like a boiling waterfall, pooling between her thighs.

He smiled slowly.

Carrie suffocated the urge to dissolve under the white slash of his teeth, his full lips. Lips she yearned to taste, suck and bite, claim and win and dominate.

She tipped onto her toes until their faces were inches apart, nose brushing the tip of his.

They'd been dancing around it, running like kids at the pool. A lifeguard blasting a whistle at them. They hovered right at the water's edge, wondering if it'd be cold or hot. If they could touch the bottom or if they'd tread, necks straining to breathe.

Wondering if he'd taste of ice or heat, if he'd clutch her as tightly as he grabbed the ball, protect her as fiercely. Carrie needed to know, to dip her toe in.

A toe.

A kiss.

She shut her eyes. Closed the distance between their lips.

A kiss. A sample. A test.

Asher heaved her into the deep end.

Before she could breathe, could gasp, could scream at the cold, the immersion, he swept her deeper, tongue splitting her lips, hands spreading pure liquid heat down her spine. She dropped her glass. A faint thump on the grass.

He smelled like the mountains. Cold air and crisp leaves. A brisk sharpness that woke you up, hit the back of her teeth, and coaxed her to inhale. Quit oxygen for this. Survive on this.

Fresh and addictive and something she knew not to venture out into the night with, and yet here she was. Pouring herself into him, taking his lips with hers.

He tasted like gin, rich and pristine and marvelous. His tongue brushed over her, teased, coaxed and…. and heat.

Heat that was always present with him.

She was wrong.

He wasn't a mountain. He was a volcano, on the verge of eruption. Air hit her the bend of her shoulder as Asher's wide hand forced its way up the back of her shirt to grasp her nape, arch her, haul her forward, and tangle his fingers in her hair.

Goodbye oxygen. Hope you find someone new. Carrie thrust her tongue into his mouth to meet him stroke for stroke, as she stretched to stay glued to him, bending, near climbing. Her body rebelled at the contortion, shoulder screaming. In the past, she put a band-aid on after stepping on a Lego, but this sweet torture—the harsh strain on the bones of her ribcage—it was too good to end.

Asher's knee pushed between her legs, lifting, moving. A jolt of shock tingled her spine as she collided with something hard and sturdy. Scratchy.

She barely had a moment to consider the hay pricking her skin before she was lifted in his arms, pinned between his chest and the maze. A shuddered cry pulled from the back of her throat.

He'd known.

Known what she craved without her saying. No more bending or arching. He held her face to face with him. No. *Higher.* She broke from his kiss to gaze down at the solid ridge of his brow.

Lord and heaven and Shonda Rhimes above, she may enjoy looking down on him even more than looking up.

Again, he knew. The curl in his languorous smile, the sink of midnight lashes.

She scraped fingers into his thick hair and reclaimed his lips. Wading now, into the shallows, waves rolling with her, shivering as she tasted. As she let her tongue explore, let it taste every corner of his mouth, moaning at the hand pressed hard into her hips. Her prone arm trapped between them should be smushed from her reaching, but he never pushed or pressed in the wrong place. As if she was an extension of him.

Asher withdrew to groan, to trail open mouth kisses down her neck, biting, savoring, chasing her goosebumps.

Don't ever stop.

As if she said it aloud, he released a chilling, coarse chuckle at her neck, little puffs of his breath stinging like hot coals.

That quickly. That easily, Carrie longed for more. Her hips angled, found his, tried to find the rhythm that she needed, craved. More.

"Asher." His name dripped from her lips, sweet and aching.

But he was lost in reverie, not listening. "Slow," he murmured to her collarbone. "Slow or I'll forget that I shouldn't— That you're not— I haven't. Wanted to—" He was babbling, so lost in her, voice ragged and husky. "I haven't wanted in— This isn't the right time."

It wasn't. In a maze at a party. Her arm throbbed, and she tasted like bad beer. She'd only just caught her ex doing this, but she'd lost all capacity for reasonable thought. "More."

"Slow," he snarled against her throat. "Or I'm going to fuck you against this wall. I'll—" Teeth on her ear, hands squeezing her waist. "I'll forget your shoulder and it'll hurt." Hot breath on her neck. "I can't hurt you again."

Even as he denied her, he returned to her. Deepened their kiss, tongue sliding over hers as if he couldn't get enough of her. The scalding, thick length of him strained between them as he forced more and more drugging kisses onto her mouth. More and more frantic, desperate, delicious.

Carrie shook as she burned over him, clutching and clinging. More. More of Asher. The fingers of her free hand fisted his hair, and she gave his lower lip a demanding suck.

His answering groan unleashed her own. *More.*

Her trapped hand reached and grabbed his shirt with greedy, hungry tugs. He'd be incredible in bed, a force, a reckoning.

But she couldn't wait. Not as his deep voice poured honey into her ear. "I can't get you out of my mind, your fucking smile." He ripped at the straps of her corset, grinding into her. "I need to feel—"

He stopped, dropped her to her feet, and lowered to his knees.

Chapter Twenty

Asher

SHE WANTED MORE.

Might have been smoother to tease her into it. To tempt and touch, to warm her up with gentle, rising touches. Fingertips and tongue, backtracking up the luscious flare of her hips.

He'd never know.

He'd shut out the whimpering voice that begged him to slow down. To savor. Told him he hadn't done this before and to figure it out. To be methodical and precise, make it perfect.

It seemed Asher always shut out reason around Carrie. Mind overrun by baser desires. Whatever washed a blush on her cheeks, coaxed her to let out a startled breath, made her arc as high and powerful as a Hail Mary.

And beyond desire was suffocating need. A yearning to see the white of her delicate green eyes and the pulse throbbed in her neck.

He could tease it out of her with a thinly veiled insult, a crass word, or, as he'd learned tonight, the dark lure of adventure. A game with stakes and risk. Just like him, Carrie was a thrill seeker.

He relished seeing challenge shatter across Carrie, almost as much as he relished tasting it.

Down on his knees, hay poked through the silky material of his slacks. He ignored it, let it harrow his skin. He didn't care if he wore dotted scars for the rest of his life, if he got hard at the state fucking fair, or at the mention of hay fever. He didn't think about the fact that this was the first time he'd ever done this, and he was doing it here where anyone could discover them.

He didn't examine the fact that it only made him crave it even more. The twisted rush of hoping Rhett would stumble upon them and find Carrie receiving exactly what she deserved. A queen of passion undulating above him.

He'd held back.

She wanted more.

"Tell me why you wore this." His palms coasted up the length of her leg, higher and higher, covering goosebumps.

"Diana," Carrie said, watching him, eyes resembling blades of grass. "It's hers. She insisted I represent her bar."

He didn't know whether to punish or praise the bar owner.

Reaching up, Asher ran hands over her bare thighs, marveling at the smooth skin, olive flecked with black. He grabbed the hem of her leather skirt and pushed up with the same force he used to rip off his pads after a brutal victory. The leather split.

He swore.

Carrie gasped. "Diana's going to kill you,"

"She can have a free shot if she waits until I'm finished." Until god willing, *she* finished.

His teeth grazed the side of her knee, and a heady giggle show-ered over him. Encouraged, Asher licked up the outside of her thigh to tangerine cotton panties.

"There you are. Hidden under all that." His fingers wouldn't wait. They slunk underneath the fabric, and he went from aching hard to fucking stone at the discovery of wet heat under his fingers. And over them. Soaked through the layer of her underwear, he sucked on her inner thigh and found the taste of her there. Deli-cious.

"I thought I lost you," he murmured as he pulled the panties aside and blew chilly night air against her hot, slick core.

Messy.

Asher hated messy.

He'd raised himself to be exemplary, well groomed, house bro-ken, and mannered. She'd reduced him to this, a man wild with hunger, snapping for it. She'd freed him.

Asher wanted to burn, to raze and expose.

Tonight, he'd devour messy.

He spread her thighs and dragged the pad of his finger of her swollen core, staring as she convulsed in response. His lungs were on fire, his pulse pounded.

"Don't," she whimpered, and his touch stopped instantly. He pried away from his favorite view, terrified he'd done something wrong. "Don't look at it ..."

He met her eyes, engulfed in petulance as he said, "If you want to rob me of such a view—"

"Just take them off," she whispered, face blazing red. "They're not sexy. I didn't think—"

Without hesitation, he guessed the next line, "That I'd be shredding your skirt and begging for your pussy in the dead end of a maze?"

Her lips parted and her eyes narrowed. Her hold tightened on his hair, pulled. "You can see over the hay. You cheated."

Yes. Or he'd never have let her out of his sight. He turned and sucked a dark ring onto her thigh. "You didn't set rules."

Her surprised smile shifted into a gasp of pleasure as his lips moved higher, closer to where he longed to be. "Do you ever fight fair?"

"Fair," he repeated, watching her chest heave. She was pure want. Unbridled need. And a fraction of what rioted through him. "Nothing about you is fair. Since we met, you've played dirty. Marvelous tempting mouth lacerating me. Every violent and lascivious emotion plain as day on your face. I never know if you'll cut me or cup me. And I don't know which I fucking want more from you. Mocking freckles, hair that gets everywhere."

He licked long and firm at the crease in her thigh, hot breath fanning her center. "Fair," he rumbled, "would be taming you, sending you three rights and a left and sitting you down for cider."

"I like cider."

"You like gin," Asher countered darkly. "And chaos. And me." She gasped, eyes flying to his. "Admit it, and I'll find you a fair agreement."

She gave a piercing look. She wanted to fight. She bit her lip.

She wanted him more. Asher filled with devious satisfaction.

"Just pretend they're lace and gold and tight."

Did she wear that for other men? Sparkle and shine and red lines crisscrossing her skin in nauseating patterns?

He detested the idea.

"No. I like these."

"You're being cruel."

"Cruel would be depriving me of cotton soaked by the brat herself for a man she hates."

Then, with an almost crude, crushing need, he wrenched those panties aside and latched onto her core with his mouth, sucking and swallowing, devouring. She arched against him, fingers clutching his hair, pulling too hard and he didn't care. Didn't notice. Just attacked.

"*Yes.*"

The whisper rioted through him. He wanted to hear it again and again, louder, crying out. He wanted it as she spread out under him in satin sheets, her fingers caressing his cheeks, pressing down as she drew back for air after a delirious kiss.

Asher may have never eaten pussy before, but he knew how to read signals. To move with her arches, to slow when she quivered, to spread her wide, hike her leg over his shoulder and take her weight until he only tasted Carrie, saw Carrie. No stars or moon to guide him, just the bend of her hips, the flex of her thigh at his ear.

On his knees in front of her felt as familiar as stepping onto the field, feeling pressure in his chest, adrenaline flooding.

His fingers wrapped around the cool skin of her upper leg, smooth and bare and soft under his grip. Nerves raced up his spine as she rocked into him. "Say something," he whispered, biting into her thigh. "Talk to me."

Distraction. So he couldn't overthink, only listen and learn and do.

She sighed, fingers tugging at his hair.

He dragged teeth across her clit. She hissed and shuddered. "Talk, brat."

"You were right," she gasped as his tongue returned to her, as he licked and swallowed a groan of pleasure, hiked her leg further up his shoulder. "I hate black." Fingers scored his scalp as he drank from her, savored the undeniably sweet lust of Carrie.

"It's—" Another gasp as he plunged one long finger into her, felt her drive down against him. "It's misanthropic and morose. Funerals and storms."

Dead ends and dark corners. Asher was darkness. Irascible and gruff.

He sucked at her harder, tongue moving in the slow circles that made her breath hitch. Added a second finger into her tight, wet heat. Nearly lost it.

Draped over him, she moved as if she were the reaching flames of a blazing fire, pure and potent and dominant. She tipped into an arc, only her head on the hay wall, her body falling onto Asher's as though terrified she might set the entire maze aflame.

Burn it down. All of it. Everything. Leave scorched earth and them, black ash under his knees.

Burn me, he wanted to say as he pumped into her, as he lavished at her with tongue, sucking and stroking. *Burn me, I deserve it. For fueling fire. For stirring embers.*

Releasing a string of breathless moans, Carrie ground against him, dug nails into his scalp.

"I like the light," she moaned, riding on his face, building. Taking what was hers. Asher kept the slow circles over her clit as her eyes squeezed shut, and he thrust into her.

"Yellow," she gasped. "I like yellow. The burst behind your eyes when you smile. White at its core, color crowded there."

She stroked his hair, fingers trembling in time with her thigh wrapped over him, heel bearing down on his shoulder blade.

Close. He was getting her close. He could feel her clenching and fluttering around him. *Fuck* he ached for her.

"Asher."

The name broke him. Compelled his hunger into craving.

"Asher," she exhaled softly. "*Yes*. Like that."

He hated her. Hated how his body singed at the sound of her feverish gasps. The rapturous pants as she pulsed around him.

Surreal. He was dizzy with her, exhilarated and drunk.

He closed his eyes. With each touch, he read her sinful desire, and tackled it. Slow firm circles, deep thrusts into the swollen center of her. She moved against him, and he groaned, lent himself to her, desperate for more.

No, he didn't need to see her to deliver her pleasure, and yet his head tipped back as he scissored his fingers within her. Watched as she growled into the air and flew apart, constricting around him and unleashing.

Asher fell over the ledge with. Pulsing, groaning, sinking teeth in the flesh of her thigh.

Only when the painful grip of her fingers loosened did he pull away, sit back on his heels to find her eyes, stroked his wet knuckles down the line of her calf on his shoulder.

"Why the outfit?" he asked, kissing her ankle. "Not for me." No, she'd been surprised to see him. Shocked. And then came the flush.

Carrie searched his face for a long moment, skin dewy, eyes glowing. "I told you—"

"Tell me the real reason." He blew a stream of cold air over his kiss. Smirking at the shiver that exploded up her body. "You could've matched Diana. Shorts and a tee. But you put on leather and chains."

You tortured me.

For the shortest breath, violence glimmered in the air.

Asher braced for the outbreak, to lose the progress they'd made, to get thrown back where he belonged.

She pulled his hair, dropped her leg from his collarbone and urged him up with only a finger under his chin. "The same reason I hate you. Because we're the same. I don't do anything halfway either."

His response was a growl, his hand on her throat, and a kiss so deep he hoped to steal her brightness.

But it was too good to be true.

A chainsaw revved, and a scream pierced the air.

***

A S THEY SPRINTED THROUGH the darkened maze, careening to the entrance, narrowly avoiding a nest of laughing jack-o'-lanterns, Asher had a revelation: he was having fun.

At a pumpkin patch with no kids, surrounded by strangers, a wet stain on his favorite pants, cum on his lip, a fuckload of hay in his shoe, and he was laughing, squeezing Carrie's hand.

Fucking laughing.

He couldn't remember the last time he'd been out of breath without a defenseman chasing him down.

Now shrieks and rotating blades tracked him.

"They're getting closer," Carrie called, missing her step when the damp leaves gave out underfoot. Her cheek smacked his biceps, and instead of letting go, giving them both space, she clung to him more firmly, pressed closer.

Around her hips flapped Asher's jacket, tied in a knot against her belly button to shield the three-inch tear in her skirt. "Hurry up then," he scolded, yanking her tighter into him.

If Jason or Freddy or Mike, fuck even that tricycle riding little bastard, was on their tail, they'd have been long dead. Cut into a thousand never-stood-a-chance pieces.

Half to blame was Carrie's continued yelps and screams. Half Asher's laughing.

Even kissing her was fun. Fuck, he could've kissed her for an hour. Dry humping, hickeys, swollen lips and coming up for air. Hours. Days.

A lifetime.

When was the last time he actually enjoyed making out?

Did he want to fuck Carrie—ask the re-hardening rod knocking on his zipper. Rhetorical.

But first, he wanted a week of making out, of learning what every part of her tasted like, if the soft skin under her ear made her toes curl, if she liked a little hair pull, a nip on her lip.

"You want the chainsaws to get us?" he teased breathlessly, untangling a strand of hay from her hair. "Do you want to be chopped up and frozen like pizza bites?"

Her forehead kissed the side of his neck, and she grumbled, "If that's what you're scared of, don't worry, you're too gamey to bother slicing. They'll dump you in a ditch."

Smirking, he curled a hand around her nape and yanked her to a stop, crowding into her, stealing a quick kiss. "Brat, I'll launch a flare."

A scream. Close.

Carrie yelped, her face lit up with a huge smile. "Save me, my Lord?"

Maybe it was the whisper of her plea against his lips, smelling like pumpkin and hops.

Maybe it was the feel of her, the clutch of her fingers on his, a hand that no one had ever held so tightly.

But it was most likely that the words pouring out of Asher's mouth had to do with the nickname alone. An inside joke. A rite of passage he'd rarely been privy to. He took her lips in a vicious kiss, pinning her chin in his fingers. "Nobody gets to you without going through me."

She smirked. "I don't think chainsaws have a hard time discriminating between people. They're made to cut through oak trees."

"You calling me weak?"

She beamed at him. So fucking beautiful. "Calling you flesh and blood, and I'm not scared of the chainsaws. She peeked behind him and shuddered. "I'm scared of who's holding them."

"Nocturnal lumberjacks?"

"Teenagers." Carrie uttered with the resonance of Voldemort. "They're merciless and they wield so much power."

"Your Achilles heel is people without the ability to vote?" Asher cupped her closer, guiding her to the wall. "I won't allow that. I'm your mortal enemy."

Carrie scrambled in his grip, laughing as she thrashed under him. "Stop. They'll massacre us."

Both arms hooked around her, he led her straight to the haunted portion of their Heady Halloween. "I'm not afraid of chainsaws or teenagers."

She clutched his chest, sling nudging his third leg. "What about teenagers with chainsaws?"

"Not scared." His teeth went to her ear. "Offended you'd put them above me. What do I have to do Carrie? To haunt you?"

"You're terrifying, let's go."

He chuckled, dark and slow. "You're a filthy liar, and I won't stand for it."

"You're the biggest, fittest, scariest man in the world. Now let's go." She yanked on his collar. "*Asher.*"

Fuck, it was adorable when she tried to take charge.

"I think you're placating me." He threw her a look of comical indignation. "And there's only one way to show that I'm the real monster."

"I'll schedule a ring match between you and Paul." A pause. "*Asher.*"

"I have to do this for you. You forced my hand here, brat."

"Oh my god please." A tiny shriek unleashed as the rattling noise increased, the haunters creeping closer. She stopped attempting to break free. Now she was angling to crawl through him, into him. "This isn't funny."

It was precisely that.

Seeing sweet Carrie clad in leather, looking freshly fucked squirm over a couple of teenagers making minimum wage. They'd more likely worship her than kill her.

"Do you hear that?" Asher whispered about fucking nothing.

It worked.

With surprising dexterity, she wound around him to mimic a backpack, face buried in his shoulder blades, fingers scratching at his stomach.

"Don't hurt your arm," he warned. Wholly prepared to end the fun if she put herself at risk.

"Shut up," Carrie muttered violently, leg hitching up his hip.

Chuckling, he spun around and caught her, bracketing her squirming form in his arms. "Look right." She glared. "C'mon, brat. Right." She tipped. "Now left." Again, she followed his direction. "There," he smiled. "I can see you."

"Asher."

"You should trust me. I know what I'm doing. My job is fifty percent evading attackers."

"I do," she rushed, fingers hooking on his belt loop, eyes darting. "I trust you so much."

"Placating liar."

Her gaze cut to his, then her lips were brushing his ear, hot breath making him groan and fist her shirt. "You think I'd let you enter my body if I didn't trust you?" She nipped at his chin. "Think I'd come if I was scared of you?"

"No, brat. I think you came twice as hard for just that." His attention wandered to her mouth, the smile she kept sucking down. "Want me to prove it?"

"Asher—" Still chastising, but less I'm-going-to-spank-you-for-this and more I'm-going-to-spank-you-for-this.

He shut his eyes and breathed her in. "I like when you say my name. Like—"

Light flashed over them, searing Asher's retinas. "What the—" He shot out his hand to block Carrie, ready to tell a few preteens to fuck off. He was about to perform an encore.

Until Diana said, "Thank sodding hells."

CHAPTER TWENTY-ONE

CARRIE

S HE'D LOST HER FUCKING mind. And no amount of retraced steps would help her find it.

The ambient noise of Sunday Night Football leaked from the TV in her living room all the way into the kitchen, a hangover from College Game Day. Sitting on the chipped linoleum, back on her cabinets, Carrie was dissecting a wikiHow on how to fix your fridge cooling unit. Backwards.

Unplugging hoses, and stuffing socks inside.

For him.

For Asher.

She fell back on her butt and pressed her head to her knees. *Where's a pillow to scream into when you need it?*

She wanted him.

Wanted him now and tonight, wanted him in the morning with coffee and a sore throat, wanted him smirking by her side on the bus, wanted him pushing her across the wet lawn, storming into her house. Wanted him in her bed. Now, in the dead of winter, on top of the satin sheets in summer.

She wanted him forever.

Intensity. Asher burned her up with it.

"Why don't you call him?" Jill asked, skating into the kitchen. The cardboard box in her arms said *Warm Shit.*

Carrie dropped a corrugated plastic hose into her lap. "Why can't he call me?"

Jill pushed her readers to sit on her purple crown braid. The turquoise frame clashed exquisitely with her traffic cone orange sweater and baggy green corduroy pants. "Perhaps he's buying a fridge in anticipation?"

Not likely.

Carrie kept seeing his face when Diana and Riley found them. The sheer panic on his features when the darkness receded. Like he'd thought she was someone else the entire time they'd been together. Like all the laughing and teasing, all the fucking savoring and passion had been shared with another, and Carrie had swooped in at the last moment. Offended the crown.

"He's not," Carrie said, pushing to her feet and dusting off her jeans. "He calls me a brat. He's trying to kick me out."

"Darling, I've been called far fouler by much sweeter men and never found it remotely demoralizing." Jill set the box on her popped hip, stack of charm bracelets jingling. "In fact, I've found it quite tantalizing. Like a masquerade. Playing a whore or—"

Can't unhear that. "He's not sweet."

He was mean and domineering and aggressive. Never listened, didn't have a romantic bone in his body.

And she was quite worried she loved him.

Loved his words whispered into the hollow of her throat, the feeling of being tucked under his arm, feeling his laugh on her temple, his eyes blaze down her body.

Jill raised a beautifully shaped eyebrow. "Good. Who craves a toothache?" Then she was gliding down the hall, using her Birkenstock to open the door. "Stop looking for a reason to call when you know there isn't one."

Alone, Carrie felt even crazier.

She stared at her phone, sitting on loud next to her abandoned formerly hot tea. Anti-inflammatory, the green box said. Thoughtful.

She dialed and before the second ring, got his voicemail. She could kill him. "Call me back."

A text rolled in.

No.

                                        My fridge broke.

Your fridge isn't covered in the lease agreement.

Well fuck. Time to re-read the article.

                                    My oven's broken too.

No, it isn't.

Why don't you come

over and find out?

Flirting. She could flirt.

No.

That word. She resisted the urge to strangle him, to call him imperious and contrary and a giant bloody gaping thorn in her side. Her heart.

I hate you.

You miss me and you hate that.

So matter of fact. She wanted to slap him, poison him, maim and kiss him.

Are you alone?

Like she was a pathetic loser with no weekend plans? She started for the door, for her keys and purse to go to The Hand with the intention to prove him wrong, or have a bit of truth when she responded: No. Fuck you, I'm thriving. I'm—

Unzip your pants.

Her heart stuttered. No. He couldn't mean—
He would never—
Asher Laughlin would *never*—

C'mon brat. We both know why you called.

Carrie slumped against the wall, stranded in the entry hall, moonlight streaming onto her socks. She could hear his smug voice, the low command licking through her. She shut her eyes.

No bubbles and read receipts is a good sign. You might get what you want.

Another text.

Who the fuck uses read receipts?

She did. Accountability. Clear communication.
She slid down the wall, socks skidding over the runner.

You don't know what I want.

If he did, he'd be here. He'd be here, barging into her life, getting in her face, shoving ice under her sling and kissing her like she stole his air. Infuriating her. Melting her.

Me. Whether or not you can admit it.

Him. Always about him.

Electrocution. She'd tell him the drain broke, throw a hair dryer in it.

And I fucking want you.

Oh god. Her butt hit the floor, her pulse quit. She stayed leaning over her phone screen for as long as she could hold her breath, unbelieving, reveling.

You make me furious, you know that? Every time you call, I want to punish you for it.

Her stomach clenched, her fingers ran to the cold swell of her lip. It was bent. Smiling. She was smiling and insane and this was a bad idea when it started but now—*punish*.

She read it again and again, picturing his hands leaving imprints on her skin.

I want to throw your clothes on my floor. Burn them so you can never leave. I want to wrench the taste of sun from your lips and spit it on the floor. Lay you in it, fuck you in it. I want to stop being a fucking steel rod around you. Constantly, and you don't even notice, selfish little brat. What do you give me? *Pain*.

Her heart wrenched. She pressed her thighs together.

Put me out of misery.

Carrie stared. *Pain*. She swallowed past the sting in her eyes. Pain.

Good, was all she could think. Pain sounded a whole hell of a lot like what scored her chest. The tender ache she carried around, wishing she could numb it with ice.

You want me.

She texted, hands shaking.

What I desire is irrelevant.

Because of the pain?

She tipped her head to look at her door, the horrible, whistling patch he'd made. The other side bearing his name. A claim he'd staked. Words she saw every time she closed it and faced the monstrosity next door.

Because need trumps desire.

And he needed her out of her house. He needed her miserable too. He needed her to break, not bend. He needed—

I need you to come. I need you to come so hard thinking of me that I can feel the pain ease.

A sudden, overwhelming rush of lust soaked her underwear through. Carrie unlocked her knuckles from the death grip on her phone, watched it hit the hardwood like it scalded her.

She couldn't decide if she hated or loved the fact that she needed exactly what he'd said. That her hand was fumbling with her jeans, that her core clenched.

I need to feel you. Tight and hot and wet, clutching my fingers. I need your taste to give me reason to swallow. I need your gasp more than air. I need your light.

Sinful thrill broke through her like crackling fire. Storms of lust sweeping in with vengeance.

Carrie scrambled for her phone. Using her weak side so her free hand could slide underneath her waistband. The underwear she'd wished she'd worn for him. Lace and sheer and sexy. Lilac.

Light.

Her face burned, the word she gave him, the ones he'd asked for while he—

God she'd barely known she was talking with him buried between her legs, laving across her nerve endings beneath thick smears of clouds clotting the night sky.

Fucking light.

He replied.

It hit with no warning.

Agony, not pain.

Carrie capsized into an endless sea of confusion. Drowned under Asher and his words, his hands, his hatred. The echoes of his laughter. Agonized under how badly she wanted to touch him, be touched by him.

Take it.

She sent back, panting on her floor. Giving in.

Tell me how.

His reply was instant. Her request unnecessary. He would've taken it without her permission, would've told her exactly how.

I'd sit you on my lap so you could feel how fucking hard I am, spread your legs over my thigh so wide you were straining.

You better be touching yourself, Carrie.

Carrie. Not brat. Whatever hesitancy she had shattered.

Yes.

I'd shred your flannel. Buttons littering the ground, spread my palms over your tits, let myself play until you pushed into my grip. Snapped at me to hurry. Your fucking tits. I can't believe how pink they are, the same pink as your lips, as your pussy. Pink. I fucking love pink.

Touch your clit, slow. Trace my name.

She did, splaying out across her floor, hair stuck to the wall, tailbone aching on the hard wood.

I'd wait until you whined, until you shut your eyes and slid up my thigh like you were tortured. Then I'd devour you. Take your mouth the same time I found those pretty panties. The ones I've imagined a thousand fucking times. My tongue in your mouth, my fingers in your wet, tight pussy, palm on your swollen clit, knee rocking under you. You'd buck on me. Fight. Because you live to fight. *Christ*, and I live to make you writhe. To take your throat and suck every freckle into a fucking hickey.

The filthy words rioted through her, crushing pleasure coursing, pooling at the throbbing spot at the center of her.

She listened to her own breaths in the empty hall, just her, the sound of her fingers circling her clit, and the quiet buzz of Asher's incoming texts.

The silence felt louder than her shutter as her fingers dipped lower, as she stole wetness and spread it, quivering at the touch, picturing Asher looming over her, his lips at her temple, whispering threats and compliments as he moved his hand over her. Warm skin. Solid muscle. The rigid length between them, revealing he was as affected as she was.

Maybe more.

I'd need you to come. I'd need to make your eyes flutter and roll before I stood up, before I brought you with me, twisted you around and fucked you, Carrie. Fucked you deep and hard and as pathetically long as I could while

you were still trapped in your orgasm. Minutes, brat. I'd get fucking minutes, that's it.

That's how blinding you are, a destroyer with light. A blazing star across my fucking retinas.

It had barely begun before the climax wrecked her.

A current raking over her with iron talons, piercing her skin and dragging her down and down and down until the pressure and depth of the world overwhelmed her, until there was no light, only darkness, until he'd stolen it from her, scraped it out of her soul. And she imploded in the black.

His name fell from dry lips as she writhed and groaned, fingers pushing near painfully against her.

When she opened her eyes, her breaths echoed. The moon had drifted behind a cloud, left her in shadow.

She called him.

Wrist trapped behind her zipper, thighs squeezed tight. The ring echoed. She was shaking, sweating.

Two rings.

Voicemail. "The oven broke. I'm breathing in noxious fumes," she told the receiver, voice a rasp. She paused, panting. She wouldn't beg.

Don't say it, don't.

"Asher. Come over." A pause. She ended it. "Asher—"

A robot cut her off. "The voicemail box you are trying to reach is full." *Beep.*

Call ended.

A text.

You're light headed because I made you come. No other reason.

Her heart fell, pinched and ripped.

Pain.

She bent forward and tucked her chin on her knees.

The carpet's still wet.

Fine brat.

It was impossible to tell how long she sat there, fixated on her phone. Hand still in her pants, confusion swirling in her gut. Between six minutes and ten hours.

The moment she heard footsteps on her stoop, she was up, buttoning, brushing back her hair, ready to punch Asher in the throat or kiss him until she could see again.

She tore open her door. "You?"

Chapter Twenty-Two

Asher

"**I figured it out**," Riley said, glancing up from his phone.

Asher stayed quiet. Riley could be addressing many things.

Since they'd stepped foot inside what would eventually be the laundry room, he'd listed four dire problems. What to bring to thanksgiving, when he should cut his hair, was No Shave November still a thing, and whether Diana was hot or crazy.

"Hot," Asher decided finally, knowing she'd rip his nuts off if he said otherwise. Fuck, maybe even if he said that.

"Crazy, blistering, mouthwatering hot." Riley let out a howling whistle. "No, I meant Halloween."

Asher tensed, fingers stilling on the wall.

Halloween had become a dark, dangerous word, an end and a beginning. The culmination of his existence. He avoided thinking about it. About how close it was, about how fucking complicated his life was.

Four weeks ago, Asher would've clawed out his heart to speed time up, to yank Holmes through time. To sink into her peace and start the life he'd always wished for.

He should crave it still. And he did. In pieces. If the next week vanished, he could be with her, forget the entire month, forget everything before Holmes.

Who, though, could forget Carrie Huston?

She'd stopped calling.

For the best. He loved another. A perfect woman who didn't curse, didn't break in to homes, didn't cry or hoard.

Didn't keep a photograph of him at her bedside. Didn't leave him voicemails, didn't insist on them, didn't taste like fucking candy.

Thank the football gods they'd been playing in Philly. Winning no thanks to him. Too distracted.

He'd have appeared at her door, tried to tell her he didn't belong to her, and she should start packing before he got cruel. But he'd end up inside, trapped in her rainbow reeking of burned sugar, and he'd forget all of it. He'd see her and crack. He'd fuck her. Regret it.

Come over.

Five days. Five excruciating days he'd stayed away. Could he survive seven more?

Seven days. He wanted to step across the week with his eyes closed.

He never wanted it to end.

Either way, Asher was bracing for pain, vicious and penetrating.

He grabbed a clay tile from the backsplash pile and weighed it with his hand, avoided Riley's gaze. "Burton's searching."

Searching and failing. No matter how much gold Asher acquired, Burton was officially evading him. Road runner style.

"No, not that. I've got a theory." Riley popped his head through a gaping hole in the drywall. A window, if Asher had to guess. He couldn't remember anymore. "What if it's someone we know—"

"Hey. Don't go in there," Asher snapped, catching Riley's elbow.

The receiver's eyes scoured the raw wood door like it led to Narnia. "Why not?"

"Because ..." Asher shoved his hands in his pockets. "Because the floors are done, and you'd mess them up. All it needs is paint."

"So I only get a tour of the shitty half-finished stuff?"

"This is not a guided excursion. You said you needed to talk. I told you where I'd be." Asher watched as two sets of closet doors were hauled into the primary and steered Riley the other way, toward the kitchen. "So talk. I assume this is about your hellion."

Riley sighed, easily distracted. "If she was mine, there'd be nothing to say. I wouldn't be here following you around." He flicked the white chandelier hanging in the hall. "She's harder to crack than I originally estimated."

Asher didn't reveal his surprise. "And reality isn't living up." Asher tilted his head. "Hard to get makes for blue balls."

"You'd know." Riley pulled a bar of chocolate from his pocket and broke off a piece. "I thought she'd hate me. Which I can work with. I dig the murder-you-in-your-sleep energy. Scary. Sexy.

Whips and ball gags. Ropes. Floggers. Melting wax while I get her off."

A few workers in hard hats flashed Riley freaked out looks, and he winked. What did they expect from a guy in flared corduroy pants and a Santa Baby Mariah Carey tee?

"What's the problem?" Asher asked, shaking his head at Riley's candy square offering. "Did she take you home and show you her Care Bear collection?"

"First of all, I'd love to compare with someone." Another wink, chocolate on his tongue. He lowered his voice. "But kind of?" It sounded like a question. Asher paused outside the pantry. "I told you she was at Heady Halloween because she's working with my mom's company. They're friends. They did fireball shots together."

"Killed the boner?"

"No fucking way. I love a girl who gets on with my mom. It's just ..." he steepled fingers over his chest. "She was nice. Didn't swear once. Just bloody and shag and hells. And she's super close with her brother. She keeps a collated business plan in her truck and ..." He glanced at the kitchen island, where new Carrera marble counters were being sealed. "Are those donuts?"

"How can you eat all that crap during the season?"

"Unlike you, my workouts go past dark," he taunted, swaggering into the kitchen and throwing back the orange and pink box lid, fingers wiggling over the choices. "But Diana— when the haunted house stuff started, she genuinely panicked." He scooped up a black and orange frosted donut hole, complete with bat sprinkles. "I tried to tell her it was fake, but she went full John

Wick. Yelled at me to leave and then started screaming for Carrie. Do you think something happened? Maybe to Carrie—"

"No." She'd run in the street wearing a bath towel, let Asher into her house. She'd laughed at the chainsaws. Laughed against his skin, holding his hand.

"Then it's Diana. What could it have been?" Riley moved to the counter and took two napkins from the pile. "I've never seen someone made a shiv from a woodchip and the way they sped off together was odd. No goodbye."

Asher felt a surge of relief. She hadn't left because of him.

No. He didn't want relief. He wished she'd hate him.

What a fucking mess he'd made. Losing control. All for a woman he'd never intended to meet.

Without realizing it, his hand was on his phone, swiping through to his call log. Habit. To hear her soft voice again. The breathless gasp. *Come over. Asher.*

No one said his name like that. Whispered, welcoming, soft with just a flicker of anger, of desperation, a strained whimper.

Sounds he'd never wanted to hear from her.

Sounds he thought about every time he was in between sentences, snaps, and breaths.

She had no idea how much power she had over him.

All of it.

"Chuck," Asher called, spotting the signature spit bottle.

In stained jeans and a St. Michael's sweatshirt, Chuck sauntered over and smiled. "She's looking great, eh?"

"Coming along," Asher conceded.

Riley and Chuck shook hands and exchanged names. "You looking to build Riley?" Chuck asked, fishing white business cards from his wallet. "We're finishing up on this place in the next week."

"I bought a turnkey on the water," Riley informed regretfully. "But if you know anything about installing decks, I'm in the market."

Asher laughed. "Diana did mine."

His donut hole slipped off his napkin and hit the floor, rolled. "What?"

"And Carrie," Chuck added. "Our donut fairy." The contractor turned to Asher. "I need you to confirm the paint colors you sent me so I can submit the order. We'll spray her down and then it's final electrical before we put a bow on the front door."

Asher avoided Riley's glare as he approved his selections. Purposely kept his gaze on the door when he asked, "What do you think happened to Diana, then?"

"Fuck you," Riley growled, blowing dirt off his donut. "Carrie was here? You had her working on Holmes' house? That's messed up."

"I wasn't here." He wished he could look away. Couldn't. "I didn't know she was coming over. She and Chuck are"—*fuck how did he*—"They know each other."

More so now since he'd sent Chuck to her house with a wet vac ten minutes after he'd jacked off to Carrie's voicemail.

Messy.

Riley studied Asher for a long moment, and then said, "Talk as in she's seeing multiple people? You guys are casual?"

No. Absolutely fucking not. Asher would never let another hear those sinful, strangled sounds. Someone else's name trickling from her lips. He wadded his fingers into a fist, clenched his teeth. "We're nothing."

"I've never seen you talk like you do to her, not even to me." Riley paused. "You hold back and keep shit to yourself. With her—"

Asher looked at his best friend, letting his fury into his gaze. "She's not mine."

Riley's brows rose, then pulled together. "But you like her. You were smiling and laughing. I saw you two. She makes you happy. Dude it's perfect. Me and Diana, you and Carrie."

The idea stung.

"No Riley. Jesus." His molars cried out. "Look where you're standing."

Riley blinked twice, didn't move. "The kitchen?"

"*Holmes's* kitchen." Asher's voice was thick with gravel, pained. "She's the one. She's my everything. The person I can build a future with. The perfect woman. I can breathe with her. There's nothing with Carrie."

Carrie was messy.

Riley went to the sink and washed his donut off. "That's it then? Done?"

"I don't even know if she likes me." She shouldn't.

"Do you really want to wonder?"

"I've been wondering for three years."

Riley spun to face him. "And it's made you fucking miserable. C'mon. Open your eyes. There's a beautiful woman who wants you, who you want back."

"A week until Holmes. Riley. It doesn't work." He wouldn't miss his chance. Beyond the window above the sink, Asher spotted a navy BMW pull in across the street. "What the—"

Riley turned and squinted, a donut in his cheek. "Lincoln gets a tour?"

"No." But that was undoubtedly Lincoln Wray walking around the hood, thumb hooked in the pocket of his jeans, sunglasses tucked into his shirt, bending down to open the door.

"Shit," Riley muttered.

She was crying. Carrie was crying. Fat rolls of tears down her face as she took Lincoln's hand, allowing him to help her gently from the car.

Asher's heart pounded. He forced an inhale.

His first thought should have been, *what's wrong?* Instead, he mapped out a twelve step plan to dismantle the man who dared hurt her, accepting that it'd ruin his career, his life. Outrage, visceral and lashing, stripped him of his concerns.

"You didn't say she lived next door."

He'd never heard anger in Riley's voice before. "It doesn't matter," Asher muttered, staring as his QB and tenant exchanged words on the sidewalk. As she wiped her cheeks and smiled at him.

It had always been like this. Asher on the outside looking in. He'd accepted it long ago, and yet. This pierced especially deep, pricked vital organs.

"You're keeping tabs on her."

Asher couldn't deny it. "I'm inspecting my house. She and I are—"

Electric.

Doomed.

"She's a nice girl, Asher."

"It's not that simple. I love her!" He couldn't tear away from Carrie, from the dip of her chin, her hair fluttering in the wind.

Riley laughed, and it wasn't the laugh of a Moore. It was cold and dry. Humorless. "You don't mean Carrie. You mean Holmes."

"Carrie and I just met." It took him an instant to repent. A flash of her cuddled under his arm, her smiling over the foam of her beer, standing outside his door.

"You don't even know her name," Riley pressed.

"Carrie hates me!" he burst, seething as she dove into the arms of his QB, pressing her cheek to his sternum.

Riley said something, but it hit deaf ears. Asher couldn't think. Breathe. Not with a rage rioting inside his skull, a twisted repeating verse of *what the fuck, what the fuck, what the fuck.*

She hated him.

And she'd made sure it stuck.

Chapter Twenty-Three

Carrie

BLISTERING RAGE MENDED A broken heart ten times better than a motherfucking puff pastry ever had.

Releasing Lincoln, Carrie fumbled in the expanding nest of papers tucked in her sling for his ticket to the Green Mountain Cancer Alliance's Annual Auction.

"There you go," she said, smearing a smile on her face. Lincoln deserved it. For the ride, for the help. Definitely for the white line of snot on the center of his chest.

Rage also caused Carrie to cry quite a lot. An unfortunate side effect, for which she'd apologized profusely. One last crying fit. Not for her broken heart. Because she had that totally under control. Swaying the gallows handled. The outburst was strictly because Lincoln Wray, quarterback, was a wonderful hero.

"I really am sorry," she said, passing him the ticket and a spare brown McDonald's napkin—only slightly dirty from a too hot cinnamon roll.

Without his helmet and pads, Lincoln incited thoughts of the devil. Not in what he wore—jeans and a dark purple Rip Curl shirt—but his suck-the-air-out-of-the-room presence. The striking hue of his deep blue eyes seemed to darken his chestnut hair, elongate his face, and pull his mouth taut, as if he were waging internal war. He was the type of man Diana would tell Carrie to avoid in a dimly lit alley.

Which was unfair, because he'd only been nice to her. Kind and generous. She dabbed at his chest, trying to minimize the damage. His long fingers enveloped her wrist. "Carrie. It's a shirt. Not one I particularly like. Don't worry about it."

"I feel bad. You're doing me a favor and I went kamikaze on you."

"It's an important issue. And personal to you. I'd consider you heartless if you didn't react emotionally."

The ensuing silence made Carrie think she'd cry again. Swiftly smothered when she spotted the obnoxious gunmetal black car on the curb.

Rage.

Missed you baby.

"Thank you again." She scrunched the napkin in a fury fist. "I think you coming will really help sales. Maybe we'll get a picture of you and the buyer. Only if you want to. You've already—" Signed three prints, delivered them to the Burlington Gallery, coddled a pitifully hysterical Carrie without saying *please holy hell stop, I'll give you everything I own if you just stop*, like Declan had. "You've done so much."

"I enjoy supporting the community." Lincoln's smile was crooked under his straight, aristocratic nose. A smirk Carrie would find captivating if she weren't vibrating with rage. "You have my number?"

"Yes," she confirmed, dispersing the dust floating in the air, small grains visible as the sun's dazzling gold hue shifted toward pink. "Why?"

She snuck a glance across the street.

Lincoln moved in her direction, getting near enough that she could smell the spice of his cologne, feel it slither into her nose. "Am I missing the rest of the question?"

"Why do I have your number? You're famous." She'd scoured the web for Asher's contact information and found squat.

"I prefer to handle my own business."

It was precisely what she'd thrown herself into. Business. Scheduling November shoots, updating her website, detailing all six lenses. Then, when the lonely feeling transformed into delicious rage, she'd tracked down Lincoln to his home in the country. Donned her comfiest jeans—should hand and knee groveling be required—and refused to leave unless his name was on her picture.

He'd answered his door without a shirt, shook her hand, and invited her inside for tea, which evolved into dinner. Broccoli and broiled chicken, not a starch in sight. She felt like she could lift a car.

Vegetables. Who knew?

Or maybe rage. Glorious cherry red rage.

"Doesn't the season keep you busy enough?" she asked. Asher was extremely busy. Too busy to answer the phone, to stop by, too busy to tell her he was a fucking liar. Too busy to admit it was his house across the street, his property dwarfing hers, his workers keeping her up at night.

"Not by half." Lincoln's voice was wry, frustrated.

The response set her back. "Are you single?"

He scanned the blacktop and clung to the parallel parked G-wagon. His thick brown eyebrow raised as he tucked a hand deep into his pocket. "Interesting question, considering your attention hasn't strayed from my receiver's car."

Her cheeks splashed pink, even as she feigned innocence. "You saw that?"

"There's little I miss. Especially when it's him, of all people."

"You don't like Asher?"

"He doesn't want me to," Lincoln told her, gaze sweeping up and down Nice Way, checking for other things he might've missed. "Having people hate him is easier. It's his choice. People don't like him because he set the rules, not because they saw him and didn't like it. It's a shield."

A shield. Carrie's chest pounded. "Yes. That's exactly right." Her breath came out quickly. She scrambled closer to the quarterback, tipped her head back to ask. "But why?"

"Why put a steel door on a safe?" Lincoln opened his door and tossed his Ray Bans in the passenger seat. "Must be something worth stealing." In two graceful movements Lincoln folded himself into the driver's seat, long legs crammed under the steering wheel. "I'll see you on the second, Carrie."

She waited ten entire seconds, waving at Lincoln's rearview before she sprinted up her stoop, and threw aside the door. She scowled at the his name printed for all to see.

Don't think of him. Don't. Don't.

Busy. Rage.

A shield. Yes. It was a shield, because Asher was thoughtful and kind—

No. Carrie stomped down the hall, past the box fan drying her carpet and dove into the costume closet, pulling out yards of silky amethyst ribbon.

Her costume. She'd put it off long enough. Worries and fears clipping at her heartstrings. Jack was the answer, the glimmering silver lining to this ruthless storm. If she needed perfection, he'd give it to her. Drown her in perfection.

On her toes, she yanked the cobalt sewing tin from the shelf above her head.

A ceramic mug of pine cones toppled onto the floor.

Reginald.

Before she could shout for him to clean up, she registered the increasingly common slap of her door on the wall.

She squeezed her eyes shut and fisted her ribbons. Diana or Jill or Declan. Didn't matter. She wasn't up for a chat.

"Not now!" She pushed through the fabric coils, winter coats, and puffy, enormous skirts.

The door shut with a bang. "You break my door, you buy it!"

"That's hardly a threat you can follow through on."

Carrie whipped around. Knew exactly who she'd find. Not that it changed the way her heart skyrocketed into her ribs when she discovered Asher in her home. Clad in opulent black, storm clouds in his eyes.

Her breath caught. "You."

Asher ignored the odious tone, marching towards her, intense gaze searching her features, muscles in his jaw flexing wildly. "Forget my name or do you only use it when you're begging?"

"I've never begged—"

"Asher, come over." He pressed her into a wall of clothes, silks and cottons and chiffons tickling her, molding around her as he took a handful of her hair, brought it to his nose in a deviously predatory display. "You still smell like me."

Impossible. "Leave me alone, jackass."

"Now you're doing it on purpose."

"I'm not," she hissed, a plastic hanger jabbing at her nape.

"Liar."

Jackass. She shoved him away and stormed into the kitchen, her ribbons trailing behind. "Fine," she growled. "I am. Because I'm done. With *you*. With this. With calling."

Asher's voice lashed like a crack of lightning. "You're moving out then."

Over her dead body. She whirled to face him, holding smug court in her doorway. She glared. "No. You'll have me as your neighbor for eternity."

His shoulders fell, and she advanced, harnessing five days of loneliness and anger. Rage.

"How long did you think you could keep it from me? That every time you've been here, it wasn't for me. I was a side project, a detour. Whenever Chuck complained about his boss, I should've known it was you. You never once made an effort. Never once came here for me." She was consumed by fury and violence. Brimstone and white hot fire.

He'd let her think it though. Let her imagine fate or destiny kept placing them together, coincidences and surprises. When every visit had been for his house, not her. She was angry enough to raze it.

And in return, Asher was bitter, marrow breaking cold. "Why should I?" he asked evenly. "When you've proven I'm replaceable? Was Lincoln's place easier to break into than me? How quickly did you dismantle his security?"

"Lincoln answered my call. He picked up the phone. And because he abstained from threatening me with the police, or shoving me like a child, he's my date to the GMCA benefit."

There was a drawn-out, icy pause.

His jaw ticked. "Date?"

A technicality. A date only in that Lincoln would be seated in the same row as her. But since Asher didn't look the least bit pleased with her success, she turned to her cabinets, and used more strength than necessary to yank open a drawer, vision too clouded to even search for her fabric shears. "Drinks. Dancing. Bidding. Artwork. Raising money for cancer research."

"And I couldn't do that for you?"

Carrie's jaw unhinged. She scowled at her oven mitts and twisted to look at him. "Fucking excuse me?" Before he could repeat himself, she was off. "I came to you. First. I hiked three miles with a print of your fucking face to ask you. To use *please* and *thank you* and invite you to join me to make a difference. And what did you do, Asher?" She drew in a piercing rattling breath. "*No.*"

"Ask me now."

She banged the drawer shut, moved to the one next to the sink. Batteries and pins and glue. Her pulse pounded, her jaw ached. "No."

"Goddammit Carrie. Ask me."

"*No.*" *Slam.*

"You absolute brat."

She could feel his eyes boring holes into her. But she kept scrambling, kept opening drawers she'd already searched in hopes of finding something new. A subterranean ditch she could hop into. One she could push him down. Somewhere gloomy and dank and teeming with spiders and snakes and a starving carnivore.

Slam. An edgy, twitchy sensation scarred her skin, gave her tunnel vision. How dare he come here and ask her. She wanted blood. Splashed in the corner, dripping down the walls. She wanted to feel his pulse fade under her grip, watch his gaze bulge and then slowly close.

She'd be alone then.

Her fingers slipped on the cabinet handle. She took a deep, centering breath, and heard only silence.

He'd left.

She dropped her chin to her chest, fingers struggling to stay hooked on the shiny gold pull. He left.

Which made perfect sense. The only reason he'd come was for his house, then to shred her apart for Lincoln. He didn't care for her.

"I hate him." The nasty confession echoed, and she wished she could stop her pulse from skipping. "I hate him," she said again, convincing herself, cementing it. How many times to memorize something? Seven? "I hate him, I hate him, I hate him—"

"I do too."

She jerked in surprise and found Asher right behind her.

Before she could scold him, scream or shriek, he hauled her into his arms and his mouth came down to capture hers.

Chapter Twenty-Four

Asher

The kiss was precisely what Asher wished to avoid. Soul sucking and deep and clawing. Too rough to be pleasurable, too addictive to change it. He had Carrie by her hip and her jaw, their every in between aligned, and still he gathered her closer.

He'd known. He'd known as he'd crossed the street, this would happen. He couldn't look at her without tasting her, taking her. He'd just never imagined it like this. Picking her up in his arms, setting her on the edge of the sink and mauling her.

He had imagined it.

Vivid fantasies and painful dreams. He'd obsessed, dick in his hand, Carrie's voicemail on speaker. He pictured silk sheets and flickering candles. A slow, sensual stripping of her clothes. He saw her fingers crooking him forward, stroking his chest, his lips on her cheek, the sweep of her bare shoulder. Indulgent. Elysian.

A union of lovers. A Dashboard Confessional song and a selection of lubes for the lady to choose. A knotted black tie hanging off the door knob and a handful of those self-conscious laughs as they fit together for the first time, as they learned and explored, cooperated.

This kiss was a hostile takeover.

Raw and toxic and dirty.

Hedonistic.

An exchange of anguish. A display of the corrosive pain she'd rammed inside him, seething acid collapsing his ventricles, gunning for the chest.

The pain of his resilience, his refusal, his warring paths shackled to her wrists and ankles.

Pain.

It was winning. The agony dominating. Severing connections in his mind, twisting synapses back to his heart, stinging and biting, shooting pangs of acute pressure and tightness down his spine, twinging every muscle as he twisted his hands around Carrie's waist.

"Why can't you try?" she pleaded against his mouth, pulling back so sharply, her elbow struck the sink behind her.

Cold water sprayed onto the counter, on Asher's knuckles. Leaked to the linoleum.

"I'm falling and I'm tired, Asher." Her fingers fumbled with the chrome faucet, cold to hot. "I keep picking myself up off the floor because you're not here. Because you quit." Her face burrowed into his chest.

Could she hear how fast it beat? Like bullets spraying into foot thick glass, clawing to reach her, to take her out once and for all.

"You leave and leave and leave." She slashed at his shirt, her tongue stroked down his throat.

He swore and kissed her savagely. Pulled back too soon and pressed his forehead to hers. "You are precious. More than you know."

Precious to him. More than he could admit.

A beat and then she was stepping back, shaking fingers pushing off his chest, lashes heavy with unshed tears. He knew she wanted to wipe them away, but she didn't want to draw attention there. Too proud, iron willed. "Not enough."

Too much. So precious he had to protect her. So precious he marred her with his every touch.

With a gentleness he'd only ever used to comfort his temporary siblings in the middle of the night, Asher stroked his thumb over Carrie's dark lashes, collecting the water. And all the while, he told her what he'd told no one before. To stop her from ever crying for him. Because of him.

"Leaving was the goal growing up. Leave the orphanage, leave foster care, leave the system. Get out, get free. Don't look back, it might suck you in again." He watched a new tear form at the corner of her eye. "The good kids got picked, bad kids got left. So we all tried to be good." His gaze fixed on the tiny backyard beyond the sink's window, brown grass poking through bright orange leaves. "I wanted to leave. I didn't care about having a house or toys or my own room. Just clothes without my name stamped on the tag, a pillow with a case. I tried—" He choked there, stomach lacerated in memories.

Carrie's fingers were on his cheek now, caressing. The water was still running. Steam rising.

"I tried every day to leave." Every minute.

She curved her fingers over his ear, tucking hair back. "There are thousands of kids who don't get adopted, Asher. It's not you, it's the lack of support, the lack of opportunity."

"You're wrong," he said harshly. "I stayed."

"You were a child. What choice did you have?"

"I could've screamed for more." He was staring into her eyes, laying the nasty truth bare. "I could've demanded it. Fought. Told somebody what I wanted. Instead, I kept trying to be better, but it didn't matter. Nobody wanted me."

"That's a lie," she said softly. "You had odds against you."

"No, I stayed, Carrie. I stayed and waited until the entire fucking system forgot me. Because I was nice and good and polite like all the kids who got to leave, except I didn't time it right. It took me too long to figure it out. I aged out."

"It's not—"

He closed his eyes. "Do I even like football, Carrie?"

"What?" Her shock was palpable, and it occurred to Asher that he'd never asked himself before.

"I played because my foster dad watched it, but do I? Did I ever fucking wonder? Did anyone ask? Dave didn't give a shit until I got signed."

"I know you like it." He clenched his jaw, and she shook her head. "I do. I know. Look at the photograph, look in it, because it's obvious how much you love it. Just because you started it for the wrong reason doesn't mean you don't enjoy it."

"Like you."

She shook her head again. "You don't need to be someone else for me."

He needed her to understand. "I'm poison to you."

Whenever he was near, he hurt her. He'd do it again. It was written in stone. He'd be the person to destroy her, and here he was seeking her comfort.

"*Christ*," she hissed on an exhale. "You're such an idiot." She was pressing her forehead to his, her lips on his. Once. Twice. Her knees bracketed his hips. "You're not poison, you're morphine. The pain—" Her hold was so tight, he wondered about the cost. The damage. Five purple and blue spots. "I only feel it when you leave, Asher."

It overwhelmed him. His name on her lips, her body tangled with his. Steam enfolding them, drenching their skin.

"End it," she whispered. "End the pain."

He stopped denying himself.

Quit evading and half living.

Asher made his kiss everything he was. Brutal and probing, utterly wicked.

In turn, Carrie whimpered in her throat, and clung to him, tongue entangled with his. His match. It stole so much of his sanity, her feverish mouth and cloying soft lips. He shot an arm to brace them and smacked a puddle of hot water, slipped, hand catching on a open drawer, pushing. Wood snapped.

Forks and spoons, butter knives clattered to the floor. Splashed there.

Carrie buried her face in his neck, licking and sucking. Asher kicked the silverware aside, and cinched an arm around her waist, ran his hand into her back pocket to rock her into him.

Fuck, she looked like a dream. Skirts, leggings, sweatpants. They did a disservice to her ass in jeans. Blue and tight and gripping. It was like finding gold in the sand. Full curves to pair with long limbs. Swells built over time, arcing bends you leaned into without realizing.

Asher wanted to bow her over her ridiculous cluttered couch and sink his teeth into that ass, bury himself in it, then yank her to the floor and fuck in the most primal, hungry, depraved manner he knew. The way he wanted to take her every time another man's name fell out of her mouth.

He wanted his thighs and hers to be pink and raw.

That wasn't an option. It wasn't a version of an option, not a distant cousin. His jaw ached from grinning, from gnashing his molars.

He tugged her closer, needed her faster.

She yelped. A fleeting echo, but more than enough. "Stop," he rasped. "Wait."

"I can't." She spread kisses down his throat, lingering over the corded tendon, slow and languid and tortuous. "Please don't."

"Stop now. We can't."

She shoved him. *Hard.* Hard enough, he had to counterbalance, lean in. The back of her head hit the window, the pane cracked.

She was furious, pendant lights bathing her in amber fire. "Leave then." She jumped off the counter, sliding down his body. "You don't really want me. You want to toy with me and—"

He cut her off. "Carrie." Yanking on his hair, he flashed her a beseeching, self-deprecating look. "Your shoulder. The shoulder

I fucking wrecked. I—" His thumb traced over her cheek and his voice lowered to a whisper. "I need a minute to figure out the best way to properly fuck you without hurting you and I can't because every time I look at you, I want inside you, I want to thrust, ram, and fuck, make you cry out my name. But I made you a promise that I won't hurt you again."

A promise he'd break.

But not yet.

Lashes low, she took a deep breath before she spoke. "I want you Asher. No waiting. Too much waiting. The distance is as good as strangling me." She paused. Swallowed. Said roughly, "I can't breathe without touching you. Can't figure it out unless you're with me. I've never felt so helpless. I need you."

The words settled between them, in her crowded, messy kitchen, flooding and breaking under them. Every detail, from acorns on the stove to needles tucked in the microwave door, would stay with Asher forever. He'd treasure the messy.

He shut his eyes at the confession, eagerness pouring into his veins. Her trapped hand angled from the sling, slipped two fingers into the slat of his button down.

"*Fuck*," he muttered, hands ending up buried in her silky hair. "It's worse when I close my eyes."

He kissed her. Devoured her mouth with his, cutting off any more pain. Sealed them together to stumble through the pleasure.

The resulting rush pumped a hundred magnifying emotions into his blood. Yearning, longing, desire, desperation. A maelstrom erupted, need whipping. Out of control.

He raised her into his arms, licking into her mouth, grabbing a cabinet door to brace them and ripped it clean off the hinges.

"Fuck."

He was an athlete, a master of movement, kept his body in precise control, and he was fracturing under Carrie's undivided attention.

Her chuckle wiped away his frustration, his embarrassment, left him to drag them back together. He dropped the door, heard it splinter, and set her back on the counter. Heat, pulsing and decadent and sinful sizzled between them, a flame protected from the wind eager to raze as their hips pressed flush. Rocked. Grinded.

Tongues, teeth, lips. She tasted like his favorite drink, and AA didn't start until tomorrow.

A deep, roiling pain rioted through him at her touch, the tease of her fingers brushing his bare stomach as her hips swiveled over his overeager cock. He couldn't fuck this up. Couldn't—

Not touching—clawing, ripping at his buttons, nails scratching.

Plans to dominate, seduce, to savor and lavish deteriorated as half his shirt split open.

His hands dropped from her hip to slow or speed or follow.

Follow. Because she knew what she wanted. She ditched his shirt to tackle his belt buckle and anticipation struck like a rainstorm, so thick and gushing, he couldn't see, just felt every jolt that hit his skin, every slip of her finger under his waistband.

Lust lashed him like fresh lightning, wrapping spiteful stinging volts around his torso and singeing, yanking, telling him one thing.

Touch. Share. Pain. Split the pain, the sting, the blistering that didn't hurt, didn't burn. Asher kissed her harder, propping her on the counter to attack her pants button, the zipper. Tilting to yank denim and panties over her ass, shove them down her thighs, peel them off the rest of the way. Twisting, throwing a tangle of clothes across the room.

He wanted her sounds again, the whimpers, the hushed murmurs, the swallowed moans. He wanted them now. He rid her of her flannel.

Steam fogged the window, poured sweat under Asher's palms, down Carrie's neck. He snapped the faucet off, knocked her Marshmallow Fireside hand soap in the water. Sent a prayer for its service.

He was too frantic to save it. To stop the bubbles already exploding over the edge, the reek of caramelizing sugar and syrupy smoke. He needed to see, to understand.

What would it be like if he stayed.

And she seemed desperate to discover too. Unbuckling his slacks, unzipping, nearly falling off the counter.

His hand raised from her waist up the swell of her breast, brushed over her small, peaked nipple. His control snapped, his hips arched upward of their own accord, searching to get closer to her core. He urged her higher, pulled her against him until his tongue moved over her nipple. His fingers slid down the ridges of her spine, locking them tighter.

"Asher, I want—" She whimpered, clawing at curve of his neck.

His body reacted with a surge of urgency, a spike of want and anticipation. He wanted to lift her up and fuck her, completely suspended in his arms, at his mercy, press her perfect ass against the cracked windows and ram into her, see if her freckles left smudges, splay her across the floor and roll his sleeves up for the best meal of his life.

Sliding up her soft inner thigh, his fingers found her core slick with desire.

The dark prideful beast inside him relished the low noises escaping her throat. He slowed, doubled back to any place the sounds grew, charting a languid path to her clit that left them both gasping. He planted the pad of his thumb against her.

It was the manner in which she went pliant, collapsing into him, choppy hair cloaking his shoulder, the complete surrender to his hesitant touch, that freed his control. Killed the monster that lived to fuck and devour.

Rising from its ashes was a creature no less deadly. One that roiled in the promise of deep, slow thrusting, decadent torture, long looks and gasps.

More tender than he'd been, he slid a finger inside her. She pulsed. Purring at his tremulous debauchery.

He lost the faded light of her chandelier, the sparkling soap bubbles, the glow of the rising moon. He only saw the shimmer of her skin, smooth and soft everywhere. Delicate and kissed by the darkest brown freckles, dots up her left forearm, below her knee, where he wanted to grab her thigh.

He wanted to mark them on his own body, reminders that he'd seen each one.

Her hands, freckled too, lovely, slipped inside his fly.

His lust became a hungry gnawing nightmare, thirsting to taste, aware of only one road to satisfaction. Tasting every freckle and laving over the bare patches.

"How are you already this wet?" he asked, wanting her to take it back, never wanting less than this.

Carrie's fingers wound around his length and he groaned.

Fingers slipped. She jerked. Sensitive.

Teeth scraped his neck. Carrie's voice was void of tenderness, it was angry and thrilled. "You don't understand what you do to me," she panted into his ear, clutching him.

He did. He understood. Felt the same way, like she'd lit a firecracker and aimed it at him point blank range. Made his blood liquid flames, stamped thought and reason.

He stroked his finger further up, arm bending around her thigh. She moaned, and he yanked them together. A hard snap.

Her mouth was parted, waiting, vulnerable when he kissed her. Needy and deep and endless.

He wanted to fuck her like this, every part of them touching, soft breasts bouncing against his chest.

Carrie mumbled into his neck, something incoherent, something that sounded like *yes* and *more* and *now* and a fist pounded his chest when he bit her lip and sucked it better, when their thighs kissed and he pinned her there against him, grinding, slipping over her.

His atoms vibrated, anticipating wreckage.

She groaned again, arching to control, to take, pressing frantic kisses to his temples, his cheeks, his throat.

He took her chin, held her there to watch him, see the rise of his chest as he lifted her again, fingers digging into her hip.

"You're shaking," she murmured.

"Ignore it."

Licking down the delicate curve of her shoulder, he stroked her clit with his thumb. Ravenous. He was ravenous. Locking her into him, ensuring she couldn't jostle, he teased her, plunged another finger inside her.

Heaven.

Fuck, they were too close. He couldn't get the right angle. In a frantic burst, he released her to crash to his knees. "Light me up, brat."

Chapter Twenty-Five

Carrie

"A SHER," CARRIE CAREENED FORWARD, bending awkwardly on the few inches of ledge she balanced on. "Wait. You're shaking."

Broad, inviting hands, dirty with black ink, coasted up her bare thighs. The eyes that watched her were hazy with desire. His mouth curved, blessing her with the smirk of a man who could see exactly how wet she was for him.

Asher indulged in the sight, lips curling and spreading, the sleek muscle in his jaw ticking. His tongue offered a preview of what played in his mind, flicking gently at his sharp, white canine. "So are you."

Yes. Shuddering.

Trembling. Because she was trying not to come at nothing more than the promise flaring in his dark, unfocused gaze. Because there were no shadows here, no clothes to hide behind, no screen she could turn off. She had Asher unabridged. His husky whisper and her panting. He teased a single finger through her damp heat.

She forced her knees together.

He was fast, hand ripping freed, eyes flaring. "Brat."

"Ash. Why are you shaking?"

"Nervous tick." He didn't look up as his fingertips skated across her knees, tapped as if to say, *let me in.*

She pointed her toes to push him away. The give of his chest to her slight pressure threw power into Carrie's blood. In this position, seated high above, she felt like a queen and him her most faithful subject. "You're nervous?"

"Aren't you?"

Not even a little. "Worried I won't be able to keep up?"

Dipping his head, he shook back and forth his an-swer—no—and licked the hot skin he'd created under his touch.

Carrie stopped his languid sweep to reach out and brush sweat damp strands of hair off his forehead and cup his cheek. Stare at a man who'd struggled his entire life to satisfy. Feel her heart break a little.

"What's there to worry about?" she asked breathlessly. "Even the bad is good with you. When we're fighting, pushing, when I want to knot bricks to your feet and dump you in Shelburne Pond, there's always ..."

Intensity.

Hazel eyes didn't blink.

"Friction," she settled on, face warming. "Hot glittering fric-tion embedded in your touch." She felt her lips creep up with his. "Why are you smiling?"

He buried his face against her locked knees and groaned. "Be-cause you're making it worse."

Dread was a sharp stone in the black pool of her stomach.

Maybe they didn't work like this. Agreeing and playing. Maybe he needed the fight.

Sadness scored her, tempered her rising boil to a languid simmer. Couldn't they stop fighting? Just this once? Couldn't they lay down weapons, pull their blows? "Tell me how to make it better."

Don't ask me to fight. Not when we're vulnerable and clumsy, holding open, bleeding hearts.

"Stop doing that."

Carrie's mouth sprung open.

"Stop getting goosebumps, stop holding me, no pushing or pulling, stop sounding like—I can't—" His head popped up, chin on her knee. From the angle, she could capture his features perfectly—straight nose, swollen mouth, hair in his devastating hazel eyes—but his attention was on the door. "If you keep reacting, this will be over before it stops, alright? I won't last."

Her brows furrowed.

"I don't sleep around." His teeth sank into her thigh. "So I'm trying to hold it together."

She leaned her head back and laughed. "That's it?" She was pulling him up into her, wanting to kiss that smile, feel it mold onto her.

He was steel, rammed into the earth, immovable. Not looking at her, not smiling.

"Hey—"

"There's no one else." Dark lashes shuddered over his eyes. "I never—" He scrubbed his face harshly. Tore his gaze to hers. "I never even considered it. I haven't slept with anyone."

Silence.

Carrie's eyes were frozen open. A thousand urges bubbled up in her system. Comfort and hold and cuddle, mutter promises to.

Wreck. Ruin. Conquer. Steal.

She stroked his hair and sucked on her lip. How many times could he demolish the vulgar image she had of him? Slice apart her veins and make her bleed?

It wasn't the right time for any of it. He was lowering his shields, she couldn't pity. He'd hate her even more.

She flicked his ear. "I know you've considered it," she challenged playfully. "I have the proof. Something about turning me around and fucking me?"

I'd get fucking minutes, that's it. That's how blinding you are.

Darkened eyes locked on her, lips parted in shock and delight. "Brat."

"You should've answered your phone." She caressed his cheek, softened her voice. "It's me, Ash." A gentle smile. "There's no pressure."

"No one Carrie. What if—"

She'd had enough what ifs for a lifetime. "What if it's better? The best?" She squeezed his nape. "Get up here and kiss me."

A flicker of indecision and then teeth were grazing her thigh, and her legs were thrown apart like they'd only just remembered they were opposing magnets.

A devilish curve shaped his mouth. Hot breath tickled her core. "*No.*"

How did she tell him she missed him like a missing limb? Missed him like her soul had tried detaching from her heart, peeling from her bones. Missed this, how his tongue licked over her core while her head fell against the broken window, cold air whistling at her temple. Missed something they'd never done, but she saw continuing until their hearts gave out.

Carrie hated how the confessions tangled on her tongue. Every time a revelation coalesced into words, he'd wreck it with a suck that made her blood boil.

He'd lied. Mocked. Abandoned. She wanted to suffocate him between her legs.

She wanted to drag him to her lips and pour her last sacred breath into his lungs.

Sinuous, splintering pleasure licked up her spine, chased by a stab of iron hot pain. Her shoulder crying out.

She puffed through the throb, arching to ease the sharp burn.

Strong hands yanked her closer to his mouth, greedy, ravenous as he licked at her. Past shame, past shyness.

She groaned and rocked hard into his face, palm slipping on soap bubbles. Her elbow slammed into the countertop. "Fuck!" she yelped, slapping her thigh at the same moment he plunged two fingers into her. "*Fuck.*"

She watched her skin welt and pink next to his head. Too rough on skin too delicate.

She choked out a shaky laugh, struck with a strange sense of karma. Asher and her, fighting their constant tug of war. Kicking hard whenever the other hit the ground. Spitting. Yanking back only when the pain cut bone deep.

Tough. She heard his words whispered into her ear again. *So tough.*

Something tore in her shoulder and she bit her tongue when Asher sucked her swollen clit into his mouth and buried his fingers to the hilt. Shameless. Messy and shameless.

White hot desire cut across her brain. Fractured lust, every color of the rainbow shattered down her spine.

Tough. Not a soul dared to accuse Carrie Huston of being tough.

But she was.

Asher had cracked her open to show her.

His whispered *tough* echoed though her as bliss and torment blitzed overtight muscles. *Tough.*

She wasn't a flower. She was a damn stick of dynamite and between her legs lay the fuse. "Asher, *fuck.*" She gritted her teeth as the sling scratched her hardened nipple. Inhaled a shaking breath. "Asher."

He couldn't hear, not with her thighs clenched around his head, not with him pinning her there. All virtuous, monstrous hunger.

"I want—" She whimpered. She needed him here with her, at this oxygen thin level. Overwhelmed with blinding pleasure, stalked by pain. She wanted him to have more hands, more fingers, more tongues. She wanted *him.* Inside her, big and pulsing, thrusting. Maybe all of it at once.

His hands flexed, and then she was spread apart, knees splayed, chin falling to her chest, panting. And he thrust his tongue inside her, hot, wet and not enough.

Carrie groaned her despair, feet jerking, breaking her grip from his hair to hold on to the counter. Something loud fell. Water trickled.

The saccharine aroma of vanilla and sugar drenched them. Warm, slippery water seeped into her hip, leaked down her calf, her foot, down Asher's back and dripped onto the linoleum, pooling, staining the knees of Asher's custom suit.

A throaty chuckle rose from between her thighs and hazel eyes snared hers as he licked a stream of bitter water from her ankle to her knee and spat it into his hand. Sunk that hand into the waist of his pants.

She moaned.

Time became an issue. A commodity she was running out of. With a clumsy, feral stretch, she shoved her arm free of its sling to grab him. "Asher," she pleaded. "More. I can't wait."

"Yes." His hand smacked the marshmallow foam as he stole her lips, tasting of her and bitter soap. Of adrenaline and desire. His hands left her to rip open her drawers and Carrie whimpered at his distance, past desperate, shoving the sling over her head. *Tough.*

"Where the hell—" Asher groaned as she threw his boxers down, driving it down powerful thighs. Stared.

He slammed a drawer shut. "Carrie. Where."

"Takeout." She was breathless, gasping, wishing she'd taken geometry more seriously. *Would he even fit?* "By the fridge."

He growled, pulling away, throwing open the drawer, knocking aside chopsticks and soy sauce packets to grab a condom, ripping the foil and sliding it on as he returned to her.

"I'm putting one in every drawer," he murmured, kissing up her throat. "Two." He took her lips, and carefully lined them up, pulled her up and up. Even with her perched on the counter, he towered over her, tipped her hips to accept him.

A hollow blue moment sank between them, emotions hanging like wet sheets on a line. Nervous. Scared. Excited. Terrified. She could practically hear him swallow.

She didn't move save for a small nod, and an angry curl of her fingers around his half open shirt. "I can take it."

"That's never been a question to me."

His hands were still shaking, almost fumbling as he brushed the hair off her cheeks, eyes searching hers. "I can't remember not wanting you." He breathed as he pushed inside her. Slow. Searing.

Carrie hissed.

He didn't blink, not even as his throat bobbed, as his gaze darkened, slaughtered the favorite of her colors. "I want to stay," he muttered, burying his face in her neck. Licking, pushing, stretching. Until finally he was inside her.

Pain.

Wondrous, sinful pain.

Then he moved. Delivered the deep, rolling thrusts she craved, each plunge mimicking the tightening of her soul to her bones, latching onto her muscles, sticking, gluing.

Foreheads together, Carrie panted over his lips. Too long she'd felt empty.

Her wet hand slipped on his face, cupping his cheek, and he smiled. The kind of smile that destroyed, killed. A smile secret and wild. He hauled his shoulders back and, with his blackened hand, drew tiny popping bubbles over her bottom lip. Pulled out and pushed in. Again.

The pleasure became too much, stomping her pain, torturing her with enough heat to fuse iron chains around her heart. Carrie groaned, climax barreling down her spine before she could suffer the dark, bitter dream. It was impossible to contain herself with him, to stifle and bite her cheek to quiet.

Grappling. Hands biting skin. Close. Closer. Needy fingertips. Squeezing hips.

Carrie gave into it, the world stalling, bliss blurring her vision as she rocked forward, taking the orgasm like it was the last one he'd ever give, wanting to make it last. His thrusts skipped and quickened, and then his face was in her neck, his groan shaking her body.

She cried out his name.

A moment passed. Then Asher laughed, warm breath tightening her nipple. "Next time," he licked the point. "These are getting more attention."

He pulled back, *out* with a ragged hiss, kissed her cheek, and vanished down the hall, tight ass flexing unabashedly. He returned wearing boxers, carrying tissues and a pair of Carrie's favorite white sweatpants and methodically spoiled her. Helping her off the counter and into her underwear, pants, socks. He kissed the tender spot on her shoulder. "Couch."

She giggled, grabbing paper towels as he shucked his pants on, buckled his belt.

"And where are you going?" she asked, mopping up the bubble explosion.

She couldn't feel all ten toes, and two of her cabinet doors were broken, her window cracked, a drawer in pieces. A shiver wracked through her. *Tough.*

There was something deadly, sorely wicked about proving how tough, about outlasting her house.

"Nowhere, brat." He swatted her ass. "Couch."

He met her there in minutes. Shirtless, skin gleaming with a beautiful sheen of sweat, hair flopped on his forehead. "Tea." He passed her a steaming mug. Then, "Ice." And a bag of pepperoni pizza rolls draped over her shoulder.

He sat on her ottoman, knees spread, shoulders level, nail marks on his pecs, bites on his neck, and a blush on his cheeks.

He smiled.

Her chest swelled, contracted and burst. Contorted painfully. Hollowness cramming full of the man in front of her.

Tears obscured her vision. She felt her stomach cramp, lost her breath, like she'd been punched in the solar plexus.

Everything twisted, warped. Tough and strong yanked from within her reach. Shifted. Sidestepped beyond grasp. Tough, yes. But not without him.

"Asher. I— I've—" She didn't realize she was hyperventilating until his stare speared wide, didn't understand she was sobbing until wet landed on her hand.

Terrified, Asher bent forward, two fingers crawling up her arm. "It's hitting you? The pain? We should've gone slow. *Shit*." He started adjusting the pseudo ice pack, taking the tea from her, fussing.

No. The pain was far away, fleeting snow on a mountaintop.

She loved him.

It wasn't a question or a concept or a possibility she could send to the back burner.

She loved him, mind, body, soul, consumed. Him. She felt stretched in too many directions. Seconds from shredding.

Jack, was all she thought, in the haze of pain and pleasure. Jack was getting shoved aside.

Jack was nice.

Asher, this quiet comfort, his hand caressing her shoulder, sent a terrible disorienting sensation over her.

"Carrie. I need you to answer me." His voice was serious as he angled her face to his.

She blinked. *Don't tell him. Wait. Say anything else. Don't say it. Don't say it.*

Her lips screwed into a wobbly smile. Terror shocked her veins.

Say something nice. Don't frighten him. Light. Fun. Tease. Don't scare the man you're gone for.

She pulled her cheek out of his reach. Somehow, it felt too intimate.

He waited, hand hanging midair, fingers drooping. "I was too rough."

Her eyes filled. *Don't say it. Don't tell him. Don't make him run.*

"You were perfect." She had to smile, couldn't ruin this for him. "What now?"

"Ice. Repeat."

She nodded, mind clearing, lungs filling. Deep breaths. "Paul will hang you if we keep him up all night."

"He'll have to catch me first," Asher teased, sliding onto the loveseat next to her, ignoring the blankets toppling into his lap. He grabbed her remote. "What's his split time?"

"He's gotten a lot faster since he added tennis balls on his walker." Except now when he went too quick, his hair stood on its ends.

"He has a walker." He looked at her, mouth open. "And you thought I'd fight him?"

"Are you saying you'd refuse to fight somebody with a walker?"

"Yes, dammit."

Easy. Light. She smiled and pinched his thigh. "Not very ablest of you. Paul can fight anyone he wants. And win."

"Ye of little faith." He raised his arm for her, and she snuggled under. Warm. He was so warm. Even in her cold house. "What are we watching? The royal wedding? Downton? The"—he snapped his fingers—"slutty one. With the duke."

Bridgerton. "I have no idea what you're on about. I only watch very serious documentaries about global health crises."

He kissed her. Quick. Easy. "You're such a fucking liar."

She snuggled closer, ignoring how easy this was. How comfortable they were. How there'd been no awkwardness after, no regrets.

She laid her cheek on his shoulder. "What's my tell? Twitchy eye? My fingers aren't crossed. Voice change?" He scrubbed his jaw, blush back on his high cheekbones. "You have to tell me. What if you kill Paul and I have to cover it up, but I've got a lisp and crossed eyes? You'd have life in prison."

"Please, you would blame me before the police finished asking the question." He tugged their hips together again, spun the remote in his fingers. "You don't have one."

"What?"

He swallowed, arm rigid over her. "I can't tell when you're lying.

"But, you—"

"I just say it when I hope you are."

I hate you, she'd said.

Liar.

Chapter Twenty-Six

Asher

Asher's jaw sealed tight under the unwavering focus of Burton's scowl. He was losing enamel faster than the ice caps were disappearing. But there was no scenario—building swallowing fire, killer bees, aliens among us—in which Asher was going to ask about the slip of black paper Burton had tossed on his desk.

If he showed interest, he might as well hand over his balls.

"Got it." That was all he'd said. Burton's chilling greeting continued to circle in Asher's mind as he took twice as long to dial 1-0-31 into the wall safe.

The tight end pounded his heel into the tile. "Stop fucking around."

Apt words. "Cutting it close, don't you think?" Asher turned and leaned against the wall, folding his arms. "Information first."

Burton's demeanor shifted, gaze hard, incisive, locked to the paper in front of him. The office smelled like wood and bitter black tea with sprinkles of fresh snow. And whiskey.

Thanks to his guest.

Burton narrowed his eyes, stared.

Asher smiled. *All day, old man.*

"Little shit," Burton growled, shrugging big shoulders against the leather back of Asher's desk chair. "I played mine first, busted my ass to get to you. You better ante up."

Asher could see the white curly cue numbers from here. A phone number. Definitely not Burton's writing. His PI handed it off directly. Spinning digits, connected by flicks of the pen. Only seven. Local.

"My down payment covered a name, not a number. I have a phone book."

Burton rubbed his jaw, a solid block under his wild beard that had started to salt and pepper.

"She's not in it." He lifted Asher's MVP trophy into the light and spun it, feigning interest. As if he didn't have four sitting in a box somewhere. "But I'll double down."

Asher resisted the shock, battled the squeeze of oxygen from every cell in his blood. Name. Number. He'd found her. Years. Years in the shadows, searching, and now he'd know.

He'd found her.

Unbidden, a vision came. Of Carrie. Three nights ago. Her rolling into him on the couch, her mouth against his throat, the mewled *no* when he moved to stand. Bleary-eyed, his murmured *I have practice at six* and her corresponding bite on his pulse, the lick against the small, sensual hurt. Her hand fisting in his hair at his nape. Flashes of a Victorian ballroom on the TV bathed Carrie in shimmering gold and silver, making her hair into a milky way and her eyes rare gems.

He'd stopped moving when she swung a leg across his lap. Shared a kiss that took over his mouth. "I need sleep, brat," he'd whispered, clenching her hip, refusing to let go.

She'd bit down on his lip next. Water from her thawed pizza bites stained her sling, a midnight shadow on the blue, black ink running. "Not nearly as much as I need you." She'd slid their hips together, a perfect cradle. "It's only a few hours anyway, hardly worth the trouble."

He'd agreed as she'd tightened her thighs. He'd had a feeling she'd keep coming up with reasons if he argued. List them off without ever having to say the word he was terrified to hear.

Stay.

Yet stay he had.

Holmes never stayed. She was always leaving.

Asher yearning to follow.

"Adelaide Heatley." Burton's growly voice jerked Asher back into the present. "Fits most descriptions. Twenty-five. Summers in Europe. Went to boarding schools in Cambridge. Comes from wealth. Tall, blonde. Skinny. An event planner. Confirmed she'll be at The Hand."

Walking carefully to his desk, Asher dropped off a silk bag. Burton's payment. Gold set ruby ring. Burton fit it on the tip of his pinky finger, twirl it. Raised his hand. "Exquisite."

A jarring moment was Burton the Boar marveling at hand crafted beauty.

He stood and put his hands on his hips, pushing aside his warm-up jacket to uncover ripped jean shorts. "Like taking candy from a baby."

"I mean this with as little respect as possible: get out and never come back."

Burton paused in the doorway. "Tell Riley I found the weasel, too. He was a lot easier."

Asher clenched his fist. "Where?"

"Hospital. Doing physical therapy with his grandma if you'd believe it."

Asher reached for the safe, but Burton was shaking his head. "It's on the house. This time."

Adelaide.

Asher snatched the number.

Chapter Twenty-Seven

Carrie

I T WAS LIGHT AND warm inside Asher's apartment, paneled in a cream board and batten and void of any life. Boxy windows were encased with ivory linen curtains, ironed into pleats and pinned aside with gold hooks. Such exactness she expected from him.

The same precision she deemed certifiable, annoying and yeah, sexy when he meticulously cleaned the cum from her thighs.

The furniture was crisp, cushions that'd never seen the crunch of a sloppy sit down or belly flop. One couch, a lonely chair. A glass coffee table that Carrie could wrap in cellophane and return full price.

No pillows, or blankets, no old US magazine with really juicy articles on Selena Gomez's love life.

Hollow.

Carrie's stomach wrenched at the realization. She'd learn more about Asher by falling into a wormhole than visiting him here.

No knick knacks or memories, no toad figurine playing the ukulele. A gift he may have never wanted, never hinted at liking, but someone had seen it in a store, turned it over in their hands and thought of him. Scanned the price tag and only grew more confident that this present, this porcelain toad, was perfect for Asher.

There was no toad that he hated, yearned to give back, contemplated re-gifting, flat out returning, but every time he considered it, looked in the googly eyes and thought *why, why would they get this for me?* he'd change his mind. Because they *had* thought of him. No matter how misguided, he'd been in their thoughts, so he'd kept it. Dusted it. Named it Sheldon and told guests he played Somewhere Over the Rainbow poorly on his three string ukulele.

But there was no toad. That existed in the wormhole.

In an alternate reality.

Because that had never happened to Asher. Because his dad didn't drink tequila sunrises and scroll on eBay. His mom hadn't conflated a love of otters for toads.

Carrie wanted to get him a toad. A mariachi band of toads, each wartier than the last.

She'd never been to a five-star hotel, but she imagined it felt like this. A place so lacking in personality that it felt futuristic, otherworldly. So out of touch, she couldn't relax until she saw it—a gleaming bar cart. She strode through spotless glass French doors into an expansive office. Desk-chair, standard but the cart—

Immaculate. Ornate. Vintage. Restored meticulously. It reminded Carrie of something her mother would drag home in her hatchback. She'd polish it for days, vow she'd sell it, and a month later it'd be holding candles in the upstairs bathroom. Carrie reached for the mirrored shelf.

"Put your hands up."

She grinned, twisting, caught.

Asher leaned nonchalantly in the doorway, his legs elegantly crossed. Charcoal slacks, camel belt, and an ivory button up, all wrinkle free. His hair was wet, slithering onyx raked back. His eyes were tangled in color, chocolate and mint and framed by midnight lashes. Perfectly sloped nose, cheekbones sharp as jagged glass. Lips a dream come true.

Carrie loved him.

She'd buy him a thousand toads.

She strolled across the room and locked her arms around his neck. He smelled heavenly good. Fresh and clean. Almost identical to her favorite shower gel—the one she'd bought—

No.

"A storm destroyed my kitchen," she pouted. "Feed me."

Asher wasn't smiling. He was prying her off him.

Her heart wrenched, humiliation building. She'd pushed him too quickly with a visit. He didn't feel the same. It was over—

"Where's your sling?" he asked, voice laced with concern.

Her heart resumed its beating. She cleared her throat, swallowing down panic, letting relief wash in. "I took it off."

A preemptive maneuver. Because the last time she'd been within screaming distance of Asher, she'd punched free of it.

"You need at least two more weeks."

"I'm tough. It doesn't hurt anymore." Plus, she wanted to do *this*. Cinch her arms around his middle, tip her head back and plant her chin on his sternum. "I think you should kiss me now."

"Suddenly I find myself wanting to catalogue your thoughts." A flare of mischief in his eye was the last thing she saw before her feet lifted off the floor and he was kissing her. Hot and heavy and heady. Fingers in her hair, arm wound around her waist, hands kneading her ass. His skin was still supple from the shower, and she drank him in. Pleasure slammed through her in his embrace. The man who'd given himself to her, laid down his shield.

She pulled tighter into him, smiling into his mouth until she was grinning too big to kiss.

His tongue softly flicked the pulse in her neck. "You break in?"

"No."

His teeth grazed her shoulder. "Liar."

"Your door was unlocked."

"I employ 24 hour security.

"I pre-ordered the Fa-la-la Nutmeg granola, and Artie's loyalty shifted dramatically."

"My first instinct," he murmured against the underside of her jaw, "is to be furious, but that almost sounds healthy."

She smiled, working the clasps of his buttons. "I'll eat it over ice cream. With sprinkles." She'd share, spread chocolate swirl down her stomach.

His phone rang, and her feet smacked the tile.

"*Shit*. I have to take this." He was already sliding the green bar, backing up. "Help yourself to anything."

There wasn't a thing she'd find in Asher's washboard-abs-cider's-too-sweet fridge she'd consider edible, but Carrie let him storm down the hall, anyway.

Because he'd just left her alone. In his apartment. Like a damn fool.

***

S HE DOVE RIGHT IN, no testing the water, full-blown cannonball. Sprinting like she was in heat one of a cutthroat Easter egg hunt, she went for the obvious finds.

Diana said be wary. Carrie listened.

But there were no coins between his cushions. Not a single stray hair on the carpet.

His view lacked any sort of compromising image, no flash of the naked neighbors going at it. Just a million dollar panorama of Church Street. Students striding determinedly to campus, heavy backpacks and oversized headphones.

In two days, the puffy coats and Uggs would be gone, the cobblestone would bloat with people in costumes violating open container laws and shriek-singing the Monster Mash.

Frowning, Carrie hurried to the kitchen. Maple cabinets, granite counter, recess lighting.

There.

Beside an elegant French press—classy prick—she uncovered the first sign of life. A single wick candle. Before thinking, she pried off the lid and inhaled deeply.

Whipped vanilla, cold air, and a freshly opened packet of the white sugar. The wick was black from use and when she overturned it, fingers making prints on the frosted silver glass, she rolled her eyes. Spun confection and winter spice.

Rich people words, a fancy version of her ultra sumptuous special occasion body butter. Vanilla Dream. A lotion so thick, it required naked dry time and a hundred tiny circles to seep into her skin. A lotion for mindless, undeserving self-care days and post The Shower showers, when not a hair existed nor a pore was visible.

Of course, he'd cherish the scent. Stealing yet another one of Carrie's simple pleasures. Gin, whipped vanilla. Next thing she knew, she'd be splitting the extra crispy fries with him.

And she would.

Happily.

With hopes to find a lighter, match, or flamethrower—wasn't her apartment—she opened the nearest drawer. Discovered a single silverware set. Spoon, fork, and knife.

She stared, heart breaking.

At least when they moved in together, there wouldn't be excess.

The idea curled around Carrie like thick toxic smoke. *Living together.*

Her and Asher carrying boxes. He'd label them all in his boxy capital letter writing. Kitchen comma drawer comma singular fork comma fragile. Double tape it at every seam for guaranteed travel protection.

Only to slice open the box and find that Carrie had put in Singular Fork, and in the empty space chucked along paintbrushes and toothpaste and her egg timer and the navy ramen bowls.

He'd give her that frustrated, I'll-kill-you look, jaw bunched with tension and growl something like *you've ruined the entire schedule. How am I supposed to unpack this? Where in the kitchen do paintbrushes go? Am I brushing my teeth in the fridge?*

And she'd have to stop him from squirting Artic Mint on the tile by claiming she'd made moving fun. Each box it's own present. When really, she'd done it for this. For the dilated pupils, the angry snap of his tongue over his teeth. For the fight, the explosion, the friction.

His and hers sides of the bed. A thousand of her blankets folded in his tight, tucked corners. Gin and football and Jane Eyre. Rows of serious midnight suits and Carrie's paint smock and camera harness.

She found envelopes in the next drawer. Perfect. Pulling the fundraiser ticket from her back pocket, she snatched one and opened it, ready to slobber all over the seal and write a dirty innuendo about a surprise inside until a tube of paper snared her attention.

Blueprints.

His house. She glanced at the doorway Asher had disappeared through and worked double time, grabbing the roll and spreading it across the dark countertop, smoothing it with her fingertips, squinting.

Twenty Nice Way, but which way was north? Despite how she spun it, it was wrong.

Missing her place.

No, not missing Twenty-one Nice Way. Gone. Replaced with a garden, complete with impermeable walking path and hedgerows.

Heinous black oil brewed in the pit of Carrie's throat. Her stomach rolled. The candle dropped to the floor, shattered on the tile.

She was moving again, less direct, stumbling, reading, squeezing the papers, shaking her head, vaguely registering the passing rooms, the hall, the guest suite, his bedroom before she heard him, whispering in the closet.

He'd taken the call in his closet, huddled over the receiver, hand over his mouth.

Discussing this? Her ruination? Her worst nightmare?

"What is this?" she asked, her voice not her own. Shrill and shaking. The papers were limp in her grip, crunching and tearing. "Asher?"

Hazel eyes lifted to hers, tracking over her face, and then dropping down, locking onto the evidence. "Where did you find that?"

Blood rushed to her ears. "It doesn't really matter, does it? Because I found it."

He gazed directly at her, with eyes devoid of any emotion. "You weren't meant to see it."

"You're tearing down my house?" Heat surged behind her eyes. There was too much spit in her mouth, and her knees ached. Rage. Red and vicious, it filled up the room and flooded into her. "Were you ever planning to tell me? Or was it a fun game? Torture me and then once I'm out on the curb, send in the wrecking ball?"

"That place is a death trap." A growl sounded from low in his throat and he started to reach for her, but Carrie stumbled back. "Come on, Carrie. You know that. Fuck, it's a miracle hasn't collapsed around you already. It's dangerous."

"So this is chivalry?" She threw the papers at him, ice in her tone. "I don't fucking want it."

His eyes flashed. "No one should live there."

"You've decided. So that's that? How"—she raised her hand at him, snarling, crumbling—"dare you. It's the only tie I have to my mother. I told you." Regret thrummed through her, hacking her soul into flimsy shreds to blow away in a breeze.

Asher stepped forward, mumbling an *I'll you call* into his phone.

Suits surrounded them. Black suits, navy suits, black again. All paired perfectly. All sorts of fancy, slick shoes lined the wall in neat pairs.

Carrie wanted to shred them, tie knots in the sleeves, pour used litter in the brogues.

"It's not habitable, Carrie. It's that simple."

He didn't know how the words stung. "My dad sold our home as soon as she died. He ran. He didn't take anything. This is my only link to her. Just this house. Three years of her life. She painted the door herself. Hung the chandelier in my bedroom. This is it and you—" The words caught in her throat. She couldn't breathe. She grasped a suit sleeve as her legs wobbled. "You want to take her away from me." Her voice was small and perplexed and devastating.

"Of course not," he told her, advancing again.

"I'm alone without the house!"

Her shout stopped him, and in the closet bigger than her bedroom, she heard his teeth slam together, saw and grind. "Your mother's dead? You never told me. I—"

"Oh my god," she sank her nails into the thick fabric, realization like a knife to the chest. "You weren't going to tell me. Of course not. You didn't even mention that the mansion across the street is yours. You were just going to blow in, this elusive, intoxicating hero intent to hack me apart. My home—oh my god." The room was spinning around her. She couldn't breathe. Asher's hands were touching her and they made her flinch. "Don't touch me. *Don't.*" Her voice cracked on the command.

"Let's talk about this," he said too slowly. "You never told me about your mom."

Her gaze tracked over his face for a sign, running over the sculpted cheeks and his long nose, the inky brows. "Does it change anything?"

His mouth opened.

Silence.

"Oh, god." She shoved him, staggering out of the closet, tears streaming down her face. Briefly, she registered the massive white bed. Wanted to throw crimson latex paint on it. "You ruined my cabinets. We broke a window," she rasped. "Oh my god, I thought it was romantic and sexy, that we were living in the moment. I thought you were—" frantic, obsessed, in love. "You did it on purpose."

"No," Asher barked. "Absolutely not."

"You did." She didn't think she could bear it. Anguish pulled her down.

"No. Carrie." His footsteps chased after her. "Nothing with you has ever been planned."

Planned. When she'd found literal plans for her greatest fear. "The only place I feel at home." Where was she? How did she leave? She stormed rooms and swallowed a laugh. Another maze. Same wretched ending. "You're so methodical." She was shaking her head. The knot in her throat pulsed with emotion. "You planned every detail. I don't know why I couldn't listen to you. I'm so stupid. You told me."

"Carrie, slow down. Stop. You need to talk to me."

She wouldn't look at him. Couldn't.

"I can't keep doing this," she croaked, storming through the broken glass in the kitchen, charging across the living. She wasn't talking to him anymore, he didn't get more.

"Men tell me they're bad and I don't listen," she hissed. "You told me and I didn't believe you." She needed to get out. She needed to escape. She found the door. Cracked it wide. Heard Asher kick through the glass, a curse on his lips.

"Carrie. Stop! Carrie, come back here right now."

But she was at the door, slamming it behind her as hard as she could. Stairs. Get to the stairs. At the end of the hall, the elevator doors opened and Jesus took that fucking wheel as she burst inside.

Asher flung open the door behind her. "Carrie, goddammit!"

She hit a tall hard body and a sheet of plastic wrap.

"Hey, whoa." Riley caught her in a bear hug, sporting summer green from top to bottom. Plastic encased gray garment bags in his hand. "Is that Asher?"

"Close it, close it, close it, close it." She was clenching the front of his sweatshirt, making knots. Her knees were locked and the pain in her shoulder was back and brutal.

"Riley!"

"Okay, okay." He moved quickly, finding the right button.

"No!" Asher's shout was cut off.

And she went to the ground. Crying out.

She couldn't feel her heart, but she knew it was shattering. Shards digging into her veins and corroding. She didn't want to feel a thing. She didn't want to love the man she hated. But love wasn't a reasonable emotion. All it saw was Asher chasing after her, repeating her name.

"Holy shit." Riley set down his bags. "Are you okay? What happened?" A pause. His concern morphed into worry. "Did Asher tell you?"

Her throat felt so thick she couldn't talk, she couldn't think. She looked at the clothing bags creased in half on the cold ground.

And then she was feral, pushing Riley to the side, tackling the long garment bags, shredding the plastic as her synapses short-circuited. She jerked down the zipper, threw back the fabric. Trembled.

"Is this yours?" she asked, lifting a charcoal sleeve.

"It's just a Halloween costume. What's going on? Why are you running from Asher?"

"It's his." Her mind was blank. Her fingers strangled a gentleman's cravat. White linen shirtsleeves, a fitted waistcoat, and trousers.

A Lord. And wasn't that the perfect fit? As Carrie had spent months crafting the ideal Lady.

The elevator dinged down another level. Slowly descending.

"I'm dying," Carrie panted, collapsing to the floor, burying her face in her hands. "*Hew*," she snarled, shoving the costume away, letting it bunch and wrinkle.

"How?" she cried, hunched over her knees. "How could it be him? Jack detests gin. How could *he* be Jack?"

"What are you—" Riley glanced at the costume and then at her. Gulped. "We should have known it," he muttered, falling back against the silver wall. "How didn't we fucking guess? Diana's your best friend. She owns The Hand. *Fucking A*, I do the Times crossword and I don't see this?"

"You didn't know?" she asked quietly. Frozen with pain.

He shook his head, scrutinizing her as if she were a rare specimen trapped under a microscope.

"Diana uses old British curses. And says you're obsessed with that shit. How did I miss it? She told me Asher never stood a chance with you. Said it like she knew it. Because you were in love with somebody else." He covered his face. "*Fuck*."

Carrie grasped at her knees. "You can't tell him." She was bleeding out here on the elevator floor. Her present and future deteriorating with every dropping level.

"Don't tell him. Please don't tell him. I can't face it." She scrambled to him, clasped his hands. She should've been embarrassed, pleading on her knees to a near stranger, but she'd rather strip herself naked in the middle of The Peak than lose anything else right now.

Riley sounded pained. "He's my best friend."

Guilt had him avoiding her eyes. Carrie made herself inhale. "You want Diana?" she asked, past desperate. "Done. Whatever you want. A kiss. A date."

"She'd kill you for bargaining with her."

It wasn't denial. "She'll agree."

Diana would let Carrie push a broadsword through her fifth and sixth ribs if she had a reason.

Usually wide eyes narrowed. "Why?"

"I'd do the same for her."

"Why don't you want him to know?"

She wished there was a clean, pink bow tie, curled ribbons answer. Wished to check a box on a long list of inevitable behaviors. *Betrayed by the man you love? First things first: haggle your bestie's virginity (kinda) and swear his friend to a duping of the century. Check.*

The truth was, he'd hid from her, and now she wanted to haul bulletproof sheeting over everything he didn't know about her. However little was left.

Wetting her lips, Carrie's nails pierced half circles into her shin. "I lost my mom when I was seventeen to ovarian cancer. We'd known. She'd been battling for years. But knowing doesn't make it any less sudden. My dad—" His wrinkled hand clutching her mom until she was cold. "A child is expected to lose their parent. It's inevitable. But no one expects to lose their soul mate. I wanted a love like theirs my entire life, and I got it. The pain. The worst pain I've ever felt."

They peered at each other, Riley sorrowful, Carrie breaking, listening to the slow tick of passing floors. She wished she cried less, could explain how it felt like every happy memory she'd ever had was unraveling and the strings inside were black with mold.

"He's fast," Riley told her as the elevator's momentum slowed toward the lobby. "And I'll try, but I'm not a blocker."

"Will you tell—"

He nodded. "Two days."

"Thank you."

"He'll come for you," Riley warned, helping her stand, tucking hair behind her ear. "I don't think he'd stop chasing you, whether or not he figures it out."

Why couldn't it have been Riley? On the barstool, in the end zone, on her doorstep? He'd have made her laugh, treated her with utmost respect. There'd be no passion, but there'd be no destruction either.

She managed a tiny smile and leaned into his warm, gentle palm for a moment. Pulled his wrist away. "He doesn't even come when I beg."

The elevator doors parted, and Carrie wished she had time to embrace Riley. Thank him again, but she saw him.

As if he were the only light in the lobby, her eyes fixated on Asher. Tight fist pressed against the open door of the stairwell, breath sawing, jaw tight.

She charged. Converse slapping the marble floors.

"Running, Carrie? You really ought to know better." His voice was void of any warmth as he moved to intercept her.

"You," she rasped, vision wonky, clouded and dark, lungs empty. Her shoulder throbbed, but she was glad she didn't have her sling so she could put her full power into her swing.

The slap echoed.

Asher didn't flinch.

Not as a grotesque pink bloomed over his cheek, and a muscle jumped under his eye. He didn't move as fresh tears came down Carrie's cheeks, as she shook out her hand out.

"You're dead to me."

From behind his desk, Artie yelled *cops* and *calling* and *freeze*.

Asher didn't look away from her, but he told Artie, "Don't. She's earned it."

Maybe the most decent thing he'd ever said.

CHAPTER TWENTY-EIGHT
CARRIE

"M EGAN'S A LOT TALLER than you." Crouching, Diana gathered more gauzy shamrock green fabric in her hands, folding it over, and presenting a palm to Carrie. "Pin."

It was their second package of safety pins. The first was spent making sure the wings held tight.

Magnificent jade wings Carrie had never wanted, wings that busted door frames, whacked heads, left that vicious red streak on Diana's forehead. Heavy, starched wings with glittering gem patterns and barbed tips as savage as fish hooks.

A fairy.

In a haunted forest. The Hand had transformed. Radiant black candles threw shadows on the floor. Rich ruby and emerald bulbs feigned the atmosphere of a canopy high above, trapping partygoers in the starless and ominous wild. Enormous, carved tree trunks protruded from the walls, fat branches home to owls and fox, scared faces half hidden, eyes black. Horrifying and beautiful.

Diana had peaked.

The staff were fairies. Most were glorious and killer and nasty, but a few, like Megan, were merely devious tricksters.

"Will Ethan be okay?" Ethan, Megan's youngest, had eaten all the mystery flavor AirHeads after their trick or treating and quickly ruined the mystery by vomiting so intensely Megan's babysitter called her home.

Silver lining, Carrie had a costume that needed no match.

"He ate too much candy. He'll get over it. I drink too much every day and I haven't been to the doctor in ten years."

"You are a beacon of health."

Diana tipped her head.

Wicked, winding vines crawled over Carrie's arms and up her neck, creating the illusion of a high collar, but the dress was sinfully low. A Lady would cake her freckles, braid coronets into her hair, and rouge her cheeks.

Carrie wore a peridot head band and thorns. Diana didn't keep a mirror in her office, so they were working with a blush compact. From what Carrie glimpsed, she resembled kid playing evil queen. Swollen and bloodshot eyes, chapped lips, locks prisoner to a sad, straight bob.

Why did she get a bob?

The flared leafy skirts draped past her knees, turning what was meant to be a sexy and dangerous and whimsical into childish.

Diana rose slowly, inspecting her work, squeezing between the wings and her solid walnut desk to yank Carrie's bodice closed. "That's the best I got. I wouldn't recommend running, reaching, or dancing. Also, be careful sitting because you might end up stabbing yourself and absolutely no metal detectors."

"The wings are heavy," Carrie twisted slightly, trying to find her new center.

"And they're rentals. I will remove your kidneys if you damage them. That's how expensive they are."

Costumes—not for the sake of exploitation—were not in Diana's vocabulary. She wore her signature black, dolled up with a silver eyebrow stud, chain-link belt, and brass knuckle ring, equal parts deadly and stylish.

"Drink?" Diana rounded her desk and retrieved her Casamigos. A compromise between her taste for larynx melting whiskey and Carrie's romance with gin. "I don't have limes in here," she warned, filling two stubby glasses.

"I'm far past needing a lime." Carrie drank hers on a reverse inhale. Shuddered.

She expected a reaction from Diana, whether it be a laugh, smile, or slow clap. Maybe a ten second bottle pull to prove she was reigning champ. But Diana set her shot and folded her arms. "Are you certain about this?"

Diana had taken the news of the Jack-Asher paradigm with far less crying than Carrie.

She'd nodded, paced, asked 'and you're sure?' half a dozen times, then she'd smiled and reclined in her chair. "You are the only person who can fall in love with two completely different men and find out they're the same."

Then Carrie dropped the bomb. The site plans. Her house.

The smile vanished and in a fit of marvelous feminine rage, Diana'd kicked her door clear off its hinges.

The sweet gesture only caused Carrie to erupt in fresh tears.

"If you want," Diana said, folding arms across the shrieking skull on her chest. "I'll shut this whole thing down. I've got a canister of starter fluid in the truck, Declan's packing lighters. We'll start over in Maine. It's easier than it sounds."

"No, absolutely not." Because one, it was arson. Two, Maine was essentially Canada. And Three, he wouldn't win. "Asher doesn't get to steal Halloween from me. He can take my job and the neighbors and my house, but not this."

"Hells yeah."

She suppressed tears, not wanting to ruin her makeup. "You don't think he'll show, do you?" Did she want him too? He'd chase you forever.

"If he does, I'll introduce his molars to my bat and tag Declan in for a game of break the arsehole into fun sized pieces."

"No. You can't."

"Please don't protect him." She'd never heard Diana's voice so soft.

"He won't come." Carrie snatched Diana's glass. Shot it. Burned internally. "He won't and if he does, it means he never wanted me. He only wanted the fantasy." She dabbed her cheeks. "And that's..."

Worse.

It was worse.

To have him see her wholly—tears and laughs, and slaps—and know he still yearned for the perfect version. Someone she could never be.

"Why couldn't I pick someone good? For once?"

"You picked me," Diana replied. "Carrie, you chose me, and I will never hurt you. It's not you. It's the world. It's tragic and rotten and you're too sweet for it."

She wasn't. She'd slapped him.

The blue towel—nailed to the header and masquerading as a door—slid aside to reveal Declan in black on black. The Lovatt siblings rarely strayed.

"We've reached capacity." He peered at Carrie, the empty glass she cradled. "Say the word. Doesn't matter who he is. I'll end him."

"Dismembered style," Diana added.

"Flayed and freezer packed."

"Fed to the earth's molten core in screaming strips."

"Make his browser history public access."

Because of the wings, Carrie couldn't hug them, so she reached out, resting a hand on each of the Lovatt's cheeks. "I love you too." They never said it, but she could interpret it well enough. "Thank you. But I'm okay. It's our night. I want to have fun."

Diana retrieved her glass, filled it and shot it. "You still have a vomit bucket at your place?" she asked her big brother.

"If you're referring to my favorite blue salad dish, yes, I have it."

"It's held more vomit than salad, therefore it's a vomit bowl. And I think it's getting a workout tonight."

"Reminds me," Declan pulled out his phone, and asked Carrie, "What else do you want me to bring from the house? I have clothes and blankets."

Carrie shrugged. Crashing at Declan's sketchy studio was mostly a blur. Diana rubbing her back, vowing to massacre mankind, feeding Carrie fries, restarting Pride and Prejudice (2005) over and over.

"Clothes and blankets?" Diana flashed a you're-an-idiot look that only a sibling could survive. "That's not a list. Those are nouns. What are you going to do, pack all of her clothes?"

"How many can she have?"

Diana clearly thought he'd lost his mind. "It's Carrie!"

Declan frowned. "I don't know. Should I wish for a fucking scrapbook? She's not really a fairy, D."

"You do not D me, D."

Amidst the tangle of another sibling showdown—incredibly often after any charged emotional event—Carrie snuck out of Diana's office. She wanted to see Diana's vision. The smoke machines, and poison apple martinis. Dance with a wood nymph.

See if he'd come.

With the windows taped over with paper, it was hard to believe the Hand had ever been a bar. Gnarled branches, moss-covered walls, flashes of scaled masks and rounded ears and black tipped tails. Dragon scales and wands. She smelled cedar and rain and, in spurts, horrendous axe body spray.

The unsettling fragrance floated to the far corners of her mind when she saw him.

A man she'd thought she knew. Twice over. And now felt like a stranger.

A man only content with perfection.

Fumbling with the wings, Carrie stared from the safety of the dancefloor. When he turned, she held her breath. His shimmering onyx hair was tousled handsomely, and he bore a five o'clock shadow, but it didn't conceal a jaw she'd memorized.

She'd been so dumb to not recognize him. too in hate and then love to open her eyes, too distracted with his words. She never saw the man. But there he was. Asher Laughlin. Same broad shoulders, same chiseled jawline, hazel eyes.

A purple glazed lowball glass sat in front of him, a lemon curl drooping off the rim. She knew what it was, and her gut turned at the idea of gin.

No more gin.

Never.

She wanted to scrape her body wash off, the one that had reminded her of Jack, the one she'd inhaled off Asher's skin. Dumb.

Carefully, with her heart in her throat, Carrie slid across the smooth wood seat of her chair. Stared at her drink, imagined rinsing the tequila from her mouth, and letting gin whisk her away, give her amnesia. Allow her to swivel and smile, see Jack as he used to be. A hero.

The Hand had a strict policy. Written on the wall in waterjet cut steel. Look each other in the eyes.

The tourists found it prophetic and profound, and a bunch of other pompous P words, but the regulars knew Diana had had it made because she was sick of people yelling at TVs in bars.

Tonight, they didn't obey.

"Don't look now, but your costume's one of twenty."

Carrie's mouth fell open as Asher's low, gravel raked voice as he nudged The Aviator to her.

He didn't know.

Gathering strength, Carrie channeled her best duchess accent. "Better than a disheveled rake."

"A Lord."

Lord Jack. "A Lord would room temperature port."

"Yeah." he scrubbed a hand down his face. "You're probably fucking right."

"Nor would he ever use such callous language in the presence of the fairer sex."

"It's a costume, Holmes. The callousness has been tempered to its limit."

Her cheeks immediately pinked. She used her straw to submerge her cherry. Struggled to stay upbeat as she asked, "Not drinking tonight?"

"I have your number." A folded strip of matte black paper tumbled across the counter and Carrie lurched to grab it, peel it open. Weight crashed down upon her shoulders, seized hold of her limbs.

"I hired a PI to find you. I couldn't wait. I missed you and—" he wiped his face again, as if he couldn't believe he was talking. "I couldn't wait. I guess that's the brunt of it, right? Impatience."

Her fingers curled around the phone number. "You tracked me like a dog?"

"I tracked you like a highly trained hound addicted to the scent of your blood."

Carrie's stomach wrenched with longing. Misplaced and penetrating.

"To be fair," his voice took a hard edge. "I assumed you were searching for me too. I made myself easy to find, if you'd have looked. But like I said," he chuckled. "I was impatient. So I took charge."

She shot him a glare. "You're drunk."

"It helps." He undid his simple leather watch. Laid it on the counter. "This is for you."

She didn't want it. Paper crumped in her hold. Overwhelmed. She was overwhelmed. Asher had even wrecked her Jack.

"A gift, a token of my appreciation. To represent our time together."

"You're leaving."

"Yes." His low voice sounded distant, but he was there. She could feel him, warm and inviting, smell the mountain air.

"Do you love me at all?"

"I thought I loved you."

It hurt like a hundred pins stabbing. She winced. "But you don't?"

He waited, as if he considered lying or sparing her feelings, this stranger he'd claimed to care about. But no sugar coating came in his rumble. "Not enough."

Carrie took it like a physical blow, a hit to the chest. She jerked back off her stool, stumbled, wings tugging her around.

Asher caught her biceps, steadying her, hands warm and familiar. And when she finally looked into his eyes, she uncovered red ruining the white, and darkness overtaking color.

Asher stilled. "You."

Carrie ran.

Her feet led her into the crowd, wings slapping bodies, catching on tails, earning disgruntled shouts. She kept running, aiming for neon EXIT and bursting outside.

In seconds, Diana was a shadow at her back, boots pounding behind as Carrie fell out onto the sidewalk, scraping her knees, destroying the skirt.

Something warm and heavy smelling of a bonfire and spa draped over her shoulders. Diana's leather coat. She wished it were a black hole.

Diana didn't speak, didn't ask why she cried. She helped Carrie up, pulled three dark strands off her lips, and nodded. "It's over now."

Chapter Twenty-Nine

Asher

Asher's dream twisted and warped into a nightmare. The endless cycling nightmares where he got stabbed and revived only to feel the knife again.

Barbed ribs drilled into his lungs, suffocated him. The waistcoat and trousers surrendered to the frigid air, let the chill creep into him, tunnel and cut the farther he got.

He kept dialing, kept calling. Kept leaving those rambling voicemails that he'd mocked her for.

She'd flinched. Ran.

He'd lost it. Shredding wings searching for her. Shouting after her, his voice swallowed by the dance music.

Two men in orange shirts kicked him out for harassment, for bothering the servers.

His fingers were numb, his end of his nose stung.

Where was she? He needed her.

He'd realized it the moment she surprised him at his apartment. Watched her inject color and noise into the space. And goddammit, if Riley hadn't called fifteen times to double check the measurements on his waistcoat, he'd have told her.

Showed her.

He should've understood unleashing Carrie into his home would cause chaos.

The shoes weren't made for running. Glossy soles of the wealthy upper class of old England scraped and skid over the cobblestones. Rubbed twin blisters into his ankles as he sprinted through the sleepy North End neighborhoods.

He'd never wanted Carrie.

He'd never entertained it.

He'd had a plan, his perfect life within reach. The house, the picket fence, kids. Love.

Until Carrie entered and ruined him so fantastically.

He'd wanted to ruin her back. To puncture her heart and burrow until every heartbeat bore his name.

She'd known who he was.

He cursed darkly into the night, slowing down as he hit the sidewalk of Nice Way. The run helped clear his mind, sucked the tipsy from him. Truly, getting drunk hadn't been his intention. Going to The Hand wasn't his intention. He'd been content at the house, terrorizing the workers, locking rooms off, staring across the street, wondering where the fuck she was.

Riley forced him to go. Convinced him, rather. Said Holmes deserved a goodbye. And when Asher grabbed his keys and a ball cap, he'd clarified a proper send-off. In full dress.

Thus came the drinking.

Asher leaped up the front steps.

His paper window patch fluttered in the wind. Broken through. His name split.

Rage thundered in his blood. Carrie knew who he was, who they were, and she still ran. Why? He shoved his arm through the ripped pane and threw the deadbolt, helped himself inside.

"Carrie." He tripped over a red craftsmen toolbox in the hall. "Carrie, It's me."

Music played in the kitchen, guiding him forward with a sultry guitar solo.

Instead of Carrie's great green wings and inky freckles, he found skinny black jeans sticking out from under the broken sink.

"Who the fuck are you?"

A wry laugh bounced off the inside of the cabinet. Smoothly, the intruder stood, and without having ever met, Asher immediately recognized him. Ratty black sweatshirt pushed up to his elbows, tattoos scattered down to his wrists. Dark hair, too thick to curl right. Thin, pale face.

The same I-carry-a-gun smirk as his sister. And it was equally convincing.

Declan tossed a silver wrench, alternating hands, and then ditched into the sink. Crossed his arms. "Did I miss your fucking knock?"

"Where is she?"

Unlike his pint-sized sister, Declan had blue eyes. Bright beside Carrie's thin mint cabinets. "She thought keeping me from the bar would somehow protect you when you destroyed her. But I know how to play a long game, me and baby sis have been playing our whole lives."

Asher wiped sweat from his face with the back of his hand. "Where is she, Declan?"

A flicker of surprise brightened his gaze as he surveyed Asher from his polished jet-black shoes to his charcoal cravat. "You realize Jill likes me too much to call the cops. No matter what she hears." He leaned back on the counter—right where—

Asher looked away.

Declan buffed his nails on his chest. "Getting to know the neighbors is always a smart move."

"You're trespassing," Asher returned sharply. "It looks like you broke in, and I'd bet from how comfortable you are threatening me that you've got priors so if you don't want an ankle monitor completing your look, you'd better fucking answer my question."

"Help," came Declan's dry response. "Another entitled asshole's trying to threaten me."

Asher lifted his chin to glare. Something brutal and primitive heated his blood at the idea of being kept from Carrie. With deadly clarity, he knew what he had to do.

He seized Declan's hood and pulled it forcefully around his throat, embodying Asher's choking feeling. With brutal force, Asher smashed him into the cabinets, yanking on the fabric. Wood groaned.

Declan dug fingers into Asher's arm, separating the muscle.

The sting of pain was nothing compared to how Carrie had left him. Fishing the wrench from the sink. He forcefully struck it on Declan's hand to release his hold.

"Maybe she didn't tell you this," Asher growled, tightening his grasp, cutting off air. "Because you like being the hardest, coolest guy and you're fucking fragile about it, but I'm a foster kid. Not one who got the teddy bear. So if you think I'd ever fucking fold when someone attempted to keep me from the only woman—the only person—I've ever loved, then I should ask, for your sake, if you'd like to be buried or cremated."

Declan saw the sliver of truth in Asher's story, not that he wanted to fight, or even threaten, but that he would. That this was far past desperation. For Asher, it was life and death.

"She doesn't want to talk to you," Declan wheezed, face red.

"Then she can listen." He didn't know what he'd say. Only that he wouldn't stop talking until she heard, until he solved this. "Speak or—"

The vicious click of a switchblade rang in Asher's ear. Followed by a ruthless confession, "I would have loved foster care."

Asher flinched and Declan asserted dominance, shoving free, looking manic. Asher hit the wall. "She doesn't want you, and she doesn't have to listen to you."

"You can't keep me away from her."

Declan glanced at the door leading to the stairs. "The fuck I can't."

It was a toss-up on who would win if they fought. Asher had trained strength and incredible stamina. He was no stranger to pain or hits, and he had fifty pounds of muscle on Declan.

But he lacked a knife.

He bolted for the stairs. "Carrie!"

He was sprinting, missing steps, skipping others, hands yanking him up with the rail.

The impact of Declan's slam sent them both flying through the door.

***

B LISTERED, BRUISED, AND BATTERED, Asher pushed Declan off him, but he didn't stand. Didn't look to see what Declan hit as a dust cloud exploded between them.

On his hands and knees, blood trickling down his nose, Asher entered a staring contest with an extremely chubby raccoon.

His tiny hand-like paws were paddling in a My Little Pony pink dish, water glowing under the reflection of the moon. Tucked behind his pointed snout were wide, terrified eyes, smoke black in the shadows.

"What the—"

It took off, tearing across the room, hauling itself up a stack of cardboard boxes and launching itself out the window, wiggling frantically to get its gut past the frame.

Declan coughed from his position on the ground, splayed flat, legs tangled up the wall. "Great. You scared him."

Asher blinked, adjusting to the dark and spotted the knife spun out on the dusty floor, waiting.

Declan didn't seem aware he'd lost it as he curled up, rubbing his chest. "Now I'm going to be roaming up and down the street all night, shaking a bag of Cheetos."

"For the raccoon?" He didn't take his eyes off the knife.

"He's not a raccoon. He's Reginald, the Marquees of Nice Way, and Carrie's completely domesticated him. You ever seen a raccoon that fat?"

Asher had never seen a raccoon. Period.

"Hand me that, will ya?" Declan gestured to the blade. Asher didn't move. "We're solid, man. For now, at least. Just don't corner me. It's not good for your health."

Asher swiped the knife and found a light switch, offering a hand as he stood.

He wasn't sure who gasped. Logic begged him to understand it was his, because Declan knew Reginald well enough to list his favorite snacks, but out of the side of his eye, Declan looked just as shocked as Asher felt.

He scraped a hand through his hair, looking at everything and focusing on nothing.

It was entirely possible no one got used to it. Not even Carrie. Each time she trudged up the steps with another box, turned her fingers on the doorknob, she gasped too.

Most of the windows were covered. And the ceiling light's glow stopped short, obstructed by overturned furniture, metal chairs stacked on a table. Big yellow bins nested nearly eight feet high. Mismatched tubs teetered onto each other, the lids sunken and breaking.

Small cardboard boxes filled gaps and then in those gaps, trinkets, beige lampshades, a bottle of wine with a golden silk bow, old black boots. Massive white sheets covered what they could, hiding messes that should've made Asher's skin crawl. The bleak scent of stale dust brought to mind drywall and saw horses.

"She's not here," Asher deduced.

"Whoa, you have seen some shit." Asher jerked to give Declan a questioning look. "If I stumbled on this hoard, I'd have some damn questions, and probably get sprayed for fleas."

"Carrie's messy, not dirty." Though, in the mind's recesses, he added vet appointment for Reginald to his life plan, as well as bulk cheese puff purchase. "What is all this?"

Thin brows raised, Declan shrugged. "Well, from there to there"—he pointed to a credenza painted with silver roses to a dismantled sleigh bed frame—"That's what she smuggled out of the house before her dad sold. Her mom did all the artwork, just like the door you busted."

Asher's heart punctured, but Declan kept going. "Those boxes are mine. I move a lot, so I tried to get rid of all my shit. And before I could do a Salvation Army dump, Carrie had my ass hauling it up the stairs in ninety degrees." In three strides, Declan attacked a cluster of bins, removing a red lid. He smiled faintly at the contents. "She said I'd want it someday. The back rooms are filled with Diana's shit, stuff they've been compiling for the new bar. The rest is— Whatever she can't let go of. Memories."

"She's your private storage shop?"

"She had a studio here before. This building used to be an art commune."

"And now she houses your crap?"

"Diana says it's a ransom, so we can never leave her." Like her mom, like her dad. Like him. "But I think she knows how badly we need roots." Bright blue eyes cut to Asher.

Roots.

Asher plucked the edge of a sheet and yanked. Paintings, and sketches, a mirror foiled with gold leaf. He ran his fingers over its gilded edge. An antique. She'd kept everything. Held on. Proof of her happy memories.

Her mother's things. Things Asher would kill to have from his family. Any sign he'd had one.

"Cover it back up," Declan said, adjusting his sweatshirt. "Reggie is scared of his reflection."

Asher pulled it taut, but not before he caught the thick wad of green behind him, clutched in Declan's hand.

"Rent," the guy said, passing it over.

Cash. "Singles."

"Ask, but you won't get a fucking answer. It's for two months."

"You can't pay her rent." Asher wasn't collecting it.

"She'd never agree to me taking care of her rent, but she's as good as my sister and this is where she feels loved. So get used to dirty, sweaty singles." A hand slammed on his shoulder. "And if she asks why her checks bounce, say it's out of the kindness of your goddamn heart."

Asher was fixated on the room. He wasn't sure what made his heart stop—that Carrie had been abandoned by so many, or that she'd stayed for those who deserved it.

He needed to see her. So he used a word he rarely used since his eighteenth birthday. "Please, where is she?"

"Not fucking here."

Chapter Thirty

Carrie

Diana's engine choked out with an archaic howl. Carrie clutched her seatbelt tighter as the wheels popped over the curb and Diana slammed into park, not the least bit concerned with the thin stream of smoke escaping the hood.

She had a soft spot for the useless beast and yet Carrie's latest rescue down-turned her lips. "That's not a pumpkin," Diana told the orange lump, line of earrings cresting her lobe jingling with indignation.

"Same family," Carrie insisted, covering Gourdo's—Lizzie McGuire's friend-zoned gourd—imaginary ears and whispering, "You're just as precious." And she'd go to the grave saying it.

"Okay, we need to reintroduce you into society quicker than planned if you're Golluming root vegetables."

How could she leave it? The last gourd in the bin at Hannafords, on clearance because November had struck. A measly calendar flip and now no one liked it. They wanted red and white glitter, snow and stockings. Shinier, prettier, more elegant.

Halloween two point oh.

Carrie trailed her fingers over Gourdo's raised growths. "I have a practice shoot with the Essex marching band tomorrow." She inhaled through her nose, spinning the gourd over her lap. Cold air, biting enough to be called winter, pierced the holes in the knees, hip and thigh of her daisy jeans.

"Can you be without your sling that long?"

Carrie's prone arm flexed before her mottled blue and black sleeve. "I can handle it in spurts. I'm tough." Plus, she couldn't spend another day holed up in Declan's loft, hiding his cigarettes. There were only so many dark holes she could reach into before something bit her. "It'll be quick. It's not a full band. Just four trumpets and a ribbon spinner. They want to look bold and daring."

"Black," Diana advised sagely, swiveling on the torn leather seat to smirk. "When in doubt— Holy. Sodding. Sunshine. My retinas are melting."

Carrie was ardently ignoring the house across the street, fearing the emotions it'd spur. Fearing acting on those emotions. Being charged with violent and disturbing homicide.

However, at the promise of singed eyeballs, Carrie twisted in her seat.

Diana's horrified voice filled the cab. "It looks like melted butter oozing from the walls."

It did.

"Oh my god," Carrie was outside, running before Diana could say *butt-ugly*.

"Chuck!" she called, pulse racing. Maybe she should exercise more. "What's happening? What are you doing?" It was even brighter closer. Banana peels, lemons, egg yolks.

"Painting, girl." Chuck hooked his thumb in his tan work pants. "What else? Where have you been? No donuts yesterday."

"This is the wrong color, Chuck." She stared at the siding of Asher's home, face slack. Were her ears ringing? Or was that noise coming from the paint sprayer? It felt like she was wearing earplugs. "You have to stop." Her voice was hoarse. "He hates yellow."

"Who?"

"Asher!"

"No. No. We confirmed a week ago. Hell, I double confirmed. The plans said white. Then he changed it to Sunshine." Charlie touched the base of his neck and shrugged. "Two yellow houses on the same block seems strange. But I'm the builder, not the designer."

"It's a mistake." Her breath fogged in the chilly air between them. She squeezed her palm to keep from grabbing him. "You need to call him. This is wrong."

"Can't do it."

"You have to."

"You hear that?" She frowned, brows pulling together. Then, modulated shouts, a whistle. Her stomach dropped. "That's the sound of the Mountaineers' game, honey. Winning. No getting to the boss today."

"But it's *yellow*. Chuck."

"He said you'd like it."

No. "Me?"

The contractor flipped through his phone, tongue picking his teeth. "You're the girl, aren't ya?"

The girl? "What?"

"Lookit." He pocketed his phone, leaned into her, breath smelling of tobacco and sugar. "The boys are painting the inside once we finish this. Why not walk through before we go in? Might help."

The solid oak front door was propped open on a cement block, and Carrie didn't waste a second before storming through. Sheetrock walls taped and mudded. Soft honeyed wood floors. White cabinets and counters. White stone fireplace.

Hollow.

Carrie felt it suck at her soul.

Then she saw it and it struck like vertigo

Five black words on the hearth. **You burn me brutally. Beautifully.**

She blinked at the words in Asher's neat, frustrating scrawl, like a typewriter taken to the wall. She swallowed back a painful throb in her throat and when she turned, she saw more small almost invisible markings. Under the windows. **I watch and sting.**

By the entrance. **Slam the door as long as I'm in it.**

She found more. Clinging to a wall corner. **Your heat lingers**. In the nook of the kitchen, windows papered over on the outside, but hazy afternoon light seeped through for her to read. **I brew coffee for two. The steam rises and tangles. You are somewhere else.**

Everywhere she turned.

Words above the sink, by the fridge, stamped on the end of the island. **Marshmallows** and **Frost** and **You**. She found that in every corner. **You** and **Here** and **There** and *You*.

Part of her wanted to take a hammer to the walls, to break and make swallowing clouds of dust and chemicals and breathe them in. But she wouldn't. She'd take the words instead, destroy the wall, and take the words.

Beside the door, vertically, like marginalia in a favorite book, she found, **I never hated before. I hate this.**

"What's taking so— Fuck." Diana froze in the entry. A pillar of black in the white, harsh and nasty and the words seemed to draw to her, like stars in reverse, glittering obsidian on endless white.

There were tears in Carrie's eyes. "He wrote me."

Diana's fingers pressed against the wall. She read, "Drown it, wreck me, strangle the walls with color, bury my floors. Infect it to match me." She looked across the room. "What did you do to him?"

"He's painting it." He'd written her the letter she'd asked for and he'd thrown it out.

Diana stormed through the house, pushing down a short hall, kicking in a door, chalky black prints in her wake.

Carrie gave chase, reading as she went, a riot in her blood.

You ravage me

I surrender

Shatter my heart

She'd murder him, kiss him, and slit his throat. Cry as he fell.

Diana grabbed her the strap of her sling and swung her around. "Look."

No bed, no nightstands or books, not a chair for clothes on the cusp of laundry. But a bedroom. Undoubtedly. Picture windows facing two sapling apple trees, trembling in the November breeze.

Black. So much, it pricked her skin, sunk in, laid ink on her bones. The blocky notes were struck through with big straight lines, but also thin scribbles and x's. Slashes to eradicate the text beneath. Smothering his voice. ~~Your hands. Your composure. Your smile in the corner of my eye. Gin~~

~~Gin~~

~~Gin~~

Lines telling Carrie not to read. Words not about her.

But she did. Jumping between the same word over and over, she read the condemned musings. ~~Your laugh. Flowers. Smoke. Vanilla. Vanilla.~~

"Stay."

Carrie froze. The word bigger than the rest, the word written in between every X. **Stay. Stay. Stay.**

Stay with me.

The back of her throat hurt. She couldn't swallow. Her face was hot. Carrie turned around. Black in her stomach like churning acid. "We should go."

"Carrie." Diana gestured helplessly, palms up. "This is—"

"No."

Stop. No. She wanted to fight and thrash and bite and punch. Two nights ago, she'd crashed to her knees in Declan's. Peeled off her clothes, sat in the shower, and wrapped herself in a robe that wasn't hers. Slept on wet hair, Diana's boots on the comforter.

She hated him. He consumed her and she—

"He wasn't going to tell me."

"Love—"

"He did all of this." Carrie threw her arm out. "Everything." her voice was a harrowing whisper. "And he was never going to tell me."

Diana stroked her arm. "Sweetie, you're upset—"

"I'm bleeding!" she shouted. "Everywhere, from every part." She rubbed her burning eyes. "Let's go. There's a home game today. Traffic's going to be bad." She wiped her face, but there were no tears. He'd pushed her too far, leagues past her breaking point.

"Did you get it?" Carrie asked, voice like an echo.

"Options are in the car."

Cruel determination wove through Carrie, steeled her spine. "I require Declan's unique expertise."

Diana's angelic face betrayed nothing. Comfortable with whatever carnage Carrie sought. "I'll start on an alibi."

***

"THEY'RE UNDERSTAFFED." DIANA'S VOICE drifted over Carrie's shoulder. On dagger sharp stilettos, Carrie could see almost right into her best friend's caramel eyes.

Accepting a glass of bubbly with a twirl of her skirts, Carrie arched a brow. "No shop talk. It's girl time."

"It's not a switch," Diana muttered. "And it's painfully obvious. The lines around the bar, coat check fumbling, the cluttered empty glasses. This is a museum, not a dumping ground."

"I'm going to kill you if you keep talking about this. We are two smart, interesting women. We should have a thousand better things to discuss than how many champagne flutes belong at the top of a statue." Carrie tilted her head to the intertwined amorphous shapes, unsure if she was viewing the universe's creation or disgusting bestiality. Both.

They were restricted to the contemporary art wing of the Burlington Gallery. A former airplane hanger turned gem of New England. Forty-foot ceilings and cement floors left for the art to be the focus and tonight, white chairs in long rows faced a temporary stage.

Black tie, according to the wealthiest of New England, was sleek and sexy and subdued. Draping emerald velvet, cinched burgundy. Sheaths of onyx, midnight, obsidian, and ebony.

"None," Diana replied. "And you couldn't kill a gingerbread man." She swirled her champagne like the best of the wealthy, but she Carrie refused to believe anyone else was discussing murder so breezily. "Not even if you ate him. He'd tumble around in your intestines until he gum dropped out."

Carrie bit back a smile.

"Hello." A stylish man in a suit cut in between them. All Giorgio Armani and oil baron. "I couldn't help but notice how beautiful—"

"Not interested." Diana didn't let him down easy. "Scurry off before my heel craves scrotal annihilation."

Carrie snorted into her flute as the suit tucked and turned.

All night she'd been approached.

It was the suit. Jet-black and suctioned to Diana's curves. She'd worn it without a shirt, just a shiny gold chain dangling between her cleavage all the way to her belly button. She'd pulled her thick, wild hair into a high, full ponytail that Carrie could lose her wallet in.

Combat boots replaced with stilettos, Diana embodied lust and envy and every other diabolical, desirous sin, and men were so weak, so accustomed to following their every dark intention, they floated around Diana, waiting for their eyes to accidentally meet, to get a chance.

It was all for Carrie.

The heels, the missing nose ring, the hovering, the absolute avoidance of her photograph on the other side of the room. Diana had become a shelter in Carrie's shitstorm and instead of holding on and praying, Diana had fortified the walls, replaced her windows with shatterproof and reinforced the shingles. She was Carrie's safe harbor and she, like her overprotective brother, took the job seriously.

Carrie would too. If ever given the chance, if ever Diana's defenses slipped, Carrie would pick up the pieces, dust them off, shine them on her shoe and sew her back together.

"You could be nice," Carrie droned.

"Have you met me?"

That meant Diana *was* being nice. Carrie switched subjects. "Does anyone have your eye? It's been a while for you, hasn't it?"

Diana cricked her neck, staring into her glass. "I'm not yet desperate enough to sleep with a trust fund baby. Besides"—she linked their arms together—"they're only interested because they think we're lesbians and being sandwiched between Little Bo Peep and their first Alt girl gets them raging hard."

Carrie laughed. It wasn't a bad comparison with the frills of her dress, the draping cream lace, the cinched lilac bodice. She was chastity to Diana's lust.

It was a perfectly acceptable dress. Wasting it seemed simply ridiculous. It wasn't the ballroom piece she'd imagined storming into The Hand with, but who would know without a Lord beside her? She'd tailored the ruffled layered lilac skirts to a delightful tea length. A shimmer began at the hem and thickened up the squeeze of her bodice, darkening to to the rich purple of dusk. Beautiful. A shade that invoked power and prestige. She'd left the delicate sunset azure lace mask at home, as well as the bonnet, elbow high gloves, and shawl. She didn't want to be someone else today.

She'd thought herself bold, captivating when she was at Declan's. Every yank of her corset like knives sheathing in a harness.

Now she felt like a cheap plastic loofa in a room of silk.

"Well." Diana finished her champagne and pulled a blue paddle from her back pocket. "Should we sit and wave this thing around?"

"You got a bidding paddle?"

"In the name of cancer research, I'll force every rich prick here to up their bid." She tugged Carrie toward the seats, saying loudly, "If the Huston piece goes for less than ten grand, it'll be a steal."

Ten grand. Carrie would dig a grave and lie in it. "You're going to get us kicked out."

"I'm curing cancer," Diana shot back, picking at her chipped nails, the only crack in her glammed up facade. "What group is it in— Oh shite."

Carrie echoed the sentiment as her new muse walked inside, stroking a hand through wet hair.

He wore black, like most of the room, but he'd skipped a jacket, in favor of an onyx button down with breathing room left at his throat. Blue eyes blazed and thick eyebrows arched when he saw Carrie and then he was beelining for them. Lincoln Wray dressed up well.

"Have you told him?" Diana whispered.

"I actually prayed for them to go into overtime."

"Prayed to who? The sodding football gods? They've all got brain damage, and prioritize ED and beer prayers over—"

"Lincoln!" Carrie greeted, smiling as wide as she could.

"Carrie," he purred. "You're a vision in lavender." Sparkling eyes skidded to Diana, flared. "Lincoln Wray."

Diana stared at his outstretched hand, pursed her lips and tipped her head up. And up. "Lady Macbeth. How do you do?" She spun to Carrie. "The dogs are barking. Let's sit."

Lincoln gestured to the chairs. "Lead the way. You can tell me more about your interest in erectile dysfunction."

Diana's smile was pure wicked delight as she evaded his proffered hand and sat next to Carrie in the second row. "An area of expertise for you?"

"Not since you walked in."

"Romance *is* alive," Diana crowed. "Please tell me more about your public boner."

Carrie swatted her thigh. "*Diana.*"

Instead of being embarrassed or offended, the suave Lincoln was smiling, leaning into Diana's ear, saying something that led to best friend's eyes narrowing. Made her shoulders straighten, and her fingers tighten around her glass.

"Let's sit somewhere else," Diana whispered to Carrie.

A man chasing her off?

"Group B begins with an original print—"

Carrie went red, leaned over, talking over the auctioneer, "I'm so sorry, Lincoln. I couldn't—"

The thin white sheet over her print fluttered to the ground and silence hit the room.

It was like shock therapy. Each time she looked, it broke her a little more, but it would strengthen her. Staring, hating, loving.

Her best.

Her worst.

The moment before her life irrevocably changed, before the tears started, before darkness swallowed her. She'd gotten the shot.

He was miserably happy. Harsh eyes framed by spiked lashes, light flashing off violently straight teeth, hollows in his cheeks shrouded in damning shadows. Exhaustion, agony, loneliness in the photograph, no other jersey in the end zone, just him, staring down her lens.

Darkness and hard work and payoff—*there* in the corners of his mouth, the upturned edge. Barely a curve. Vulgar predatory satisfaction.

"We'll open bidding at one thousand."

No one bidding had not occurred to Carrie. Not that she thought she was an undeniable success, but she'd figured a paddle would rise.

It was for charity.

Most likely, a paddle would've if she'd submitted the Wray piece. The photograph of him grinning like a man of power, his signature spiral shooting across the blue September sky.

The print on stage was half the size. It didn't bear a signature.

Diana raised her paddle. "One thousand." Her hand curled around Carrie's, as if to say, *worth every penny*. Even if Carrie knew Diana would rather tattoo Scooby Doo on her forehead than own a photograph of Asher broke-my-best-friend's-heart Laughlin.

Slowly, unlike the other items for bid, paddles raised. Trailed languidly with incremental bids until Lincoln landed it at five thousand. Carrie leaned across Diana to tell him. "You're being too nice."

"No, he's not," Diana bit, raising her paddle. "Six grand."

Lincoln's came up right after.

And then a third rose. "Ten."

His voice electrocuted every individual cell in Carrie's body.

She felt her atoms rush together, like kids on a boat trying to see a mermaid, and her entire body tipped toward him to glimpse something magical.

The tone, though, kept her from turning her neck, locked her face forward. Too dark and serious and not fitting of the man in her photograph.

She wanted to remember *that* man. Not the one flickering with recognition in a mystical, cursed forest.

"Twelve." Diana squeezed Carrie's palm.

"Fifteen." Not magic. She hadn't imagined it, she hadn't wondered or wished. It was his voice, even more menacing. She capsized, twisting, skirts ruffling over, pouring onto the lap of the gentlemen beside her. A purple taffeta and stapled lace flood.

He didn't mind. He was already looking over his shoulder. Their entire row was, Diana included, tightening her stranglehold on Carrie's fingers.

Whispers rose.

Connections fired. *Is that him? It's him. The man from the photograph.*

Scandal. That was what Carrie would lean over and whisper in Diana's ear, if she didn't know better. If she'd never been involved. She'd do it in a posh duchess accent, fanning her face, voice full of appall even as she grinned and tried to glean more information from the crowd.

"Eighteen."

"Twenty."

He wore a t-shirt. Plain and white, thin enough Carrie felt like she could watch his heart beat. It was the shirt one donned under a button down on a humid day. But never alone.

Too thin, too plain, too rudimentary for a man who bid twenty thousand dollars on a photograph of himself from the empty back row.

More people turned, following Carrie's gawking. And she should turn away because Asher didn't like attention. He didn't want eyes on him. But she couldn't spare him that. She missed him too much.

Missed the way he tugged at his collar, like it was shrinking around his throat.

She wanted to button his jacket, and softly whisper he'd forgotten to tuck his shirt in, and his pant leg had rolled up in the car.

Because those were all things he'd want to fix.

But Carrie catalogued each and every single one of them. She added them to her heart with hash marks, like she was solving for X. A shadow of scruff lined his jaw and creases around his eyes suggested he'd had a long day. Perhaps even longer than Carrie's.

Her eyes lifted as his paddle did. She couldn't hear the numbers anymore.

He'd found her.

No, he'd seen her the entire time. She'd just finally made it to his piercing hazel eyes. Eyes she'd mistaken for black.

He'd come. He'd come here. He'd stolen words from her and then come.

As he lifted his paddle, his mouth moved, and she focused on the black wound over his fingers. Smudges. Smudges from a man who considered leaving seconds on the microwave to be an offense worthy of the death penalty.

Again, his paddle raised. The room was growing more and more quiet. The mingling guests admiring art had caught on to the bidding war.

The rebel goth Diana and the rumpled man from the photo.

Eyes darted back and forth. Carrie felt a tear slip from her eye because she refused to blink.

"One million." Asher's paddle, his voice. Loud and harsh, the same tone he'd used to tell her no when they first met. *No.* Obstinate and rude, and she'd wanted to kiss it out of him even then. Except now he was offering a world to her.

Diana paused, the auctioneer's fingers angled to her.

It was utter silence now. Not a breath, not a sneeze. Bodily functions ceased to exist at the concept of one million dollars being spent on her tiny, measly, unsigned photograph.

Diana let go of Carrie's hand.

"One point one." Diana's voice, but she wasn't holding her paddle any longer. She'd bent across Lincoln's lap, her fingers wrapped around his wrist, black nails cutting half-moons into his bronzed skin.

The auctioneer shifted their point, two fingers on Lincoln. Waiting.

Diana looked up and Carrie heard the tiniest, softest "Please" slip out of her best friend's mouth.

And Lincoln Wray, who'd come to see his face on stage, only to be duped by Carrie, who'd been resolutely dismissed by Diana, calmly locked eyes with the goddess in black and nodded. "One point one."

CHAPTER THIRTY-ONE

ASHER

"Two."

Chapter Thirty-Two

Asher

T HE PEN WAS RIPPED out of his hand before Asher had the chance to sign his purchase agreement. Fingernails dug into his skin, a beautiful, furious voice hissed quietly in his ear. "Have you lost your goddamn mind?"

Yes.

He would have paid triple to talk to her.

And he'd have emptied the coffers to get her fingers to brush his, even this crushing grip.

Go far, try new things, put yourself out there.

"Mr. Laughlin."

He refused to look at her. He didn't want to say *yes, yes, yes.* He didn't want to ask, *why didn't you wear it?* He didn't want to say that you're the most beautiful thing here, and you're purple. *You're freckles and you're purple and you're everything.*

Because he didn't deserve her. He didn't fucking deserve her.

But he could do this. Pay. Spoil. Spend. Because she deserved the world.

A woman who saw people leave and only wanted to stay all the more. Stolen from all of her life, torn from the mother she loved, forgotten by a father. Alone and filled with so much longing that she'd been resolute to make sure those she loved never felt the same agony.

A woman who held on to things she cherished.

The woman he couldn't write letters to.

He'd mocked her.

All his life, Asher wanted to belong and never felt it, gazed across the fence and seen greener grass. Turned bitter. Rotten. Vowed alone was better. Alone meant no one to abandon you, reject you, no one to see you and bark no.

Do you say anything other than 'no'?"

"Pen?" he croaked to the auctioneer. After his bid, he and his photograph were swept from the contemporary exhibit, down the hall of Indigenous artists to a small office, smelling of vellum and stale coffee.

Banished by vanilla.

Asher tried not to inhale as he blinked between the promise of purchase and the worker.

But a giant poof of purple distracted him. "He's drunk," Carrie was saying. "Has a real problem. I noticed you were understaffed and perhaps that's how you so gruesomely over-served him and can in no way hold him liable for this purchase."

The auctioneer looked at her like she was deranged. "You want to rescind a donation?"

"I'm not drunk," Asher managed roughly. "Get me a pen and I'll sign. I just want the photograph."

"Asher," Carrie was tugging on his elbow, cheeks cherry red, the hand in her sling tearing at the glittery fabric on her stomach. "You are losing your mind. You cannot do this."

She'd pinned her hair up with small white clips, face clear and bright, neat. Freckles and dark lashes and soft chin.

He swallowed. "I want a Carrie Huston print."

She cupped his cheek, eyes wide as saucers. "Then I will give you one."

"I want to pay." He had to.

"No." She shoved him backward, and pointed at the auctioneer, who was undoubtedly getting paid by the hour. "This is off the record!"

"Lady, there's no record."

A Lady. A Lady in glowing purple. They would've been a perfect pair, and it would've been so wrong.

"Asher." Carrie was clutching his crimped lapel. No—smoothing it, fixing the pleats like he liked. "I have a bigger, better one in my bedroom right now. Please, help yourself to it."

"I want you to have that one. I want this one."

He wanted to remember smiling.

"Asher!" She was whispering. The angrier she got, the quieter, the more hair flicked past her clips, and spilled onto her face. "I'll kill you for this. Do you understand? Dead. Burn your fingerprints off, erase you from the internet, feed you to a very handsome raccoon—"

"Okay ma'am. that's all very illegal and the GMCA cannot condone—"

"Now you care about the law?" she clipped at the auctioneer's objection, her grip on Asher's sleeve tightened. "We just need a moment. You just—" She made a very violent gesture for him to wait, tossed the pen on the table and hauled Asher through the door.

Curse him to hell for following along.

"I am—" She puffed up her cheeks. "I can't even—" She balled up her hand into a fist and shook it, all while shoving him down the hall. "I have never been this angry. I can't even speak. Do you realize how infuriating that is?"

She was seconds from clocking him, yanking him closer, glaring, breathing fire. "You're antagonizing and deliberate and you came here just to prove your fucking point." She was slamming him with the heart of her palm. Walking faster. Rushing them. Turning to hit and then striding again, skirts singing.

"And this is what you wear?" she snarled. "To a fundraiser. What? To provoke me? Two million dollars?" She choked on the last part.

She was still laying into him, still flinging curses and hate. And he came for her, her name on his lips, his hands in her hair, spinning her into the closest room as he kissed her, needy, and hopeless and frantic.

Chapter Thirty-Three

Carrie

C ARRIE GASPED AGAINST ASHER as he pulled her tighter, as he licked over her lips, claiming her with long, decadent stokes until she was trembling against him, clutching him.

A door slammed. Automatic lights flicked overhead. Carrie had no memory of passing through a door, but she thanked the stars and heaven above they had.

She clung to him, knees weak, drunk with him, wild under his touch, completely aflame. He was crushing twelve layers of skirts, and she was trying to shred them off, utterly desperate for the man who'd come for her, who'd wrote to her.

His mouth skated down her neck, hands gripping her waist, nipping, licking, sucking. Carrie's head rolled back, her eyes falling shut at the sensation of his hands dipping under the straps she'd made, hot and devastating.

Too late, on an exhaled moan as he trailed kisses over her cheek to her eat, breath thick and tragic, she remembered the fury coursing through her body.

She shoved at his hard chest, hating—loving—how big he was, how solid, and how easily he gave way to her anger, pulling back with darkened eyes, chin dropping, awaiting his punishment.

"Money?" She shoved at him. "Money, Asher? What kind of sick fucking amusement is this?"

"It's a donation. In your mother's name."

She wanted to slap him again. But just glared, heaving. "You think I want your money?"

"I've never entertained the idea."

"I don't." And he was nodding, not fighting, not breaking eye contact. She shoved him again. "How could you take this to me?" His lips parted, but she was talking already, aching, letting hurt seep from her lips. "You hide the words I covet all to throw cash in my face? Why? To humiliate me? To prove you're detached?"

"What are you—"

"I went to the house. I tried to stop Chuck from wrecking it with yellow paint."

"Sunshine yellow," Asher corrected, jaw clicking. "You went inside."

"I have only ever desired a word from you. A sign. Proof that I'm not alone in this— And you—"

"I love you."

Her heart slammed into the floor. "No."

"*Yes.*" He was pulling the pins from her hair, letting them clang on the floor. "Yes," he repeated before she could front an argument. "And now you'll listen to me. Because I will keep spending your future until you listen."

She tried shake out of his cupped hands. Half-hearted, shocked, aching.

"I love you," he rasped. "And haven't I always? From the moment we met. Each time. You've had me."

She clung to her fury. "You don't get to do this. March in here and give me sweet memories when I saw it. What you did. Kept from me." She couldn't figure out if she was pushing or pulling. Just touching. Feeling. Inhaling snow and outside, skin heating. Clutching while trying to stay afloat.

You burn me brutally. beautifully

He pressed a soft kiss to her temple, reeled her into his chest, and spoke into her hair. "I wish I could write you letters. I want to send them from as far away as possible, stamp them with every country between us. I want to list everything I love about you and watch you read it. But that'd mean I have to leave. And I don't want to leave."

Carrie went stiff.

Before she could hurl accusations, he was talking again. "I wish I could send them to the farthest corners of the world to find you. So that you understood whenever I'm jotting notes on a napkin, listening to your day over breakfast in your tiny kitchen, I'm writing I love you. I love you, I love you."

His gaze held hers, sharp and uncompromising. Showing more than she ever thought to hear. He looked past her then, over her shoulder. "I want to write that every time, but I can't. How do I admit it to paper without ever seeing you hear it? Because I want to see your face when you hear that I love you. That I'm gone for you. That I fought it and lost."

The admission had Carrie thrumming with pleasure, leaning into him, his warmth, his scent.

"So I don't write you letters." The words, a simple fact that shouldn't gut her, stole her breath.

He clutched her like she might run and went on, whispering in the empty room, voice broken, weak like she'd never heard him. "Because my letters aren't poems or prose, they're robotic and repetitive. I love you," he was whispering into her ear. "I love you. *I love you*. You've reduced me to a man of seven holy letters. And I want to be there, watching your fingers curl around the paper, follow your eyes across the words, but I'm too impatient. I'll say it first and ruin it. Spoil the contents."

She took a deep breath, willing herself not to cave. How long had she yearned for this? And now it'd come, and it stung like a needle through her nail. "You love *her*."

She struggled in his grip, throwing her wrist, twisting skirts beating her calves. But he didn't release her.

Perhaps because she couldn't bring the command to her lips, couldn't get them out of her throat. *Let me go.* Because he looked like he loved her, kissed her as much. "You don't love me. You want perfect. You want a house with a garden. I won't give it to you. Let go."

Damn him for listening.

Cool air swept her up like an ice storm.

Asher stepped back, chin lowered, predatory, eyes incredibly dark.

He was shaking. Shaking, even as he stepped back further. Honoring her wishes. The black spots on his hands shuddered like they were trying to leap free.

Carrie had always seen Asher through the lens of an athlete. As a man who fought and tore and cut through others. She'd seen him get thrown to the ground and never cover his head, never tuck, never lose sight of a goal despite the physical wreckage.

It never occurred to her he could tremble.

Yet when she thought of Jack, alone at the bar, creasing his napkin, waves of do-not-approach wafting off him—she understood.

Two sides of the same coin were a reckless man and one who pushed all away for self-protection.

His fists clenched. "I loved Holmes."

The confession nearly brought her to the ground.

"But loving her was like loving a reflection on a still dark pond. I never saw all of her, but I was happy with the cross section I got, with two-dimensions, because it was all she offered. And I never thought I'd get more until I met you."

She sliced him a fierce look. "And you hated me."

"Of course I did." One side of his lips lifted in a small smile. "You showed me I was living underwater. In cold, murky darkness. And I was terrified surfacing would end in suffocation and I'd lose the both of you." His expression did damage for its honesty. "I'd rather have a fraction of you than none at all."

Carrie swallowed around the knot in her throat.

He watched her for a long movement until she shifted uncomfortably under his assessing gaze. Still, he stared. "It was pointless," he croaked. "The fighting. Every time I cut you, all it did was sharpen you."

"I want to do worse than cut you."

When he didn't reply, she said, "I want to burn you. Brutally."

The air between them thickened.

"Beautifully," Her eyes went wide at the steel in his tone. He reached for her, fingers pushing a lock of brown hair behind one of her ears. "Burn me, brat. Shred me, slice me, don't leave me."

She kissed Asher like she'd wanted to kiss Jack. She rested gentle fingers on the harsh slant of his cheek, above the stubble, and she took his mouth carefully with slightly parted lips. She yearned to feel her soul ignite. She wanted to feel a connection burst in her.

She wanted to kiss him under the shroud of music, with gin on her lips. Wanted to float away. But she couldn't.

Carefully, she retreated, sending distance between them. "It stings," he rasped.

She understood. The kiss wasn't them. "Fix it then."

CHAPTER THIRTY-FOUR

CARRIE

THE KISS HE GAVE her was lush and heavy, packed with aching desire and nips of pain. His hands, instead of luring her closer, as he'd always done, encased her as he moved to her. Came to her. As he always would.

She was desperate for him like she'd never been.

The unforgiving floor in her entryway, the foamy counter, she'd been wild in lust, and it didn't register on this new scale he'd forged. Snowflakes compared to the blizzard whipping through her now.

It'd always be like that. She knew it.

That this hunger for him would only grow, build, become increasingly urgent, until they died from it.

She ached for it.

Taking his lips in harsh and cruel sucks, licking into his mouth, she clutched to him. Furious and utterly enamored. She ripped away and spun, waved wildly at the stays of her gown. "Off. Take it off."

Broad hands covered her shoulders, followed down the curve of her waist, over her skirts. "Asher," she hissed.

He kicked up her hem. Trailed blazing paths up her legs, poured laving kisses down the side of her neck. Hooked fingers in the line of her underwear. Teeth sank into her.

"Should I guess the color?" he teased.

Teasing. While she ached. "Rainbow," she panted. "Tie-dye. You'll hate it."

The band stretched on her hipbones, smarted and then tore, resonating like a gunshot in the empty room.

"I hate plenty," he murmured darkly, twirling her to face him. "But soaking fucking wet will always be my favorite color."

Carrie's mouth dropped as he shoved the colorful underwear in the chest pocket of his jacket. Absurd and dirty and pure sin.

"Do you have to break everything?"

"You broke me first," he told her, voice so rough it was difficult to understand. Coiling his hand around her neck, he crashed them together. His kiss was hard and ferocious. He drank from her like she was the most decadent wine ever bottled, and he was a selfish man intent on delirium. No drop spared. Every lick, gasp, and sigh infected his blood, cured the shake in his palms.

Strengthened him.

He needed her. The salve to his torrent of unfamiliar emotions. The cure to his whipping, strangling love.

Her heart thundered. One of his powerful hands fisted her hair.

The black across her eyelids moved. Twisted and exploded in flat, straight lines. *Stay*.

Begging lines, scratched lines. *Stay*.

She felt it in his hands. The firm press of him, the unyielding grip on her waist, the hand pinning her neck to him.

Stay, stay, stay.

Raised to leave. Punished for staying, and now he begged for it. For her.

She kissed him harder. Pushing him back, sweeping them across the cold gray floors until he collided with the wall. At the first nudge on his shoulder, he kneeled, dove for her skirts, a pleasured groan emanating from deep in his chest, flooding the room. Burning Carrie.

"Stop," she said, freezing him instantly. "Lean back. Sit."

Frustration raged in his stare, but he obeyed. His breathing was ragged, fast and shallow, cheeks flushed, inky strands of hair tousled wonderfully, slinking into his eyes.

"A well-trained hound," she murmured. Earning another flash of fury. So petulant and pissed off, she couldn't help but bend and take his mouth.

His hand snaked up along the curve of her good shoulder, crept to her nape and pulled.

She toppled onto him, skirts flinging purple in every direction, her knee hit his thigh, her elbow his armpit.

Asher laughed low against the shell of her ear. "That makes you a floppy-eared rabbit." A buck of his hips sent them into alignment. Carrie's thighs spread over his, her hand on his chest, her core resting on a wicked ridge.

The floor was cold on her shins, stung her knees. Painful until Asher's tongue darted out to trace her earlobe, slid up the arch to whisper, "Think you can outrun me?"

Threat and promise and vow.

Stay.

She kept reading it, reading it, reading it as she kissed him, as she plummeted under her skirts to wrench the button of his pants open, slide down his zipper, reach inside.

His body jolted when she gripped him, too hot, impossibly hard and smooth in her hand. His teeth scraped her lips. The sting wrangled a little noise from her throat.

Inexperienced, she reminded herself as she stroked and his breath caught audibly in his throat.

Oh, how she longed to corrupt him. To teach him how to be greedy and dirty. Demand he fuck her face, beg him to come on her. Paint vulgar words on her skin, wrench her hair back and tell her the kind of filth he'd planned for her. Darkness and shadow. Lust and yearning. Shameless obsession.

Until then, she'd savor his frantic hands, his sensitive body. Cherish it the way he deserved.

Foster care could've destroyed him. Slewed his morals, sunk nasty poisoned claws in him. Made him mean and unfeeling. But he didn't let it. Odds against him, Asher tightened up ship, tried harder, cared for those he could, yearned for it in return.

He hummed as he suckled her neck, moving down to lick at the swell of her breast. Her body pulsed in response, hips rolled, and she squeezed his thick length and lurched forward to cling to him, lust spinning through her, making her groan.

Steps ahead, Asher's big hands cupped her bare ass under her dress and tugged her up, trapping her hand between them so he could take her mouth again, knead her skin, fingertips teasing the wet, aching center of her.

Maybe he was already corrupted. Because on the floor in a public museum, Asher yanked her to her knees and sank his teeth over her bodice, sucking so hard she felt the heat of his tongue on her nipple. She moaned and he sank his fingers into her, gliding in how wet she was for him.

Violent lust ravaged her.

Hand stuck between them, Carrie was helpless to him as he held her up, muscles solid and hot around her, fingers plunging deliciously deep, his angle hitting her just right.

"Fuck, you're so sweet," he breathed into her mouth, filling her faster, tangling his tongue with hers. "Tell me how you need me."

As if wasn't written on her face as his fingers curled inside her, as she let out a little shriek of pleasure. He muffled her with a filthy lick, groaning, dark lashes impossibly low.

"Inside me." Her voice was ragged, high. Unfamiliar.

His fingers pushed harder into her, severed her sanity.

"I'm not laughing, brat." A murmur against her jaw. He slid another finger inside her and she sobbed at the pressure. Pushing back to ride him.

His nose trailed across her throat, inhaled. "Let me get on my knees," he rumbled in a covetous tone. "Let me fill you with my tongue. Let me taste you. Fuck, I want to taste you."

Carrie clenched around him as her blood blazed. She buried her face in his neck, licked the sweat on his tendon, latched her teeth there. Pleasure folded in on her, swelled.

Hungry, frenzied encouragements flew between them. Soft, simple things they'd never have said a week ago, were thrown as quickly and harshly as their insults. *Yes. So good. Like that. Hold on. Let go.*

"Stay."

She couldn't tell whose words, whose moaned plea. She couldn't ask, couldn't stop as Asher's rhythm doubled, long wet fingers unrelenting. Her mind reeling, she exploded around him, crying out. Sparks scattered behind her eyes.

It had been frantic. Now it was twice as fast. Carrie's breath on his open mouth. She was rasping, croaking out a thousand things. Telling Asher she had an IUD, telling her she was too empty. She needed him, flailing with her obnoxious skirts, all while feeling the aftermath of her orgasm dripping onto his thighs.

In front of her, hair wild from her tearing, eyes rimmed with red, mouth swollen, bruised, Asher stared. Silent. Her soul splintered.

She loved him.

He could steal her house. He could raze it if it made him happy. If it filled his hollowness. It if made him smile. She'd give it all up.

"Carrie, I'm sorry," his voice was hoarse. Broken. "I'm so—"

Her mouth landed on his. In the insane mess of her skirts, it took maneuvering—Asher lifting purple until the skirts were piled up to their necks, Carrie fumbling one handed to free his hot rigid length. Then eye contact.

Unbearable, carving relentless *intensity*. Not a flame, a forest fire.

Carrie's heart grew so big it threatened to pop.

Asher's gaze flickered once—enough for Carrie to recognize it. *Pain*. She reached out, but he was quicker. Always quicker. She cried out as he thrust up into her, yanking her down at the same time, impaling her.

Right. It was so right, how he filled her, his damp breaths on her neck, his hands nailing her to him.

The lights went out.

One by one along the walls.

And Carrie cried.

Chapter Thirty-Five

Asher

Asher thought he hurt her, despite the slick, wet glide between them.

But then Carrie kissed him, soft and slow and luscious. Broke apart to lay her forehead on his neck, rising on his raging hard cock.

He expected it to be over. He'd put himself out there and it was over. *Good try. Not everyone wins.*

He may have been a virgin two weeks ago, but he understood sex and tears didn't mix.

Understood regret when it stared him dead in the eyes.

It shattered him, his lungs crushing, pulse staggering. He lifted her hips to pull her off when she sank back down onto him, moaned into his shoulder. Bit.

Pain. He took it. Fed it to her as offering, as penance.

She peeled back, rose again and lowered, and it was so fucked up—he was fucked up—that he met her next descent with a thrust.

They moved too slowly for the lights to turn on. Maybe she did it on purpose, wringing her pleasure without having to look at him.

A scalding tear glided down her cheek to sear his wrist, cut down his arm. He couldn't do this. Couldn't—

"I hate you," she murmured, rolling her hips over him.

No. No, he couldn't do this. No. He loved her. He loved her too much to do this.

Her forehead fell to his, pushed hard. He smelled vanilla and salt. Fingernails clawed his chest, right over his heart. "I can't—" he croaked.

"You're supposed to call me a liar."

"Carrie."

"Call me a liar," she whispered, rocking over him, moaning. "You always get it right. Tell or not."

Which meant—

A wild jolt speared him. An animal reaction sent his hips rearing up and his hands to her face, desperate to see her. A muffled groan went between them. "Carrie—"

"I love you," she told him, pressing as tight as she could despite the ridiculous dress between them. He wished they were naked. Wished he could feel her bare skin. "I love you so much," she repeated. "For weeks." She started moving faster, panting. Hot, soaked flesh closing around him. Inviting him to bliss.

He kissed her, not long enough, not deep enough, before she pulled back. They stayed close, two people sharing breaths and wonder. "God, maybe before we ever spoke."

She clenched around him, gasped.

Asher drove into her, hand braced on her shoulders, plaster scratching his back, ass numb on the floor, he unleashed, fucked her until he found oblivion. Kissed and licked her, clutched her like the sun, as he pounded into her. Out of control. Unbelieving.

His body was on fire, his blood roared, and his heart so damn full, he wondered how it didn't slump from his chest, splat out onto the floor and make a big red stain. "What do you need?" he growled, rearing into her, sweating, pleasure scouring his bones, winding like chains pulling to break. He couldn't find her under the fucking skirts. Couldn't reach her to give the pleasure she needed. "How can I?"

"Ash," she whined, meeting his demanding thrusts, hair bouncing.

"Tell me." He'd shred the dress, rend it apart to give her what she needed. "Whatever." He vowed against her skin.

"*Stay.*"

He didn't stand a chance. Kissing her, plunging into her, he exploded, marveling at how she shuddered and cried out in response, clenching around him, panting and gasping.

The door burst open.

The lights snapped on.

CHAPTER THIRTY-SIX

CARRIE

"GOOD AND BAD NEWS," Diana said, heels rapping violently across the floor.

Asher twitched inside of Carrie and sent her a frantic, horrified look, red on his cheeks.

Sweet gods above. She wanted to see him blush every day for the rest of her life.

Aside from the wet stains on her bodice and teeth marks on Asher's neck, nothing looked untoward thanks to the swaths of Carrie's skirts. If anything, her plopped on his lap in a thousand layers, looked sweet and innocent.

Still, Carrie said, "It's not a great time."

"It's creepy in here." Diana spun around, nose wrinkled.

Carrie followed her gaze, taking in the room for the first time, and finding nothing but chalky busts atop white pillars. Shining silver plaques produced their namesakes and origins. Simple, understated, creepy. Like an abandoned mannequin factory, but on the good side of town. No rats, just dozens of dead stares.

Figured she and Asher would exchange I-love-yous in front of a bunch of severed heads, though.

Diana poked the end of a large white nose at her eye level, and asked, casual as can be, "Which do you want first? Good of bad?"

Asher shot Carrie a look she interpreted as, *let's get the fuck out of here*. Unfortunately, they had to hash a couple of things out now, and with Asher pinned under her—inside her—Carrie hoped it would minimize bloodshed.

"We've got some of our own news," she told her best friend, adjusting her hips with a sucked in breath. "How about bad first?"

"I bought a duck painting for thirty grand."

Carrie's mouth popped open. Of all her guesses.

"I promised you'd go on a date with Riley," she blurted.

Asher's hand wound around her wrist, brows knitted together, hips pressing upward.

She hissed through a moan, raked her fingernails over his chest, and told him, "He realized you were Jack before I did. I swore him to secrecy."

Asher had to swallow three times before he said, "You're in trouble, brat. I'm going to—" His threat ended with the flex of his thighs, a deep plunge inside her.

Carrie clenched her teeth. "Punish me later."

His eyes darkened with malice and anticipation.

Across the room, Diana spat a horribly inventive PG curse. "Sure. I'll take the bullet for love. I'm a regular Cupid." She steepled sharp nails on her bare sternum, eyes like daggers. "Diana gets double bad news," she droned. "Sodding typical."

"What's the good news?" Asher growled, clearly getting impatient. Probably feeling the come slowly pour out of her.

Diana leaned against the wall, chipped polish off her nail. Smirked. "You first."

She knew.

Carrie ran her fingertips over Asher's lips, liking the way his eyes closed at the touch, his dark lashes dusting his cheeks. He hardened insider her, pushing against sore muscles. She stifled a groan. "We're in love," she rasped.

"Wonderful. Declan's been arrested."

"What?" Both Asher and Carrie turned. Carrie gasped at the pressure.

Luckily Diana was too busy scraping a price tag off the bottom of her shoe to notice. "Yeah, apparently he was caught stealing from your"—she pointed to Asher—"house, and the cops were patrolling and snatched him." She didn't seem the least bit concerned, just annoyed.

Carrie felt a trickle of guilt, and slashed a shameful look to Asher. "That's my fault. I asked him to hide all of Chuck's paint sprayers."

"Why?" he asked.

"Because thy were going to paint over everything you'd written me. And I couldn't let that happen." She'd never cover them up. "We need to bail him out. You have to go and tell them you're not pressing charges."

Thoughtful, Asher slowly ran his hand up and down her spine. "I can't."

"The fuck you can't—" Diana snarled, leaning over them, ready to eviscerate. "He's my—"

"Down Cerberus," Asher boomed. "Declan's Carrie's family, which makes him mine too." His mouth twitched up at the corner. "And it's my fault he was caught. I requested extra patrols so you'd feel safer. However"—he locked eyes with Diana—"my hands are tied with his release. Carrie has to do it. It's her house."

The air sucked out of the room.

Diana lifted her chin. "Explain."

He didn't. Instead, he lifted his hips and reached into his back pocket. Carrie bit her lip to keep quiet at the sensation of him deep inside her, swelling. Asher panted once and handed her a small, white envelope. Folded in half. Perfect corners, crisp line.

"It's yours." His gaze was steady and resolute. "20 Nice Way. I put it in your name. You have to pull the charges."

"No." Carrie furrowed her brows at the envelope, feeling it grow heavy in her clasp. She pried it open and her heart stuttered, her pulse raced. A deed. With her name. And—

His voice lowered. "I also changed 21 to you, and there's shipping confirmation for your car from Pensacola. It's arriving tomorrow."

She was shaking, couldn't read any of the important cursive words on the fancy embossed paperwork. "My car?"

"I met Travis. We spoke." Spoke in that dark, grizzly tone sounded a lot like threatened bodily harm.

"You got my baby Camry back?"

"I can't write you letters, Carrie." His jaw clenched. "This is the best I can do."

She dropped the important, fancy papers and reached into her sling, past the bunched brown napkins until she felt the silky sheen of her paper ball. She put the receipt in his palm, waited patiently for him to unravel it. "You wrote me this the night we first met. Ice and Repeat. That was enough for me." She tucked a smile to her chest. "But then you had to go and outdo yourself. Which is so maddening."

"Back to hate?" he croaked, cradling the receipt, blinking fast.

"Never," she promised. "You wrote to me. Asher, you wrote me a house. You filled it with words. You ruined me for letters. Spilling your thoughts across walls in random beautiful places." She ran her fingers through his soft hair. "You can never sell."

He leaned into her hand. "It's not mine to sell. It never was. I built it for you. I didn't think you'd come without a bribe." The admission, told in his dry, honest tone, was like wasp stings on her heart.

"Ash—"

"And they're freckles," he went on, tipping her head up to his. "Black marks on the walls, I call them freckles. I wrote one for every one I've tracked on your body."

Carrie felt briefly overcome with him. Heart near to bursting. "I'm going to kill you for trying to hide it from me."

He hooked an arm around her waist and tipped her closer yet. Inky brow high as he delivered a wild, hot lick up her throat. "For hiding the psychotic ramblings of a desperate man?"

"Ramblings I want." She shut her eyes at the feel of his lips on her pulse, breathing shallow, head spinning. "It's all I ever wanted. Letters were a mode of transportation. But I don't need pen and paper. I just wanted to know what you thought of me, and instead you ripped your soul out and served it on a platter."

She pulled his hair as his mouth closed over her throat. "One upper," she rasped.

"Are those underwear in your pocket?"

They jolted at Diana's cold accusation.

Asher's lips left her neck. "How much did you spend on the ducks?"

"Thirty grand! On two bloody gory ducks." Diana groaned, raking a hand through her hair. "Declan called. I stood up to answer because I'm filled with class. Except standing is apparently an acceptable form of bidding. So I owe twin mallards." She slid down the wall to pout. "What the fuck is wrong with me? That was my down payment. Carrie—"

Asher's hip lifted.

Carrie gasped. "Yes. They're my underwear."

Diana jack-knifed up, stormed for the door, yelling. "This is my living nightmare!"

"Devious," Asher purred when the door slammed, hips driving up.

Carrie smirked. "Learned from the best."

EPILOGUE

CARRIE

"WE SHOULD'VE DONE THIS from day one," Diana said, setting her steaming coffee down on the windowsill to reclaim her paintbrush.

Carrie swirled brown and cream together to find a tan that worked and frowned. It wasn't right. "Agreed. It feels like we were prolonging the inevitable."

Outside, the thinnest layer of snow doused the cobblestone. Falls were short-lived in Vermont. Winter had come.

First Winter. The soft winter that involved delicate flurries and wistful breezes before the frigid air truly packed a punch to start Real Winter.

"Is Riley Coming?" Diana nodded toward the extra canvas and easel nearest to the door. An additional pan of oil pants waited, still wrapped in glossy red saran. Oil paints. So they wouldn't dry out. They cost three times what the Crayola water colors did, but Carrie could buy anything she wanted. Just about.

It had nothing to do with the credit card in her purse. Black, metal, weighing approximately twenty pounds, linked directly to Asher's accounts, despite her objections. She didn't need his money. Truly.

After selling a single piece for two million dollars, she'd made the state newspaper. The article went viral on ESPN, and before she could hyperventilate, her website crashed. Everyone either wanted to buy a Carrie Huston photograph or be photographed by Carrie Huston. The Vermont Maples baseball team had begged her for a photo shoot. Paid in advance. With a whole lot of zeroes.

She vowed to never take pictures of instruments again. Not with the calls from Sports Illustrated, and her upcoming contract with the New York Flame's soccer team.

"He bailed." Carrie dipped red into her mix. "Said it would be too weird to come."

"Lame." Diana stuck out her tongue. "I have a key to his house, so whenever we get sick of this, let's go over there and wreak havoc."

"How did you get a key?"

"When the Mountaineers were in Texas, his mom sent him a great touchdown basket with every apple known to man and she asked me to bring it in from the snow." Her brush flicked against the canvas. "Obviously, I made a copy. For emergencies."

"Did you make copies of my key?"

"Honestly, I've probably lost more copies of your key than you've ever had."

"Comforting."

"Please, it's not as if you're ever there anymore. You need to move out. Asher keeps saying it and he's right." Diana recoiled at the words. "That feels unnatural coming out of my mouth, but it's true. What are you waiting on? The house is finished, isn't it?"

"Not quite. The paintings dragging." Because after returning the stolen paint sprayers, Carrie requested every black line of Asher's be preserved. Apparently, hand painting four thousand square feet was time-consuming. "But the crew started on Hubert's place."

Chuck hadn't been excited to work with Asher again until Carrie offered a bonus and daily donut deliveries. By the spring, 21 Nice Way would be beautifully restored into a community art space, complete with darkroom, kiln, and stripper pole—Jill claimed ballet bars were for prudes.

"Think you can really leave? What about your mom?"

"I think she'd be happy to see it as an artist's retreat again. And I can put her furniture to better use at the new house." New place, old place. Renovations, catered photo shoots, interview with Elle magazine. A month ago, Carrie was stealing salt packets from China Fusion and dismantling a cooling unit.

Goes to show. Crazy wins. Every time.

"And sod off to Reggie?" Diana asked through a locked jaw. Her hand clenched so tightly around her paintbrush, wood cracked. "Thanks for the memories. I have a boyfriend. See you never." The malice dripping from her didn't relate to Reginald's care plans.

Girls' time had dwindled to scheduled meetups and football games. Diana—by her dark standards—had taken the change well, by stealing the wheels of Asher's G-wagon and selling them.

"Reginald's moved into the new attic already," Carrie said. "Asher bought him a collar with a tracker, and I gave him my mega blanket. He's gone from Marquess to King."

"Neat freak living with a trash panda," Diana mused. "Brings light into my life. I got you a housewarming present."

"No, you didn't." She refused to have a portrait of two preening ducks in her home. She dropped her paintbrush on the easel's wood ledge. "So it finally shipped, huh?"

"Sitting in a crate in my office. Arson's back on the table."

"How's the property hunt? Have you found The Doctor?"

"Abysmal." Diana snagged her coffee from the sill for another dose. "I keep searching for a dark creepy corner to stash Buffy and Spike and there's nothing. All the buildings look promising until I step inside and find rusted pipes, an active crime scene, or a ghost that looks like me. And those are at the top of the budget."

"If you need a loan-"

"Don't invest in restaurants. Fifty percent fail."

Carrie smiled. "Yes, but one hundred percent of yours succeed."

"I'd love to spend your boy toy's cash, really I would. but eventually it'll be yours. So no."

Fuck the money. A thrill coursed at the concept of Asher being hers. She swirled gold into the mix. "Maybe you can call at The Duck. Then at least, they'd fit in."

"Interesting idea, but then I'd have a duck themed bar."

"Give and take."

"I prefer to take. I do have some other names. The Neighbor. The Instigator. The Enabler."

"Meta," Carrie mused.

"I'm hoping it'll come to me once I find the place, like mom's naming their baby on the operating table." She frowned. "If I ever find one."

"You will."

They each surveyed their canvases. Carrie wanted to peek, certain they weren't drawing the same thing. Half certain Diana had slashed something wild and raucous across the pulled ivory. She'd only touched the reds and blacks and blues. None of which existed in Asher's clinical white bedroom.

Diana sighed. "I can't believe it's been a month."

"A month together, in love for three years. It fits."

A low rumble rippled from the center of the bed and a smile burst across Carrie's face as Diana flicked her brush in surprise and threw red splatter over the wall. The women froze, arms halted midair as Asher stretched, rolled, sheets pulling and moving.

With a yelp, Diana ditched her paintbrush, grabbed her canvas, and dashed for the door. "Next time we're dong Riley!" she called mid-escape.

Carrie finished the final stroke, smiling as Asher's rich hazel eyes blinked open, uncertain and hazy, slowly absorbing the sight of the easels lined at the foot of his massive bed.

His eyes sharpened on her, and he smirked, sliding down impossibly soft sheets until his legs hung off the end.

In the slanted buttery sunlight, broad chest bare, all rugged muscle and steely sinew, splotchy black bruises on his ribs, hair dark as raven's wings, he looked like a monster escaped from a fairy tale. Like he'd tear apart Hell to wrench the damsel into his hold.

Her monster. Vicious and cunning, who'd happily burn the world if she left it. His knees were all scars and scabs as he notched them on either side of her legs, and with gentle fingers, he tucked hair behind Carrie's ear. "Is this my punishment for sleeping in?"

"This," Carrie murmured, spreading sunset orange over his brutal jawline, "is what you get for asking Diana to include you on our outings."

He rolled forward to nip her mouth, palms sliding up the back of her thighs, kneading. "I missed you, love."

He'd been gone for 40 hours and Carrie had mourned every one. Falling into his arms, she set her cheek atop his hand, nails skimming the top of his spine. "Not like I missed you." Her hands spread over his back, the warmth of his muscle seeping into her. "But you can make it up to me."

His dark chuckle shook her, and he licked the inside of her right biceps, skin that had been hidden from him for so long. "So—" He pointed to the empty easel. "If that's Diana. Who's the third voyeur?"

"Who else?" Carrie smiled, biting the tip of his ear. "Our next victim. Riley."

"Should I worry about you sneaking into the other men's bedrooms to paint them naked?"

"I'd never paint anything so untoward."

"Alright, brat." He scooped her into his lap. "Then what did you paint?"

She remained silent, watching the muscles in his arms jump and shift as he stole her canvas.

She wasn't a painter. Not like her mother. Her artistry started and ended with photography, but she'd put heart and love on the blank page.

"What do you think?" she asked.

It was from memory. The veins in his hand, his powerful hold, the calluses dotted over his palm, smudges around his forefinger and thumb, ink driven in the crevices of his nails. Tan lines from the gloves, the scar on his left index knuckle, and the telltale white pads of a harsh, uncompromising grip.

She'd painted fantasy. The future. A band of gold ensnared one very important finger.

Asher's lip tilted and spread. "When do I get to paint one on you?"

"There's no rush." She draped over his him, soaking in his smell, his feel, everything, melting into her monster.

"Give me a day and I'll make you mine," he vowed. "I'll brand myself with your name. Give me a note or sign and I'll wait on my knees."

"Oh yeah," Carrie faced down his challenge with an arched brow. "If I said tomorrow, what would you do?"

He kissed her softly, nose brushing her cheek.

And dumped her onto the crumpled white comforter before rising, bare as anything to stalk unabashedly into his closet. "You say tomorrow, and I walk in here"—he opened a slim drawer hidden under his suits, pushed aside a line of watches, and Carrie's favorite hair pins—"find this little velvet box." He lifted the very thing. "And I get down on one knee and wait until midnight."

He moved his fingers to open it, and Carrie jumped up. "No!"

"No?" he growled at her. Not hurt. Angry. Because he'd never let her go. He'd become whoever she wanted to marry, do anything to keep her. Her greedy monster.

"I mean *yes*, but no. Not yet."

"As we've found, brat. I much prefer yes out of your mouth than no." He stalked forward and seized her with a kiss. Slow, heady, and toe curlingly cruel, hand rough on her throat, lips reverent. Enchanting her, ruining her the best way he knew how.

"Why?" he whispered when she yanked back for air.

"Because it's too much. The houses, my photography, everything. I can't be engaged too. I'll die of happiness."

He smirked, kissed her again, planting hands on the bed to trap her. Dragged his mouth down her throat. Sucked. "Then, let's skip the engagement and jump straight to marriage. "

She sighed under his ministrations, breathless when she told him, "And rob me of an out of touch, ultra extravagant Marie Antoinette dress? Have you even met me?"

"Problem solved, brat. You'll be a Bridezilla, drive me up the wall, make me fucking crazy and we'll fight every day. Fuck to soothe the pain." He licked her neck. "I changed my mind. I want a tediously long engagement."

She scowled at him. "I want a mountaintop wedding."

"Wherever, brat. So long as I get to fuck you in white."

Thank you for reading.

9 781958 374085